THE FEVER TREE

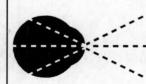

THE FEVER TREE

JENNIFER MCVEIGH

THORNDIKE PRESS
A part of Gale, Cengage Learning

GALE
CENGAGE Learning·

Detroit • New York • San Francisco • New Haven, Conn • Waterville, Maine • London

LIBRARY OF CONGRESS CATALOGING-IN-PUBLICATION DATA

McVeigh, Jennifer.
    The fever tree / by Jennifer McVeigh.
        pages ; cm. — (Thorndike Press large print historical fiction)
    ISBN-13: 978-1-4104-5938-1 (hardcover)
    ISBN-10: 1-4104-5938-1 (hardcover)
    1. Women—England—Fiction. 2. British—South Africa—Fiction.
3. Diamond mines and mining—South Africa—Fiction. 4. Smallpox—South
Africa—Fiction. 5. Large type books. I. Title.
PR6113.C835F48 2013b
823'.92—dc23   2013009071

Published in 2013 by arrangement with Amy Einhorn Books, an imprint of G. P. Putnam's Sons, a member of the Penguin Group (USA) Inc.

Printed in the United States of America
1 2 3 4 5 6 7 17 16 15 14 13

For Alice Rose

ONE

The first indication that her father was unwell had come in June.

Frances woke in the night and stared into the dark, listening. The house held its silence for a moment, then exhaled in a murmur of low voices which drifted up from the landing below. She drew a shawl from her bed and pushed open the door.

"Lotta?" she called down. Quiet for a second, then the creaking seesaw of Lotta's weight on the stairs, and the bobbing light of a candle. A billow of white nightgown, and the maid's broad, placid face swam into view.

"It's your father, Miss. He's back but he's not been himself." She pressed past Frances into the bedroom.

"How do you mean?"

Lotta bent to light the candle by the bed, her chest expanding and contracting like bellows, the flame flickering as she breathed.

7

"What's wrong with him?" Frances demanded, grabbing at her wrist.

Hot wax spilt over their hands and Lotta drew back, wincing in pain. "I don't know exactly. A coachman brought him in. Said he'd had a collapse."

Frances struggled for a moment to imagine this. Her father, the sheer bulk and power of him, didn't seem capable of collapse. He was, in every way, a man of strength. The errand boy, so they said, who had conjured his furniture empire out of shillings like a magician pulling banknotes from the pockets of paupers.

She took the candle from Lotta and went down to the ground floor, her feet sticking on the checkered stone tiles in the hall. Her father was in his study, sitting in an armchair to one side of the cold fireplace. His shirt was unbuttoned and a grizzled beard was beginning to cover the deep grooves that lined his cheeks. He looked pale against the green walls and glossy rosewood furniture, but when he saw her his face broke into an affectionate smile. He was exhausted, she decided with relief, but otherwise fine. A glass of brandy hung casually from one hand. If it tipped any further it would pour out onto the carpet. The breadth of his chest was exposed, and she saw that his body was tighter and more compact than she remembered, as though it had withdrawn into itself with age. She had admired his brute force as a child, the strength of his hands as he drew her wriggling onto his lap.

"Ah, Frances. I asked Lotta not to wake you," he said, holding one hand out to her in apology for not standing up. She took it and smiled, bending to kiss him. He had been away on business, and it was a relief to have him home.

"When did you get back? Are you ill?"

"Not at all, just a little tired."

Then, because it occurred to her that it might all be his fault, "Have you been drinking?"

Her father laughed, a rich, deep sound that soothed the edges of her fear and made her, involuntarily, smile. He glanced at the armchair which sat opposite him. "You see, Matthews, how sharp she is, my daughter?"

Frances turned. She hadn't noticed the man sitting in the chair behind her, on the other side of the fireplace. He had a neat, angular face with a narrow forehead and greased brown hair cut close around his ears. It took her a moment to recognize him, but when he stood up and stepped towards her she remembered. "Mr. Matthews."

"You must call him Dr. Matthews now,"

her father said.

"Of course." He was a cousin on her father's side who had stayed with them for a few months when he was a boy. He had the same serious expression she remembered as a child. "Where is Dr. Firth?"

"Dr. Firth is out of town," Edwin Matthews said with careful articulation. Even at sixteen he had sounded as if he were a master giving the lesson at school.

Frances was standing on the floorboards by her father's chair, her back to the empty grate and her feet nudging against the edge of the carpet. The dark, polished oak was coarse on the soles of her feet, and she rubbed her big toe across the smooth butt of a nail. She was dressed inappropriately and she shivered, too cold to be standing in the study in her nightdress. She had the feeling that she had interrupted a private conversation, and the silence of both men seemed to be an invitation for her to leave. Perhaps she ought to have been grateful to Edwin Matthews for coming out to see her father in the middle of the night, but she felt only frustration. It had been a long time since she had seen her father, and she wanted to talk to him properly, which meant alone.

"Well, now you're back," she said to her

father, "we will make sure you are well looked after."

"Frances, I am fine." He waved his hand, suddenly impatient. "And you must go to bed. I am overworked, that is all, and I called for the doctor to give me something to help me sleep."

She looked at him for a moment longer. He raised his glass as if to say — that's enough concern, leave me — but his hand tremored as he brought it to his lips. He hadn't mentioned a collapse. Perhaps Lotta was exaggerating. Either way, she wouldn't push him on the subject, not now. She bent down, kissed him again, and went upstairs.

She paused on the landing outside her father's room. Lotta was turning down the bedcovers. "I would like a few words with the doctor once my father has gone to bed. Would you ask him to wait?"

The window in her bedroom gleamed pale and cold behind the curtains. She drew her shawl from the back of the chair, stepped behind the red damask folds, and stood looking into the street below. The rain had stopped. It was perfectly quiet. Too early yet for the butcher boys in their blue aprons. The lamp at the end of the street throbbed a dull yellow through the milky fog, and she watched a lamplighter appear out of the shining gloom, lean his ladder against the crosspiece, and turn off the dial. The flame shrank to an orange ball, guttered, and went out. He paused, one hand on the post, and gazed along the street behind him as if waiting for the city to stir itself and shake off sleep.

The candle wax had sealed itself in a smooth, hard film over the back of her hand. When she flexed her palm it cracked in shards onto the carpet. She trailed her fingers across the burnt skin, to the soft inside of her wrist. Her pulse came in a quick, restless beat, echoing the dull thud which knocked against her stomach. What if he was seriously ill? This was the terror that had kept her awake as a child, when his booming voice and unruffled calm had been the only thing to puncture the gloom and silence of the house after her mother had died.

After a moment she stepped out from behind the curtain and lit the lamp at the dressing table, illuminating an assortment of brushes and combs, bottles of perfume, scented oils, and china powder boxes. She brushed out her hair until it became a crackling, fiery mass of copper curls, then dampened it with lavender water and wove it into a long plait. Her reflection looked back at her from the small mirror on the table. At nineteen years old she had the sense that her life ought to be full of opportunity, but instead she felt as if she were suffocating. She shook her head slightly, running her hand over her plait, and saw, in the reflection, the two porcelain dolls her father had given her as a child sitting on a chair by the bed. They stared back at her with glassy eyes, silence breathing from between their half-opened lips.

There was a knock at the door. "The doctor is waiting for you, Miss."

He had been shown into the morning room on the ground floor, and she found him standing at the window with his hat already in his hands, ready to leave.

"How is my father?"

"Sleeping." Then, walking a little way towards her: "I have looked forward to seeing you again, Miss Irvine, though I might have hoped it would be under better circumstances." His warmth disconcerted her, and though she couldn't have said why, she found it threatening. His eyes, she noticed, were very pale, almost gray in the half-light that warmed the green glass at the garden window. They were intent and watchful, and very bright: without them his face would have been a mask. She didn't think he was a handsome man — perhaps he looked too serious to be handsome — but he had a certain intensity which demanded your attention.

"Should I be concerned?" she asked, and when he didn't reply: "Dr. Matthews, tell me — is something wrong with him?"

The doctor stood perfectly still, almost a silhouette against the window, with the fingertips of one cupped hand resting on the corner of her desk. There was something cold-blooded about him. Where the light caught the edge of his face, she could see his skin was sallow and drawn. He must have been up all night. He licked at his lips to moisten them. "I think he is suffering from nervous exhaustion."

"Nervous exhaustion?" She gave a small laugh. "You're sure it's nothing else?"

He didn't reply.

"I don't think you know my father, Dr. Matthews. He isn't the nervous type."

"They often aren't."

"And what, in your professional opinion, has brought this exhaustion on?"

"Miss Irvine, you should get some sleep." He touched her lightly on her upper arm. "There is no use in worrying."

14

She shivered, shrugging off his hand, which might have been there out of professional concern but seemed to assume an intimacy between them. She regretted not having dressed before coming down. "Thank you, but I'm all right."

Then after a moment, she said, "Dr. Matthews, what concerns my father concerns me also."

"I suspect I couldn't tell you anything about him that you don't already know."

Whatever Edwin Matthews might think, this wasn't necessarily true. There was very little she knew about her father's life outside the house.

"I should like to know if he said something to you."

"Your father and I talked — yes — but for the most part about mining in Kimberley."

"He has investments in coal?"

"No!" He gave a thin, dry laugh. "Diamond mining, and he didn't mention investments. Kimberley is in South Africa. I live at the Cape."

She flushed. Of course, Kimberley was the famous diamond-mining town.

"Who painted these?" Edwin had picked up the watercolors of her father's roses which were laid out on the desk.

"I did." The weather had kept her indoors,

and she had spent most of the past two weeks at her easel in the morning room. There had been few visitors, and the time had been marked out by the tapping of her paintbrush as she cleaned it in the jar and the muffled voices of the tradesmen which drifted up from the kitchen below.

"They're very good." He was looking at her closely, as if adjusting some calculation in her favor, and she felt an old annoyance. This was the same arrogance he had had as a child, always judging the world according to his own criteria.

"Were you taught to paint?" he asked.

"A little." She shrugged. "But always portraits. I prefer to paint plants." Frances enjoyed the meticulous task of committing every detail — the veins, hairs, and shifts in color which most eyes failed to notice — to the page. The painting was always a compromise. It looked so little like the thing you painted, but its difference — the struggle for representation — was also its beauty. She pointed to the cut blooms in a jar on the table. "My father's roses. They're lovely, don't you think?"

"Perhaps, but I have never liked domesticated plants. There is something excessive in their prettiness." He paused. "They seem decorative to a fault."

"But splendid nonetheless."

"I can't admire splendor if the cost is sterility." He gestured to her watercolors. "These roses are either grown from cuttings because they can't propagate themselves, or they are grafted onto the stronger roots of other plants to help them survive. They have to be nurtured by the careful gardener in a perfectly controlled environment. Monstrosities, Darwin has called them. Deviations from their true form in nature."

"And if they were left to grow in the wild?" she asked, curious.

"They would either die or revert back to their aboriginal stock." He put the pictures down and said, "I should leave you to rest." As he walked past her towards the door, she stopped him, not wanting him to go without some kind of explanation.

"I don't see what could have brought it on," she said, insisting. "I have never seen my father under pressure. He isn't afraid of anything."

"We are all afraid of something, Miss Irvine," he said in a quiet voice, his cool gaze flickering over her. "Some of us are just better at hiding it than others."

His words unlocked a kernel of fear. When he was gone she felt it growing inside her, winding cold tendrils round her ribs, and

17

letting an agony of sadness seep into the edges of her exhaustion.

Two

When Frances's parents first married, her father had lived as close to respectability as he was able. They had a small cottage in St. John's Wood, no carriage, and a maid who worked overtime to keep the house from turning itself inside out. On Frances's sixth birthday, her father hired a carriage. It was a sky-blue day, the streets glistening with the previous night's rain, and they splashed through the wide-open spaces of Kensington, past half-erected streets and fields churned to mud under the wheels of builders' carts; past timber merchants, rubbish piles, and brick kilns that gave off the hot, stuffy smell of a bread oven. Everywhere were the sounds of construction; the shouts of workmen and the clinking of buckets being drawn up scaffolding. Her mother must have been sickening already because Frances remembered her excitement was tempered by concern for her pale face and bruised eyes, which squeezed shut each time the coach jolted on the potholed road.

They pulled up outside a large, stucco-fronted terraced house, and her father introduced her to a short, stocky Irishman with a wide smile and the same softly guttural accent as his own. "Kerrick, you're to do whatever Frances asks of you." And Kerrick had introduced her to the two grays, who nibbled at her fingers with soft, whiskered lips and breathed hotly into her hair. When she asked who the house belonged to, her father had laughed and said it was their own.

Eight months later, her mother had died, and the house which had seemed to promise happiness became a place of mournful reproach. Frances suspected her father was grief stricken, but it was hard to be sure. Once the funeral was over he never discussed her death, and though there were things about her mother that she wanted to know — why her lungs were diseased, and whether she had been in pain — she didn't have the courage to ask. On her father's instructions, every trace of her mother was removed. Wardrobes were emptied, photographs were taken down, and the morning room was cleared of her letters and diaries. The long drawing room, where Frances had imagined elegantly dressed women rustling in front of the gilt mirrors, was shuttered up. Her father worked a great deal and came home infrequently. His life was orchestrated around business, and on the rare occasions he brought guests back to the house, they were clients who sat with him in his study, smoking and talking, with the door firmly closed.

There was a tutor who came every morning and taught her mathematics, geography, and a little Latin. He introduced her to watercolors, teaching her the fundamentals of painting, and she ruined reams of paper before she learned that, with color, subtlety is everything. Her nurse spent long afternoons in the playroom embroidering cushions for her niece's trousseau. She tried to coax Frances to do the same, but never insisted, because Mr. Irvine had told her not to press his daughter into anything she didn't care for.

Frances stalked the house in the afternoons, finding odd corners to sit in, where she let her thoughts drift with the dust through the high-ceilinged rooms. When she thought about the house as an adult, she saw it from the strange perspectives she had inhabited as a child. A cupboard door warped with age, so that she could pull it shut from the inside, or the dining-room table like the roof of a coffin, rough and unvarnished on its underside, with the curved bow legs of the Georgian chairs boxing her in like the muscled calves of so many guests.

Her mother's family, the Hamiltons, lived in Mayfair, but she didn't meet them until a few years after her mother had died. They didn't approve of her father, with his Irish blood and poor connections, and they refused to acknowledge Frances. Her father, she learned later, had persisted in trying to reconcile the families in the hope that the connection would benefit her, and eventually they relented. When Frances was nine she was invited to visit her cousins Lucille and Victoria. She was nervous and didn't think she had made a good impression, but the invitation was repeated, and thereafter she went to see them once a month, though it was understood that the visits would not be reciprocated.

At dinner one evening, a few months after meeting the Hamiltons, she looked up to find her father staring at her. She was chewing a piece of meat off the end of her fork. His lip curled with distaste. "Frances, have you forgotten your manners?"

She was conscious of having done something wrong, but she wasn't sure what it was.

"Your knife. You don't care to use it?"

She looked down at her knife and colored. She hadn't used it before, not for eating, but he had never minded until now.

"Christ!" He brought his fist down on the table, making her jump along with the candlesticks. "The Hamiltons are right. You're ten years old and you eat like a little savage!" She put down her fork and stared at him, mortified. Most of her life was spent trying to avoid disappointing him. "If I had wanted you to have the manners of a factory girl, I would have sent you to live with your cousins in Manchester!"

He hired a governess to solve the problem. Miss Cranbourne arrived with a military sense of purpose. Every aspect of Frances's life came under scrutiny. According to the governess, she frowned when she concentrated, slouched when she walked, and ruined her fingernails with chewing. Her voice was too shrill — a sign of willfulness — and she spent too much of her time painting and daydreaming. For every minute of the day there was a task. There were lessons in letter writing, flower arranging, portrait drawing, cross-stitching, and crocheting. Etiquette manuals were learned by rote. She embroidered cushions and slippers, fashioned bell pulls, painted fire screens, and modeled a whole basket of fruit out of wax. She pressed flowers and learned their Latin names. She acquired hairpins, fancy brushes, and combs, and learned about ringlets, frizettes, and braids and how to pile her hair on top of her head in a bandeau. For her freckles — the result of a slow and enfeebled circulation — she was prescribed cold baths, applications of buttermilk, and a bowl of carrot soup for breakfast. The sun was strictly off-limits, and the windows in her bedroom were draped with muslin.

Frances applied herself to the new governess's regime, if not to please Miss Cranbourne, then to please her father, and because she knew her cousins would tease her less if she shared some of their accomplishments. She found most aspects of her new life stifling, but there was one introduction for which she was genuinely grateful. Miss Cranbourne suggested her father buy a piano, and he agreed. Her mother, he told her, had been talented. Twice a week, a teacher came and unraveled the music like a foreign language, and as Frances played, she could feel the house flickering to life, becoming for a moment the place it might have been had her mother lived.

She was thirteen years old when Edwin Matthews came down from Manchester to stay with them in London. It was hot that summer, and London sweltered. The smell of sewage came in from the streets, milk turned sour and curdled in their tea, and the air outside was choked with smoke. Her father hated the heat. He complained in the evenings that it was like living in Rome, and Frances remembered the pictures she had seen of a Roman caldarium, its floor a burning panel of hot marble.

"I'd like you to make him feel at home." Her father pushed his plate away, leant back in his chair, and lit a cigar. Now that it was evening, the window to the street below was slightly ajar, and a breeze stirred the gauze curtains. "And I shouldn't try to talk to him about his mother." Frances knew already, without having to be told, that dead mothers weren't appropriate conversation.

She had never heard of Edwin Matthews before. He was a distant cousin, had been born in Manchester, and at sixteen was three years older than Frances. His mother had drunk herself to death, leaving her husband with five boys. His father, a steelworker, had written to Frances's father asking for sponsorship. Edwin was hardworking, he said, and might do well in the right hands.

He arrived by train on the hottest day of the year, wearing a blue wool jacket stained under the arms where he had sweated through. He stood on their doorstep with his trunk of books and an air of extreme self-consciousness: a tall, slim boy with very pale skin and hands so fine-boned they might have been a girl's. His face looked hot and shiny. Pimples had erupted on his forehead, and they crept down his nose. When Kerrick — in shirtsleeves — tried to relieve him of his jacket, he shook his head, a rush of color turning his cheeks scarlet.

Her father had told her he might be uncomfortable in a London house, and he was right. Edwin looked as though he was scared to breathe in case he knocked something over. He took his shoes off before walking upstairs, he opened doors with extreme caution, and he was able to sit for hours reading a book without moving a muscle except to turn the page. He was scrupulously tidy, scrubbing his hands before every meal until they looked raw.

That first night, she remembered, he had almost burnt the house down. He'd never seen how to work a gas lamp, and he blew the flame out when he went to bed. Frances woke up to Kerrick shouting, hammering on Edwin's door, telling him not to light a match but to come straight out. She stood at the top of the stairs and watched him apologizing. His pajamas were too small for him, and his skinny ankles poked out of the bottom. He glanced up the staircase and saw her watching. His face twisted in embarrassment.

Despite his social unease he was perfectly self-contained, preferring to spend time alone studying than in company. He reminded Frances of a child she had read about in a newspaper who never said a word until he was eight and then one day at breakfast began reciting *King Lear.* Edwin wouldn't try anything unless he was sure of it first, and he watched their household with meticulous care until he could mimic how they talked, walked, answered callers, and drank their tea. Within a few weeks he had all but smoothed out the accent which would remind people he was Irish. All this, she realized later, was crucial education. He couldn't have hoped to have a successful practice when he was older unless he learned to mingle with Society.

At supper, her father would ask him about

the family. There seemed to be hundreds of relations, and she couldn't keep track of the names: Irvines, Matthewses, O'Rourkes, Dohertys, Connellys, O'Donnells. They each had a different story, and her father would draw Edwin out of his shell, encouraging him to give his opinion on the famines of his father's generation, the pomposity and greed of English landlords, the slums in Manchester, and the lucky ones — the émigrés who had escaped to America. It was a bleak picture they painted, and Frances didn't want anything to do with it. She had scarcely known that she was Irish until Edwin had come to stay, and now he was contaminating them with his talk of filth and desperation.

"Papa, he's barely civilized," she told her father when she was alone with him. Edwin had bad manners — he didn't use the butter knife and he heaped the sugar into his mug with his dessert spoon. Her father had turned very still, but she carried blindly on, trying out the word her cousin Lucille had given her. "I don't want to sit at the table with an Africanoid."

The slap — the first and only time her father hit her — stunned her. She felt as if she had been branded. He stalked out of the room, leaving her standing in his study, mouth open in shock, her cheek burning hotter by the second. They never discussed it afterwards, but she realized then that there was a difference between her and her father. Perhaps it had always been there — but Edwin had been the one to show it to them.

In the evenings, after supper, her father liked her to play the piano. Edwin watched with the fascination a collector might bestow on a fine piece of china. Afterwards, he would ask her father if he could play chess with Frances in the library. She would have liked to say no, but her father always assented on her behalf. These were the only times she heard Edwin speak confidently. He talked to her with the careful deliberation one uses to instruct a child, taking a methodical interest in her strategy, laying out the fundamentals of the game until she could put up a sustained defense. He coached her with patience, ignoring her determined silences, and when she toppled her king in defeat, wanting to have the game over with, he would talk her through, with pedantic satisfaction, how she might have won. When she looked up from the board, he would be watching her with unguarded curiosity, as if she were an equation which, when solved, might bring him some advantage.

She remembered resenting his intrusion into their lives, and when he left at the end of the summer for school, she was relieved to have him gone.

THREE

A month after her father had returned, Frances drove across London to a ball given by the Hamiltons. It was a filthy night, and the carriage lurched through the streets, its shutters closed against a driving rain. She was apprehensive and tried not to fidget as Lotta, cursing under her breath, struggled to fix a hairpin that had come loose. The pin was restored, and after a few minutes the clatter of horses' hooves on wet cobbles gave way to the slow crunch of gravel. There was a slamming of coach doors and shouts of exasperation as people found themselves drenched in the dash from their carriages to the house. Kerrick appeared at the door and bent dripping over the step, and Frances caught sight of the grand villa, light pouring out of the bank of tall windows on the first floor. It was always strange to arrive here as a guest. It was the house her mother had grown up in, and this, coupled with her natural shyness of large groups of people, made her nervous. She took a deep breath to steady herself before wrapping up her skirts and running for the steps of the portico, where powdered footmen in livery chosen for their handsome muscularity shook water out of their tailored jackets.

Guests jostled for space in the huge hall, their voices echoing off the flagstones. Women, still cocooned in furs, streamed water like ducks, their faces shiny from the cold. They were arriving in large, boisterous groups, straight from dinner parties, and Frances realized she was the only person who seemed to have come alone. The dressing room was a clamor of greetings and exclamations, the pitched voices of a swirling, glittering array of girls all talking at once. She gave her jacket and shawl to Lotta and glanced at herself in the long mirror. Red hair, impossible to control, was softened by a dress of white-spotted Brussels net. The fabric had been ordered from Paris on advice from a dressmaker, a dour woman with pinching fingers and a mouth crammed full of pins. She had claimed an intimate knowledge of what was fashionable, but Frances regretted having trusted her. Standing amidst the sleek figures of the other girls, she could see her skirts were too full and old-fashioned. She looked dowdy, as if she were already married. Two girls giggled as they walked past, clutching each other's arms, and Frances envied them. She didn't want to face the ballroom alone. She caught her eye in the glass and reminded herself that this was meant to be fun.

A sweeping curve of stone led up to the ballroom on the first floor, and she stepped into a swell of sound. Musicians, stationed behind a line of marble columns, were playing a polka. The floor was awash with a kaleidoscope of dresses, sweeping in, around, and away. Crystal chandeliers glittered from an ornately plastered ceiling, and white roses and purple violets had been woven into swags which hung between the curtained windows. A butler walked up and down the line serving champagne in silver flutes, and she took a glass in a gloved hand and brought it, clouded and cold, to her lips. She would need introductions in order to fill her program of dances, but there was no sign of her aunt. Frances had never had a flirtation with a man before, let alone been courted, and she was a little in awe of the ease with which Lady Hamilton orchestrated her daughters' string of male admirers.

She caught sight of her elder cousin,

Lucille, a porcelain beauty with pale skin and dark blue eyes. Her head was bent slightly to listen to a friend, and her embroidered fan fluttered open and closed like the flickering tail of a cat. Frances paused, unsure whether to make her way over. There was a kind of brilliance to Lucille's social confidence which could throw Frances off-kilter. She had a natural instinct for the nuances of Society, and she never looked more relaxed than in the midst of a crowd.

"Darling Frances," Lucille said when she approached, her eyes glancing over her dress. "Have you come all on your own?"

"Lotta is waiting downstairs," Frances said, though it didn't really answer her cousin's question.

"And how is your father?"

"Well, thank you." This wasn't strictly true. He hadn't been himself since he had come back from Manchester, but Frances didn't feel like discussing his health with Lucille.

"Ha!" Lucille's lips parted in triumph. "I knew he'd take the news all right. He's not the only one invested after all. Though Mother was convinced he'd have some kind of . . ." Lucille opened her hands to imply an unnameable catastrophe.

"What news?" Frances asked. Lucille, with

34

her sensitive ear for Society gossip, always seemed to know something that Frances didn't.

"You don't know?" Lucille arched her finely drawn eyebrows and considered Frances. Not for the first time she felt as though she were being scrutinized under a microscope, Lucille marveling at her naïveté as if she had discovered the attributes of some strange new species.

"Oh — just some minor skirmishes over railway stocks," Lucille said eventually, shrugging. "Nothing serious, I'm sure." She smiled, conciliatory, then glanced across the room. "Isn't that your cousin, who stayed with you all those summers ago?"

Frances followed Lucille's gaze, trying not to be surprised by her singular ability to place everybody in a room. Dr. Matthews was standing on his own, staring straight at her. His hair was combed back from his narrow forehead. He held her gaze for a second then looked away. She felt a flicker of irritation at finding him here and hoped he wouldn't try to dance with her.

"I suppose Mother felt obliged to ask him," Lucille said, "out of loyalty to your father."

"He's a doctor now," Frances said, feeling somehow responsible, "living at the Cape."

"You've seen him?"

"He came to our house a few weeks ago."

"What is it with the Irish? You extend a charitable hand, and they're forever nipping at your heels."

Frances opened her mouth, but before she could say anything her cousin said, "Oh, Frances, *please.*" She placed a hand on her arm. "You shouldn't take everything so seriously."

"Frances?" It was her aunt, interrupting them to introduce her to a corpulent man in his fifties who was sweating so profusely that his hair stuck to his forehead and moisture ran in beads down his neck.

"Never married, but not for lack of funds," Lucille whispered in Frances's ear as he led her away to dance.

"Too damned hot," the man wheezed, smiling at Frances as he stuffed his gloves into his pocket and clasped her hand in a moist, fleshy palm. He guided her over the floor, scanning the faces of the other guests over her shoulder. "Some notable absences this evening."

"What do you mean?"

"The bust-up over the Northern Pacific Railway." He smiled at her. "It's sent a few worthy gentlemen back to their beds."

When the same man tried to insist on

dancing with her again an hour later, Frances feigned dizziness. She wandered into the adjoining room. Here was a glut of food. Tables piled high with jellies, biscuit towers, cherry trifles, and myriad cakes in lurid colors. There were carvery boards carrying morsels of guinea fowl, slabs of ham, and slivers of cold tongue. A vast salmon looked as though it had been picked apart by a cat, the soft pink flesh torn away from underneath its silver skin. Men and women sat in small groups, grasping tiny silver forks and dabbing at their mouths with white triangles. It would be awkward to sit and eat on her own. She thought about leaving the ball, but that would mean admitting that she hadn't enjoyed herself. She wanted just a few minutes alone. The door to the library stood slightly ajar across the hallway, and she crossed over to it and stepped inside.

The walls were paneled with gray oak, and shelves stretched in arched alcoves from floor to ceiling. Rows of neat, leather-bound volumes were stacked side by side in perfect symmetry. She walked across an intricately worked Turkish rug to one of the two sash windows that looked out onto the back of the house. The shutters had been closed. Frances lifted one of the latches with a click and folded it open. It swung smoothly on its hinges, the heavy wood surprisingly light in her hand. She leant her head against the glass for a few moments, enjoying the cool firmness against her forehead. From the quiet of the library she could hear the steady rolling of a waltz, the ripple of voices when the music stopped, and the rhythm of steps on the marble floor when it started up again.

She remembered this room well. Once or twice as a child, when her father was away on business, she had been sent to stay with her cousins. She had longed to be alone, but she was rarely left to her own devices. Lucille and Victoria fingered her as if she were a rare specimen to be dissected, untying her ribbons so they could tease out her cloud of red hair and pulling off her gloves to look at her freckled hands. When they grew bored, Frances wandered through the house turning over objects, opening drawers, and examining the backs of cupboards in the hope of discovering something that had belonged to her mother. Lady Hamilton disliked Frances poking through the rooms of her house. She caught her once and snatched up her hand, scolding, "Fiddle, fiddle, fiddle." Then, twisting the skin on the inside of Frances's wrist into a sharp pinch, she said, "I won't have you turning everything over like a shopkeeper looking for profit." The insult, Frances realized later, was that she was just like her father.

A thread of fresh air pressed through the seams of the window into the leathery damp of the room. There was the smell of wet grass, but when she cupped a hand to the pane all she could see was blackness and, blacker still, the dense shapes that must be trees. She pulled away from the window, and the outline of her face emerged, distorted into a milky apparition. White skin glowing in a swath of hair, her eyes black hollows punctured by circles of light. She ran her tongue across her lips, but their full curve was lost in the murkiness of the reflection. A glimmer of light from the lamp caught the edges of her narrow chin and high cheekbones. Her father had called her a pixie as a child, cradling her face in the palm of one broad hand. His fingers had smelt of warm skin and tobacco. He said she was too small and delicate to be all real. She had grown tall since then, but she had kept the fine bones and sharp angles.

There were times when her face didn't seem to belong to her and she felt as if she were eyeing a stranger in the mirror. She couldn't identify herself beneath its brash colors, and she resented the way it drew attention. It was too obviously Irish. People treated her differently because of it. She watched them taking in the coils of russet hair and green eyes. Girls became prickly and standoffish, boys kept a fascinated distance, and her mother's family, for whom she was too obviously the daughter of an Irish pauper, visibly recoiled. It would be nice, for once, to blend in.

Lucille's question nagged at her. Was her father invested in the railway? How serious could it be? She had glimpsed him at home this evening caught in a moment of distracted stillness, and it had seemed to Frances that he must have aged without her noticing. He gripped the back of a chair, pushing himself upright out of the stoop that pulled his shoulders into a gentle curve. His hair had crept back from his forehead, and his cheeks looked gaunt. When he saw her looking at him, his face transformed, mobility erasing the cleanness of the image that had presented itself to her. He smiled at her and winked, and in the effort of that expression she had felt a pang of concern and something that felt awkwardly like guilt.

She shivered. The fire had burnt down in the grate, and the logs, crumbling into ash, showed small corners of dull flame. Only two lamps had been lit in the room, one on a card table. Its varnished surface revealed a thin edge of the green felt that lined its underside. Two small, hard chairs were thrust away from the table, and a chessboard showed a game won by attrition. The second lamp stood on a large mahogany desk which sat between the windows on the far wall. The leather inlay glowed a dull taupe. There was nothing else on the desk except a small globe. She spun it carelessly and on a sudden impulse put her finger on the spinning ball. She felt it thrum under her fingers, slowing down under pressure.

"A dangerous game, tempting fate."

Frances swung round. A slender man was standing in the doorway, framed by light. He came a little way into the room, and she saw it was Edwin Matthews. He was the last person she wanted to see. She didn't want to talk about her father's illness, and she didn't want an Irish cousins' reunion. If she was being honest, his presence at the ball slightly embarrassed her, and she realized she didn't entirely disagree with Lucille. She didn't say anything, hoping he might leave. He would assume, finding her here, that she hadn't been enjoying herself, and this would give him some advantage over her, though she couldn't exactly say why.

Despite all these things, as he walked

towards her she felt a subtle pleasure in being found. He looked at her with pale, gray eyes and made a sweeping motion towards the door. "Their conversation doesn't interest you?"

His face lacked any of the mobile excitement and flushed enthusiasm which had marked the faces of the other guests. He looked uncomfortable in his tail suit, like a bird in borrowed plumage, yet confident, as if he hoped to extract something from the situation.

"All anyone can talk about this evening is the collapse of railway stock."

"I thought your father was an investor?"

This came as a small shock, that he knew when she hadn't. "What if he is? My father is a careful man."

The doctor tapped a cigarette against the back of a silver cigarette case. "Do you mind?"

She nodded her assent, and watched him lift a match from a small glass globe that stood on the mantelpiece. He struck it firmly against its ribbed edge, dipping his head to bring the cigarette to the blue flame. Despite herself, she was curious. Would a doctor from the colonies really be presumptuous enough to flirt with her? She didn't imagine he had found himself here by mistake. He didn't look like the kind of man who did things carelessly or arrived at places by chance. For a moment his features were hidden by a cloud of smoke. When it cleared, he motioned to the chessboard. "Do you care for a game?"

She hesitated. It could be compromising if someone walked in and found them alone together, but in the end curiosity got the better of her. She wanted him to reveal himself, so she agreed to play.

He picked up an ashtray and placed it on the card table. There was a cigar ground down in the bottom of it. She could smell the rich, sweet tobacco. He pulled out a chair for her, and as she sat his knuckles brushed against the back of her dress. He began setting out the pieces. She remembered his tendency towards silence. "Is it true," she asked, prompting him into conversation, "that if all the diamonds at the Cape were sold at once, a diamond wouldn't be worth more than a pebble?"

"Perhaps," he said, straightening up the pawns so that their rectangular bases ran parallel with the squares. "If they could all be sold at once. But most of them are still in the ground." He glanced up at her. "To be honest, I am more concerned with the people who mine the diamonds than the stones themselves."

"The magnates?"

"And the natives who work for them."

"Are they very savage?" she asked with a dramatic flourish.

He glanced at her but didn't answer, and irritated by his disapproval, she turned her attention to the board. The chess pieces were intricate imitations of the Battle of Waterloo, the upper torsos of the soldiers flattened into ivory, blue uniforms against red. He took up a pawn and put his arms behind his back, then brought them forward in front of him for her to choose. His hands were white and hairless, and when Frances touched one lightly it turned and unfolded like a flower, revealing long fingers with the ivory piece resting on a creased palm.

Frances didn't concentrate on the game. Instead she watched the doctor play. There was a contained satisfaction in his body, an accuracy of expression in the way he moved his pieces around the board that frustrated her. She was ashamed to find herself wanting him to acknowledge her position, and she regretted agreeing to play. Occasionally there was a swell of noise as the door to the ballroom was opened, and they heard low voices and the steady footsteps of men going out into the night to smoke.

When the opening moves had been played out, Frances deliberately moved her bishop so that he could take her, but he avoided her and instead slid his knight neatly around it. She countered quickly, opening up her board, exposing herself over a series of moves, but still he wouldn't take her, not even when her queen was open to his bishop. She became more reckless, but still he held back. Finally he executed a perfect checkmate, removing just one of her pawns from the board in order to bring his queen into attack. When it was over he leant back in his chair and studied her.

"I don't interest you, Miss Irvine?"

He was looking straight at her, and she met his gaze. "Quite the opposite. You convincingly proved yourself the better player." She felt a small satisfaction in refusing to engage. She stood up to go, but he motioned for her to sit.

"I have to return to the Cape before the end of the year." He was looking steadily at her, eyes calm, but a blue vein pulsed across the surface of his forehead.

Voices and rapid steps came down the corridor. They paused outside the library door and then moved on. "The Cape, Miss Irvine, would interest you." He moistened his lips. "I hope, in time, that I could interest you." For a brief moment the music had stopped, and all Frances could hear was the slow ticking of the clock on the mantelpiece.

"Interest me in what, exactly?"

"In marriage. I am asking for your hand in marriage."

Frances blinked back at him in surprise. She had expected an artful declaration of passion, perhaps, but no more than that.

"There's a chance I'll make some money." He leant forward, his eyes flickering over her face. "Others have done it . . . if I can establish myself in certain circles . . ." He paused, lowering his voice. "You could help me. Introduce me to the right people."

"Introduce you to the right people?" she asked in disbelief. "What do you think my father would say if he were here now? Don't you think you are rather taking advantage of his charity?"

"Are you happy living in London?"

The question threw her, and it took her a moment to say, "I can assure you my happiness is no concern of yours."

She drew back her chair and stood up. It was possible she had encouraged him, certainly she had played his game, but now that he had delivered his lines, she realized their situation was completely inappropriate.

He stood up and walked with her over to the door. "If you change your mind . . ."

He was too confident, and she suddenly disliked him. "You play a good game of chess, Dr. Matthews, but I'm quite sure it will have been our last."

She left him standing by the door and walked quickly out of the room.

FOUR

Frances waited for her uncle in the drawing room on the first floor of his Mayfair villa. Lucille and Victoria hadn't appeared, and though manners dictated they should greet her if they were at home, she suspected, from the occasional squeals of girlish laughter and thrum of feet upstairs, that they had simply decided not to come down. She was nervous and would rather be standing, but had instead chosen to position herself in the corner of a deep, rust-brown velvet sofa. She didn't want to seem confrontational, a criticism that her uncle might have applied to her father, and which she supposed could be extended to herself. Her father had been dead two weeks, and her uncle had called her here, she hoped, to offer her a place in his household.

The drawing room was an impressive space, with high, corniced ceilings and an excess of dark, claw-footed furniture. Varnished mahogany tables with curving, white marble tops and gilt lamps stopped up every gap in the sea of velvet. Her aunt collected De Morgan vases, and the luster-glazed, ocher-red images of dogs chasing a variety of beasts gleamed from the corners of the room. The easy grandeur of this house had enthralled her as a child. It had been in the family for over sixty years, and Frances wasn't sure whether it was this fact, or the convincing size of her uncle's family, which lent it an air of invulnerability. How flimsy the trappings of her father's life had proved in the wake of his death. There was none of the stability that Frances saw here. More than half a century after the family had moved in, this house seemed as resistant as ever to calamity.

The pattern of green and maroon stained glass on the windows facing her cast a gloomy light over the room, keeping out the brightness of the August day outside. There was no fire burning in the grate and the lamps hadn't been lit. Her uncle admired what he called *quality,* but he had a distaste for excess, another criticism which had been extended to her father, who had loved cigars and long nights at his club with a passion that suggested he hadn't believed in a correlation between indulgence and longevity.

After a few minutes, she stood up impatiently, her black crepe skirts rustling, and walked to the far side of the room, where a piano stood to the right of a wide bay window. She leant an elbow on the mahogany and looked into the Wardian case that stood embedded in the bay. It was a large ornate structure made of glass and lead with a rock garden at the bottom barely visible beneath a riot of ferns. They grew too closely together, palms pressed against the glass as though appealing for escape. The case had steamed up with a clammy heat. She bent closer and smelt the sweet rot of damp vegetation. A few lime-green shoots were unrolling themselves in the bottom corners, sprouting dense buds that looked like a collection of soft, furry snails. The glass case offered protection — the ferns wouldn't last a minute exposed to the pollution of London air — but it would also, eventually, suffocate them.

"You share my daughters' fascination?" Frances turned and saw her uncle walk a little way into the room. "They are quite passionate about natural history." Frances didn't contradict him, though she seemed to remember her cousins had long ago abandoned their interest in the natural world; a passing obsession that had lasted long enough to convince him of their diligence.

"Uncle, thank you for finding the time to see me."

He was dressed in his customary black suit and was frowning slightly, like a man under threat, not a little afraid of what the world might be mustering to throw at him. He was someone, she thought, who might be cowardly in all things except in the protection of his family. This single passion precluded close relationships with outsiders, and Frances, who had never had reason until now to test his feelings towards her, was unsure whether she would be considered one of those to be protected.

He waved her to a corner of the brown sofa and sat down in a chair opposite. "How is Mrs. Arrow keeping?"

"Quite well, thank you." He had leapt straight to the heart of her problem, but she wanted to avoid having to spell out her fears. Her father's sister — Mrs. Arrow — had arrived two weeks ago from Manchester. She took a shrill pleasure in denouncing her brother's fall into penury, and demanded a gratitude from Frances which exhausted her. Every conversation began with a veiled criticism. "When we get to Manchester, I shan't want you. . . ." She had five children, three of whom needed a nurse, and she had agreed to take Frances with her to Manchester on the understanding that she fulfill that role.

"Good. Now, I have received a letter that pertains to you." He unfolded a piece of paper from his waistcoat. "From a Dr. Matthews."

Frances felt the muscles in her face freeze up.

"He asks for your hand in marriage." Her uncle smiled at her. "What do you think of that?"

"I think nothing of it." She tried to keep her voice level, conscious that too much emotion unsettled him. "I can't marry Dr. Matthews."

"I understand it might not have been what you were expecting, Frances, but on reflection it is a good match. And he has written a convincing letter. He talks about his friendship with your father, and your father's charity towards him as a child. He is a qualified physician with a practice in Kimberley, and while he has little money right now, he is young and there is every chance he will do well in the colonies."

"Please, Uncle. You don't understand."

"Frances." His voice was cautionary, tipped with steel.

"I barely know him."

"He tells me he saw you not long ago, in this house? You played chess together? That sounds almost like a courtship."

"I don't like him." Frances took a deep breath, trying to suppress the panic which was welling up inside her. She needed to appeal to her uncle on a practical level. "You can't imagine what he is like. He is all ambition. From the moment he came down from Manchester to stay with us he has wanted to sidle his way into our family."

Her uncle looked unmoved. He put his palms together, placed the tips of his fingers under his chin, and spoke in a measured, even tone. "I have spoken to him myself. Ah — you are surprised? Yes, I asked him to call on me here. You see, despite what you may think, I have taken your future very much to heart. He spoke warmly of you, and I was reassured that he is a good man with appreciable prospects. Your father exposed you to a great deal of privilege and your life will — undoubtedly — have to change, but he will see that you are well looked after."

"And if I say no?"

"Then you will live with your aunt in Manchester."

"You know very well I can't!" Desperation

crept into her voice. "I'll have to work for my aunt for the rest of my life."

Her uncle looked at his hands and said nothing.

"She is so different!" Frances stood up, biting her lip.

"Not so different from you, Frances," her uncle said carefully. "She is, after all, your father's sister."

Frances caught sight of herself in the gold-crested mirror over the fireplace. She regretted standing up. Her uncle would take it as a sign of bad breeding. Beneath the eagle with his wings unfurling, the dark, convex glass threw a distorted impression back at her. Sparks of red hair swirled away from her in dense curls, and the narrow, angular lines of her face warped so that her mouth twisted with bitterness. Her Irish blood was too visible for her uncle's liking, reminding him of everything her mother had given away, and she wondered whether he would be happy never to see her again. "So — you won't have me?"

"Good God, Frances! You are just like your father," he said in exasperation, turning down the corners of his mouth in distaste.

"Imagine Lucille living with her!" Frances raised her voice in accusation. "Do you think she could stand it?"

He paused for a second. When he spoke, it was with a certain detachment, his voice freezing up at the edges. "I have been very careful to make sure that my daughters are provided for should anything happen to me. And I must remind you, though I struggle to see how you have forgotten, that neither Mrs. Arrow nor Dr. Matthews is any relation of mine. But, since you ask the question, I hope I have brought my girls up with grace and humility enough to accept what life throws at them. The last few weeks have been difficult for you, Frances, and of course I sympathize, but I would also encourage you to accept that life cannot always be easy."

Either he hadn't quite understood the position she was in or he had chosen not to engage with it. She felt misunderstood. In his distrust of others he had drawn a circle around his family, and it was clear to her now that she had been excluded. With nothing left to lose, she approached that part of her which was most appalled. "And what about your loyalty towards my mother?"

"Your mother thought your father's family was good enough for her, and I'm sure if she were here today she would think they were quite good enough for her daughter.

Your lack of resolve does her a disservice."

He sighed and stood up, signaling the end of the meeting. "I think you know your father left behind some considerable expenses. I wouldn't want you to think we haven't been generous. But this isn't an issue of cost. I won't say I approve of your frankness, but since you have been honest I will give you honesty in return. My wife and I have discussed your situation at length. We are not sure it is in your nature to play second fiddle, as it were, to anyone. You should ask yourself whether you would really be happy living here under the umbrella of your cousins. I am inclined to think you would not."

Frances didn't tell him that she would do everything in her power to please her cousins if it would save her from living as a servant in her aunt's house. She saw that he wouldn't change his mind, and her pride had been wounded enough. "Please write to Dr. Matthews and tell him I can't accept his offer."

"If that is your decision."

She nodded. How could it be otherwise? She couldn't marry a man for whom she felt no affection, a man who was prepared to use her sudden fall in fortune as an opportunity to coerce her into marriage. She

56

turned to go, and her uncle said, as if piqued that she was leaving so soon, and in a sudden remembrance of magnanimous generosity prompted not so much by Frances's situation as by paternal pride, "You must come and see the family before you leave London. They are very generous, my girls, and I know they will have all sorts of things they will want you to take with you to Manchester." She glanced back once as she walked out of the door, and saw her uncle deadheading a geranium bush that was beginning to droop, his attention already diverted to the safe running of his household.

It was late in the afternoon by the time she got home. Her aunt stood in the doorway of the morning room clutching her youngest child. She was a stout woman with wiry red hair streaked with gray, and a red rash that crept down her nose and across her cheeks when she was upset. Frances could see herself dimly reflected in the older woman's features, and wondered whether this was what age had in store for her.

"What on earth took you so long?" her aunt asked, casting a neat, sharp slap across her cheek. Before Frances could react, the woman had thrust the child forward. She had no choice but to take the placid weight of him in her arms. His face was white and shiny like a porcelain jug, and a thin mucus streamed from his nose. When he made a grasp for her mouth with a wet hand, she smelt the creases in his fingers, damp and sour like soft cheese.

"Poor Jimmy! What he needs, Frances, is a nurse who can keep the time. Honestly, you behave as if I weren't doing you a favor, taking you with me. Heaven knows it's only out of the goodness of my own heart. It's not as if you know the first thing about bringing up children. Just look at you!" she cried as Frances struggled to keep hold of the wriggling boy. "You're no stronger than a child. You've never done a hard day's work in your life."

Frances bent down and placed the boy on the floor and, ignoring her aunt's protests, walked quickly upstairs to her bedroom. She locked the door, barely registering the howl which had started up downstairs. For the first time since her father's death she felt something stronger than grief take hold of her.

Her father had taken her once to her aunt's house; a small terraced cottage in a street so long you couldn't see to the ends of it. There were so many people crammed inside its four rooms, wailing and crying and climbing up her skirts, that Frances thought her head might explode with the noise. It was winter and the windows dripped with condensation. The walls were covered with a cheap imitation wallpaper which the gas lamp had turned from orange to black, and the rug was matted with damp. The maid had red eyes that streamed as if weeping were a fact of life. Frances had stepped out to the privy in the back-yard. Its door had frozen shut and she had to kick at it to loosen the hinges. Cock-roaches nestled their wriggling bodies between thin cracks in the wood. She had stood there, hands pressed together, re-nouncing this place as a kind of personal hell.

Now her father was dead, his protection was gone, and she was being sent back to where he had come from. Unlike him, she didn't think she would ever escape. It wasn't unusual for a household to keep an over-worked relation, who sweated for her keep and had no family of her own, until she was too old to be of any use. She couldn't rely on her aunt's children to keep her in her old age. They wouldn't remember their obligation to her father. More than likely, she would be cast out to the workhouse. If she didn't find a way to escape going to Manchester, she would spend the rest of her life regretting it.

FIVE

Frances smoothed down her mourning dress, sucked the ink stain from her finger, and read the letter again. *Dr. Matthews. There is something I should like to discuss with you.* She still wasn't sure she wanted to send it. Could she ever feel anything except dislike for a man whose proposal had been born from pure opportunism? If he hadn't asked to marry her, then her uncle might well have taken her in. But his letter had ruined every chance of that. He had made it too easy for her uncle to be rid of her, and it was quite possible that he had known it would be the case.

Sunlight streamed through the window. It was too hot for September, and the heavy weave of her dress was making her sweat. It was more wool than silk, and its seams chafed against her skin. She ran a finger around the cuffs, easing the material away from her wrists. What would he make of her change of mind?

The writing desk, worn and polished, was almost entirely covered with letters of condolence. It faced the window and she looked out onto the garden. The grass, usually carefully trimmed, had overgrown its borders. It would need cutting, but not by Kerrick. Another heap of envelopes had arrived this morning. Not the letters she might have expected, from the politicians and businessmen who had fêted her father when he was successful and deserted him when his money ran out. These were people she had never heard of, governors and trustees of charities and ordinary men and women who wanted to acknowledge her father's benefaction. She hadn't known about his work for charity, and it was a consolation that there were people who loved him for it, who hadn't abandoned him as soon as his fortunes had turned. She might have had a chance to meet some of these men if convention had allowed her to be at the funeral, but instead she had been forced to spend the day at home with Mrs. Arrow.

Frances dropped the letter onto the desk and rested her head in her hands. All morning she had listened to the milling of feet through the corridors of the house. Gradually, the noise had subsided, and now all she could hear was the occasional ripple of applause when something went under the hammer for a good price. Most of the furniture would be gone by tomorrow — only the morning room and her bedroom had been spared — and her aunt had already left for Manchester. It was a blessing to have her out of the house. She couldn't have borne her running commentary on the event.

There was a knock on the door.

"Tea, Miss?"

"Yes, Kerrick. Thank you. How many is that now?"

Kerrick's forehead crumpled into an expression of deep disgust. "Over one hundred since this morning." He stood not quite straight in the doorway, his shoulders bunched together with age.

"And the sale?"

"It seems good, Miss. Your father had no shortage of beautiful things. But there's an awful lot of gentlemen happy just to gawk."

The contents of the house, and the house itself, wouldn't bring in enough to cover her father's losses. There would be nothing left over for her. "Heavily and unwisely invested" was the verdict delivered by her uncle when he had emerged from a protracted meeting with her father's lawyer. When she asked to know more, he polished his nose with his thumb and forefinger and delicately avoided the word "bankruptcy."

The newspapers told her more. Her father, it turned out, had been borrowing money against his company to invest in the Northern Pacific Railway, which was building a line across a vast, untracked stretch of land up near Canada. Six weeks ago, the railway company had filed for bankruptcy, defeated by the remoteness and scale of the terrain. There was a map in the paper. They had meant to extend the line almost across the breadth of America, from the Great Lakes to the Pacific Ocean. Frances understood why the idea of a railway across the wilderness might have appealed to her father. When she was a child, he had loved to show her his collection of maps. He would unfurl them on his desk and point out uncharted territories in Canada or Africa. His face would become animated as he described their remoteness, and she had the sense, as she listened to him, that he felt trapped in London, hemmed in by the conventions of Society.

Now his debts had to be paid, the lawyer's fees and the staff wages. Her uncle had stepped in to help, and she was grateful but also unnerved by his efficiency. The funeral, his arrangements for the staff, and the sale of the house had all been accomplished in a little over a month. Kerrick had been with them for fourteen years, and in just a few days he would be gone. There was almost nothing left of her father's life. Irvine & Hitchcock, his furniture business, one of the largest in England, had been sold off for less than the value of its stock. And now the auction, as if in opening up the house to Society he could satisfy its appetite for scandal. Even Frances was to be tidied away, and once she was gone her mother's family could get on with the business of forgetting.

If she sent the letter then she would have to accept Edwin's offer. She was intrigued by Africa. It could offer her a fresh start. And she could get used to a less affluent life, going without the things she was used to. The problem was that she didn't think she would ever come to like him. He was too serious. Always analyzing everything until he had squeezed all the joy out of it. When she was with him she felt he expected something from her, a kind of moral rectitude to match his own. And she couldn't imagine letting him touch her. Worse than that, she distrusted him. He had appealed to her uncle, unashamedly using her father's death to strengthen his claim, even when she had made it quite clear the last time they had spoken that she wouldn't consider his proposal. It was ambition. He wanted her not because he cared about her, but because she would be a mark of his success.

She remembered him as a boy, dazzled by this house with its broad garden and white Kensington façade, by their hushed rooms and walls lined with books. Unable to have these things for himself, his ambition had crystallized into marrying the girl who had grown up with them. He really didn't know her at all, and it was these parallel motives of worship and control which unnerved her. It was possible he equated these feelings to love, but to her it looked like little more than grasping self-interest.

Yet it had to be better than living with her aunt in Manchester. At least she would have her independence. She read the letter again and in a moment of quick decisiveness folded it and slipped it into an envelope, held it for a second more between her fingers, then dropped it onto the silver letter tray. Kerrick came in with the tea, set it out on the low table, picked up the letter, and was gone.

Frances turned back to the window. She

blinked into the hot glare of light and caught sight of two figures standing on the lawn; ladies from the auction looking for something to report back to their friends. They peered through the windows, and when they saw her watching, one of them waved at her guiltily. Frances leant forward quickly and closed the shutters, boxing herself up in the dark.

It hadn't occurred to her that he might not come. She waited all day in the morning room. The house was hot and silent. Groups of men arrived from time to time to remove furniture, and the quiet was broken by their thick, labored grunts and the scrape of wood on marble. When she was sure that he wouldn't come, she went up to her bedroom to begin packing. But she felt defeated by disappointment. Piles of dresses, open drawers, hatboxes, and a muddle of shoes had turned her room into disarray. Two small suitcases gaped open by her bed. How could she possibly decide what to take with her? Her aunt had been very deliberate in her instructions. There wasn't room in her house for a Society girl. She must keep her belongings to a minimum.

At five o'clock Lotta knocked at her door.

"Dr. Matthews to see you, Miss. He is

waiting in the morning room."

Frances found him standing with his back to her, cap in one hand, looking into the garden. She stood for a second watching him. He was perfectly still; a slight figure in a suit worn thin at the edges and cut too short for the fashion. She took a deep breath and stepped into the room.

"Dr. Matthews. You are very kind to have come."

He turned at the window. "Miss Irvine. I'm so sorry for your loss."

She nodded and motioned to one of the low chintz chairs pulled up on either side of the cold grate. They sat opposite each other, and he drew his hands into his lap and looked at her intently. His silence felt like scrutiny. She had forgotten his ability to disarm her. Gone was the shy, unsure boy of sixteen. He was no longer her guest, reliant on her father for charity. She needed something from him, and she suspected he knew what it was. The window had been pushed open, letting in a thin stream of cooler air and the gentle grind of traffic from the street.

"You must be enjoying seeing your family after so long away?"

"Yes, but I sail tomorrow from Southampton. That is, if the weather holds."

She was surprised. "Back to South Africa? So soon?"

"My plans have changed." He gave her a tight, compact smile. "And yourself? What will you do now?"

"My aunt has offered to have me. I am to take the train up to Manchester next week." She talked to fill the silence. "Truthfully, I am a little scared. She has three children under the age of eight, and I am to be a nurse to all of them. That is until I can find myself a position or a husband." She blushed, realizing her mistake. "My uncle manufactures soap. So at the very least I shall be clean."

He smiled, as if waiting for something. She felt a flush rising up her neck. Then he looked away, stood up, ran his hands through his hair, and walked over to the window. His movements were quick and agile, and she realized his stillness was deceptive. After a few moments he came back and stood by her chair, looking down at her.

"Shall we have an honest conversation?" He paused, waiting for her approval before going on. "The Cape is a very different place to England. When I saw you last I had just arrived in London. My excitement to be home clouded my judgment. I had

69

forgotten how Society works here, how rigid it can be. I had no reason to expect a different answer to the one you gave me."

He crouched down beside her, picked up her hand, and held it lightly in his. His skin was pale, almost translucent. Beads of sweat had broken out on his upper lip. "And yet, I was sick with disappointment. I would like to have you, Frances, as my wife." He paused. "If circumstances have changed your mind, they have not changed mine. The decision is still yours to make."

Frances was silent for a moment, conscious that everything depended on what she said next. In a whisper, embarrassed by the sudden intimacy her answer would throw up between them, she said, "I would like to go with you to South Africa."

He pulled her gently towards him, whispering her name. When he kissed her, his lips were unexpectedly cold, and she drew her head sharply away from him, but he stayed crouched awkwardly in front of her, leaning his head into her shoulder and kissing her neck wetly. She hadn't expected this. He groaned softly and she shivered, gazing over his shoulder towards the window. The sun had passed behind the trees, and she saw a fly, dizzy with heat, turning itself in circles against the pane. I have done the right thing, she told herself, as she felt his fingers press into the waist of her dress. I will forget England, and I will try to be happy.

Six

Frances closed the front door and stood for a few seconds in the hallway of the house. It was early October, a month after she had accepted Edwin's proposal. Outside she could hear the driver's grunts as he loaded her trunk onto the cab. The servants had all left for their new positions, and the rooms had settled into a quiet, dusty emptiness, their walls a pattern of dark squares from the pictures which had been taken down and sold. Lotta, who left this morning, had been the last to go, and for the first time since she could remember, Frances was utterly alone. She stood rooted to the spot, unable — now that the moment had come — to bring herself to leave. As long as she was here she could hold on to her father, but when she stepped through the front door she would be leaving behind everything she had ever known.

The last month had been spent on her

own in the house. The cook had left not long after the funeral, and her meals had been taken at the desk in the morning room, prepared by Lotta. Frances had hoped Lucille would visit, but her cousin never came. She wanted to tell someone about the dread which was bearing down on her. She was frightened of leaving England, and needed reassurance that she wouldn't be forgotten. She called on the Hamiltons, but the maid told her they had gone to Bath for the month. Frances had taken to waking up in the dead of night, her heart pounding. It was always the same dream. She was floating on the surface of a black sea, and when she screamed no one could hear her.

After a few minutes, she walked down the hall, her boots clacking on the stone floor. She pushed open the door to her father's study. The hinges creaked, and the familiar sound conjured an image of him sitting at his desk, but when she stepped into the room it was empty. The curtains had been stripped from the windows, and the rug had been pulled off the floor, exposing raw, unpolished boards. The room smelt of him. Of cigar smoke and something else that lingered.

The only piece of furniture left over from the auction was his chair, which stood alone in the center of the room, almost as if his ghost sat upon it. The green leather on the seat had wrinkled, and there was a dip from the many years of bearing his weight. She placed a hand on the hollow, half expecting it to be warm, but it was cool and slightly tacky against her palm. She sank into the chair and pulled her knees up to her chest. When she thought she might cry, she clenched her jaw and pushed the heels of her hands into her eyes until the blackness was punctured by shards of light. Perhaps if she stayed exactly where she was, the world would come to a halt and she would never have to leave. But a moment later she heard a hammering on the door. It was the cabdriver, impatient to be off, and she uncurled herself and — for the last time — walked down the hall and out of the house.

Paddington Station was a heaving roar of noise and smoke. Crowds surged in all directions. Frances, unused to such a rush of people, was momentarily overwhelmed. She had only a few minutes to get herself and her luggage on the train, but she couldn't find a porter. Cursing the cab which had flung her down on the side of the street, she lugged her trunk toward the station concourse. Men pressed against her on all sides. A boy selling the *Penny Paper* walked up and down the line shouting the day's news. Usually she would have had Kerrick or her father here to help, but *usual* didn't count. She would have to make do by herself.

"Watch where you're at!" Two young porters in caps ran past, wheeling trolleys piled high with cases.

"You'll get run over if you stand there!" one of them shouted, knocking her sprawling onto the wet station floor. She stood up, brushed the mud off her skirts, and pushed her way along the edges of the throng until the crush eased. There was a pie shop, closed for business, and she stood for a moment resting in the doorway. There was no porter here, just two businessmen in black frock coats who walked past her without a second glance. Something tugged at her sleeve and she swung round, bumping into a thick-waisted man who wore an old coachman's blue greatcoat, buttonless and blackened by damp. His hair was matted with grease, and his breath smelt of drink. "Sewin' cotton, Miss?"

She shook her head with an attempt at authority, but he bent closer, thrusting forward a rack of dirty cotton reels. His hand was swollen with cold; black grime

75

etched between bulges of tight red skin. He edged forward as she backed away. "Cotton, Miss?" He took a step nearer. "On'y one for a penny."

Frances turned, but he was too agile. "Cat got your tongue? Too fancy to talk?"

He waddled towards her with exaggerated steps, laughing and gyrating his hips until she was backed up into the small doorway with her shoulders pressing into the knocker and the man's coat, stiff with age, brushing the front of her dress. He snatched at her wrist and held it, and when he smiled his mouth was full of broken, yellowing teeth.

"I need a bit of cash," he said, leering at her. She shoved him away with her free hand, but the strike had no impact on the solidity of his body. He grasped her wrist and twisted it with the other into the grip of one hand. Then he felt around her waist for a hidden purse. Frances screamed, and a moment later his body was being dragged away from her by a tall, well-built man in a tweed jacket with wild black hair and a thick beard. The cotton seller stumbled away.

"Are you all right?" the man asked, putting a hand on her shoulder and looking at her closely. He had dark eyes, like pools of ink. "Did he hurt you?"

"No. Thank you." Her voice shook slightly.

"Could you help me? I'm meant to be catching the one o'clock to Southampton, but I'm afraid it leaves any minute. I need a porter."

"That's my train," he said, swinging her trunk effortlessly onto one shoulder. "Platform three. We'd better hurry or we'll miss it." He shouldered his way through the crowds and across the concourse, and she followed in his wake. Their train, still motionless, belched clouds of steam, while men in uniform walked down the platform shutting up the doors.

"Lucky I happened to be there," he said, handing her up. There was a piercing whistle, and the train shuddered into life.

"Thank you," she said, turning in the doorway, but he was already gone, darting up the platform to the first-class carriages.

The train careered through the outskirts of the city too fast to make anything meaningful of her last glimpses of London, but there was no use wishing it to slow down. Her life in England was over. In her portmanteau was a ticket stamped "Female Middle Class Emigration Society." Edwin had paid for her passage to Cape Town under the protection of the charity, and in a compartment at the end of the carriage she found the group of girls traveling to South Africa. She stepped inside, and an absent minded-looking, middle-aged woman with round eyes and florid cheeks looked up reluctantly from her Bible.

"Miss Irvine?"

Frances nodded.

"Good. I was worried we had lost someone already." She dabbed at her nose with a handkerchief. "I'm Sister Mary-Joseph, your matron for the journey."

The girls shifted along the bench to make room, and Frances sat down between the window and a girl with blond curls, who gave her a broad, white-toothed smile and offered her a mint.

"Thanks," Frances said, dipping her hand into the paper bag.

"I'm Mariella."

"Frances."

The girl leant in and breathed a wave of peppermint into her ear. "She's not reading the Bible, you know. There's another book hidden inside the cover."

"What is it?" Frances whispered.

"That's what I've been trying to figure out."

Sister Mary-Joseph was employed by the charity to safeguard the moral health of her eight charges, ensuring they didn't fall in love with the first seaman who smiled at them. Frances knew that these girls, like her, must be apprehensive about the kind of lives they would find in South Africa, but she couldn't help envying them. They had signed up to teach or to nurse. Their lives were to some extent their own, and they would more than likely marry someone of their own choosing. She traced a gloved finger through the condensation on the window, revealing a flickering strip of green. There was no changing the future towards which she was rapidly hurtling.

Only yesterday she had given up her mourning clothes, folding them into a box which would be sent, with the last of her possessions, to Lucille and Victoria. Edwin had written telling her to bring only the simplest things. He had hinted at limited means, saying that their day-to-day lives would be basic. Colonial girls, he wrote, were different to their counterparts in England. It wasn't beneath even the best of them to cook, sew, and do the washing. She wouldn't have any need for fine dresses and white gloves. Instead, he told her, use the space in your luggage for things of use which couldn't be found easily in South Africa. At least two pairs of strong boots for walking, gloves for gardening, a good sewing kit, some muslin which could be sewn into nets to keep off flies, and fabric — at least ten yards — to make curtains. Her trousseau should be as practical as possible. Don't be tempted to bring silverware and expensive linen; instead pack cooking utensils and one or two good iron pots. If you possibly can, he wrote, bring a sewing machine. It will be an enormous comfort to you. Frances struggled to imagine any scenario in which a sewing machine would be a comfort to her. She hadn't the first idea how to use one.

Edwin's list was so outlandish that when she tried to picture her life in South Africa, she kept coming back to an image of herself sitting at a sewing machine wearing canvas gloves and heavy-duty leather boots. It might have made her laugh if he hadn't been so clearly serious. He obviously didn't have any idea of her capabilities. He had insisted on having her because she was Sir John Hamilton's niece, and now he wanted her to become some kind of missionary's wife. Still, she had done her best, conceding to the boots and gloves and using up precious space in her trunk for two iron pots. Almost everything fashionable had been left behind. Alongside her two cotton dresses, her black woolen bodice and skirt, and her stockings and undergarments, she had brought only one pair of white kid gloves, a bundle of lace, and a silk evening dress — there was bound to be an occasion at Kimberley when she would want it. She had packed a white muslin gown for the wedding and a pair of straw hats to keep off the sun. She wasn't sure what she would be able to find in South Africa, so she had brought a few pots of oil of cacao, two bottles of tuberose perfume, enough powder to last six months, and some bath soaps. There was a book on household management — a gift from her aunt, Lady Hamilton — and finally, stowed at the bottom of the trunk, her easel and her watercolors.

The two girls sitting on the bench opposite had struck up a quick friendship. They were debating which was worse, a Boer or a Bushman. Their voices clattered over the fragile silence kept by the rest of the compartment. Occasionally, a tunnel shuttered them in momentary darkness and they were quiet, only to start up again when the train burst out into the light.

Cornfields gave way to rolling green downs, the sky became overcast, and rain began to fall in spats against the window. A cemetery was backed too close to the railway track, gravestones gaping out like broken teeth. The train cut through a chalk escarpment down into an open, verdant valley floor, past a forest of hawthorns and an ugly flat-roofed brick building which loomed out of a clearing in the trees: Southampton's poorhouse. All of a sudden the landscape opened up and they were skimming along the edge of Southampton Water to the mouth of the Itchen. A beach of clean white shingle curved away from the track, and they were there.

Porters darted onto the train, offloading their trunks onto trolleys marked "The Cape Run." Frances stepped down behind a scrawny boy who was clutching a birdcage half his size. His mother snatched up his hand and scolded him for dragging his feet. The girls walked down the platform, past the first-class carriages, where servants in livery were handing down luggage. There was no sign of the man who had helped her, and she wondered whether he had been too late to board the train.

The station led right onto a promenade, an open expanse of sea and sky framed by green hills rising up on either side of The Solent. The wind snatched at their umbrellas and made sails of their skirts. The air was damp with rain and held the sharp, metallic taste of salt and, beneath it, the cloying stench of rotting fish. Mail wagons belonging to steam-packet companies with names like "Oriental" and "The West India" surged up from the docks. Coaches and luggage wagons competed for space, offloading cargo and passengers, who scrambled out onto the wet cobbles shouting for their footmen to follow. A man with a wheedling voice called "Iced ginger beer" to a cold, uninterested crowd. Sister Mary-Joseph ushered the girls over to a sailor who was shouting above the commotion, "The *Cambrian* this way! Passengers for the Cape run!"

They joined a group of bedraggled figures waiting to be handed down into a small steam tug. A stretch of canvas had been drawn across it for shelter. The sea looked dark and ugly under the blanket of fine rain. It moved with a lurching swell, swilling corrugated boxes and submerged newspapers up against the side of the pier. When it was Frances's turn, she stepped forwards and gave her hand to the ship's boy, put a foot carefully onto the slick wood, and stepped down into the belly of the boat. Black smoke pumped up into the dark, wet sky. A steam packet maneuvered its way out from behind them, and the tug heaved in its wake, grinding itself against the algaed bricks of the pier. As they headed out into The Solent, the sky brightened. Seagulls wheeled and mewed above them, flashes of gray in a high white sky. One of the girls pointed out the Isle of Wight, and they all strained to look at the faint shadow of hills etched against the horizon.

The tug chugged over to the docks and into the shadow of the *Cambrian.* The steamship towered over them, motionless on the surface of the sea, like a huge factory with its steel plates and black funnels. Two squat collier ships were pulled up next to it, and their crews heaved sacks of coal onto pulleys. Frances lifted her shawl over her shoulders to prevent the fine black coal dust from settling on her dress. It was cold, and a forlorn gloom had fallen over the girls. Excitement had given way to apprehension. The seawater swilling around in the bottom of the boat seeped into their boots, and when Frances scrunched her toes, water oozed out from between the leather seams. The colliers finally finished, but they had to give way to a smart little steamship which had pulled alongside carrying first-class passengers. More waiting under a drizzling rain. The women from the Female Middle Class Emigration Society were low priority in the scheme of things.

An hour later, their clothes wet through to the skin, the girls clambered up a ladder onto the deck. A turmoil of passengers from all cabins, first down to steerage, milled together, impatient to find their berths. A woman, looking anxious, clutched her shawl and demanded to know where she would find her luggage. Casks, barrels, and crates were being loaded onto the deck by sailors whose voices carried above the racket. Wire boxes stuffed full of squawking chickens were stacked one on top of another, and a cow, supremely calm, licked the fresh paint from the balustrade.

"Miss Irvine?" Frances turned to see a florid-faced gentleman with orange whiskers bearing down on her. "Well, what about this!" he cried. "I didn't know you were traveling on the *Cambrian.*"

"Mr. Nettleton." She gave him her hand, and he turned to the group standing behind them at the stern.

"Liza!" He waved to his wife. "Look who I've found!"

Mrs. Nettleton, a friend of her cousin Lucille, was easy to spot. She was a tall woman with a manicured beauty: no eyebrows, and a neat, fashionable hat trimmed with brightly colored parrot feathers, now beading with the rain which blew in under her umbrella. The hat looked pathetically jaunty against the iron-gray sea. She was talking to a broad-shouldered gentleman whom Frances recognized as the man who had helped her in the station. He had made the train after all. Neither of them looked up, although Frances was sure Mrs. Nettleton had seen her.

"Liza!" her husband called again. "It's Miss Irvine!"

His wife said something in a low voice to her companion, and stepped over to them. She gave Frances a thin smile. "How do you do, Miss Irvine?" She didn't offer her hand. "I was sorry to hear about your father."

"Thank you."

The gentleman joined their group, gazed at her, and — when she caught his eye — winked. His eyes, dark lashed and heavy lidded, weren't black, as they had looked in the gloom of the station, but a rich amber flecked with green, like stones glinting underwater. She smiled at him. There was an awkward silence while everyone waited for Mrs. Nettleton to make introductions. After a moment, Frances realized that Liza Nettleton, who had known her since she was a very young girl, was refusing to introduce her. She froze in embarrassment and felt a deep flush rising up her neck.

Ignoring her, Mrs. Nettleton turned to her husband. "Can you believe they still won't show us to our cabin? I think you should have another word with the steward."

The other gentleman ran a hand over his jaw and looked at Frances. "We have already had the pleasure of making each other's acquaintance, but there wasn't time to ask your name."

"Ah, so you've met already," Mr. Nettleton said, looking pleased. "Miss Irvine, this is Mr. William Westbrook. Mr. Westbrook, Miss Frances Irvine."

Frances gave the man her hand. He didn't look English, though his voice carried no accent. He had a well-trimmed beard, wire-black. His nose was straight and fine-boned, but his nostrils flared slightly and his mouth had a wide fullness which was curling into a smile as he looked at her. She realized he understood her awkwardness and it amused him.

"Miss Irvine is Sir John Hamilton's niece," Mr. Nettleton said, glancing anxiously at his wife, who was looking unhappy. Then he said to Frances, "Did I miss your name on the passenger list? Who are you traveling with?"

"I have assisted passage to Cape Town." Her hand went to her throat, where it began to pull nervously at the soft skin of her neck. Awkward questions were sure to follow the revelation that she was traveling second class.

Mrs. Nettleton glanced over at the huddle of girls by the balustrade. "With the Female Middle Class Emigration Society?" Frances nodded. "I've done some charity work for them in London. A wonderful organization. In fact," she said, laying a hand on Mr. Westbrook's arm, "Mrs. Sambourne, who chairs the society, is a very good friend of mine." She gave Frances a smile, both sympathetic and dismissive. "You must let me know if I can help with anything. Mrs. Sambourne asked me specifically to keep an eye on her girls.

"Now, Mr. Westbrook," Mrs. Nettleton said in a confidential tone, leading him away, "you promised to help us with our little theatrical presentation. Do you know *The Palace of Truth*?"

He ignored her, and instead said to Frances, "Miss Irvine, you're traveling without family?"

"Yes."

"Then you should certainly join us for dinner one evening."

Mrs. Nettleton frowned, two fingers pinching the fabric of Mr. Westbrook's coat.

"A lovely idea and well meant, but I'm not sure Mrs. Sambourne would approve of you making favorites of her girls."

"Nonsense! You know Miss Irvine, and I'm sure if I speak to the captain he would allow her an invitation to dine with us in the first-class saloon." He looked at Frances with a warm, open smile, and his eyes shone conspiratorially. He was being kind, but he was also enjoying frustrating Mrs. Nettleton's finer social principles, and Frances couldn't bring herself to join in the joke. There was no pleasure in being used as bait to rile Mrs. Nettleton. She was stung by the woman's reluctance to introduce her, and it had reminded her all at once of the humiliation attached to emigration. You didn't leave England without leaving Society.

"Thank you, but I'm afraid Mrs. Nettleton is right. Dinner wouldn't be possible. Now, if you'll excuse me."

As she left, she heard Mrs. Nettleton say, in a voice that dropped to just above a whisper, "Mr. Westbrook, you must promise me not to start up any kind of flirtation. It would be too unkind. You can't imagine how difficult it is for some of these girls. Mrs. Sambourne tells me . . ."

Frances had hoped that traveling to South Africa would be a fresh start, an escape from English Society, but the *Cambrian* offered no more protection than her uncle's drawing room.

SEVEN

There was a squall out at sea and the ship was kept in port for two days waiting for better weather. Entertainments were planned for the voyage. A weekly paper was started called the *Cambrian Argus,* and a concert was decided on by two elderly ladies in first class. They held auditions in the saloon, and Frances, wanting to keep her thoughts away from her father, went along. They declared her a nice little player, and gave her permission to practice on the pianoforte in the music room at four o'clock every day.

On the way to her first practice, a voice called to her from the stairwell. "Miss Irvine?" She turned. A man was standing above her, coming down from the deck. The bright day made him into a shadow. Her eyes took a moment to adjust to the light. It was Mr. Westbrook, his square jaw set to one side and his dark brows bunched into a frown.

"Are you cross with me?"

"Cross?"

"You thought I was making fun of you yesterday." He walked down the steps until he was standing beside her, quite close, in the small well at the bottom of the stairs. That was clever of him, to have read her so closely.

"And you weren't?"

"It's not an easy journey to make, to a new continent, by yourself." He leant a hand on the wall above her. She could feel the heat rising from his body. He blocked out the light from the stairwell, and they stood together in near-darkness. "I remember feeling very alone when I first went to Africa."

It was a long time since someone had offered her any comfort, and the ease with which he understood her made her want to confide in him. She shrugged her shoulders and smiled. "To be honest, it probably makes no difference whether I am in South Africa or England."

He considered her for a moment. "Irvine. Is it Irish?"

"Yes," she said, bristling at the question. "My father was Irish."

"A merchant?"

"No. A shopkeeper. He made and sold

furniture." She wasn't going to dress it up for him. Let him think what he liked.

"Some of my greatest friends are Irish. Wonderful drinkers."

She laughed. "Yes. My father had a talent for it."

"It wasn't your father who started Irvine & Hitchcock?"

"Yes. That was him."

She steeled herself for him to say something pointed about her father's losses, but instead he said, "What a coincidence. So it was your father who started up the Charity for the Houseless Poor?"

Frances nodded. "I didn't find out about it until he died. He never talked to me about his public work. Do you know the charity?"

"A little. Your father was generous with his success. He had a reputation for being openhanded. This particular charity is unusual, you see, in that anyone is allowed through the door, regardless of sex, race, or criminal history. I'm partly Jewish, so I like the idea of a charity that doesn't discriminate. It houses some six hundred people every night who would otherwise be on the streets. Well, we donated some money, and were invited to dinner. Your father seemed a very charismatic man." He looked at her kindly. "You must have been proud to be his daughter."

She hadn't been proud, not for a long time. There had been recrimination and disapproval from all sides in the aftermath of his death, and she realized with a surge of relief that she had been waiting for someone to name the qualities of the man she had respected and adored.

"There are lots of people who would say otherwise," she said.

"There are lots of people who are fools. Your father was a genius in business. So what if there are men who resent him for it? A man should be judged by his achievements over a lifetime, not by a moment's ill judgment." He straightened up, flexing his hands so his knuckles cracked. "Besides, it's not as if he was the only one to take a punt on Northern Pacific. I would rather achieve greatness as your father did, and lose it all at the end, than set my sights on mediocrity and risk nothing."

Mr. Westbrook had given her father a better, more honest tribute than she had heard from anyone who had known him personally. For the first time, someone had spoken about her father's background — that he had been born Irish and poor — not as something to be ashamed of, but as a mark of pride. The huge burden of her grief shifted, making way for something lighter. She wanted him to stay. She hadn't had a chance to ask him about himself, but he was already moving away. "Good-bye, Miss Irvine. I wish you all the best at the Cape."

Eight

The hot, crowded little cabin reeked of shame. They were cargo being shipped for export. Women without choices. Their families had thrown them out to save the embarrassment or expense of keeping them at home, and emigration was an acknowledgment of failure.

"I'd rather die than spend my life looking after other people." Mariella unlaced her boots, lifted a foot onto Frances's bunk, and began to unroll a stocking. Anne stood next to her, unbuttoning a petticoat. There were three girls in the cabin, and only just enough room between the bunks on either wall for the two girls to undress. Mariella grunted as she struggled to lever the stocking off her foot, and her thick, glossy blond hair spilled onto Frances's bunk. She spent hours pinning it each morning, teasing out two ringlets with curlers heated over the fire in the fore saloon. When she took off her clothes she seemed to swell in size, her ample pink flesh springing loose from a tight corset. She was quite happy to walk around their cabin showing off the full weight of her breasts with their expanse of creamy skin and darkened, stretched areolae. Frances, unused to living with other girls, was surprised and a little revolted by this casual lack of modesty.

Anne slept in the bunk opposite. She was a petite Catholic girl with an oval face and black hair parted down the middle, which gave her the look of an Italian Madonna. Her hands were small and delicate, and always busy with a skein of wool, knitting shawls or bed socks for her mother. She looked younger than eighteen, spoke rarely, and laughed even less. Frances suspected she was homesick already. She was going to South Africa to be a nurse, and Mariella was needling her.

"Imagine breathing in other people's diseases all day long." Mariella stepped out of her dress, unstrapped her bustle, leant her forearms against the bunk above Frances, and waited for Anne to loosen her laces.

"There's a man in steerage who had his arm blown clean off in the mines. Two nurses had to hold him down while they sewed his shoulder blade back in. He said their dresses were so red you couldn't have paid for scarlet that color."

"Mariella!" Frances scolded. Anne was biting her lower lip and looked as if she might cry.

"Well what?" Mariella bent her head to look in at her. "I should just like to know why, that's all."

"Not all of us, Mariella, are going to the colonies to be married," Anne said, working on the last of Mariella's laces.

"I shouldn't think you'd turn down an offer if it came your way."

Mariella wriggled out of her corset and into a nightdress. She planted a wide, pink foot on the edge of the bunk, her big toe inches from Frances's face, and heaved herself up. "There aren't enough men in England to go round. They've all escaped to the colonies. I intend to redress the balance." Despite themselves, the girls laughed. Mariella had a way of getting at the truth.

Sister Mary-Joseph looked into their cabin to check that the girls were in their beds, and a few minutes later the ship's bell rang, the signal for all lights to be extinguished. Frances blew out her candle. It was their first night at sea. Finally, that afternoon, the guns had sounded, the sails had been hoisted onto the yards, and they had lost sight of Southampton as it receded into dusk. The second-class berths were towards the bow of the ship, close to the steam funnel, and the room was thick with the heat of the engines. Frances, used to sleeping alone, disliked the warmth and the damp stuffiness of the other girls' bodies. She asked for the porthole to be left open at night, but Mariella had been shocked. What if a wave came in and drenched them?

"How can you be so confident that you'll like what you find in South Africa?" Anne asked when they had settled in darkness. "You've no idea what to expect."

"No," Mariella said, "but it can't be any worse than what I left behind in England."

"What about your father? Surely you'll miss him."

"My father is a drunk. I worked fourteen hours a day for three years sewing buttons on coats in a factory in Bristol to support him, and when he finally found work he threw me out of the house to make room for a girl half his age." Mariella was older than them both, and usually imperturbable. It hurt to hear her sound so bitter.

"I agree," Anne said, breaking the silence. "South Africa has to be better. At least there'll be work. That was the worst thing when my father died. The helplessness. Not knowing how my mother and I would feed ourselves."

"I thought you were trained as a nurse?" Frances asked.

"Not then I wasn't. My mother took on work as a seamstress, and earned just enough to send me to nursing school. Only for a year, though, and I couldn't find a hospital to take me at the end of it. Too many girls with more experience."

"But you have a position in South Africa?"

"Yes. I'll have to start in Cape Town, but I hope to go to Kimberley eventually. There is a nurse there, in charge of the hospital. Sister Clara. She is famous in South Africa. They say she is tireless in her helping of others. Almost a saint. At the age of ten she declared that she wanted to be a missionary, and she managed it, against her parents' wishes, through sheer determination."

"Well, Frances," Mariella said after a moment. "What about you?"

"What about me?" she asked, reluctant to tell them.

"We've both bared our souls. Now it's your turn. What's your story?"

"There is no story. My father is dead." She swallowed. It was still difficult to say it out loud. "And my uncle wouldn't take me in. I have no qualifications. There was nothing I could do in England."

"So you took the first proposal that came your way?"

She was surprised at the ease with which Mariella understood her situation. It was strangely comforting to have it distilled into a few words. "Yes. That's pretty much it, I suppose."

"Well, aren't we a cheerful bunch! We'll have to do our best to enjoy ourselves on the *Cambrian,* while we still have a chance."

When Frances woke in the night the cabin was dark. She had no idea how long she had been asleep. She could hear the heavy revolving of the screw in the engine room, the timbers of the ship grinding against each other, and then, much closer, the quick, shallow breaths of a girl crying.

"Anne?" she whispered.

The breathing stopped for a moment, then gave way with a choked sob. Frances stared out into the darkness, waiting for the room to take shape. "What is it?"

"Did you hear about the *Castle*?" Anne caught her breath. "The boatswain says it's a mile to the bottom. It makes me feel dizzy imagining it." Frances had heard about the *Castle.* It had hit rocks off St. Helena some time after midnight, sliding to the bottom

101

so quickly that the crew didn't have time to rouse the passengers from their beds. Four sailors survived.

"There's no shame in being afraid," Frances reassured her, but it was a shallow truth. They were all, in their different ways, fearful and ashamed. She thought about her uncle's reluctance to take her in, the ease with which he talked disparagingly of her father, and her cousins' embarrassment over her change in status.

"But you must be excited?" Anne's voice was full of generous pleasure. "You'll be married in South Africa!"

Frances didn't reply, giving the conversation up to the throb and pull of the engines. She stayed awake long after Anne's breathing had merged with Mariella's into the soft, heavy rhythm of sleep. She thought about her aunt's filthy, cramped house in Manchester and her brood of children who would have made her into a servant, always fetching, bathing, and scolding. Edwin Matthews had offered escape, and she had taken her chance, but he wasn't so different from her uncle. He had picked his moment carefully and caught her in a cage. It might be better than living with her aunt, but it felt like entrapment, nonetheless.

And yet, there was more to it. He had

managed to unsettle her. Their meeting hadn't been as simple as she had thought it would be. She had expected him to be embarrassed by the corner he had penned her into, and had presumed he would acknowledge the awkwardness of his situation. But instead he had looked at her with a quiet expectation and an attentiveness that she found oppressive. When he kissed her he had tried to be slow and careful, his fingers barely pressing against her waist, but he couldn't hide his urgency any more than he could hide the weight of his possessiveness, with its awful note of triumph. It was humiliating. He would want to own her completely, to expose every part of her, and she would have no choice but to open herself up to him.

Panic made her skin crawl. She pulled her hand out from under the sheets and looked at its whiteness in the dark, reassuring herself that she was still there, as a ship might fix its coordinates on a star. What does a person become when they have nothing left to hold on to? She sat up and, defying ship's rules, fumbled for a candle and lit it, breathing deeply to suppress the dread which was welling up inside her.

When her mother had died she had felt limp and hollowed out, like one of the rabbits hanging up in the pantry with its guts in the sink. But her father had been there to face the awfulness of their grief and take it on himself. He stood between her and death, and she had felt safe as long as he was there. Now he was dead, and Frances wasn't sure she could make do without him. His absence left a cold, black place inside her which seemed to be growing as the days went on, and there was no one who knew her well enough to stop it.

She reached into the shelf over her bed and pulled out her copy of Tennyson. Between its pages was a photograph. It had been, for as long as she could remember, tacked to the wall of the morning room; the only evidence of her mother left in the house after her death. Frances had taken it with her when she left, easing it out of the frame and wondering as she did so whether the last fingers to have touched the picture had been her mother's. The edges of the photograph were curled and yellowing. Frances knew it had been taken at the zoo, on the day the first hippopotamus had arrived from Africa, and you could see the metal bars of a cage to the right-hand side of the frame. Her mother, narrow-faced and strong-jawed, clearly not a beauty but with a certain physical stature, leant on her father's arm. She looked up at him, her mouth half open, lips curved into a laughing smile. He was looking at the photographer, but there were small dimples on his cheeks and you could tell he was trying not to laugh. What had been said in the seconds before the photograph was taken? Frances felt a jolt of pain. He was gone and their happiness could never be re-created.

She didn't know how her parents had met, but she did have some idea about her father's childhood. He had never discussed it with Frances, but his sister, Mrs. Arrow, who thought she was a spoilt child, had made a point of telling her how it had been for them growing up. Her father was the eldest and only surviving son of an Irish Catholic family who had emigrated during the worst of the potato famines and ended up in Manchester. He was six when they came to England. They had been farmers, comfortably well off, but in Manchester they had to make do with the ground floor of a cottage with one window and a horizon of bleak, gray stone. The four daughters, who all came later, shared the bed with their parents, and Tom, her father, had slept on the floor. They shared the yard and the outhouse with six families and a plague of rats who came inside in winter. Frances's grandfather had gone to work for a tannery, collecting feces off the streets, and the daughters had learned to stitch by the greasy light of a tallow. Mrs. Arrow told her all this while she fingered through Frances's clothes, her eyes assessing the vast wealth stored in the cupboards of this young girl who had never known what it was to boil huge vats of water over an open range or pick lice out of the seams of her underwear. But how did he meet Frances's mother? Her aunt's cool eyes told her nothing, but Frances didn't need her for that part of the story.

The Hamiltons' cook was getting on in years, but she had a fierce memory, and she had been with the family so long that her loyalty was oblivious to changing generations. She had arthritis, and Frances discovered that she would talk to her if she helped her with the jobs her fingers could no longer manage. So she shelled beans and listened.

"She was always Sir John's favorite," the cook told Frances, pounding dough on a slab of white marble. "And that's the root of the problem. When your grandfather found out, he couldn't forgive her. He refused to let her out of the house. Said she would marry a shop boy over his dead body." She paused to blow out air and wipe

106

a floured arm across her forehead. "Your father came, but they wouldn't let him in. It was your mother who slipped out to him the next day, and she never set foot in this house again. Your grandfather wouldn't let us speak of her, and he wouldn't let anyone in the family visit her. Not even when she was clearly dying. It wasn't until your grandfather passed away that your uncle felt able to have you in this house."

The dull clang of the ship's bell rang overhead, calling the watch, and Frances blew out the candle. Two o'clock. A cockerel, not wanting to be caught out, made a strangled cry into the dark. Something cold and hard which she didn't recognize was beating in her blood. A thin veneer of anger had calcified around her grief. Why should she feel ashamed of her father's bankruptcy? Why should she be banished to the colonies? She let herself imagine, briefly, the pleasure of having enough wealth to be independent.

NINE

At some point in the night Frances must have drifted asleep. When she woke up the ship was rolling. A glass was sliding backwards and forwards on the floor between the berths. There was a rancid smell in the cabin, which she couldn't place until she heard a choking retch from the bunk above. She whispered into the dark, and Mariella's voice came back to her in a wet cough, asking for a bowl. Frances allowed herself a few seconds then forced herself up, clinging on to the bunks in the dark as their cabin heaved from side to side. She lit a candle and in the flickering light found a bowl under the bunk. She passed it up to Mariella, who grasped it just in time, and Frances saw the sheen of sweat on her face, and her fingers, clogged with vomit, as she lurched over it.

She pulled her wool shawl over her shoulders and felt her way along the narrow corridor to the bathroom: a box cubicle with running water and a small zinc bath. Anne was inside, kneeling on the linoleum floor, vomiting into the toilet bowl. Frances stepped around her and came back to the cabin with wet cloths, cleaned Mariella's face and hands, and didn't resist when the weight of her head rolled into her shoulder. The girl's skin was damp and she moaned softly, clouding Frances's neck with a sour stink. By the time she had pulled the wet sheet off the mattress and changed her nightdress, a dirty glimmer of light was showing at the porthole. Anne came back and crawled into her bunk. She was a better patient than Mariella, administering to herself and never breathing a word of complaint.

Only once, the next day, when Mariella asked her to read aloud in the cabin as the ship listed from one side to the other, did Frances feel nausea creeping over her. It pulled at her stomach and made her head spin. She went up on deck and stood for a few moments under the squalling rain until it passed. The captain caught sight of her and asked her name.

"Well, Miss Irvine," he said jovially, "at least someone's on their feet. Though you'll not have much company at dinner tonight."

He was right, and she had eaten in the fore saloon alone except for a group of English soldiers who came in late. The lantern on the beam above swung a murky light over the tables, and the soldiers didn't notice her sitting in the corner. They were young but toughened round the edges, like fresh leather left out in the rain, and they had spent the last few days contriving ways to flirt with the girls in the second cabin, somehow getting their hands on fresh flowers, which they delivered up to them in baskets of eggs. Frances was interested to hear them talking alone. Their words were coarse and unfiltered by a sense of propriety. Two of them peeled apples, and a bottle passed between them. One soldier was telling how he had bought a native girl from a friend in return for a bottle of Cape brandy.

"Best deal I ever made. There weren't many flies on this one, I tell you."

The bottle clinked against a glass as it was pushed along the table. "They're a darned sight easier to keep than white women."

"What about those kaffirs they hung for being spies? They sent them up a tree with ropes round their necks, and told them to hang themselves."

"Where was that?"

"In the Transvaal. One of them wouldn't

jump, so they shot at his buttocks. The nigger caught hold of a branch as he came down and kept hold of it until they shot his hands free."

One of the soldiers grunted. "It's not right."

"No, but it'd make a man laugh."

Frances had seen an African serving in a hotel in London, but he had worn clothes and spoken English. She couldn't imagine a country peopled by men dressed in skins.

When she went up on deck the following morning, the light was dazzling. A high wind scuppered what was left of the clouds, rattling the clinches and filling the sails. Waves tore towards them, six or seven feet high. They reared up over the deck, but the ship always rose on the swell, staying just ahead of them, and they rolled on in a torrent of foam. A fine spray was thrown off the sea and she licked the salt off her lips and laughed. This was a wild, empty place, and it filled her with joy after the stuffy heat and wrenching sickness of the cabin. There were few people. She caught sight of the boy with the birdcage sitting cross-legged with his back to the cargo hatch. He held on to the cage with one hand, encouraging the bird to sit on his grubby finger. There was no sign of the stern woman who had chivied him on the platform. "Where is your mother?" she asked.

The boy was concentrating intently on the bird, which hopped from bar to bar, bobbing his head at the boy's finger. "My aunt? She's not feeling well."

"Are your parents in South Africa?"

He shook his head. The bird held on to the bars with one claw and with the other took a delicate step onto his forefinger, testing it for stability. Satisfied, it shuffled along until both claws were wrapped around his skin. The boy looked up at Frances and grinned. "I knew she'd do it eventually."

"Have you had her long?"

"Not very. My mother asked me to look after her, but my aunt says she won't survive the cold nights."

"Can't you take her below deck?"

He shook his head. "She's not allowed. She chatters too much."

Frances let her hand rest on the boy's head. It was like ruffling a pile of downy feathers. After a moment she produced a sugar lump from her jacket pocket and gave it to him. He smiled, and she said, "Do you have a name?"

"Gilbert."

"Well, Gilbert, can you tell me what the

worst vegetable is to have on board a ship?"

"Miss?"

"It's a riddle," she said, smiling. "You'll have to work it out." She left him puzzling over it, and walked towards the stern, stopping at the chalked line that was drawn each morning across the deck. Beyond was the area reserved exclusively for first-class passengers. Two sailors were up on the mizzenmast trying to reef a sail which flapped viciously out of their hands. She heard shouts, broken by the wind, and saw a group of men — three sailors and a passenger in shirtsleeves — gathered about twenty feet from where she was standing, leaning out over the water. They had rigged the gangplank, and a group of white birds circled them, dipping and diving.

A steward walked past and saw her watching. "Baited a fish. Mr. Westbrook's been fighting it for gone an hour."

She was curious to see William Westbrook in this new guise of fisherman, and she watched for half an hour under flickering sunlight, until they had hauled the fish on deck. It was at least six feet long, and broad. A swordfish, she realized, admiring the long, pointed spear. Its body was slack and its mouth gaped slightly, revealing a rusted iron hook the size of her forearm. The sailors grinned and slapped Mr. Westbrook on the back. His sleeves were rolled up, his collar was open, and his hair fell in damp curls to his neck. He handed the rod to one of the crew then squatted down to wash his hands in a bucket of water. His shirt, drenched with sweat and seawater, clung to his chest. He glanced along the ship to where she was standing. She saw him register her, and felt caught out. Her ears were full of the roar of the sea. He watched her, his mouth opening into a wide smile. She looked away, embarrassed. The sailors had strung up the fish with a hook through its tail. Its gills heaved open and shut, the thick white flesh breaking rhythmically to reveal a rib of scarlet gashes. Two crew boys winched it up and another dug a knife into its belly. Blood gulped out onto deck. Frances, revolted by the sight of the fish turned inside out, put a hand to her mouth and swallowed. When she glanced back at Mr. Westbrook, he was leaning against the ship's wheel talking to the captain, laughing and shaking his hand.

Mr. Westbrook appeared beside her a moment later, one hand supporting himself on the rail, the other shielding his eyes from the sun. "You think I'm a brute?"

She denied it, but he said, "You can be honest, Miss Irvine."

So she nodded and said, "It seems a mean thing to do."

"And yet, I don't think you would think so if you had been the one reeling it in. It's a wonderful thing to fight a fish that size. The dark body thrashing beneath the surface, the two of you locked in battle." He laughed. "You look doubtful."

"I am."

"Your sympathy is misplaced. The sea looks fairly benign today, but she can be a mean mistress. You can be sure she'll have her sport with us when a storm blows up."

Frances smiled. "All the more reason to placate her."

"Ha!" He laughed. "Yes, perhaps you're right. But I've never been very good at placating."

He had the same poised confidence she had noticed in him before, but it was softened now by a boyish enthusiasm. He looked pleased with himself after his catch, balancing on the balls of his feet, squinting into the sun, one hand thrust into his pocket. She wouldn't have been surprised if he had launched himself up the ladder to the crow's nest just for the fun of it. He smiled, rueful.

"Now those . . ." He swept his hand to the stern of the ship, where sailors were

115

throwing line out for the group of diving birds. They had baited one of them. The boatswain was drawing it in, flapping frantically, until he had a grasp on its wings. Then he tore the hook from its stretched and gulping throat. "That's nothing but petty cruelty."

"I'm afraid I don't see the difference."

"Have you ever tried eating a gull?"

She couldn't stop herself from smiling, and he grinned back. His enthusiasm was contagious, and for the first time since her father's death she was full of a complete, effortless joy.

"I would like to have painted it," she said, suddenly.

"Painted what?"

"Your swordfish," she said.

"Well, why don't you?" he asked, looking pleased.

She laughed. "I couldn't. Not when the sea's like this."

He leant his elbows back against the railings, and they were both silent for a few seconds, looking across the deck at the sails and the rolling blue of sea and sky. She felt entirely content in his company, just as she had been with her father. They were similar, these men, both large in stature and full of charisma. They both had an easy charm and an infectious ability to enjoy life. She suspected that Mr. Westbrook, like her father, was indifferent to the petty sermonizing of Society. And Frances was sure that there was more to him than met the eye. He could be serious as well as amusing, and he had talked passionately enough about her father's charity to convince her that he had high ideals.

"Miss, Miss, I have it!" Gilbert threw himself breathlessly in front of them.

Frances crouched down. "Whisper it."

He leant into her ear. After a second she nodded.

"Whisper what?" Mr. Westbrook asked.

Gilbert broke into a delighted smile. "Sir, what is the worst vegetable to have on board a ship?"

They both looked at Mr. Westbrook as he thought about it. He paused a long moment, then groaned. "A leek?" Gilbert gave a cry of delight, and Mr. Westbrook shook his head, smiling. "Did you think that one up, Miss Irvine?"

She laughed, and Gilbert tugged at her sleeve. "Another one. Give us another one!"

Later that afternoon, she found a note on her bed. It was an invitation to dinner: *Since Mr. Nettleton and I appear to be the only members of the saloon well enough to dine, I think you must consider it your duty to enliven our company. W.W.*

Frances looked at the quick, confident writing, and gave a private smile. Her hands were sweating slightly, and her fingers left a damp print on the fine linen paper. On an impulse, she smelt it, and caught the faint muskiness of sandalwood; then put it down, embarrassed. Mr. Westbrook was being kind. He pitied her traveling alone and wanted to make her feel included — which was admirable, but it was just this quality of easy-handed generosity which made her like him more than she had reason to. The letter was a clever concoction of intuition and lightheartedness, designed to put her at her ease. He had looked at her standing on deck in her simple cotton dress and seen through the prickliness of her pride. He had captured in an instant her grief, her loneliness, and her reluctance to go to South Africa. And now he seemed to be telling her, subtly, that he understood these things. Her throat tightened, and to her surprise she found herself brushing away tears. His kindness made her vulnerable, and though she wanted to talk to him again, she couldn't bear to be the object of his pity, or Mrs.

Nettleton's scorn, so she wrote out a short letter declining the invitation.

TEN

The following day the weather improved to placid gray skies and calm seas. The ship, so quiet before that you might have been forgiven for believing she carried only a handful of passengers, began to hum with activity, like a beehive struck to life by a stone. As time went on, a routine of sorts established itself. Breakfast at eight, a slow meandering walk along the deck, lunch followed by backgammon — there was a tournament in process — dinner at four, and tea at seven: sardines and boiled eggs.

Frances experienced a sense of freedom and independence on the *Cambrian* that was entirely new to her. In England she had rarely, if ever, been allowed out of the house without her father or Lotta accompanying her. Now she explored the ship on her own and talked to whomever she wished. Sister Mary-Joseph showed little interest in the girls as long as they didn't disturb her. She was reading romances disguised between the covers of her Bible, Mariella had discovered, and she had been forced to emigrate to escape a scandal in England. It made sense. Why else would someone agree to chaperone a group of women out to the colonies for the little money the charity could afford to pay?

The second-class saloon was home to a diverse collection of humanity. The girls traveling with the Female Middle Class Emigration Society all had positions at the Cape as governesses, teachers, or nurses, but there were other figures Frances grew to know by sight. A genteel woman with red eyes and a hacking cough was headed for the sanatoriums near Cape Town. The air in South Africa was second to none for those suffering from pulmonary complaints. Two Swedish cousins with white-blond hair and sunburnt foreheads talked diamond buying to anyone who would listen, and a brisk, efficient-looking young man plied a good trade taking passengers' portraits with a camera.

There was a trader from Natal with an overgrown, grizzled beard and cheeks crumpled into thick folds by the sun. He laid out his skins every day, hoping to sell the last of his wares on the trip back to

South Africa. He had various cat skins, zebra skins, and the head of a lion, which must have been badly preserved because it smelt of putrefying meat, and Mariella swore she had seen a maggot wriggling between its nostrils. He sold ostrich feathers, intricately carved ivory ornaments, and jackals' tails bound into fly swats. In the evenings he sat on deck with a lantern, and men and women gathered round to listen to him telling tales about fever swamps, elephant hunts, and mountains infested with leopard.

The Reverend Ames was the only member of the clergy on board. He couldn't have been older than twenty with a smooth, pale face that was prone to sudden, acute blotching when he was excited and hands that fluttered around his face when he talked. He was on his way to establish a mission in East Africa, and he led a zealous service on deck every other day and on Sundays gave the sacrament.

A thick-set, heavy-boned Italian man with a drooping mustache and watery eyes kept a dancing bear and a monkey. He said he was emigrating for a better market. No one wanted a dancing bear in London anymore, and Frances could see why. The monkey, dressed up in military uniform, spent the day riding on her master's shoulders, but the bear looked seasick and unhappy. She wore a muzzle and chain, and when her master cried "Round and round again," she would tumble head over heels across the deck and then waddle her hips around his stick in an awkward dance. Occasionally the monkey scampered onto the bear's shoulders and tweaked her ears. If the bear swiped at him, the Italian thrashed her with his stick until she bellowed.

The third-class passengers looked drab and poor. Everyone knew they were crammed into steerage too many to a berth, and on hot days the stench of sewage drifted across the ship and caught in the back of your throat. The women spent all day mending, scolding, and sluicing their children down with buckets of seawater to prevent lice. There was a group of shaft sinkers from a coal mine in Lancashire, a tough-looking set being shipped out to work the new machinery which had been exported to South Africa. They whittled tools for the fields and swapped diamond-smuggling stories, which were passed along the deck: the lady who took a carriage out of Kimberley nonchalantly clutching a bunch of grapes, a diamond concealed in each lobe of fruit; or the carpenter who managed to smuggle £200,000 worth of stones in the handle of his chisel, only to be caught in Southampton by a private detective.

Mariella stood with a group of girls every afternoon near the chalked line that marked the first-class deck. They propped themselves up on one another's shoulders, leaning against the railings, laughing and nudging one another as they watched the first-class passengers. They noted the names of politicians, their wives, Lords and Ladies, filing away gossip and turning over every aspect of every woman's dress. Frances was drawn to the camaraderie of the girls, but when Mariella beckoned to her to join them she stayed away, not wanting to be seen gawping by the Nettletons or Mr. Westbrook.

She rose early in the mornings and took her coffee above board. There were few passengers around at this hour, and she enjoyed watching the sailors scrubbing the decks, shaking out the sails, and polishing the metal until it shone. It was cool, the air was fresh, and the deck was uncluttered by the canvas chairs which sprang up after breakfast. George Fairley was always there before her, greedily inhaling his first cigarette of the day. He was in his forties, small and compact, with a soft flop of tawny hair and an anxious habit of chewing the side of his nails until they bled.

He liked to talk, and Frances enjoyed listening, grateful not to have to tell her own story. He had been a small landowner but had lost everything in the depression. He talked to her about the rivers on his farm in Devon, shearing sheep in a snowstorm, and his hatred for the new cities with their vast factories pumping black smoke into the horizon. Frances hadn't realized that the steamships importing wheat and refrigerated meat from the Americas had done such damage to English farmers.

"I ended up in Sheffield, working for a steelworks making parts for the very steamships which had done me in!" George laughed wryly and rubbed at the stubble that bristled across his face. "Which gave me the idea to emigrate."

He hoped to find diamonds and make his fortune — or, if not a fortune, then enough money to live comfortably. Frances was captivated by his tales of the diamond fields. The Vaal River was a utopia in the desert, George said. Huge boulders clung to the banks of a swirling mass of green water. When you rolled them away a clutch of diamonds glistened beneath, each as fat and round as a plover's egg. George had an uncle who had spent two weeks digging on the Vaal. Long enough to make his fortune.

They stood one morning, watching a troop of swallows which had been following the ship since they set out. The birds, lightning quick, swooped and dipped in a shifting cloud, skimming the surface of the water, never left behind for a moment.

William Westbrook crossed the deck in front of them, and George called out, "Sir, could I detain you a moment?"

"Certainly." Mr. Westbrook stopped, nodding at Frances but not greeting her. She wondered if he was cross that she had declined his invitation to dinner.

"I have heard you're a man who knows about diamonds?" George asked expectantly.

"I know a little."

"I have contacts on the Vaal River. Do you have any advice?"

"What did you do before?"

"I was a farmer."

"Well, then, I advise you to go back home and farm."

George stared at him for a long second. "What do you mean?"

"The Vaal is no good. The sands have run dry."

"Dry?" George Fairley was incredulous.

"They haven't been digging there for years. The camps have moved to New Rush, Kimberley, though you'll not have much luck there. It's a thousand pounds a claim, and even if you could afford it, the earth is hard as rock."

George was silent, taking this in, and Frances saw how awful it was for him to hear it.

"How hard? Can a man dig it?"

"You'd have to work like a mule, and even then . . ."

"But how do most men do it? I've heard with a bit of luck you can get rich."

"In the old days, yes. Now the claims are being consolidated it's too expensive. You need a team of natives, guards to make sure they don't steal, influence on the mining board to stop them squeezing you out, and, of course, men you trust to sort the good stuff from the bad."

"There must be other sites?"

"And you think there aren't men who have looked? Men who know the ground better than you?" William Westbrook must have been ten years his junior, just a boy to George, but it was clear he had more experience, and it was hard to doubt he was speaking the truth. His voice was respectful but firm. "I'll be honest, Sir, since it might save you. I've seen men broken by prospecting. They end up worse than kaffirs, crawling round in the bottom of the mines without even a shirt on their backs."

George Fairley looked at him, speechless. "But even supposing you are right, I can't go home. There is nothing for me there."

Mr. Westbrook shrugged with a touch of impatience. "You'd be better off in an English workhouse."

"I don't believe you, Sir," George said, his voice cold with anger. He flicked his cigarette overboard. "You'd rather not have the competition, is that it? You should be ashamed of yourself." He turned on his heel and left them both standing there.

"Why did you do that?" Frances demanded.

Mr. Westbrook looked at her coolly from under heavy-lidded eyes, and she realized she had never seen him serious before. His jaw had locked and his face was impenetrable. All humor had drained from his face. "I told him the truth."

"Did you have to make it so bleak?" He didn't answer, so she said, "He has put everything into this venture."

His nostrils flared, and his eyes were blank when he turned to look at her. "And do you care so very much about him?"

The question was ridiculous. "He needed hope, Mr. Westbrook, not someone trampling over his future."

"I told him the truth, Miss Irvine. If it sounded harsh, it is because it is an unpleasant truth to have to deliver. South Africa can be a difficult place to make a living. A man of his age would be better off in England, with his family."

He was gone before she had the chance to apologize. It wasn't until she thought it over later that she realized she had been naive. It was quite possible he was right, and she wished she hadn't disagreed with him when she hadn't the slightest idea what she was talking about.

ELEVEN

Two days later the captain issued a gale warning. At five o'clock the wind began to blow and the sky turned dark. The light was sucked into a mass of granite clouds. The timbers of the ship creaked as she climbed the waves. Frances went down to the cabin and found Anne perched on the end of Mariella's bunk. The room was cold and damp, and Mariella was vomiting into a bowl.

"What are they saying in the saloon about the storm?" Anne asked, looking at her with wide eyes. Frances gave her hand a squeeze. "We're to keep our cabin windows shut."

Anne stroked Mariella's hair and gave her a cloth to wipe her face. Then she wedged the bowl in next to her and climbed into her own bunk, defeated by the swell. Frances lay down, letting her body be rocked with the sickening heave of the ocean. She tried not to think about the prospect of a gale. When Mariella begged one of them to get some more tonic for her seasickness, Frances volunteered. She was relieved to have an excuse to leave the cabin. Sister Mary-Joseph had a berth to herself a few doors down. Frances knocked and stepped inside. The narrow space beside the bunk was strewn with dirty linen and half-finished plates of food. When Frances asked her for tonic she waved her away, either too sick or too scared to talk. Frances insisted, and she said, "There's none left." She turned to face the wall. "You girls have taken it all."

The doctor would have some. The surgery was at the stern of the ship, past the engine rooms. It was difficult navigating the narrow passages below deck, with their guttering lights and swinging doors. When the ship rolled, people were propelled towards you like balls down a cannon. She stepped through corridors swilling with water and vomit, then climbed the narrow stairs onto the deck. It would be quicker to cross to the stern this way, and she wanted to gauge whether the weather was really as bad as it felt down below. The wind was fierce. It snatched at the door when she opened it and blew it back hard against its hinges. She stood for a second, steeling herself against the noise, then stepped out.

The deck was a dark sweep of wet wood. Night had come on, and the weather had driven everyone but a few of the crew down to their cabins. She was at the center of a torrent of sound: the roar of the ocean, and above it the cleats rattling, and the wind screeching through the ropes. She caught hold of the rigging to keep her balance, buckling her knees to take the impact of another wave. A light curtain of spray swept over the ship, stinging her eyes. She clawed at her hair, scraping it off her face. It was rougher than she had expected.

She ran the few steps to the railings which ringed the deck and looked out over the water. The lantern at the tip of the mizzenmast dipped to the sea starboard-side, rolled up and swung down again port-side. The pocket of light swooped over the ship and out to sea, catching the surface of the broiling mass before swinging back again. It cast a fractured light over the swell, illuminating in flashes the tips of great riders thundering towards the ship.

The wind stepped up a notch, and a stinging rain flew at her in bright sparks under the circle of light. She edged her way along the deck, holding on to ropes as she went. Two sailors called to each other, their voices muted by the wind into the wordless mewing of gulls. Then, quite suddenly and without warning, the ship leapt. The deck pitched, rolled, and became a vertical. Her face slammed into the railings. Seawater surged over her, sweeping her off her feet. She tried to scream, but her mouth was full of water. It was cold, like melting ice, and it had fingers which pushed down into her throat. Then a sharp pain under one arm and a force pulling against her fall. A hand, like a vise, held her upright. She snatched at the figure, caught at a coat, and pulled herself against it. The man pushed her hard against the railings, so she knew where she was and felt safe from falling.

The wind roared. She felt the strength of the man, and the rain driving against them, soaking her skin. She pushed her face into his chest. He pulled his jacket up around her head and spoke into her ear, his lips brushing against her skin.

"We're safer here for a moment. But you must move when I say so. Can you run?"

She dreaded having to walk across the open deck, but she nodded her head against the wet wool of his coat. The storm had risen up in an instant. She could hear the hoarse shouts of the sailors and the screeching of ropes. The engine groaned. Her legs felt weak, and there was a dull ache above one eye where her head had struck the railings. The ship felt as though it had no more strength than the leaf boats she had launched as a child into the small rapids of a stream, spinning desperately across the surface until the water sucked them down.

The ship plunged into a wave, righted itself, and the man said, "Now," in her ear. He moved, flipping her round so that she was in front of him and his back was against the railings, then he propelled her forwards. They stumbled and slid with the motion of the ship, his weight behind her until they reached the stairs. He wrenched back the door and pushed her inside, and they slipped down the steps to the deck below. Her stomach contracted and she doubled over, retching. Bile and salt water poured from her nose and mouth.

"That was interesting."

She looked up, her face streaming water. William Westbrook was studying her, the corners of his mouth curling with amusement. "Some people might even have called it suicide." Then he shook his head, running a hand over his hair, and water flew off him like rain from a dog.

She was dizzy and sick, and she bent double, retching again, then stood up. Her legs felt light and very cold, and when she put out a hand she missed the wall. Mr. Westbrook caught her with one arm under hers, propping her up. "Oh no you don't."

He sat her down at a table in the first-class saloon, found blankets to wrap around her, and ordered coffee from a terrified steward. When the coffee didn't arrive he went off to hunt the steward down in the kitchens. She was numb with cold. There was no feeling from her feet to her thighs, and her upper body was gripped by convulsions. Once she started shaking it was hard to stop. Four men played cards in a corner of the saloon, passing a bottle between them and laughing as the ship threw them sideways, wreaking havoc with their game. The room was otherwise deserted. Most of the lights had been left to go out, and the red velvet and gilt mirrors which lined the walls were a mockery of grandeur in the midst of the dark storm blowing them across the sea. A few bottles of wine had escaped and were rolling loose across the floor. With every lurch of the ship, remains from dinner, left abandoned on the tables, clattered onto the carpet.

Frances thought she had seen bad weather in the first few days they had been at sea when they had pitched and rolled, and the captain had praised her for having good sea legs. Now she understood. This was a tearing, terrifying thing. A storm that whined and howled, that swept them up and slammed them down again so hard the timbers of the hull sounded as if they were splintering. It blew in dark funnels, like water roaring down a tunnel. She held on to the edges of her seat to keep herself from being thrown across the room, and tried to stop herself thinking about how cold and black the water was outside, and what she would do if she was thrown into it. She was scared of dying. Not of death itself, but of the truth that dying delivered. It released a fear inside her which was corrosive, and it ate into all her certainties — that life was a noble, worthwhile thing, that her parents' deaths had meaning, that it was something other than fear which lay at the root of every action.

Mr. Westbrook came back carrying the coffee in a large mug with a saucer held over the top to stop it from spilling. He sat down next to her, pulled a bottle from his coat pocket, and splashed a little into the mug. He spooned the hot, dark liquid into her mouth, holding the cup under her chin to catch it as it spilled. The weight of his body, the heavy line of his thigh, hip, and chest, pressed against her, holding her in place, and the spoon clattered against her teeth. The coffee was strong and it fired up her insides until her blood thickened. When she stopped shaking he placed the mug in her hand, took up a seat across the table opposite, and grinned at her. "Perhaps I shouldn't have caught that fish?"

She couldn't believe that he could joke at a moment like this. She had the impression that he was enjoying himself. The extremity of the storm appealed to his restless energy and gave him a sense of purpose. He didn't seem at all afraid. Like her father, the thought of death was leaving him unchanged, and being near him gave her courage.

She managed to smile back at him. "Thank you for pulling me off the deck."

His eyes didn't leave hers, and a slow smile crept over his face. "How are you planning to repay me?"

She looked away, embarrassed. Her teeth chattered, and she was afraid. "I may not have to."

"You'll not get away that easily." He touched the back of her hand lightly in sympathy. "A steamer has a better chance than a sailing ship. Unless the weather gets much worse, it'll hold its course."

Then he said after a moment, "I was

disappointed when you didn't accept my invitation. Why didn't you come?"

"I don't know." Her words were jerky, and it was difficult for her to move her lips. The coffee mug burnt into her hands, and her fingers had begun to ache. "I think I felt awkward accepting your kindness. It was charitable, but . . ."

"Charitable?" He laughed. With the fingers of one hand he was turning a teaspoon from end to end, over and over, on the table. "Frances, I asked you because I like you. I wanted to see you." He had bypassed formalities and was talking straight to her. She had the feeling there were no rules for where they found themselves now. He was staring at her, and she felt she ought to say something but she didn't trust herself to speak. He put down the spoon and rubbed at a thin red scar on his cheekbone with the thumb of his right hand. She hadn't noticed it before.

"How did it happen?"

"The scar? I was with my father."

"When you were a child?"

He took her hand loosely in one of his. She felt the roughness of his skin across her fingers, and watched his mouth twitch into a smile. "Frances, your concern is charming, but my father didn't beat me. He did, however, have a furnace. A spark of metal buried itself in my cheek."

There was a noise behind them and they turned in their seats. A woman ran past in her nightdress. She lurched from bench to bench, trying to keep herself upright. Her face was contorted into a silent wail. A man followed, wearing nothing but his shirttails.

Mr. Westbrook laughed. "Respectable men turned into lunatics. They'll all be ashamed of themselves tomorrow."

The storm showed no signs of easing, and when she had finished the coffee he took her to her cabin, using his weight as a wedge in the narrow corridor to keep them from falling. The lamps had gone out, and it was hard to tell in the dark which way was upright. When they reached her door, she didn't open it but pushed herself round to face him. She was scared, and didn't want him to leave. The blood pounded in her ears, louder than the screaming of the ship. "We'll be all right," he said, reaching out to touch her cheek. "There have been rougher storms than this, and people have survived them." And then he was gone and she had to face her fears alone.

The storm blew in even worse overnight. It was a brutal, raging force. It felt as if they were hurtling towards destruction. She lay

139

in her berth fully dressed, gripped by a nausea which forced her to vomit again and again into a bowl which she held beside her. When the ship rolled she was thrown across her bunk and couldn't stop the bowl from tipping. The thin bile slopped over onto the sheets, giving her skin a vile slipperiness. The only sounds from the cabin were Mariella's sobbing and the clacking of Anne's rosary. Frances grasped the edge of her bunk and found she couldn't cry and she couldn't pray. Instead, in her terror, she conjured up an image of William Westbrook. His confidence and disdain had seemed strong enough to hold back the storm. She tried to remember the strength of his body when he pulled her off the deck, fighting against the force of the sea. The bitter taste of coffee was still on her tongue, and her lips were burnt from where he had brought hot spoonfuls to her mouth. She held on to her vision of him, and braced her body against the waves.

Late the next morning Frances woke up and knew that the storm was over. The ship was barely swaying, the engines had subsided to a dull throb, and when she looked out of the porthole above her bed the sea held a perfect level. The cabin was empty. She went to the bathroom to wash, and when she came back Anne was mopping the floor. Mariella put her head around the door. "Morning, Sleepyhead. Here's toast and marmalade. You should thank me. Everyone has an appetite all of a sudden, but the ship is in chaos." She handed Frances a plate and stood swaying in the doorway.

Frances licked a blob of marmalade off her finger. "What chaos?"

"The gale got hold of a lifeboat and now it's hanging all in pieces, the cook is still drunk, two berths were flooded, and a steward has broken his leg. Oh, and someone very grand in first class has been burnt by lobster sauce."

"What was anyone doing eating lobster sauce?" Frances asked, and the girls laughed.

"There was a woman last night, rescued from going overboard. William Westbrook saved her."

"Who is William Westbrook?" Anne asked.

Mariella looked at her in astonishment. "Only the most eligible man on the *Cambrian,* Anne. Where have you been hiding yourself?" Anne smiled and shrugged her shoulders.

"Who was the girl?" Frances asked, standing up and stretching her arms to ease out the tight pain across her ribs where she had fallen.

"Not sure." Mariella leant into the cabin and tickled her under one arm, and Frances buckled, laughing. "But she's no doubt lost in a fit of passion. Knights in shining armor don't come any better-looking than Mr. Westbrook."

Twelve

Later that morning she saw Mr. Westbrook playing deck tennis with Emma and Joanna Whitaker. They were cousins, and Frances had heard that they were performing a flute duet at the concert. She watched, unable to tear herself away. The girls were plump and pink-faced, with large mouths and raucous laughs, and they vied with each other for Mr. Westbrook's approval. She hadn't realized how much she wanted to talk to him until the game ended and he walked straight past her with Emma Whitaker leaning on one arm, her racket spinning a circle in her other hand. Frances stood and stared, thinking, If he doesn't look at me, there is nothing between us. Just when she thought he would walk past without acknowledging her, he glanced up and winked. She felt a surge of relief and gratitude. He had known she was there all along.

She tried to be realistic. William Westbrook was well liked, and she suspected he was willing to grant his affection indiscriminately. Women and men alike were drawn to him. He was charming and cultured and good at playing games. There was a backgammon tournament on board, and she had heard he was the favorite to win. She knew that if he had shown an interest in her, it was in the same way that a man might play with a child on a lazy summer's afternoon. It was an amusing way to pass the time. But all her attempts at forgetting him were useless. She couldn't put him out of her mind.

She found she didn't need to ask to find out about him. He aroused people's interest in the same way that a classical sculpture might were it to be unveiled on board. They wanted to examine the sum of his perfections and seek out his faults. By all accounts, he was a man of contradictions. He had perfect manners, but he seemed not in the least restrained by formalities. He had the kind of determination and ambition that was a hallmark of being Jewish, but he wasn't afraid of enjoying himself. Despite his Jewish blood, he had strong social connections — he was a member of the Kimberley Club and his cousin was Joseph Baier, perhaps the most influential and certainly the wealthiest man in Kimberley

— and yet Frances knew that he drank in the sailors' quarters, and had even held a wrestling match with one of the furnace stokers (he had taken defeat graciously). Although not independently wealthy himself, he had all the backing of Baier's money, and he was talked about as a man who already wielded considerable power.

It wasn't until two days later that she spoke to him again. She was practicing in the music room when she saw, out of the corner of her eye, that he had come to stand beside her.

When she stopped he said, "You never mentioned playing the piano."

"Why would I have done?"

"To impress me?"

"Are you impressed?"

"Not yet." He reached forward and turned the page of the music book. His hand was broad with square knuckles and strong, callused fingers. As he brushed past her, she smelt the same earthy musk of sandalwood.

"Will you play it for me?"

It was a Chopin piano sonata. She knew the piece well, and she began confidently, until she felt him circling the nape of her neck with his hand. Her skin froze, then crawled hot and alive under his touch. A ripple went down her back into the base of her spine. She faltered slightly, missing her notes. When he took a lock of her hair and tucked it behind her ear, she was so shocked by the rub of his skin against hers that she stood up abruptly, knocking over the stool. He was looking at her intently. One of her legs was trembling. When he stepped towards her, she felt his knee push against it and heard the bristling of her skirts against him. She took a step back, into the piano, and there was a dark thud of keys. She was scared by how strongly she wanted him to touch her. Her need felt destructive. It wasn't rational, and it didn't call for conversation. It was as though she wanted him to obliterate her. She pushed forward past him, but he grabbed her hand and pulled her back.

"Frances. Don't be scared." He smiled at her suddenly and squeezed her hand, reassuring her and bringing her back out of her passion. He understood what she wanted when she barely knew herself. He seemed to be taking the darkness of her desire and turning it all to light, and his words created an intimacy between them which was even more profound than when he had touched her.

"Dinner," he said. "Tonight, in the first-class saloon. Will you come?"

She nodded, not trusting herself to speak, and he let her go. Later she turned over the way he had said her name, as if he knew everything about her, understood her, and offered her his protection. The fact that he had remained perfectly in control when she had been so overwhelmed only made her vulnerability more acute.

Frances hovered at the doorway to the saloon, conscious that she was late but reluctant now that she was here to push aside the red velvet curtain and step inside. Sister Mary-Joseph had given her permission to dine in first class, as long as she was back in her cabin by nine o'clock. She could tell from the rabble of noise that dinner was already under way. Laughter rose in waves from the other side of the curtain, and a female voice warbled merrily along in time with a tinkling piano. She wore her only evening dress, and was glad she had brought it.

It was only when she had returned to her cabin that afternoon that she remembered Edwin. The truth was unavoidable. She was engaged to be married to another man. In less than three weeks she would almost certainly be Mrs. Edwin Matthews. Yet she had decided to come anyway. Was it too late to try to change the future?

The dining saloon made a stab at grandeur, but age and the evening sunlight streaming through the long skylights gave it a shabby, tired air. It had the damp, discordant feel of a winter's drawing room on a summer's evening, and it smelt overpoweringly of boiled meat and women's perfume. Stewards in livery served champagne, and mulatto girls took orders from the passengers.

"Miss Irvine!" Mr. Nettleton had risen from his seat at the far side of the saloon and was waving his hand vigorously at her. She waved back and threaded her way across the room, catching sight of herself in the mirror that ran floor to ceiling down the length of the funnel. The blue of her dress shone back at her, but her body was barely visible. Her pale, freckled skin and auburn hair blended into the golds of the room and the tarnish on the mirror so that she seemed a gaudy, shifting ghost.

The gentlemen at the table stood up as she approached, William clutching a napkin and using it to shield his eyes against the crimson sunlight which flickered over his face and turned his skin to a strip of burnished copper. She felt a lurch of concern when she saw him. What was she doing here?

She shook hands with a couple who were introduced as the Musgraves. The man had thick, wet lips and a poorly shaved beard. He sprouted hairs from his ample face like wires from a pig's bottom. His wife was very large, with a huge, swelling bosom on which was nestled a miniature black poodle. It lay with its head curled into her neck, staring out at Frances with small black eyes. Mrs. Nettleton, looking even sharper boned next to such a generous display of flesh, gave Frances a curt smile.

"Bubbly?" Mr. Nettleton asked, shouting slightly to be heard over the noise of the other diners. She nodded and he filled her glass. They were discussing illicit diamond buying in Kimberley.

"The damned kaffirs hide them in their arses!" Mr. Musgrave roared, draining his glass of champagne and helping himself to claret.

"Mr. Musgrave!" Mrs. Nettleton admonished, fingering her small, diamond-studded necklace.

"It's true," William said, giving Mrs. Nettleton a broad smile. "The finest jewels on a lady's neck have been in places you would rather not consider."

Mrs. Nettleton laughed nervously, and Mrs. Musgrave said, "They hide them in mules too, apparently."

"Yes, Madam. Even in dogs."

"Oh, how dreadful!" She buried her face in her poodle.

William caught Frances's eye and smiled. His eyes sloped down into an expression of complicit affection, and she saw that he knew she was thinking about the way he had touched her that afternoon. Pleasure and expectation surged inside her, and a deep flush rose up her neck.

"Now, Frances," Mrs. Nettleton was saying in a bustling, matronly voice, "tell us what you are doing in South Africa. Are you going on to Port Elizabeth?"

"Actually, I'm disembarking at Cape Town."

"And do you have a good position there? I know a few respectable English families. I dare say Mr. Nettleton and I could put in a good word."

"Thank you, but I'm not in need of a position." She paused. They all turned to look at her. "I'm to be married in Cape Town." She glanced at William as she said it, and saw his eyes flicker over her in surprise. There were general exclamations and congratulations around the table.

"Miss Irvine" — Mrs. Musgrave leant over her husband to look at Frances — "you are traveling with an emigration society, is that right? And yet, you're not under any obligation to them financially?"

Frances nodded. "Yes, that's right."

"Well, that makes you perfectly placed to give us an impartial view on our little debate. I have been defending the emigration societies to the present company, but I'm afraid I need a little help holding up my end."

Frances, embarrassed, looked round the table. The last thing she felt in the mood for was a discussion about the politics of women's emigration.

Mrs. Musgrave levered her bosom over the table and tapped Mrs. Nettleton on the hand. "Now, don't be shy, Liza, we're never to be ashamed of having a point of view. The progress of our nation has been built on fair discussion." Mrs. Nettleton colored and pulled back her hand.

Mrs. Musgrave turned to face Frances. "We were discussing in particular the question of redundancy. What do you make of it?"

"Redundancy?" Frances asked, confused. She glanced at William, hoping that he might intervene on her behalf, but he was staring at her as if from a distance, with an expression of fascinated reappraisal. His forehead was curled into a slight frown, and he held the edge of his lower lip between his teeth. His hands, she noticed, were moving. He was balancing a knife across his forefinger as he looked at her. Mrs. Musgrave might be well-meaning, but her self-conviction made her unpredictable. What wouldn't she say?

"Yes, redundancy. How are a million surplus women in Britain ever to be married unless they go to the colonies? What can we possibly do with them if they stay in England?"

"I wasn't arguing against emigration," Mrs. Nettleton cut in, sounding shrill and affronted. "Indeed, I wholeheartedly support Mrs. Sambourne, but she can be naive. Like you, Mrs. Musgrave, she is led by her heart. Sometimes a little more plain speaking is called for. Emigration societies are only as good as the girls they take on. Even she complains that most of her protégés lose all semblance of principle once they step on board ship. You should hear the stories she tells!"

"Come, it can't be as bad as that."

"I admire your aptitude for fair-mindedness, but really, you know as well as

I do that emigration societies are little better than marriage bureaus."

Frances sat very still, anger welling up inside her. She twisted her napkin around her forefinger. These people knew nothing of the helplessness of the girls in the second cabin, their sense of failure and rejection, and the personal tragedies which had brought each of them onto the *Cambrian*. They couldn't imagine what it felt like to be shipped out of England.

"And why shouldn't they be marriage bureaus?" she asked in a cold voice, looking round the table. William would more than likely never speak to her again, and she was exasperated by the fact that she had no say in her own future. Her hand went to her throat, tugging at the skin. "The raison d'être of London Society is to marry off eligible women. Why shouldn't those who aren't deemed good enough for England try their chances elsewhere?"

"Because, my dear, we pay our good, charitable money so that they can find work in the colonies, not run off with the first ship's steward who takes a shine to them!"

A silence settled over the group while everyone absorbed the implications of this statement. When Frances spoke, her voice seethed with anger, and she stared at Mrs.

Nettleton, trying to hold eye contact. "One would think the least these girls could count on would be the support of their own countrymen. And yet you heap prejudice on top of penury. Is it any wonder they take the first opportunity to marry?"

"Well spoken," Mrs. Musgrave muttered, reaching over to pat Frances moistly on the back of her hand.

"Of course," Mr. Nettleton broke in, trying to lighten the mood, "no one is suggesting your friends in second class are in the least bit taking advantage. Their intentions are, I'm sure, quite responsible. Even Mrs. Sambourne's fair beauties were —"

"Mrs. Sambourne's fair beauties — as you call them — were little better than common prostitutes," Mrs. Nettleton interrupted in a clipped voice. "Last year, fifty of them, all with genteel pretensions, shipped to Cape Town. The residents were so furious they wouldn't let the women disembark for a week! Mrs. Sambourne had, in her kindness, established positions for them with respectable families, but of course it didn't take long for them to go back to their old ways."

"All for the goodness of mankind, my dear," Mr. Nettleton said.

Mr. Musgrave gave a gurgling chuckle.

"Yes, an interesting linguistic conundrum. The 'pretty horse breaker' in London is known in Cape Town as a 'London beauty.'"

"The point is," Mrs. Nettleton continued, ignoring him, "if they say they are going out to work, then it is work they should do. It's next to impossible, by all accounts, to find good European help at the Cape. I know someone who had two nursemaids run off to be married within six months of each other. Now she has to make do with a kaffir."

William stopped his balancing act with the knife and spoke with a cold smile. "And, my dear Mrs. Nettleton, is one nursemaid not as good as another?"

"You'd have your children looked after by a kaffir? Perhaps you shouldn't answer that question until you have children."

"And perhaps you, Mrs. Nettleton, shouldn't ask that question until you have met a kaffir," William retorted.

Mrs. Nettleton turned scarlet and was silent.

Mrs. Musgrave fondled one of her dog's ears thoughtfully and said, "I read a letter in *The Times* which said that babies can take on the pigmentation of their nurses. Their skin turns oily and cloudy just as if they were little savages. An English mother testified to it being true."

William gave a dry laugh. "What's true is that the English mother you speak of must have had herself tupped by a black ram."

Mr. Musgrave's appreciative chuckle broke up the awkward silence, and the stewards arrived with platters of food. It was nothing short of a banquet, and Frances was astonished that the same kitchen which produced such a meager spread for the second cabin was capable of such extravagance. There was a tureen of turtle soup and another of vichyssoise, poached salmon with hollandaise, a lobster salad, and afterwards a joint of veal, roast guinea fowl, and potatoes parmentier. Frances, fed up with baked tripe and boiled beef, had been looking forward to eating well, but she was suddenly sickened by such an ostentatious display of indulgence. Who was she trying to fool, sitting here in first class? It amused them to turn over the politics of her fall in fortunes, but where did that leave her? And then there was William, sitting opposite her, and the sinking realization that anything she might have hoped for between them had almost certainly been extinguished by the revelation that she was engaged to be married. It was all she could do to accept a bowl of soup.

The conversation roamed from the climate at the Cape to the problems of giving parties. Native servants, Mr. Musgrave was maintaining, were a particular problem because they couldn't help but indulge themselves at their master's expense, often arriving at the table nothing short of drunk. "Of course," he said, wiping hollandaise from the corners of his mouth, "the raw native is like a child. He needs to be guided, and that means keeping the bottle firmly out of his reach."

"It also means protecting him from the Boers," said Mrs. Musgrave. "The way they treat their savages is a travesty. The sooner we take over the Transvaal the better." Frances wasn't even sure she knew where the Transvaal was, and she had a hazy idea of a Boer as a kind of white savage.

"The Boers were there long before us, farming the land, pushing back the native tribes," Mr. Nettleton said. "It all seems rather unfair to me."

"Yes, dear," said Mrs. Nettleton, "but the Boers are complete heathens. They're little better than the Irish." She shot a furtive glance in Frances's direction. "They don't even believe in a collective state."

"I rather like that idea of theirs," William

said. "It's astonishingly romantic for such a practical people."

"It may be romantic, but it is also absurd. How can you run a country without central government?"

"Essentially, you're right," William said. "They are uneducated and superstitious, they refuse to wash, and they stink to high heaven. Most of them don't pay taxes, and their roads are nothing short of atrocious. And yet I can't help but admire their courage. They left Holland, gave up all the comforts of the civilized world — in essence, turned their back on Enlightenment — to trek into the heart of Africa. They wanted the right to live simply and honestly, without interference. Each man the master of his own world. Did you know that the smallest Boer farm is six thousand acres? Their land is poor, often little more than desert, but the Boer isn't afraid of hardship. They believe in old-fashioned values, which we city people, who lean so heavily on the state, have forgotten."

"Such as?"

"Family, hospitality, the right to self-governance."

"I agree with family and hospitality, but I'll quite happily forgo self-governance," Mrs. Nettleton quipped, but she had missed the point. There was something whimsical and endearing in William's yearning for freedom. Frances was taken by his idea of finding a corner of the world where you weren't beholden to anybody. It reminded her of her father poring over his maps, dreaming of the untouched places of the earth.

When the jellies had been gored and the iced oranges were pooling their syrup onto the tablecloth, coffee was served. Mr. Nettleton suggested a game of cards, and Frances was relieved to excuse herself. She got up to leave and the men rose with her. She waited a moment for William to acknowledge her, but he was talking to Mr. Musgrave about fishing, and barely interrupted the flow of his conversation to wish her good night.

She walked up on deck and went to stand at the bow of the ship. The clock in the dining saloon had read eight thirty. She still had another half hour before she had to report downstairs. It was a clean, calm night, with just a sliver of moon hanging low in the sky. She leant her weight against the railings, listening to the rush of ocean coursing beneath the boat, conscious that every inch of progress brought her closer to the man she would have to marry.

Would she have the chance to talk to William again? She doubted it. The invitation to dinner had felt like an opportunity to get to know him better, but instead it had only pulled them further apart. And she had hated the Nettletons and the Musgraves, with their petty small-mindedness, complacent judgments, and obsequious genuflection to the rules of Society. She wanted to explain to William that she didn't care about the man she was marrying, and that the thought of living in Kimberley with Edwin Matthews was like committing herself to a live burial. But how did she know he even cared enough to listen?

"So, a doctor's wife." The voice was close behind her, and when she turned William was standing beside her. He struck a match, and she caught the sweet smell of smoke. "Will he make you happy?" he asked.

She looked at him pointedly. "Can't you guess?"

He leant on the balustrade and looked out over the water. "As far as I can see, engagement is a little like purgatory. You don't know whether you'll end up in heaven or hell."

"You've been married?"

"Engaged. I decided not to marry her."

"Why not?"

He laughed. "I probably should have done. She was pretty and very rich. But she never would have made me happy. I'm a bully." He glanced at Frances. "I need someone with a bit of grit."

A silence fell between them. She saw his cigarette diminishing and thought, Any moment now, he is going to drop it over the balustrade into the sea and leave me standing here, and that will be the end of it. He took a last draw on the cigarette and flicked it over the edge. "And I had you down as a desperate girl braving the seas to find work in the colonies."

"You and Mrs. Nettleton both."

He gave a short laugh. "For what it's worth, I thought you handled her perfectly. Besides, now you know what I have to put up with every evening."

"Yes, and I wouldn't be paid to sit through it again."

"It was that bad?"

She shrugged.

"I shouldn't have invited you," he said ruefully. Then, rubbing at his beard with his hand — "Not long ago they would have treated me the same way."

"Somehow I don't believe it."

"No, really. We're not so different, you and I. Irish, Jewish — we're both outsiders.

161

When I was eighteen there wasn't a lady in London who would have so much as tipped her bonnet at me. I grew up in Whitechapel in a house with no glass in the windows and four pairs of boots between eight children."

"And then?"

"My cousin got lucky. He had been working on a sugar plantation in Natal on the East Coast. It was backbreaking work, for a pittance. When they discovered diamonds in Kimberley, Baier packed up his tools and went to the fields. He couldn't afford to buy anything at first. They'd had torrential rains, and over forty percent of the Kimberley mine was underwater. A working claim was more expensive than it had ever been. When the Kimberley mining board issued pumping contracts, Baier raised enough money to travel eight days with a Boer transport rider to buy a pump for sale in Victoria West. The contract brought in money, and after a few months, he had enough to invest. He bought up claims in the right places and ran them well. He paid for me to go to Oxford. Three years later, and the power of a few hundred thousand pounds behind me, I pass the test of respectability."

"And what do you do with this newfound respectability?"

He levered himself up on top of a stack of

crates so he was sitting slightly higher than her, with his legs dangling off the edge. He ran a hand through his tangled hair and smiled at her. "I work for Baier."

"Do you enjoy it?"

"The atmosphere in Kimberley is like nothing I've ever known. It's on the brink of an economic explosion. Where else could I have a coffee in the morning with a digger from the Australian gold fields, lunch with a forty-niner from California, host a dinner in the evening for a handful of German speculators, and end up playing whist with a cockney trader who's just pulled a twenty-carat diamond from the soil and is blowing his fortune lighting his cigar with a clutch of five-pound notes? It's a filthy, debauched, lunatic place, but there's money to be made if you know how."

"I didn't have you down as a materialist."

William grinned. "I'm not ashamed to admit it." He shook his head slightly. "I'm lucky enough to be learning from the most astute businessman in the Cape. Baier's experience is second to none. At the moment we're raising finance for a deal which will make us the sole importers of the new generation of steam engines to the mines."

"And when you've raised the finance? Will you go back to England?"

"I don't think so. England's no good for someone like me. I find it stifling. Business happens too slowly and it's difficult to find opportunities. There are too many rules, too much expectation, too many Mrs. Nettletons always peering through the window to see how you take your tea. Africa has infinite potential. The rules are still being made up, by people like Baier. And it's not just about extracting wealth. The Cape needs politicians, moneymakers, statesmen. Despite what I said about the Boers at dinner, the truth is they're an uncivilized, land-grabbing people who despise the natives and want to throw us out. There is a need for men of a certain caliber to keep them in check. What could I ever achieve at home which would compare?"

He jumped off the crate, plunging his hands into his pockets in an effort to keep them still. "There are so many things I want to do. Places I want to see. Just imagine. There are men in Africa who have never seen a European, and animals who have never heard a gunshot. You can't imagine the thrill of being out in the bush all day, hunting kudu on the plains or tracking a leopard in the mountains, sleeping out at night under a sky dripping with stars. It's a brand-new land." He smiled at her. "But what about you?" he asked. "What gets Frances Irvine excited?"

What could she say? She couldn't remember a single thing that had happened to her before she set foot on the *Cambrian* which was worth telling. Yet William seemed to be inviting honesty.

"Mr. Westbrook. My marriage . . ." She faltered, frightened of saying how she felt. "The doctor. I barely know him." He looked at her, his eyebrows raised in question. She went on. "I mean to say, I don't care about my marriage. It means nothing to me." She avoided his gaze, looking at her hands and feeling how pathetic this statement was after his own, and how obvious it was that she liked him. She thought he might not respond. He waited a moment then stepped closer, so that she could feel his leg pressing into her skirts and could smell the smoke caught in his clothes.

"Do you always do that when you're nervous?" he asked softly, watching her hand, which had crept to her neck, pulling at the skin at her throat.

"Yes," she said, swallowing heavily and dropping her arm to her side.

He brought the back of his hand to her cheek. "And what you're trying to tell me is you're not absolutely determined to marry your doctor?"

"No." She looked up at him, her heart beating rapidly. "I mean yes. I'm not absolutely determined."

"And you still owe me for saving your life."

"I thought you had forgotten."

"Not forgotten." He grinned at her. "Biding my time." Then he stopped smiling, and cradled her neck in one of his broad hands, and with the same hand slowly but firmly ran his thumb over her lips, pulling slightly at her lower lip so they parted. She felt herself leaning towards him, and when he bent his head she thought he was going to kiss her, but instead he whispered in her ear, "I thought emigrating girls were warned about the dangers of being seduced on board?"

"I don't care," she whispered back, suddenly brave.

But he dropped his hand to her shoulder and said, "Frances, it's cold out here. You should go inside."

He turned then and left her standing by the railings, the sea roaring down below, the ship moving imperceptibly towards Cape Town under the cover of darkness. She watched him glide like a shadow across the deck, duck his head into the stairwell, and go below.

THIRTEEN

A hot, breathless calm settled over the Atlantic. In the afternoons she sat up on deck with Anne, trying to paint but thinking of nothing but William. She tortured herself with the thought that he didn't care about her, then remembered with a ripple of pleasure the pressure of his thumb against her mouth. A thin haze did little to screen them from the glare of the sun, and they protected themselves with parasols and straw hats. Awnings had been strung up across the promenade deck, and the first-class passengers shimmered through the heat in white linen suits and airy dresses.

She stood one afternoon talking to Mr. Nettleton. He was one of a handful of first-class passengers taking advantage of the shade on the second-class deck. The sea was so glassy she could trace the reflection of clouds sliding across its surface. William was sitting in a deck chair just behind them, talking to the Reverend Ames.

"We're playing *Twelfth Night* and we're looking for a Viola. Do you know any of her lines?" Mr. Nettleton asked.

William slipped a hand under the hem of her dress and circled her anklebone. She stood, speechless.

"I'm afraid not," she managed to say to Mr. Nettleton, and felt her leg begin to shake. William must have been able to feel it, but he kept on talking, tracing his finger in a circle across the bone, easing the leather of her shoe away from her skin with his forefinger.

"Please don't be modest, Miss Irvine," Mr. Nettleton was saying. "You should see what we have to work with. Orsino barely has one line out of three."

William, turning his head but not stopping the exploration of his fingers over her anklebone, began to recite:

"If music be the food of love, play on,
Give me excess of it; that surfeiting,
The appetite may sicken, and so die."

He held her every nerve hooked by a different string, and like a puppeteer he controlled them all at will. When he tugged at them it was a delicate, painful pleasure, and her face flooded with heat.

"Westbrook, you are infuriating," Mr. Nettleton was saying. "You refuse to play Orsino, then you trot out his lines as if they were your own."

William laughed, turning back to his conversation, but not taking his hand out from under her dress. His boldness astounded her, with its presumption of intimacy between them. Was this courtship? She knew that by standing there she was agreeing to let herself be touched, but she couldn't bring herself to move away. He dipped his finger between her skin and the inside edge of her shoe. Her blood beat thickly in her ears, and she felt her knee buckle. She raised her foot slightly, offering it up to him, but a second later he had removed his hand. Her face was flushed and she felt dizzy.

"Are you all right, Frances?" Mr. Nettleton put a hand on her arm.

She nodded, but he pulled out a deck chair and sat her in it.

"Don't talk for a minute. This heat is terrible. I'll get you a glass of water."

The Reverend Ames was talking to William in a shrill voice. His throat bulged over his dog collar, and his cheeks had broken out in scarlet blotches. It took Frances a moment to realize that he was worked up.

"Like all men, Mr. Westbrook, you have a responsibility."

"Thank you, Reverend Ames. Please be so kind as to remind me of my responsibilities." William's voice was heavy with sarcasm.

"To love and respect all men alike, be they white or black."

"You have no notion of how I treat a man. We have never until this moment met before."

"Speculators and monopolists. If you are not one yourself, then you work for them. Devouring the land, sparking wars, imprisoning men on the basis of color."

"I don't very well care what color a man is if he has a smuggled diamond in his hand. And I don't want to upset your fine sensibilities, Reverend, but it just so happens that most of them are niggers."

The reverend flinched. "And can you blame them for stealing? When their land has been taken from them?"

"Would you rather the Romans had never come to Britain?" William's voice was slow and supple, and it was clear he was enjoying the discussion. "We suffered a little, but in the end they left the marks of civilization. We abandoned our mud huts, we ate fine food, we gazed on the wonders of plumbing. Would you have had us remain half savage? And look where we English were when the Romans left. Four hundred years of savagery and superstition! This is the nature of history, of progress. So don't come over all fresh from England with your high ideals and Sunday school morals and try to teach my cousin, or myself, how we ought to live."

The reverend opened and shut his mouth like a fish. He looked as if too many thoughts were rushing headlong for the same tunnel, jamming up so none of them could be articulated. Frances felt sorry for him. He was being humiliated, but then he was a fool for taking William on.

William drove home his advantage. "There are millions of pounds' worth of diamonds in the Kimberley mine. And they aren't worth anything, not one penny, to the kaffirs without a white man to trade with them. How do you expect the black man to civilize himself, to educate himself, without money?"

"Your thirst is for wealth, Mr. Westbrook, and mine is for love."

"Love?" William interrupted, gleefully incredulous. "This can never be a question of love! How would you support our position in South Africa with love? Or would you rather we handed over Kimberley to the Boers? Have you seen the love with which a Boer beats a black man?" William leant back in his chair, kneading one side of his beard with a tanned hand. "With whose money would you educate your savages? Your own? Your love, Reverend, is an expensive operation."

The Reverend Ames, his face puce with anger, pushed back his chair and stood up, knocking straight into Mr. Nettleton, who was carrying a tray of glasses full of ice water. They tumbled straight over the reverend and broke into pieces on the floor.

"Damn!" cried Mr. Nettleton.

"That'll cool him down," William quipped as the Reverend Ames took off down the deck. Frances laughed, but weakly. The conversation was unpleasant, and though William had beaten the reverend with his natural brilliance, he had hardly given him a fair hearing.

FOURTEEN

"Miss Irvine." The boy came running towards her across the deck. "A note for you!"

"Thank you, Gilbert," she said, ruffling his hair and opening the folded paper:

> Miss Irvine, I need to talk to you for a few moments alone. There is a cabin next to the engineer's room which is used for storage. Shall I meet you there at eight o'clock?
>
> W.W.

Frances tucked the note into the pocket of her dress. Anticipation mingled with apprehension. Despite the risks of being caught alone with him, she would be there at eight. She was more desperate than ever to see him.

Someone clipped her on the shoulder, and she turned to see Mariella standing next to her. "You're dreaming again! You'll be the

173

color of a nut if you keep mooning at the sun. Here" — she handed Frances a glass of milky water — "this heat is enough to kill you." Frances took a sip and grimaced. It was warm and fuzzy, and tasted of iron from the tanks.

Mariella leant her head in close to Frances's ear, and a wave of warm peppermint washed over her. "That, my dear," she said, pointing to the doorway of the furnace, "should be enough to take your mind off whatever it is you're thinking about." Two stokers had finished their shift. They wore pantaloons and woolen shirts unbuttoned with the sleeves rolled up. One flipped his shirt over his head, and the other held up a bucket of seawater and doused him with it. The girls watched as the man pushed tired, blackened fingers through his wet hair, working at his scalp. Water, thick with coal dust, dripped down his chest, splashing onto the hot deck, where it oozed out through the gutters. Their muscled bodies glistened with sweat and their skin shone like waxed leather.

Mariella winked at Frances. "It's a hundred and twenty degrees down there, and don't they look well on it!"

Frances smiled, but warily. Mariella was frank and honest about the things that she had no language to describe. She wanted to tell her about William's note, and ask her advice, but she didn't want her to say anything which might spoil it.

"Now," Mariella said, waggling a pamphlet in her hand, "look what I have got my hands on." It was a copy of the latest *Cambrian Argus.*

Mariella turned to the last page and read, "A Fancy Dress Ball will be held on the quarter deck on Thursday, 28th October, at 8.30 p.m. Ladies and gentlemen are requested to appear at dinner in their costumes. First- and second-class passengers invited." The girls looked at each other and grinned.

"They say fancy-dress parties bring out people's darkest secrets," Mariella said. "It's only when you are dressed as someone else that you can reveal your true self."

"And what side of yourself will you be revealing?"

"Me? Oh, I'll be quite demure for once, while Mr. Fairley, normally very restrained, will be declaring his passionate love for me."

"George Fairley? The farmer?" Frances asked, surprised, and they both burst out laughing.

"What about everyone else?"

"Well. The pretty Miss Jandice" — Mariella nodded her head at a girl walking the deck with a stern-looking older woman who gripped her arm — "haven't you noticed anything strange about her?"

"Only that her clothes are about ten years out of date. She is still wearing a crinoline!"

"Exactly. The perfect disguise. Her mother insists they are on a missionary jaunt in the Africas, but I wouldn't be surprised if she turns up to the ball, swaddling a child like the Virgin Mary."

"She's pregnant?" Frances was shocked.

"Absolutely," Mariella said. "Which is why her skin glows so, and she holds her hand over her stomach in that secret way."

William just then came up onto deck, and Frances couldn't resist asking, "What about Mr. Westbrook?"

"Ah, William Westbrook." Mariella's voice became a fraction more serious, and she avoided Frances's eye. "William Westbrook is engaged to an heiress in South Africa. Her father is a diamond magnate, and she stands to inherit a vast fortune."

"You're wrong, Mariella," Frances said. "He used to be engaged, but it was called off."

"That's not the version of the story I heard. Her father asked him to keep it a secret until he came back from England. I suppose it is a kind of test, in case Mr. Westbrook changes his mind."

Mariella's words hit Frances like stinging slaps across the face. Her stomach contracted, and a hot tightness crept over her chest. How could William not have told her? How could he be engaged to be married and still have touched her the way he did? But was it really his fault? When she had told him she wasn't committed to marrying Edwin, he hadn't kissed her, and still she had practically thrown herself at him. How could she have been so naive?

Mariella put a hand on her arm, and Frances broke out of her reverie into the real world of sea, sky, and whirling birds. "A marriage of convenience," Mariella was saying. "Apparently, the girl isn't at all beautiful, but she can offer enough wealth to make up for it."

Frances nodded, and thought, Thank goodness I found out before I met him alone. Though, God, how it hurts.

FIFTEEN

Frances's world closed down around her. She spent days below deck in the cabin, stripped down to her nightdress, feigning sickness. Humiliation tortured her, and periodically she would cry out in exasperation when she remembered something she had said or done. The concert came and went, and she didn't play. She couldn't bear to see him. The ship crossed the equator and each day was hotter than the last. The *Cambrian,* the girls reported one evening, was making record progress. They would dock in Cape Town in less than a week. The news filled Frances with dread. Down in the belly of the boat, her sheets were damp and her skin sticky with sweat. She thought about William constantly — the way he had stroked her neck while she played the piano, his hand circling her ankle, his thumb against her lip — and she fought off waves of longing.

It was too hot to sleep, and she couldn't concentrate on the novel which Mariella had given her, so she lay on the narrow bunk, staring at the sea floating into the horizon, her head throbbing with the groan of the engines. She could hear the muted cries of passengers on deck as they won at tennis, the pulling up of chairs for cards, and the tramp of feet downstairs for luncheon. She imagined each noise had been made by William and found she could picture him perfectly, a dark, laughing presence on deck towards which everyone else gravitated.

In the quiet of early morning, when the other girls were still sleeping, she heard footsteps walking above their cabin, and she wondered whether their even, elastic tread was William's. Once she lay so still that a rat crawled out from behind Anne's bunk and clawed its way up the wooden frame. It was brown with a sharp muzzle and out-sized, translucent ears. She shuddered, and it turned and stared at her, twitching its thick tail like a whip, not at all afraid.

The *Cambrian* stopped at St. Helena for the day to refuel, and the passengers were invited to disembark. Mariella and Anne were eager to explore the old-fashioned little settlement of Jamestown, but Frances didn't join them. Instead she waited until the ship was quiet then padded shoeless to the bathroom, drew a bucket of water, stripped off her clothes, and washed first her body then — leaning over the tub — her hair. The dirt ran off her in soapy pools, along with some of her disappointment and shame. The sea air had dried out her skin, and she rubbed oil of cacao into her face, applied some tuberose to her throat, and combed out her hair. She dressed, then sat up in bed with her legs stretched out, sketching. From the cabin porthole she could see the island, shrouded in mist, rising in steep, forbidding cliffs from the deep.

For the first time in weeks the ship was quiet. The engines were deliciously still, and apart from the occasional shouts of sailors loading coal on board, the ship was so silent that she could hear the water lapping against the hull. Her eyes were heavy, her hair was cool and damp on her shoulders, and she let her head drift back against the pillow.

"So this is how you spend your time."

The door to the cabin had been pushed open. William was standing there in his shirtsleeves, one shoulder propped up against the frame, with the louche confidence of an off-duty corporal. His dark eyes looked fixedly at her. She shook her head slightly to clear the fug of sleep, then in a cold, still voice asked him to leave. He ignored her, searching around the room for somewhere to sit. In the cramped cabin his body had the lithe, nervous energy of a caged animal.

"I asked you to leave," she said, but he showed no sign of having heard her. "What would someone think if they saw you here?"

"They won't."

"Easy for you to say."

"Frances, there is no one of any consequence left on the boat. They are all ashore. Your reputation is safe."

He swung himself down onto the end of her bunk, trapping her feet beneath the heavy weight of his thighs. Startled, she slid them out and gathered her knees to her chest.

"Don't look at me like that. Christ! I thought we were friends. What happened?" He smiled and placed a hand on her knee. Her skin bristled. He kept it there and brushed a finger across her kneecap. The damp flesh flickered into life. She tore herself off the bed and stood, quivering with rage, between the two bunks.

"How could you come here?" The words tumbled out in accusation. "What would your wife think?"

His eyes stopped smiling and his face tightened. "She is not my wife."

"A question of timing?"

"Frances, you can abandon your tone of outraged morality. I am not the only one who is engaged to be married."

"My marriage was never a secret."

"And mine was? We have barely said two words to each other. When was I supposed to tell you?" He looked exasperated.

"When you told me that you had been engaged and that you had given her up?"

"If you think back, you might remember I turned down an invitation to kiss you." Frances found herself blushing. "I wanted to get to know you better. I didn't know how you would react." He ran a hand through his hair, sweeping black curls off his forehead. "Why do you think I asked to meet you alone? I wanted a chance to be honest with you."

"Are you sure?" she asked, wishing she could believe him.

He laughed and said, "Did you imagine I was going to force myself on you?" Her blush deepened, and he leant forward and slid a hand around the back of one of her knees, pulling her gently towards him.

"And you weren't?" she demanded, not

quite able to pull herself away.

He grinned. "I was rather hoping you would do the forcing." She could feel the pressure of his fingers through the layers of her skirts, coaxing her into life. Caution was telling her that he hadn't quite explained himself, but it didn't seem important anymore. His conviction, and the ease with which he understood her, had absolved her of mistrust.

"How could I take a risk without knowing that you cared about me first? I needed to talk to you." Desire prickled up the inside of her legs. His face was serious now, his eyes soft and liquid.

"But what about . . . ?" She couldn't bring herself to say it.

"Eloise? An arrangement organized by my cousin. I agreed to it, but then I had no reason until now not to."

"Will your cousin allow you?" The words sounded vulgar coming from her, as if she were bargaining with him on her own behalf.

"Allow me to what?" He laughed, and at the same time pushed his hand up under her skirts. There was the shock of skin against her own. "Call off the engagement? I can't see that my cousin has very much to do with it." He brushed the soft place

183

behind her knee, and she shuddered, letting her leg buckle slightly where his hand had touched her. Then he leant forward and kissed the fabric of her dress where it fell into a point below her waist.

She was too full of want to speak. He must have seen it, because he took her hand, pulling her down onto the bunk. Outside, there was the sound of a small steamer chugging across the bay. He cupped her face with one hand, his palm against her jaw. She wanted him to close the distance between them before she changed her mind.

He put a hand into her hair, bunching it up, feeling its texture.

"You are exquisitely beautiful. I want to have you, Frances, for my own." He smiled at her gently. "But you mustn't make me feel as though I am doing all the wanting."

She stared at him with wide eyes, but he didn't move, just watched her. Instinctively, she dipped her head, and the edge of his palm nudged up over her mouth. She kissed the skin, tasting its saltiness against her tongue, and she let him slide his thumb between her lips into the wetness of her mouth. He moaned softly, leaning forwards to kiss her, his beard coarse against her face and his tongue pushing very gently against her lips until her mouth became pliant under his.

Far off, beyond the current of her desire, she could hear voices. The shouts of sailors and the clunk of metal on wood. Instinct pulled her away from him. "There are people on deck."

He tried to kiss her again, but she held him back. He listened, and then after a moment groaned in frustration. "I'll go, but next time, when I ask you to do something, will you trust me?"

"Yes. I think so," she murmured.

"Good," he said, smoothing a strand of hair behind her ear and standing up. "Because I want to see more of you." She watched his strong, tanned hands adjusting his necktie in the mirror. His face, dark-skinned and broad, turned in the glass as he looked himself over. She wanted to tell him how happy she was, but when he looked at her he almost seemed not to see her. With a brisk smile he bent over and kissed her on the lips. "It pays to be careful. There's nothing people on a ship like better than gossiping about a love affair." Then he opened the door, checked the corridor, and slipped out.

The deck gleamed in the sun, light glinted off metal, and the furnace radiated a blanket of heat which made the air shimmer. By four o'clock, a lethargic calm had fallen over the ship and the pulsing throb of the engine had sent all those who were trying to read asleep in their chairs, or downstairs to their cabins. Only one group of passengers were enjoying themselves. They were playing some kind of parlor game on the first-class deck, and their laughter washed over the boat. Frances could see the Whitaker cousins, and William in the midst of them, beckoning to a steward, who returned carrying two ice buckets full of champagne.

She sighed, put down her paintbrush, took off her hat, and smoothed her hair. She had no patience for painting today. It was good to feel her fingers in her scalp, and she rubbed for a few seconds before pushing her hair back away from her ears. Anne had gone down to their cabin, but Frances couldn't drag herself away from watching William. He had kissed her, and said he wanted to see more of her, and every time she remembered she felt a rush of pleasure. She picked up her brush and went back to her painting. Another burst of laughter from the stern of the ship.

She looked across the deck and saw Emma Whitaker pulling off her blindfold and William looking past them all straight at her. He beckoned to Emma and whispered in her ear. The girl smiled and began to walk across the deck towards Frances. She was mortified. What had William said to her?

"Will you join us for a game?" Emma Whitaker looked at Frances, her cheeks flushed with champagne. "We're playing blindman's buff, but Mr. Westbrook's being a terrible bore and won't stop cheating, and it would be so much more fun if we had an extra player."

Frances shook her head. "I shouldn't . . . ."

"Shouldn't what? Play a game on the first-class deck?" The girl laughed. "No one is going to notice, and besides, if they do, we'll get Mr. Westbrook to have a word with them." She offered her arm, and Frances, unable to resist, put down her paintbrush and took it.

William winked at her when she walked up. There were five players: Frances, William, the Whitaker cousins, and Daniel Leger, a small, hard-faced man with a hook nose. William clapped a hand on his head and laughingly said he had been an acrobat in a former life. They appeared to be good friends, but when Mr. Leger handed Frances a glass of champagne he smiled a little too widely, almost knowingly, and said, "How lovely of you to have joined us, Miss Irvine."

They played a few rounds of the game, her glass was filled, and then it was her turn to be blindfolded. She trapped one of the Whitaker cousins, but couldn't name which one, and was given a forfeit.

"Say a proverb backwards!"

"Which one?" she asked.

William said, "Where there is a will, there is a way."

She stumbled over the words, laughing, finding it hard to think with William watching her. On the next round, William was blindfolded. He deliberately ignored the calls of everyone but Frances. It was too obvious that he wanted to find her, so she eventually let him trap her against the rigging. She stayed very still when he reached out his hands and touched her face. She could smell his skin, and the salty sweetness of his breath that was the taste of champagne on her tongue. He ran his fingers over her face and felt the texture of her hair, and her muscles turned soft with longing.

Eventually he called out, "Miss Joanna Whitaker." The cousins shrieked with delight.

"Mr. Westbrook, remove your blindfold!" He did, and smiled at Frances, not bothering to feign surprise that he was staring not at Miss Joanna Whitaker but at Frances.

"A forfeit!" one of the cousins declared gleefully.

"Yes. William, you must say half a dozen flattering things to Miss Irvine beginning with the letter *S.*"

William stood very close to Frances and, without pausing for thought and in a low voice, said, "Soft, suspicious, serious, stern, supple, secret." She smiled at him and thought, If I marry him, I will never ask for another thing.

SIXTEEN

The fancy-dress ball took place three days
before they were due to dock at Cape Town.
As the girls left their cabins for the ball
amidst a cloud of powder and musk, Mariella grabbed Frances by the hand and pulled
her back. She slipped a bottle into her hand.
The glass was cool and smooth in her palm.
Mariella laughed, releasing a wave of alcohol, fiery and strong. She was dressed as a
gypsy, with her glossy ringlets gathered into
a brass headpiece decorated with miniature
bells which tinkled when she turned her
head.

"Where did you get it?" Frances asked,
twisting out the cork with a squeak. Her
father had drunk brandy at home, but it had
never been offered to her. She took a sip. It
was pure and clear, and slipped around her
mouth like smoke.

"It's French. Eau-de-vie. George won it
from a man at cards."

"You're accepting gifts?"

Mariella raised the bottle to her lips and took a glug, then grinned at Frances. "He's asked me to marry him."

"Oh, Mariella, that's wonderful! But when did all this happen?"

Her friend pressed the bottle into her hand again, and Frances took another sip, this time letting the liquid slide down her throat. It burnt a hot trail into her belly and rolled around her mouth, evaporating into cold vapor on her tongue.

"At St. Helena. We walked to the top of Jacob's Ladder together."

"He proposed at the top?"

Mariella nodded.

"How romantic!" Frances hugged her. "Are you very happy? No, I don't need to ask that." Mariella's eyes were glowing. "Where will you live? In Kimberley?"

Mariella shook her head. "A passenger in first class has offered George work on his farm in Stellenbosch, not far from Cape Town. We'll stay there for a while, then we plan to go to Kimberley. You'll be there, Frances, and perhaps even Anne when the new hospital is finished. Here," she said, pushing the bottle towards Frances, "take a proper glug. It'll improve your dancing, and it's better than the stuff they'll be serving upstairs."

Frances put the bottle to her lips and tilted back her head. She let the liquid run down into her insides until it lit up her stomach with a fiery heat and made her underarms prickle with damp. Should she tell Mariella about William? The openness of her friend's excitement made her wish she could share her own. She wanted to make it real, to commit to the open world what had happened between them, but she held back. He had said almost enough to convince her that he cared about her, but she still wasn't completely sure of him.

Mariella bent down to fix the buckle on her shoe, and Frances took a last look at herself in the glass. She was dressed as Boudica in a long russet gown borrowed from one of the girls, with brass bangles and a woven headpiece which caught up her red hair and sent it tumbling down again around her shoulders. Her face looked older than it had ever done before, and there was something hard and wanting in her eyes; a strange confidence which made her feel as though — for one night at least — she was perfectly in control and could bring about any outcome that she desired.

"Look!" Anne pointed out to sea, and the

girls paused in their walk across the deck to watch the moon, a golden orb, rise dripping from the horizon. The water shimmered like a desert of black sand, and the moon cast shadows across its trembling surface.

"Aren't we a motley crew!" Mariella laughed, linking arms with them both, and the girls looked at each other and grinned. Anne had come as Spring, in a green silk dress with a white muslin gauze trimmed with pink silk flowers which she had stitched herself.

"Doesn't everything feel strange this evening?" Anne said, looking at the passengers crowding on deck in their costumes. Frances scanned the faces for William, but there was no sign of him. Robinson Crusoe, in furs and a parasol, got down on one knee and kissed the hand of a Swiss milkmaid. Laughter rippled through the hum of conversation. Stewards wielded clinking salvers of champagne glasses, and a Turk tweaked the mustaches of a cavalier. Peacock feathers swayed above the heads of Oriental ladies, and Cleopatra was kneeling to soothe the stamping rage of a little Russian tsar. It was as if the gods had cracked open history, plucking men, women, and children from every corner of the globe to entertain the heavens. The masts had been strung with candles, and their reflection glittered over the water. There was no wind, and the sea was so calm you could almost hear the heavens listening in.

"It's rather like the last dance of the damned," Frances said, thinking, Please God, let William dance with me this evening, and let us be married in Cape Town.

They took glasses of wine, and stood with their backs to the balustrade, watching the dancing. Then she saw him on the other side of the deck. He was dressed in full skirts, with a wig of dark curls which fell to his shoulders. She smiled. His skirts were too short and she could see his unstockinged ankles. He stood leaning back on his elbows, surveying the dancers. Was he trying to find her? She raised a hand to catch his attention but stopped when she saw his friend, Daniel Leger — dressed as a jockey and half his size — whispering something in his ear. William, laughing, swung himself forward. They strode across the deck and went below, and she hated to see him go.

"Why is 'emigration' such a dirty word?" Anne was asking.

"When you're in England, you think living there is everything," Mariella said. "You don't realize that there are people who don't care a bit that you've left to find work. For them, it's the most normal thing in the world."

"I didn't like to tell people I was emigrating," Anne admitted.

"How dare they judge us?" Frances asked, swallowing her disappointment. "What right do they have?"

"Give us five years and we'll have forgotten all about England." Anne smiled. "Just think where we'll be."

"Well, you'll be a head nurse," Frances replied. "Rather terrifying, I imagine, in your starched uniform."

Anne laughed. "Our families won't recognize us!"

"What do we care?" Mariella said.

"But we must stay in touch," Anne said solemnly, and she grasped their hands and put them together, and for a second the girls held on to each other, hot palm grasping the back of hot hand, fingers intertwined with fingers. The sea rushed by below them, bringing them every second closer to South Africa, and they knew that once they got there, nothing would be the same.

The evening crept on, and there was no sign of William. Frances felt reckless. In a little over three days they would be in Cape Town. They wouldn't have another chance.

She drank a glass of wine, and then another, feeling more desperate after each one.

"Boudica," William said later, coming up behind her. "Brilliant, burnished, beautiful. The *B*s would have been easier," he said with a self-deprecating smile, taking her glass from her hand and putting it down somewhere behind him. He had trimmed his beard, and she could see the square angle of his jaw and his teeth gleaming from his sunburnt face. Somehow, even dressed as a woman, he seemed more masculine than any other man on the deck. When he laughed, his ringlets quivered, and he tossed them behind his shoulder. "I don't know how you do it," he said. "The damned things are always getting in the way. You should have seen me eating my soup." He grimaced, and she broke into a smile, relieved that he was here at last.

"Is it terrible?" he asked with a look of concern, pinching at his red taffeta dress.

"Terrible?" She laughed. "Not at all. Where did you find it?"

"Mrs. Musgrave obliged."

Her hand, she realized, was in his. He was leading her across the deck into the midst of the dancers. It was difficult to think. Her mind, thick with the wine and eau-de-vie, was slow to catch up with her body. He held

her very gently around the waist, his fingertips barely making an imprint on the fabric
of her dress. His body was warm and slightly
damp. He smelled of cigarettes and pomade,
a combination strangely at odds with the
ribbons at his waist which brushed her
fingertips and the soft collision of their two
dresses as they danced. This was the heady
concoction that he created, a subtle but
beguiling mixture of humor and intensity
which had her hopelessly enthralled. She
didn't feel sure of herself when she was with
him. She didn't know the rules of courtship. He was always one step ahead of her,
and with this came the sharp but dangerous
pleasure of being out of control, not unlike
the game she used to play with her cousins
where you shut your eyes and fell, trusting
your partner would catch you.

"Frances," he said, leaning forward to
whisper in her ear. His breath ruffled her
skin like feathers. "The small matter of you
owing me your life. Don't you think it's
about time that you repaid me?"

Her heart thudded. It occurred to her that
he might propose right here as they danced.
After a moment he said, "I want you to
meet me by the stern deck door in five
minutes."

"But I can't . . ."

"Can't what?" He looked at her, eyes laughing.

She wanted to say, I need to know that I can trust you, but instead she said, "Not where we're alone. Please."

He looked disappointed in her, and she felt suddenly very ordinary. "Frances, you're all grown up, not a child." He smiled kindly. "I promise I won't ask you to do anything you don't want to do, but it must be your decision."

He walked away, and she looked at his broad back pushing through the dancers and thought, He wants me. Of all the people he could have, he wants me.

"Miss Irvine, a dance?" It was George Fairley, holding out his hand to her. She squeezed it in congratulation and his cheeks dimpled, but she couldn't concentrate on what he was saying. All she could think about was William, whether he was waiting for her, and what he would say to her if he was. "I can't dance now," she said apologetically, leaving him, "but perhaps later?"

She picked her way through the gathered crowd to the stern door, opened it, and saw with a surge of relief that he was there, standing below her on the stairs.

"I thought you'd come," he said, smiling.

She lurched a little down the stairs, but

198

he gripped her hand tightly and marched her along the corridor. She had to run to keep up. There were cabins along one side, and they passed an open door. Daniel Leger was sitting on a bunk with a girl lying across his lap dressed as a ballerina. He looked up and winked at her as they swept past. William stopped outside the next cabin. He pulled her inside and shut the door smartly behind him.

"Yours?"

He nodded, leaning back against the door, watching her take in the room. There was just a single bunk against the wall, a few jackets hanging opposite, and a shotgun in a case above them. It was about the same size as a cabin sleeping three girls in second class. The room, lit by the soft glow of a gas lamp turned down low, smelt of leather and sandalwood. She caught sight of herself in the round mirror above the washbasin. Her hair spilled down the back of her russet gown, and her arms were bare.

The cabin was very still after the commotion of the dance, and the quiet roared loud in her ears. She put a hand on the wall to steady herself. Her heart was pounding. She wanted William to say something to put her at her ease, but instead he moved to a small mahogany rack on the wall which held a decanter and a tumbler. He took them down, poured out a little of the amber liquid, took a sip, and held it out to her. His breath had clouded the glass, leaving the moist imprint of his lips. She took it from him. The alcohol tasted dank and peaty, with a smokiness that numbed her mouth.

"Scotch," he said, and she nodded. His physical presence, the height and bulk of him, intimidated her now that she was alone with him. He was at least a head taller than her, and had a contained, athletic energy which made him restless. He took back the glass, and it clinked against his teeth as he brought it to his lips. She could feel the heat of his hands, like coals, only inches from her body. Was he going to touch her? She shouldn't want him to. In fact, she ought to leave the cabin now, but the alcohol had loosened something inside her.

"Second thoughts?" he asked, brushing her hand away from her neck so it fell still at her side.

She looked at him with wide eyes.

"Do you love him?" he asked.

"Edwin? No."

"And me?" he asked, with boyish petulance. It wasn't what she had expected. He must have known that she did, and yet he looked for a second completely vulnerable in his flouncy dress, with the curls dropping to his shoulders and his dark arms thrust into pretty lace sleeves which were too short for him.

"William." She said his name for the first time, reaching up to put a hand to his cheek. His beard crinkled under her fingertips. He took a sip from the tumbler and studied her face. She let her hand drop to her side, suddenly unsure of herself. When he stepped closer she instinctively edged backwards, feeling the door handle pressing into her back. He brought his hand up and ran his finger around the lip of her dress, across the shoulders, and along the top of the bodice, dragging it between the fabric and her skin.

"If we could only talk —" she said.

He interrupted her, his voice low and hoarse. "I've tried to tell myself I should leave you alone, Frances Irvine. Let you get on and marry your doctor. But I haven't been able to sleep for days, thinking about you." He dipped his head and brushed her mouth with his. In a sudden, instinctive movement, she raised her face to his, trying to keep hold of the touch of his lips, but he was already out of reach and she kissed instead his chin, clumsily, through his beard, feeling the bristle of hair with the tip

201

of her outstretched tongue. He groaned as she did it, put down his tumbler, then turned his mouth on hers. She leant into him. His fingers were at the nape of her neck, tracing a line down her spine, and her skin burnt where he touched her.

It wasn't until he began to lever her dress down over her shoulders that she realized he had undone the fastenings. Confused, she tried to pull it back up, but he caught her wrist and held it off and with his other hand tugged at the center of her corset so that her breasts, pale and heavy, fell free of the fabric. She drew in breath, leaning against him to cover herself up, but he stepped away from her, looking at her nakedness.

She was suddenly and completely out of her depth. She tried to make a grab for the shoulders of her dress, but he held her wrists until the skin stung, and she stopped struggling.

"What have you got to lose?" he asked, rubbing the back of his hand across one of her breasts, and she trembled as he touched her. Her breath came in a heavy mixture of fear and pleasure. He pushed his taffeta dress down around his waist and stepped out of it. He wore loose cotton trousers underneath, ruched with a drawstring on his hips, just below the clustered muscles of his stomach. He smiled, drawing her towards him, into his chest, and kissed her softly on the forehead. A sob broke inside her. "Frances," he said, kissing her wet cheeks, "don't be frightened." There was the warmth of his chest against her own, and then the gentle pull of his arms drawing her down onto the bunk until she was lying, looking up at him. He propped himself up on one elbow next to her. Then he stroked the hair off her forehead, and with his other hand lifted her skirts and brushed his fingers across the tight place inside her.

She shivered, her body shocked by such a sudden intimacy, but he shushed her, stroking her face. All the time his other hand gave her caresses, very softly, until her hips began to push up against him and her legs opened wider. Then his fingers flickered inside her, she moaned, and his mouth was against hers. His weight shifted as he levered himself on top of her. There was an urgency about him now, a fumbling as he bunched up her skirts. She tried to push them back down, but he had her pinned under the weight of him. He pulled her drawers down with one hand, and a moment later she felt a sharp, tearing pain. She cried out, but her mouth was crushed into his shoulder. He thrust deeper into her, his hips bruising hers, pleasure grinding into her pain, until he stopped suddenly, shuddered, and went slack.

When it was over he rolled off her, breathing heavily. She tried to cover herself with a sheet, but he stopped her hand, looking boyishly pleased with himself. He brushed the damp hair off her cheek and said, "Your eyes are green like a cat."

His lips were slightly parted in a lazy smile, and his eyes were dark and half lidded as he looked at her. She reached out a hand and touched the muscles on his shoulder, tracing the line of their tautness with her fingers. There was a throbbing inside her, half pleasure, half pain, as if she had been hollowed out. She thought she might cry, and wished he would hold her, but he didn't move.

After a few moments, she said, "Mr. Leger. He saw us."

"He won't say anything."

"Who was that with him?"

"The ballerina?" William rolled away from her, onto his back. "Some girl from steerage."

His words stung, and for the first time she felt ashamed and realized what she had done. Was she any different to the girl she

204

had seen lying across Daniel Leger's lap? She looked around the room, masculine in its every detail. What had she been thinking, letting him bring her here? William must have sensed it in her silence, because he reached for her hand.

It gave her the confidence to ask, "Your marriage with Eloise?"

"You have to give me time. I'll need a day or two in Cape Town to smooth things out."

"The Society has a boarding house."

"You can stay there?"

She nodded.

"And the doctor?" he asked.

"I'll write to him."

"Wait until I've worked things out with Eloise's family. It'll make things easier." He put a hand to her hair, stroking her neck. A flickering, like static, ran down her body. She turned towards him, curling her head into his shoulder, but he touched her cheek lightly and said, "Time to go."

He lay on the bed while she undid the hooks at the front of her corset and pulled it up over her breasts. Then he handed her the hairpins which had come loose on the sheet. She looked at herself in the glass. Her eyes glittered back at her, dark and strange. Her face was thin and pale, and her hair had sprung loose, swirling round her face in wiry, copper coils so she looked like Medusa in a nest of snakes.

When he stood up she felt his body pressing against her back. He swept the hair off her neck, and kissed her skin at the nape so that a shudder ran down her spine and every muscle cried out for him to pull her back down to bed. But instead he began tugging at the fastenings on her dress, sealing her back up inside it. He was as good as Lotta, and she realized this wasn't the first time he had helped a girl get dressed. Then he patted her on the rump, and said, "The music will be over soon."

She turned to face him. She could almost taste the warmth of his skin, the sweat from their bodies, and his lips, red where he had kissed her. Suddenly he seemed very remote.

"When can I see you again?" Her voice quavered, and she knew she sounded desperate. She hated herself for asking.

"Alone? Not until Cape Town. We should be careful."

"Not before?"

"Frances. Be patient." He pulled her shawl off the bed and wove it around her head. "Boudica becomes bedouin. If you see anyone you recognize, say you wanted to find the surgeon. His cabin is along this corridor."

He opened the door for her, one arm resting on top of it, so she had to duck under him to get out. She turned as she went and drank in a last glimpse of him. He was smiling at her, feet bare, trousers hanging low on his hips, dark hair creeping up his chest. She wanted him to kiss her, to say something final to seal the future, but instead he slipped his hand off the frame of the door in a gesture that could have been impatience. She turned and walked down the corridor into the wheeling music and cold night air.

SEVENTEEN

Frances was terrified by what she had done, and worried that William wouldn't keep his promise. Sometimes, listening to Mariella talking about George Fairley and their plans for Stellenbosch, she burned with apprehension. She wanted to tell Mariella, but until William had called off his engagement, what was there to say? Mariella, with her efficient, practical mind, might not understand the delicacy of their situation.

At night she gave in to imagining herself as Frances Westbrook. William would become a great politician, a successful statesman, and they would explore Africa together. She would go with him on his hunting trips. They would camp in the bush, and when he came to bed at night she would feel his hands winding round her body, crushing her ribs, pulling her closer to him. He wouldn't be easy to live with, but she understood his ambition. He was restless and determined, but this was part of his passion for life. He lived closer to excitement than most people. She would offer him a steadiness that would tame his wilder moments. And in return William would liberate her. He judged people on whether they interested him, not because of who they were. He wasn't tied to the skirts of Society like her uncle, and he didn't give a damn about the Hamiltons, or where her father had come from.

The Cape drew nearer, and she realized that she needed to talk to him about practicalities. How long would she be in Cape Town before she heard from him? Where would they be married? She would need to pay for the boarding house, and although she didn't want to mention money, the truth was she had almost nothing to get by on. The little her uncle had given her had been sent ahead to Edwin as part of her dowry.

On the third day after the ball, a cry went up across the ship. "Land ho!"

The shadow of Table Mountain loomed like a storm cloud in the distance. The captain made an announcement that they would dock after breakfast the following day. Frances felt queer. Very soon now, one way or another, everything would change. In a panic, she wrote out a note to William asking him to find her on deck after supper, and gave it to Gilbert to deliver.

She waited for him for half an hour, anxiety flipping over inside her. What if he didn't come? What if she never spoke to him again? The visible reality of Cape Town seemed to call everything into question.

"Frances." Suddenly he was there, saying her name and putting his hand lightly to her cheek so that her hair crackled against her ear.

"I was worried," she said.

"That I wouldn't come? Or have you changed your mind about me already?" He smiled, his eyes glinting green as he laughed at her, and she felt relief throw off her concerns.

Now that he was here she felt foolish. He had other, more important things to think about. It was nothing for her to break off her own engagement, but he would have to make enemies with Eloise Woodhouse's family. Mariella had told her that they were very influential at the Cape. She reminded herself that he was taking enormous risks for her, but she didn't entirely forget her own position. "How long will I have to wait in Cape Town?"

William stroked her face with the back of his hand. His knuckles grazed against her skin. "So impatient." He was assured and confident. When she was with him, she could feel the world bending itself to his will.

"But you don't even know where I'm staying!"

"Frances," he said, with just a glimmer of impatience, "I have contacts. The Society's details will be down on the ship's register."

Of course. What a fool she was, always asking him to spell everything out. Why couldn't she just trust him? But she also knew from experience that when he was gone the confidence she felt when she was with him would be torn to shreds. "Will you write to me?"

"Are you always so demanding?"

She looked away from him, stung, but he put a finger under her chin and brought her round to face him. "I'm teasing you, Frances. I will write to you the very day we arrive. I promise." He took her hand and brought it to his lips.

"But what about you? What will you promise me?" he asked with a mischievous smile. He eased the glove off her hand and lifted the tip of each finger to his mouth in turn. "You must promise me" — she felt the wetness of his mouth on her middle finger — "that you will think about me every night that we are apart."

"I promise," she said, her fingers burning where he had kissed them, and her heart beating in her throat like the wings of a butterfly against a glass bottle. It was only when he was gone that she realized she hadn't asked him for money. She would have to make do with what she had.

The Cape was within touching distance the next morning, and before the bell had sounded for breakfast the deck was swarming with passengers eager to get a look at the new country. It was a perfectly calm day, and a flotilla of small fishing boats edged towards them, their crews heaving at the oars. When they were within earshot, they called out from all sides, "News? What news?"

There was a shouted relay as sailors condensed the happenings of London a month ago into a few short sentences.

Frances stood amidst a huddle of other passengers pressing against the railings to get a good view. Table Mountain rose every second larger in front of them. Its majestic bulk towered over the bay, flat-topped and imposing, like the grand gatehouse to a new continent. Soon they were so close she could make out the trees which covered its lower slopes. Looking back down the ship, she caught sight of William weaving through the crowd towards her, shepherding Mrs. Nettleton in front of him.

"There's a good view of it from here." He levered Mrs. Nettleton through the group of passengers so she stood at the railings next to Frances.

"Miss Irvine," William said, bowing to her. Frances greeted him, and Mrs. Nettleton said a curt how-do-you-do before turning her gaze back to William. He had positioned himself directly behind them both, looking over their shoulders, and Frances felt the other passengers press in behind them.

William pointed through the swirling fog to a small, bleak-looking island with a low, flat terrain. "There it is! Misery Island."

"What a terrible name. Who lives there?" Mrs. Nettleton asked.

"Mostly lepers and lunatics."

A few minutes later they could just make out a large lighthouse on the mainland and an imposing-looking building next to it. "That's Somerset Hospital, just finished for the princely sum of twenty thousand pounds. You can't say the British don't spend money on their colonies."

One of William's hands came to rest, very gently, on the small of Frances's back. She froze, every muscle in her body tightening.

"And that, Madam," William said, talking blithely on, "is the infamous Breakwater Prison." He pointed to a squat, gray building. "It's not full of your usual criminals. You'll find doctors, lawyers, merchants, all doing a full day's labor. Anyone caught stealing diamonds at Kimberley. So don't be tempted, Mrs. Nettleton, to slip any stones into your pockets when you tour the mines."

"Oh, you are naughty." Mrs. Nettleton giggled, tugging at his sleeve, and at the same time Frances felt William stroking his thumb across her buttocks. Her skin, like velvet, took the imprint of every touch. She had never wanted anything as much as she wanted William.

"Is it a horrible place?" Mrs. Nettleton asked, hoping to be terrorized.

"Terrible." William worked his foot between Frances's boots, pushing her legs a little apart so she fell forward slightly and had to support herself against the rail. She could feel his knee pressing into hers, and his thumb tracing a circle across her skin. "At least a thousand prisoners at any one time, sleeping on concrete floors. Lights are kept burning all through the night so they can't sleep, and they labor all day chained

214

between two kaffirs to stop them talking. Any indiscretions and they are put on the treadmill."

"Treadmill?"

"It's a kind of mill with steps that turns against a tight wall. The prisoners' punishment is to walk on it — sometimes for twelve hours at a stretch. Can you imagine what that feels like on a summer's day?"

"And if they don't walk?" Mrs. Nettleton asked, deliciously involved in this story of cruelty.

"The planks keep turning, scraping their shins to the bone."

"How dreadful!" Mrs. Nettleton exclaimed. Then turning towards him, she said, "Now, Mr. Westbrook, I must make sure everything is in order downstairs."

"Certainly." William removed his hand from Frances's dress and without a glance in her direction guided Mrs. Nettleton back through the crowd.

This was love, Frances realized. He filled her up with it just by touching her, and when he moved away she was nothing more than a husk, with the breeze blowing right through her.

EIGHTEEN

A small, clean room. The house set up on a hill, offering a view of a ragged, dusty street lined with thatched white houses winding down towards the harbor. It was swelteringly hot, and the sash window was open, letting in a thin breeze which came off the sea, bringing with it the smell of fish and roasting coffee. The sun, which had slipped from view, breathed orange flames into the sky, but the sea had already turned purple in the dark. All day, Frances had watched the street, going downstairs only to take lunch. When she shut her eyes the room dipped and rolled, and she felt as though she were still on the boat.

They had disembarked three days ago to find Cape Town buzzing with the news of a smallpox epidemic. It had broken out in the town a month ago, and after clearing customs the girls had been ushered into a hospital tent, where they were vaccinated

216

against the disease. The nurses said it was the worst epidemic the town had seen in years.

They spent the first night together at the boarding house and said their good-byes in the morning. Anne left for the hospital in Cape Town, and Mariella went on to Stellenbosch with George Fairley, where they would be married. Frances lied and said Edwin was meeting her here. Now, three days later, she was still waiting to hear from William.

A dwarf, tar black, sat on a slab of stone that had been laid like a bridge over the small canal which ran down the side of the road. He had been there since breakfast, whittling a piece of wood. She had the sense they were both waiting for something. Occasionally, flower sellers came by, carrying huge baskets filled with brightly colored blooms. As night drew on, the croaking of frogs started up and the air began to hum with insects.

There was a knock at the door, and a colored maid, smelling of coconuts, came in with tea. She looked more Oriental than African, with almond eyes and black hair greased and bound. The glossy coil was held in place by a gold skewer.

She preempted Frances's question.

"No letters, Ma'am," she said, putting down the tray, and Frances, unable to hide her disappointment, asked, "Are you sure?"

The maid nodded, shutting the window. Frances leapt up. "Leave it open." The little room made her feel trapped, and the thought of another night on her own with her thoughts was unbearable. But the maid shook her head. "You'll get bitten," she said, drawing the curtains over the closed window and sealing off the outside world. She laid out the tea, lit the lamp, and went out.

There was a letter on the desk. It had been waiting for her when she arrived, but when she ripped it open she saw that it was from Edwin.

I have had to give up the practice in Kimberley. I hope you won't be too disappointed. I have a good position at Rietfontein, a farm some miles away. I will explain when you arrive, but regret that I will not be able to get away to collect you. You should travel by train, then coach to Jacobsdal, where you will be able to get a cart to the farm.

He signed off, "Your soon to be devoted husband." And Frances had felt a trickle of terror. Was it possible she might have to

218

marry him after all?

Now she sat on the edge of the bed, and her eyes crept towards her own letter resting on the mantel. It was addressed to Edwin. She had been so sure and full of confidence when she had written it, in her first few hours in Cape Town. Her tone had been matter-of-fact. "There is no love between us," she had written, dismissing with irritation the thought of Edwin reading it, his cold gray eyes dissecting her affectation of breezy sincerity. And he would be right. She did feel guilty, but he was not without culpability. His love was a greedy, selfish thing. Marrying her seemed to be no more than the satisfaction of a private ambition.

The envelope sat on the mantel like an accusation, and in the half-light she had the unsettling sense that Edwin was leaning against the wall, reading it. He was looking at her with pity. *Frances, what a mess you've made of everything.* She picked up a glass from the table by the bed and with a scream of frustration threw it at the mantel. It hit the chimneybreast and shattered in a spray of crystals. The noise shook her out of inertia. She stood up, legs trembling slightly, and began to dress to go out. She had to see William. She couldn't wait any longer.

There was no more money. And as she pulled on her gloves and fixed her hat in the mirror, she began to feel better. Practicalities were not William's strength. He probably hadn't even considered what it would be like waiting at the charity's boarding house for him to write. And he might not have guessed that she was doubting him. If she could just talk to him, then she was sure he would reassure her, just as he had done the last time. She remembered her panic then and how he had laughed at her worrying. She caught her eye in the mirror, and found that when she made herself smile it came easily. Everything would be fine.

William would more than likely be staying with his cousin, and it wasn't difficult to find out where Joseph Baier lived. He was, after all, one of the most powerful men in South Africa. The cab rumbled across the dusty town, through quiet, tree-lined streets, and pulled up outside a grand, three-story house which looked like something out of a Dutch painting. It had a gable and a high *stoep* in front and railings that curled down on either side. Every room in the house was lit up, and light poured out of chinks in the shutters. Frances caught the boisterous sounds of a brass band. The front door was closed, guarded by an Oriental man in livery.

Now that Frances was here, she lost confidence. Could she really make a formal entrance? She asked the cab driver to move on a little way, and he let her out a hundred yards up the street. Gardens had been planted on either side of the road, and the air thrummed with the sound of cicadas. Frances walked back towards the house. She passed a small tree which had been uprooted. It lay on its side with its roots exposed like parched tentacles, gleaming white in the dark. Further on was a hedge that marked the boundary of the house.

Something snagged on her skirts. She turned and cried out. A creature was holding on to the hem of her dress; a short, squat native woman dressed in colored rags, with wild scrubby hair. She had a grizzly, black face which was swollen and ugly. The woman grabbed at her, pushing her face close and letting her eyes roll to the back of her head. Frances snatched her dress away, and the woman let out a scream which broke into a glittering laugh. She tried to walk away, but the woman followed, waving her arms. Her tattered clothes fluttered, fanning out in the warm night air like the

221

singed wings of a moth.

They were close to the house now, and Frances, hidden in the shadows of a line of trees, saw a carriage pull up.

"Damn you," she hissed at the woman, who smelt of sweat and filth and still plucked at her skirts. "Leave off me!" she said, desperate to get rid of her now that they were within calling distance of the house.

A second later the front door opened, and a man walked onto the *stoep.* She recognized instantly the bulk of his shoulders, his dark hair, his easy stance and casual dress. William stepped out of a halo of light as if from fire. He ran down the steps, and for a second Frances thought he was running towards her and she almost cried out. But then she saw the carriage door open, and a woman stepped onto the street. Her face was partly illuminated by the cab lamp. She was tall and heavy-boned. Frances saw instantly that she wasn't beautiful — she had a weightiness about her body, a long nose and large hands — but she held herself erect with a grace and confidence that reminded her of Lucille. William stepped up to the carriage, taking both her hands in his and kissing them tenderly. Frances couldn't breathe. It was as if a steel wire

222

were being wound around her chest. The woman whispered in his ear and she heard him laugh. A low, deep, satisfied chuckle.

The native woman, seeing Frances's attention caught up by the carriage, began to shriek like a kite. Frances, horrified, crept back into the shadows, but William had turned towards them and now peered into the dark. He would have been able to see the white of her dress but not her face. The native woman saw William looking and, eager for attention, began a slow pirouette down the street, clapping her hands. William dug into his pockets and threw a handful of coins towards them. They fell silently into the dust, and the woman scrambled on her knees to retrieve them.

Then Eloise — it must have been Eloise — stepped back into the cab, and William swung himself in after her, shutting the door. He rapped on the roof, and the coachman flickered the tip of his whip over the horses. The carriage moved off down the street.

Frances stood absolutely still, trying to close down her emotions before realization seeped like poison into the heart of her. Her body registered the *cheee cheee cheee* of cicadas from the bushes behind the road and the woman prancing down the street glucking over her handful of coins. If she stayed very still, perhaps she wouldn't have to feel the pain. But when the brass band rumbled into life for another song, a cry tore from some animal place inside her. She walked back to the carriage, her mouth salty with tears. One thought turned over and over again in her mind, and she kept sounding it out for truth. She had never heard William laugh as he had with Eloise — an easy, spontaneous chuckle born of affection — and this simple thing shattered her reality. It was clear to her suddenly, like waking from a dream, that she didn't know William at all — the simple tenderness with which he held Eloise's hands, the honest friendship between them as he bent to hear her whisper. In an instant she had seen a collusion between them which she and William had never shared. It would have been easier if Eloise's attraction had been her beauty, but this was something different. She knew nothing about William's life. How could she have believed he might have chosen to spend it with her? She let herself imagine, with a stab of pain, where the carriage was taking them. To another grand house, a party perhaps, where William would catch Eloise's eye over the heads of the other guests.

Frances climbed back into the cab, and the driver called to the horses in a short staccato, until they were trotting back through the quiet streets, their hooves clopping on the dry earth. The truth was that William had thrown coins at her as if she were a beggar, and that dismissal — no, worse — his failure to recognize her presence in the dark, when she had known him in an instant, mortified her. All the pain she had felt on leaving England — her father's death, her uncle's rejection, the sense that she didn't belong — had been soothed by William. Now she felt the old terrors crowding in on her. Perhaps her uncle was right to have refused to take her in. The way she had behaved on the ship proved she was anything other than worthy of respect. Self-loathing engulfed her. Even William had reminded her about the dangers of seduction, and she had blithely ignored him.

She sat in the back of the cab, her hands clasped together, gulping back a sadness that spilled out of some dark place inside her.

NINETEEN

The Karoo. One hundred and fifty thousand square miles of barren, unforgiving landscape. It took them four days to cross it in an ox wagon. They had a strong wind at their backs, bellowing heat like a furnace. The skin on Frances's face became soft leather. She choked on dust and ground her teeth, but by the end of the first day the wagon had shaken the fight out of her. She sat with her eyes fixed on a gap in the canvas, watching the sliver of road taking her away from Cape Town. Her only consolation was that Edwin no longer lived in Kimberley. She would never have to see William again.

The wagon was crammed with goods. Spades and metal sieves hung down from the roof, and the canvas sides were lined with pouches holding tins of sardines, bottles of water, boiled hams, and flasks of whiskey. Equipment had been crammed under the benches. There were coils of rope, a box of wood screws, and a pair of oilcans bound together with straps which rubbed against the backs of her calves. Occasionally the wagon would hit a boulder or a tree stump and a tin of currants or ginger preserve would roll out from between the seats.

On the second morning, the wagon stopped to pick up a tawny, long-limbed Dutchman with a soft-rimmed hat and a square black beard, who folded himself onto the bench opposite. He carried a cockerel in a wire cage, which he stowed underneath his seat. It preened its feathers and clucked disapprovingly. The wagon lurched its way over the pitted road, and Frances watched the man's knees bob about his ears. He revealed a mouth full of unsteady teeth, and she smiled back at him.

The rich, fertile lands around Cape Town had given way to a vast desert. The Dutchman, perhaps sensing her unhappiness, kept sweeping his hands over the shimmering expanse. "Zebra," he would say, enthusiastically, pulling his beard, "wildebeest, impala, kudu." And she understood he must have been talking about many years ago, because in all the miles they traveled she didn't see a single wild animal, only the bleached bones of livestock by the sides of the road.

There were no hedges, fences, or walls to break the space, no markers of civilization to demarcate boundaries, only line upon line of dried-up riverbeds choked with sand. The vastness of the landscape unnerved her. How could you tell where the civilized world began and ended? They passed cattle *kraals* and ostrich camps and, occasionally, farmsteads. Native huts, like swollen beehives, were scattered across the plains. Looking out from the back of the wagon, she spotted children, so dirty their race was indistinguishable, scrambling in the dust, arms outstretched for a piece of bread, or coins. Some of the Boers had built dams, which had shriveled in the heat to murky, muddy pools. Bright green mimosa trees clung to their edges.

The dust was everywhere. It rose in great ocher clouds from the road, obscuring the glare of the sun. It crept into every crevice of the wagon, worked its way under your fingernails, and gritted in your teeth. Her lips cracked in the dry heat, and when she licked them they stung and seemed to pull too tight across her mouth.

Once, she heard the fast thundering of hooves and excited shouts from their driver. "Hallo! *Goede reis!*"

It was a Cape cart from Kimberley, going by at twice their speed. Their horses were lathered and muscular. Two young men, Europeans, grinned and waved as they swept past. Frances buried her face in her shawl so she wouldn't be seen. All her money had been spent on the boarding house in Cape Town, and the ox wagon was the only form of transport she could afford without writing to Edwin for money.

She had a letter from William in her pocket, and his words turned over and over in her mind, like the treadmill at Breakwater Prison. It had arrived the morning after she had seen him in Cape Town.

Frances — I can barely bring myself to write this, after everything that has passed between us, but — loveliest — here is the truth of it. There is no possibility of us being together. Baier refused to consider the idea of us being married. He is wrong. Utterly wrong. But I need him, Frances, more than perhaps I thought. I know you will understand when I say there are things I want to do in Africa — important things — and I need his help to begin them. If I want to make a difference at the Cape — and I believe I can — then I must first make a success of myself in the industry, and to do that I need his backing.

You can't imagine what this decision has cost me. I have had to be ruthless with myself, and with you, my dearest, and I will pray that you forgive me, because I can't stand the thought of you thinking about me with anything other than affection.

It was the letter she had dreaded, and it only made her love him more. The fact that he respected her enough to be honest with her made the finality of his words even harder to bear. He would marry another woman, not her, and she would never hear from him again. Yet despite the horror of imagining life without him, the letter soothed some of her fears. It reminded her that they had shared something real, and she allowed it to erase the image she had of him laughing with Eloise. He had tried to argue with his cousin in her favor, and of course she understood why in the end he had agreed to give her up. He was ambitious. She had always known it, and she didn't want to be the one to hold him back. Yet in siding with William against herself, she was acknowledging her own worthlessness, and she felt this as a subtle shame which crept over her, sapping her mind of strength. Enclosed with the letter was a thin, gold chain which she wore threaded around her neck. The cool weight of the metal against her skin was a constant reminder of what she had lost.

At sunrise on the third day they passed a herd of cattle, at least five hundred strong. The herders whistled and shouted, flicking their whips over the animals to keep them moving, but the cattle were walking skeletons, heads bowed low, rasping their tongues across the side of the wagon in the hope of leeching some moisture from the wood. An adolescent calf, bones propping up a tent of skin, swayed at the edges of the herd, then collapsed on its side. A herder picked it up by the tail until it found its front feet and began to walk again. It took the wagon an hour to nudge its way through. The cattle jostled and pushed the oxen and brought with them a boiling cloud of black flies. They sensed the body heat within and crawled over the canvas like fat lice.

The old man opposite squashed one expertly with the palm of his hand, and held it up for Frances to see. There was a searing pain on her calf, and she had to lift her skirts to sweep them off her legs. It didn't take her long to start killing them, and her palm turned crimson with blood.

At noon they arrived in Jacobsdal, a small *dorp* on the banks of a river with a straggle of houses and a church with its shutters battened down against the howling wind. It was a bleak place, hardly a town at all, just a street etched out in the dust as if some tired old colonial at home had drawn a line on the map with a ruler. A few corrugated shacks were scattered along the sides of the road. It was deserted. Everyone must have moved on to the diamond fields.

She found a trap to take her to Rietfontein. It was open-topped, and her shawl, pulled over her head, offered little protection against the stinging cloud of grit and sand. After a few miles the driver stopped to ask directions from a native boy herding a vast flock of sheep. Their fleeces were clogged with dirt, and their eyes shut stoically against the dust. Eventually the cart put her down at a cottage with peeling white walls and a sagging thatched roof which stood alone in the middle of a ragged plain. It was surrounded by a few fallen-down *kraals* whose acacia walls had blown in. Their thorns snagged on the patchy scrub. She bowed her head against the force of the wind and walked up onto the *stoep*.

232

No one answered when she knocked, so she opened the door and stepped into a narrow hall. It was quiet inside, and she stood for a moment, rubbing her eyes and shaking rivulets of dust out of her shawl. It was more of a hovel than a house, with two beams running below a roof of reeds and mud. There were no carpets on the loosely boarded floors, and the walls, roughly plastered and bare of pictures, leveled off short of the vaulted roof so that any noise made in the house would be heard in every room. Two doors opened up to the left of the hall. In the first, to her surprise, was a brass bedstead and an oversized wardrobe made of a dark, heavy wood.

Further on was a study, which smelt of alcohol and camphor. Shelves lined the walls of the room, and on them were jars and bottles of different shapes and sizes. They were mostly filled with a murky liquid out of which peered insects, frogs, lizards, and, in one, a slack-jawed snake. Their bodies, where they pressed up against the glass, were white and bloodless. There were ostrich eggs, still whole, and butterflies of startling color pinned to pieces of card. A grotesque spider with thick, sculpted legs trailing golden hair looked as though he had been pinned mid-crawl. White, fossilized bones of tiny creatures emerged from chunks of rock. On the desk were forceps, scissors, and a selection of knives. A microscope had been set up, and two or three nets leant against the wall. It was a chilling collection of specimens; a little production line of death and entrapment. She had had no idea Edwin was interested in natural history, but then there was very little she did know about him.

A few newspaper cuttings had been pinned to the wall above the desk. Frances looked more closely at them. They were political cartoons. Edwin seemed so private, she hadn't thought of him being concerned with politics. British soldiers and diplomats were depicted with bulbous faces and thick waists. One showed a bobby, fat and smug, smoking a cigar and wielding a baton made of newspaper. He was delivering blows to a Boer with a heavy beard and unkempt hair who had his trousers round his ankles. Another showed a native, wide-eyed, being beaten by an Englishman who held a whip in one hand and the St. George's flag in the other: "Nigger flogging, my boy, is the onerous but necessary task of Empire." Their faces leered out at her, and she was caught off guard by their frankness.

Across the hall was a sitting room with a

large chimneybreast, a crude mantelpiece, and a small dining table with four chairs. Stepping out of the back door, Frances found a mud hut which turned out to be the kitchen. A pile of oranges was heaped up in one corner, two hams hung from the ceiling, and a maid was stretched out on the floor, sleeping. She leapt up when Frances came in, startling a small ferret-like creature, which scuttled out from under the sink and stood on two feet, looking at Frances with beady eyes. It crawled closer, and Frances, thinking it might scramble up her skirts and bite her, screamed. The creature darted out of the kitchen, down the hall of the house, and into the study. She followed after it, shutting the door and trapping the animal inside. A tumble of Dutch words spilled out of the maid, and Frances shook her head to show she didn't understand. They looked at each other in mutual confusion. The maid's skin was blue-black, the color of charcoal, and a deep fold was etched down either side of her mouth. She wore a simple black dress, and a fraying green scarf wound around her head like a turban. Her feet were bare. After a moment she grinned at Frances, revealing a row of yellowing teeth. It was such a good-natured smile that Frances couldn't help but smile back.

"Dr. Matthews?" Frances asked.

The maid pointed towards the front door, and Frances understood that Edwin was out. What a relief. She was exhausted, and, leaving her trunk in the hall, she went through to the sitting room to rest for a few minutes. Dust rose in a little cloud from the chair when she sat. Flies crawled over the walls. The maid came in with a glass of water and a plate with two biscuits. She was heavily built and no longer young, and she moved slowly through the room. Frances drank the water but couldn't bring herself to eat. Her mouth was dry, and a headache was unwinding from a tight coil behind her eyes. She shifted in her seat and wondered whether Edwin would be home soon and what they would talk about when he arrived. They had no experience of courtship. What did two people say to each other on the eve of their wedding?

Just the one bedroom. She had foolishly imagined having her own, retreating into her private space each night, and this was a difficult adjustment. There wouldn't be any privacy here. She would have to sleep next to him, dress and undress in front of him, and use the chamber pot in the night. But where would she sleep this evening? They weren't married yet. She watched a trail of ants threading across the floor, up one of the table legs, to the china plate. They inspected the biscuits before swarming over them. If this house was left long enough, the ants, the dust, and the cattle would slowly dismantle it.

Exhaustion settled over Frances's body. Her shoulders ached and her knees were cramped and stiff. She let her head rest against the back of the chair. When she shut her eyes her body rattled and swayed with the motion of the wagon. She hadn't thought Edwin would make a brilliantly successful doctor. He didn't have the bedside manner for it. But he had obviously done very badly in Kimberley to end up here. This was worse than she had imagined. The same house in Kimberley would have had some of the charm and romance of pioneer life, but here they would be stuck out on the veldt, living like animals off the land. There wasn't even a bathroom. Where would she wash? Her body ached for the luxury of hot water. Could one even feel clean in this house? Her bathroom in London, with its gilt taps and streaming jets of water, seemed an impossibly luxurious thing. It was apt punishment, she thought, for a woman who had aimed for too much.

Her consolation was that at least her uncle, and her cousins, would never have to see what kind of life she was living.

She woke with a jolt. The room was in a murky half-light, and she gazed blankly at the table, at the threadbare pattern on the arm of the chair and the diminishing plate of biscuits. Her headache had cleared, but it took a moment for her mind to catch up and make sense of where she was. A fly was buzzing at the bottom of the teacup. The sun, which had been high in the sky when she arrived, must have set. With a suddenness characteristic of South Africa, the room was settling into almost instant darkness. The heat, inescapable during the day, had retreated, and Frances could feel the damp of evening settling on the ground and against her skin. Voices drifted in from the kitchen. She straightened up in her chair, listening. Then she heard footsteps along the hall, and the door creaked open.

Edwin walked in, holding a lamp. "I let you sleep."

"Thank you." Frances stood up with crisp formality, acutely conscious that she hadn't washed the filth from her hands and face.

He put the lamp down on the table. "Horrible weather. These dust storms come through from time to time." There was an awkward silence while he stood looking at her. He was dressed in cotton trousers and a loose shirt. His face was damp, and drops of water clung to his hair. He must have just washed. She registered his height — he was not much taller than her — and the lean strength of his body. This was his house that she stood in, not her father's, and it crossed her mind that she was like a package of goods delivered from England. He was remembering what he had ordered. "They don't last long. The scenery is actually rather dramatic — you'll see tomorrow." He squatted down beside the fireplace, piling kindling into the grate. "We were expecting you sooner. Your ship came in last week."

"There was a girl in Cape Town who wasn't very well. I nursed her for a few days." The lie came out awkwardly.

"Everyone knows everybody in this country," Edwin said, striking a match and holding it to the kindling. It was a statement, but it carried an air of warning. She wondered what he meant by it.

The fire caught, the wood crackled, and Edwin blew into it for a moment until the smoke pulled a clear line up to the chimney. "There's not much wood here. We have to get it shipped in." He stood up and came over to stand in front of her. There was a smear of charcoal on his cheek. The silence in the room was oppressive; she could feel the weight of the night outside pressing in. The prospect of intimacy loomed between them. He cradled her hand. His palms were dry, and his fingers, long and thin, pressed into hers. He kissed the skin on the back of her hand, almost reverently, and she shuddered.

"Frances," he said, looking at her steadily, "I am glad you are here."

She smiled and took back her hand, avoiding his eye. "Is there somewhere I can wash? I'm afraid the maid and I didn't understand each other very well."

"Of course," he said, turning away from her and calling to the maid in Dutch.

The woman showed her through to the bedroom and filled the washbasin. Frances stood for a few moments after she had gone, with her back to the door, hands pressed flat against it, relieved to be by herself. She struggled not to give in to tears, and with a determined shrug unpicked the pins from her hair. She was buying time. The washstand here was simple but clean, and a cloth had been laid out along with a jug of water.

It was only when she sat, awkwardly perched on the squat stool in front of the dressing table, that she realized the mirror was missing from its frame. She found herself staring at a blank piece of sacking and wood. It was unsettling not being able to see the familiarity of her own face. She hadn't brought another glass, and so in the growing dark she felt for the lines of skin and bone; her high forehead running into the deep hollows of her eyes, gritted with dust. She traced the sockets, down and round into the long straight of her nose, and the dry, plump fullness of her lips.

Then she unplaited her hair and ran her fingers through the length of it, working out the knots. The dust and sweat had matted it together, and it felt greasy and thick against her fingers, like sheep's wool. Finally, after washing, and half satisfied that she was a little cleaner than before, she braced herself to go out and face Edwin. If only it were William waiting for her next door. She pressed her hand onto the white wall. It was cold and faintly damp, and the chalked paint left an imprint of white against her palm.

Edwin was attentive over dinner. The maid served them plates of cold mealies with sliced boiled eggs at the small table in the sitting room, and Frances, who hadn't had a hot meal since she left Cape Town, had to swallow her disappointment.

"Albert Reitz did offer me rooms in the main farm buildings, but I thought you would rather have a house of your own. You could have a garden if you put your mind to it."

"A garden?" she asked in disbelief. "I'm surprised anything can survive here."

"There's a dam behind the cottage. It wouldn't be difficult to irrigate. You know the Karoo isn't nearly as lifeless as it looks. The wildlife has adapted to the conditions in extraordinary ways. Even the lizards have films over their eyes, like windows, so they can see in a dust storm."

She didn't know what to say to this piece of information, so she went back to eating. After a few minutes, she asked, "So is that what you've been doing next door? Dissecting lizards?"

"In my study? Yes. I've been collecting specimens. Insects mostly."

"What for?"

"What for? I don't know. Because I'm interested, I suppose."

It seemed rather a drab, ineffectual answer, and they fell into silence again. He refilled her water glass. "Of course there's still a lot to do. The outside walls have been filled and painted, and we re-thatched parts of the roof, but it's still a little run down. I expect you'll want to make curtains. I have ordered catalogs from Port Elizabeth for you to look through. We won't be able to buy anything from them, but they might be useful for ideas." He was trying to put her at her ease, talking about the things he thought she cared about, but he was going too fast. She couldn't imagine spending one night in this house, let alone staying long enough to make curtains. When he asked what fabric she had brought, she had to shake her head. "It seemed ludicrous lugging yards of fabric all the way out here. Can't we order some in?"

"Of course." There was an awkward pause. "It's just that anything imported carries a premium." He glanced at her. "You did bring a sewing machine?"

"There wasn't room in my luggage. I thought we'd find a seamstress in Kimberley."

She felt sorry for him. He wanted to be kind, but it was clear she was disappointing him. Still, it was hardly her fault. What had he expected, bringing her here?

Eventually, when he didn't speak and the only sound in the room was the hissing of the candle and the scraping of cutlery against their plates, she asked, "And what is this place? Rietfontein?" The name was awkward to pronounce.

"It's a farm, but I am working two miles away, running a quarantine station to stop smallpox getting to Kimberley. You heard about the outbreak in Cape Town?"

She nodded.

"And you've been vaccinated?"

"They insisted when we arrived."

"Good. They're calling it the black pox. It's already killed over a thousand men."

"But why is Kimberley so important?"

"Diamonds. South Africa relies on the stability of the industry. And Joseph Baier is determined not to let the disease disturb the smooth running of his business."

Frances froze at the mention of the name. "And is he so very powerful, Mr. Baier?"

Edwin laughed dryly. "There isn't anyone in South Africa with more influence."

"How long will he be keeping us in Jacobsdal?" There was an unpleasant irony in them being here on William's cousin's bidding.

"Until Cape Town has received a clean bill of health from the medical authorities." Then, after a moment, he asked, "Frances, you're disappointed?" She saw the effort it cost him to ask such a direct question.

"I thought you said you had a chance of success in Kimberley?"

"I did, but Baier is paying me to be here. It's important work." Another silence. "Actually, it's rather an extraordinary place," he said, looking at her. "It takes some getting used to, but you might learn to like it."

She gave a laugh of disbelief. "You're suggesting I enjoy the experience?"

He looked at her with a fixed expression. She met his eye, but a moment later looked away, disconcerted by the directness of his gaze. She imagined the long days stretching in front of her with nothing at all to fill them. It hadn't occurred to her that he might be planning on existing like this indefinitely. A slight panic took hold of her. "Is there any prospect of ever living any better than this?"

"Eventually we should be able to move to Cape Town and start a practice there. With your connections, we can —"

"My connections, Edwin," she interrupted him, "may not help you as much as you would like."

He was silent. Then putting together his knife and fork, he said, "As for the marriage, you must tell me what you would like to do. There is a small Dutch Reformed Church in Jacobsdal. Perhaps you saw it when you passed through? The service

245

could be tomorrow. That is, if you are happy with the idea?"

"That sounds fine," she said, frustrated by how little of himself he revealed.

Sarah, the maid, came in to clear away the plates, and he waited for her to leave before saying, "Mevrouw Reitz has a room for you at her farmhouse tonight, if you would rather stay there? Or you can sleep in the bedroom here, and I will sleep in the study. It's up to you."

"I think I would rather sleep here," she said, embarrassed by the implication that she might not be able to trust him.

After dinner, Edwin said, "I have bought you something. A wedding present, but I might as well show it to you now." He walked over to the wall behind the table. A sheet was draped over a large piece of furniture, and he pulled it off, revealing a piano. He watched her as she touched the wood. It was — miraculously — in good condition. She pressed a key and it sounded well.

"I had it shipped from Port Elizabeth."

She glanced at him and saw an expression of satisfied pleasure on his face. He was enjoying this gift, and she remembered, suddenly, how he had watched her play as a child, and how she had subtly despised him for it. She had the disturbing feeling that in giving her the piano he was fulfilling some boyhood fantasy — that it completed his longed-for picture of her as his wife.

"It must have been very expensive."

"A small price to pay for our wedding, don't you think?"

"In the circumstances, it seems, well" — she paused, trying to find the right word — "extravagant."

"I'd like you to play," he said with quiet determination. So she pulled out the stool and sat down, and began on a Chopin piano sonata, remembering too late that it was the piece she had played for William. Her body recalled his fingers circling her neck, and she stopped abruptly, putting her hands over her face.

"I know it won't be easy for you, Frances," he said, placing a hand tentatively on her shoulder. "I don't expect it to be."

"It's all right," she said, standing up, and suddenly feeling sorry for him. He had put so much trouble into buying her this present, but it looked mournful in the midst of this squalid room. It made a mockery of his ambition.

Later, as he said good night to her, she remembered. "Edwin? I forgot to say. There was a rodent. In the kitchen."

He looked at her questioningly.

"Like a ferret. It was there when I came in."

His mouth twitched into a smile.

She said, "I shut it in your study."

"Yes, Sarah told me." His eyes flashed with humor, and she realized she had never seen him amused before. "It's not just any old rodent," he said. "She is a meerkat."

"A meerkat?"

"We call her Nanny. She lives here."

"In the house? Isn't that rather unsanitary?"

"She eats insects, which can be useful."

Frances bent down to unlace her boots, and lined them up self-consciously by the door. She pulled the blue silk dress from her trunk and shook out the dust which had caught in its seams. There would be no need for this now, except as a reminder of William, and she hung it in the wardrobe. She considered unpacking the rest of her things, but on second thought decided not to. It was too definite a move. She wasn't married yet. Instead she hung up the white muslin dress she would wear for the wedding. Then she plunged her hand to the bottom of the trunk and felt the sharp wooden edges of her easel. Strapped to the top of it was her sketching portfolio. She took it out and opened it. There was a half quire of sketching paper, another half of watercolor paper, and two dozen pencils. She ran her fingers over them, enjoying the way they turned in their case. Then there was her color box, with fourteen cakes of color. Their names still evoked the old romance which had captured her as a child: Chinese white, Indian yellow, carmine, Prussian blue, rose madder, raw sienna, cadmium yellow. Sitting snugly next to the color box was a water bottle and two single-bladed penknives for whittling. This was what she had brought instead of a sewing machine, and as she closed up the portfolio and slipped it back into her trunk, she felt no regret.

When she had undressed she lay down on the bed. With a leap of pity she saw what a huge commitment it was for him to bring her here. It was a strangely sentimental act for someone so rational. She was completely unsuited to being a colonial wife. She couldn't cook or clean, sew or garden. She wouldn't be any help to him at all. As a child, her father had promised her a gold-finch, and she had picked out the prettiest cage, with a silver water bath, and hung a mirror inside so the bird would think it had company. In the same way, with his customary carefulness, Edwin had tried to predict her needs. He had furnished the house in expectation of her arrival, buying this brass bed, so incongruously polished, and shipping in a piano all the way from Port Elizabeth. There was a book on the table about the plants of South Africa, and she was sure it had been placed there for her reading. But his attentiveness didn't please her; it only made her more conscious of the extent of his control over her.

She heard Edwin settling next door, blowing out his light. Her own candle, made of cheap tallow, guttered and spat, stinking of the fat of the animal that had made it. She blew it out and felt the darkness press in on her. She had never known blackness like this. Certainly not in London, where the streetlight beamed at the end of the street. She blinked, trying to make out shapes, but saw nothing; not even her hand made a gleam in the dark. She reached for the matches to relight her candle but stopped when she realized Edwin would see the light. He would guess something was wrong.

She imagined the darkness outside and the expanse of veldt that stretched out from the farm for so many miles. She felt she was losing substance, as though she were no bigger and had no greater weight than a speck of dust. She was already so far from everything she had been just a few months ago, when her father had been alive and she had been under his protection. What would he think if he could see her now? No doubt he would be ashamed. She was living evidence of his failed ambitions.

Was it too late to call off the wedding? She could leave in the morning and go back to Cape Town. But with what money? And to what purpose? Would Mrs. Nettleton help her find a position? She had no qualifications, and there could be no guarantee of security. Her finger looped through the gold chain at her neck, and she was filled with a sudden, gut-tearing hunger for William that ripped her open from the inside and left her with a simple, brutal desire to touch him. She clenched her teeth and buried her face in the pillow so Edwin wouldn't hear her sobs.

TWENTY

It was done and there was no going back. Frances hung the white muslin dress in the wardrobe, unpinning the creamy ostrich feather — a gift from Edwin. He was in his study working, giving her time to undress, and periodically she would hear the tapping of a metal instrument against the side of a glass jar. She slipped a nightgown over her head then lay down on the bed, turning the gold band on her finger, unused to its weight. Sarah, it turned out, was maid, cook, and scullery girl rolled into one. There would be no Dutch maid, as she had thought there might be, who spoke English, and who would pin her hair in the mornings and help her dress. Edwin must have been disingenuous with her uncle. Surely he would have expected more for her than this.

The Reitzes had invited them to lunch after the ceremony, and Frances had been glad to go, not because she had any particular desire to make friends with their Boer landlords, but because it would give her a few hours when Edwin was occupied with something other than her. William had branded her — lips, shoulders, breasts — she could feel the trail of his fingers across every part of her body. She was waiting for Edwin to notice that she had changed.

They had driven a trap across the veldt straight from the church to the main farm, which sat close to a large dam. White birds fluttered like flags over the water. The farmhouse had been built in the Cape Dutch style, with a handsome gable and a broad *stoep*. A huge acacia spread its shade over one side of the house.

"The fever tree," Edwin said, following her gaze. "The farm is famous for it."

"Why should a tree make it famous?"

"You don't normally see them on the Karoo. It's too dry. Someone must have planted it years ago and made sure it had water."

She had to admit that it was magnificent. The smooth, dusky yellow limbs supported a series of wide, dense platforms of foliage which cast a dappled shade over the earth below. A herd of goats nibbled at the short grasses around its trunk under the sleeping gaze of a native boy. The lower branches of the tree grazed the wall of the house, and, looking up, Frances saw a tiny attic window, its dark panes almost hidden behind a network of thorns.

"It's a good place to build a nest," Edwin was saying, pointing to the tiny birds who darted through the greenery to the domed structures which rested like beehives between the branches. "The snakes can't get at them because of the thorns."

Mijnheer Reitz showed them around the cluster of outbuildings. He was a tall, serious man with a roughened face and purpling pouches under his eyes. He wore his long, thinning gray hair in a neat parting, slicked down to one side. His jacket and trousers were black, and he held on to a black hat in one strong, wizened hand. He stank of sheep and strong tobacco, and a dirty pipe stuck out of his breast pocket. Globules of saliva flew from his mouth into the dust with such frequency that she wondered how he kept producing them.

They were shown around a group of grubby, whitewashed outbuildings with thatched roofs. Frances tried to keep her shoes from slipping into the pools of muck and the flies from crawling into her mouth. The yard reeked of cattle and manure.

There was an incubator for young ostrich chicks, a feather bank, a dairy, a smithy, and stables. Cattle knocked against empty feed bins, and ostrich strutted noisily behind dusty, wired enclosures. Children ran in laughing circles around the cook, who heaved huge batches of dough into the bread ovens, and two mongrels chased chickens squawking into the air.

The Reitzes had a large family — six boys: four at home, two at the diamond fields. Hendrik and Hermanus were the eldest boys still on the farm. They were twins; blond, big-boned, and rudely healthy. Then there was Piet, a dark, solemn-looking child who peered down at them from the dairy loft. Edwin told her afterwards that there had been an accident on the farm when he was little, and he had lost three of his fingers. The youngest was still only a baby. It was hard to believe that so much exuberant life had been drawn from such a seemingly barren land. But there they were, thriving, scrubbed clean, with large smiles and strong bodies. Not the dour, squalid farmers with their brood of uneducated children which William had led her to expect.

Mevrouw Reitz was a stout Dutchwoman with braided hair, thick forearms, and a good grasp of English. She took Frances off to her garden and showed her how it had been irrigated with water from the dam. She had planted the peach trees herself, and there were figs, apricots, sugar peas, lettuces, radishes, cabbages, and potatoes. White jasmine flowers gave off a heady, sweet perfume, and bees droned heavily from flower to flower. Mevrouw Reitz bent down occasionally as they walked to wrench weeds from the beds, and Frances saw that her nails were caked with the sandy red soil.

"Well," she said, shaking grit off a bunch of carrots and standing up to look Frances over, "you're as pretty as he said you would be."

"Thank you," Frances said, cautious of this woman with her tanned skin, muddy hands, and piercing blue eyes.

"It's not a question of thanking." Mevrouw Reitz pushed the hair out of her eyes with the sweep of a forearm. "It's obvious that he likes you. But I'll be honest with you, Mrs. Matthews" — Frances was discomforted by the strangeness of her married name — "there are some of us here who said your husband was crazed bringing a woman all the way from England, who doesn't know this country."

Frances could feel herself wilting in the heat. How much longer would she have to stand out here under inspection? After a moment the woman asked, "How are your lungs?"

"My lungs?" Frances asked faintly.

"When I was a child, we had an English governess. She came to the Cape for the climate. I thought perhaps . . ."

"My lungs are perfectly healthy, thank you," Frances replied, angered by the implication that she had married Edwin to escape England, though it wasn't so far from the truth.

Mevrouw Reitz glanced at Frances's delicate shoes, already caked in muck, at her long muslin sleeves covering her pale skin, at her pretty straw hat. "Of course, you shan't want to be dressing like that every day. Don't get me wrong. We all like a bit of finery from time to time" — Frances had the unpleasant sensation that the woman was fingering the material, calculating its worth — "but you'll have to work hard, the two of you, and there'll be no time for indulgences. You haven't much to get you started in life, and goodness knows your husband works hard enough already. You don't want to be a burden on him."

Frances bit her lip. They had only just met and already the woman was patronizing her. How did she know they had so little to get them started? And why did she seem to think her husband needed defending? "I hope, Mevrouw Reitz, that I won't be a burden on anyone."

"I'm sure you won't be." She touched the back of Frances's hand with her fingers. "I didn't mean for you to take it the wrong way. If you need help with things, you must come and ask. You'll get lonely in that cottage all by yourself every day. When that happens, you should come and see me. We'll find something for you to do."

Despite the apology, Frances bristled. "I can assure you I am quite used to being on my own."

"I'm sure you are. But I expect it's a different kind of loneliness to what you're used to."

They walked on in silence. After a few minutes, Mevrouw Reitz swept her hands proudly over her garden. "We missed the rains last year, but we're not doing badly. Most of this relies on underground water." She pointed to the wind pump turning a slow circle against an indigo sky. "Albert's father struck water with the first hole he bored. He enlarged the dam, and we've never been without."

"And the river?"

"It floods during the rains, but the rest of

the year it's as good as dry." She clasped her hands together in front of her, as if in prayer. "We need the rains to fall this summer," she said, "or the grazing will fail and the cattle will die."

After lunch, a colored nurse came in with the youngest boy, and Mevrouw Reitz made a big fuss over him.

"Family. That's the most important thing," she said, handing the boy to Frances. He was a boisterous baby with big fists and thrusting legs which pummeled against her thighs. When Frances glanced up she saw Edwin watching her with a hungry, alert expression on his face. Please God, she thought, don't let me fall pregnant by Edwin, not in this place, not right away.

Mevrouw Reitz brought Frances through to her storeroom before they left. It was a cool, dark room smelling of damp paint. Shelves were stacked high with bottled jams, chutneys, peaches in syrup, dried figs, brandy apricots, wines, and pickles. Mevrouw Reitz pressed two jars of crimson mulberry jam into her hands, and Frances had felt overwhelmingly depressed by this show of generosity. She had nothing to give in return. She didn't have the first idea about gardening or pickling, cleaning or sewing. God knows, she didn't even know how to go about washing her own clothes. It gave her the unpleasant sensation that she existed here as a purely decorative object. She suspected there was a certain danger in this. These people would despise her, unless she could conjure value out of the soil.

When they got back to their house, it had seemed too quiet. They ate dinner in near silence, punctuated by the clatter of knives and forks, the lamps throwing their shadows in dark, flickering shapes across the stark, white wall. Conversation was stilted by the expectation of the night ahead, but there was also a sort of hesitating fear hanging over them. The Reitzes, with their righteous wholesomeness, had cast an inimitable light over the loneliness of their first day as husband and wife, and Frances felt that anyone looking in through the window would have seen that their marriage was a sham and would wonder how these two people, who had so little to say to each other, were going to survive living in such isolation.

Halfway through supper Frances thought she saw, in the candlelight, something flung across the table. It was an airy, whirring thing which went back and forth in front of her so quickly she couldn't make it out. Then — *bang!* — Edwin brought a glass down on the wood. Her skin swarmed. A bright-orange spider was trapped inside. It reared up on its legs and put its fangs to the glass. She threw back the bench, sweeping up her skirts and checking the floor.

"Is it poisonous?" she asked, when she was sure there weren't any more.

"Not deadly. It's a red man. They come out at night to catch their prey. They use speed, not webs." Edwin tapped the glass with a forefinger to make the spider dance. It was only later that she found out they were known as hair clippers because they liked to bury themselves in your hair at night and snip away at it.

Frances turned down the lamp on the bureau and slipped into bed. Her hair, unpinned and unplaited, fanned out over the white pillowcases she had brought from England. They smelt of London rain and laundry starch. There was another scrape of metal from the next-door room, then the glug of liquid being poured from a bottle. Edwin must be dissecting the spider. She imagined him tweezering off its legs with the grip of his forceps. It was an odd fascination to want to take apart a creature until you had explored and categorized every part of it.

The window was open, and a jackal gave a rasping bark into the dark. The clock on the mantel ticked heavily, but eventually she heard the chair pull back next door and Edwin's light tread along the corridor. She heard the careful removing of clothes as he undressed, and the creak of floorboards as he crossed to the lamp and put out the flame. The covers were pulled back and the mattress shifted against her skin as he got into bed beside her. He blew out the candle. They lay for a few minutes in silence, and Frances wondered whether he might not touch her if she stayed very still, but then he turned onto his side to face her. She felt his hand running over her hair, which lay across the pillow. She opened her eyes, but it was too dark to make him out.

He felt for her face, touched her nose first, then her lips, his hands moving down her neck. She stared into the blackness. Then he found her breast, and she felt his body shudder as he cupped it. He let his thumb brush over her nipple. He moved closer, and his breath was wet against her cheek. The darkness seemed to release something in him.

"Frances." He breathed her name, and she braced herself against the weight of his body as he rolled on top of her. She smelt his nakedness, and felt his thigh shift against hers. "Frances Matthews." There was a note of triumph in his voice. "You don't know how I've wanted this." He kissed her cheek, her lips, her eyes, but she couldn't bring herself to kiss him back. He was still for a moment, as if bringing himself under control, smoothing the skin at her temples with one hand, running his fingers lightly over her face, feeling out its crevices in the dark like a blind man. His touch was gentle, but his fingers trembled. He was breathing heavily, and she sensed the effort it cost him to slow down.

When he pushed his hand up under her nightdress, she drew in a shuddering breath. His fingers were cold and hard between her legs, and she gasped as he began to work himself inside her, the pain familiar but no less shocking.

"Is it all right?" he asked, his face hovering over hers, motionless now, with the weight of him resting inside her.

She put a hand on his shoulder, pulling him towards her. There was no part of her that wanted him, but she needed it over with as quickly as possible.

Afterwards, he curled himself against her body like a boy and gave her small, grateful kisses on her shoulder, murmuring his thanks into her neck. This soft vulnerability was a new side of him. He was usually too controlled to show real affection. She was faintly disgusted. Why was he thanking her? It had been a bloodless, empty act of love, and he was fantasizing if he felt she had been in any way complicit. There had been little choice on her part. Yet at least he had been satisfied. She knew, now, what he expected of her, and if he didn't ask any more of her than this, then she could bear it.

She turned away from him, onto her side. What would it have felt like to have had William's hands trailing over her skin? She gave in to imagining him, and her thighs began to prickle and burn with slow pleasure.

TWENTY-ONE

They spent little time together, and this suited Frances. Edwin worked six days a week, leaving before dawn each morning and returning just before nightfall. Frances would curl deeper into the bedsheets when he had gone, drinking in the solitude. Sometimes she would imagine his walks across the veldt in the cool dark of early morning, under a sky dripping with stars. What did he think about? Whether smallpox could be stopped from reaching Kimberley? Whether his wife was content? He was full of contradictions: hardworking and meticulous in everything he did, yet oddly dispassionate; ambitious enough to want a woman of distinction, and yet content to live on the veldt like a savage; a brutal realist, and yet at the same time whimsical enough to have brought her here.

Edwin subscribed to the *Graaff-Reinet* newspaper. It was written in English, and

Frances scoured its pages, searching for news of William's marriage, but there was no mention of him. Instead she read about the arrest of Johannes Swanepoel, a Boer farmer living alone on thirty thousand acres. He had kidnapped the daughter of a neighboring farmer and kept her for five years in a thornbush stockade. When her father finally found her, she had lost the power of speech. The story was creepy, and it caught her imagination. Swanepoel had kept the girl in complete isolation, not wanting to share her with anyone. Edwin was no criminal, and yet there was something strange about the way he had coerced her into marriage and brought her to Rietfontein. Why weren't they living in Kimberley? Or Cape Town? Or Port Elizabeth? Why had he taken this position, miles from anywhere?

At seven o'clock each morning Frances had to get up and make way for Sarah, who tidied the bed, closed the shutters against the sun, and set a dampened sheet across the door to cool the room and keep out flies. She ate the breakfast laid out for her, then spent the rest of the day sitting in a chair on the *stoep,* summoning William out of the plains. Kimberley was only a day's ride away, and every dust devil in the distance could have been him. He emerged from the horizon, riding across the veldt, his hair a swath of black against the bleached sky and his eyes squinting into the white-hot sun. She could almost hear the gravel grinding beneath his boots as he dismounted. He would kneel down beside her, bury his face in her hair, and tell her that he was taking her to Kimberley. Every day she sat and waited for him to come, until her eyes stung from staring, but she couldn't tear herself away.

The landscape mesmerized her. She had arrived at the beginning of summer, when the sun breathed like an oven over the desiccated plains. It was a brutal, pitiless heat. The earth was too warm to touch, and when she picked up an ironstone boulder the skin on her palm blistered. Even the horses had their hooves greased and bound in hide to stop them from burning.

She stared for hours at the stunted grasses, like parched heather, turning from gold to silver in the breeze. Edwin had nailed a plank of wood beneath their roof, and swallows used it for their nests, swirling and dipping out of sight to the small, round dam which lay behind the house. There was a patch of green here, by the dam: a few square yards of scrubby grass watered by the overspill and a peach tree which stood in the center of it. A few weeks after she arrived it erupted in a profusion of hard, golden fruits. They turned pink as the summer went on, until they were soft enough to be picked, and she would bite through the fuzz of skin into the warm flesh, amazed that such sweetness could come from such desolate ground.

On a clear day you could see the ghost of mountains banking like clouds on the horizon. The rains didn't come, and as the summer went on the grim, parched veldt began to look like nothing more than a tangle of dusty prickles. She couldn't believe a landscape could be so endlessly barren. It was the very opposite of the lush, green fields around London with their neat hedges teeming with busy, noisy life. The only sound you were likely to hear on the veldt was the occasional belching of a lizard. Her father couldn't have imagined this place on his maps of Africa. He would have hated the dust and the heat. She felt a desperate loneliness, having to live without him, and she struggled against a yearning for everything to have been different. His death felt like abandonment. It had uprooted her, and she had been flung out here to this wilderness, where she didn't belong.

Edwin went walking every Sunday, starting out early. He always asked her if she wanted to join him, but she declined. It seemed lunatic to go traipsing around in the heat, and besides, everything on the Karoo looked the same. There were barely any trees, no shade, not a thing for miles around that wasn't covered in a fine red dust. You could set off in a certain direction and be certain to die before you met another soul. There were snakes and spiders and a constant invasion of flies. She couldn't work out why anyone in their right mind would choose to live here. It was a hostile place, barely clinging to life, with no pretensions of prettiness, utterly devoid of romance, and yet despite, or because of all these things, she found a perverse comfort in it. She saw herself reflected in its bleak, stark surfaces. She admired its resilience and found it reassuring.

Frances learnt to be wary of the snakes. There were cobras, puff adders, skaapstekers, whipsnakes, coral snakes, horned adders, and boomslangs. Reptiles, Edwin said, couldn't regulate their body temperature. They needed shade, or their blood would boil in their skins. The house, with its dark, shuttered rooms, was a perfect haven. Once, in the cool of early morning, she opened the kitchen door and a cobra glided out, straight over her feet into the dust.

Of all the insects, it was only the spiders she dreaded. The red men at night, and during the day the hunting spiders. They raced over the soil, looking for grasshoppers, crickets, and beetles. At first, Frances mistook them for balls of grass blowing over the veldt, the long hairs on their legs working as a disguise, but once Edwin had pointed them out she realized they were everywhere.

It was the spiders that endeared Nanny to Frances. She had tried to ban the meerkat from the house but soon gave in. She had never imagined they were living with so many bugs until she saw Nanny pulling them out from between the floorboards — termites, cicadas, and burrowing spiders with thick, bristling legs; even scorpions, which she managed to disarm with a quick paw before crunching delightedly at their still-squirming legs.

The problem was that ever since Frances had locked her in the study, the meerkat had treated her with deep suspicion. She couldn't be convinced that Frances was anything other than dangerous. If Frances walked into a room, Nanny left whatever she was eating, stood up on her hind legs, and edged her way along the sides of the room with her back to the wall in a curious sidestep, as if she didn't want to offend Frances but needed rather urgently to excuse herself.

One morning Frances positioned herself at the door and waited. Nanny approached and looked indecisively between Frances and the house, as if trying to decide whether she could make a dash for it. Ignoring Edwin's instructions not to feed her, Frances held out a biscuit, and Nanny, who had obviously tasted the delights of baking before and recognized it as something altogether more delicious than a termite, shuffled up to her. When she got close, she stood politely on two legs and reached out for the biscuit with one paw. She stayed in that position, swaying and eyeing Frances beadily while she crunched away in a shower of crumbs. From then on, they were friends. The creature had little black patches round her eyes which made her look very earnest, and long whiskers, and when you stroked her belly she made a wonderful throaty purr.

Nanny sat with Frances in the afternoons on the *stoep,* her paws crossed over her chest, looking out over the plain like a sentry. Occasionally she fell asleep so that the slight weight of her body rested against

Frances's leg. When she woke up it was with a jolt, her nose wrinkling almost as if in embarrassment. When Edwin was home, Nanny would delicately deposit specimens at his feet for pickling, and in return he scratched her gratefully behind her ears.

The Reitzes owned all the land around, which came to about a hundred thousand acres. The farmhouse and outbuildings were so sprawling and numerous that they could almost be called a village. According to Edwin, there were over sixty people, white and black, working on the farm, about ten thousand sheep, as many goats, and a fair number of ostrich and cattle. There was only one dam on the farm, and in the late afternoon herds could be seen from the house picking their way over the plains, kicking up in their wake a fiery, billowing cloud of dust. The scene was biblical in its simplicity, and she was reminded of the Israelites leaving Egypt for the Promised Land.

There were things she ought to have been doing to improve the house, but she couldn't bring herself to embark on anything. She should have been altering her dresses to make them more practical. There was fabric to be ordered from Port Elizabeth and curtains to be made. Edwin had asked Mevrouw Reitz if they could borrow her sewing machine, but Frances didn't want to admit to either of them that she had never used one, so she put it off.

In the evenings Edwin would come home, but he never asked Frances what she had been doing, never criticized her over the state of the house, and never probed to see whether she had looked through the catalogs he had ordered from Port Elizabeth. The piano sat untouched under its cloth. Edwin didn't ask her to play it, and she didn't volunteer. She was grateful to be left to her own devices. She wrote to Anne and Mariella, and received letters in response. They both seemed settled and happy. Anne had been given responsibility over the native ward at the new Kimberley Hospital — she wrote that the work was tiring but rewarding — and Mr. and Mrs. Fairley had made a good start in Stellenbosch. She was happy for her friends, but their letters made her feel her own discontent more keenly.

She missed England, and wrote to Lucille asking for news of the family. Her cousin wrote back, and her letter conjured the season perfectly. It had been one of the coldest winters on record: icy cheeks, frozen fingers stuffed into mittens, and an Oxford Street dusted with snow. She described the gaieties of house parties in the country, ice skating in Hyde Park, hunt balls, and shooting weekends. The letter had arrived with a copy of a London Society magazine. Lucille had circled an article that mentioned her attendance at a number of important events. The pages were full of advertisements for perfumes and dresses, and descriptions of operas, dances, and debutantes. It was strange to think that this was the life she might have had. It felt so far removed from Rietfontein that it was as if the magazine had been torn from the pages of a fairy tale.

Edwin only once asked her if she wasn't going to paint in the afternoons, since she had a talent for it. He suggested she pick some of the plants from the veldt. It gave her an idea, and she asked him to order a volume of Sowerby's *English Botany* from London. When it arrived she set up her easel on the *stoep* and began copying some of the delicate, hand-colored illustrations, compiling a whole series of flowers to remind her of home: roses, dandelions, crocuses, and daffodils.

Every evening they ate the same thing: mealy bread, a sort of steamed pudding made of ground corn, eggs, and spices, smeared with sheep's fat, which took the place of butter. Frances grew sick of the taste of it, and in an attempt to vary their suppers she secured a leg of mutton from Mevrouw Reitz. Her aunt's book on household management had a whole section dedicated to recipes. All morning Frances turned the pages, growing more and more agitated. It was like reading a different language. When did a gravy run? What was forcemeat? And what did the writer mean by "buttered paper"?

She inspected the kitchen and found almost none of the items listed as necessary for a family "in the middle class of life." Where was the bread grater? And what did a bottle jack look like? Or a dripping pan? The recipes were problematic in different ways. Either they called for ingredients she didn't have, or they asked you to do something tricky like cutting out the knuckle or sewing up the meat.

She chose a recipe for braised meat and tried her best, but the mutton was delivered to the table a shriveled, burnt crisp, with a greasy coating of flour across the top. Edwin didn't say anything, and Frances cried out in frustration, embarrassed by her failure.

"Why didn't you ask my help?" he asked.

"Because I should like to do something on my own for once!" Frances said, pushing her plate away and standing up so abruptly that her chair clattered onto the floor. He never mentioned the incident afterwards, but he borrowed a shotgun from Mijnheer Reitz and would walk home in the evenings with a brace of quail or partridge, or a *korhaan* — a type of bustard — and he taught Sarah how to cook them.

Once a week Edwin rolled on top of her in the dark and expended the passion which seemed to be so lacking from the rest of his life. It was a relief when she realized he wouldn't ask for it more often, and she let him fondle her breasts, showing neither enthusiasm nor unwilling. When it was over he kissed her gratefully, almost apologetically, as if he had defiled her in some way. He seemed satisfied by the perfunctory nature of these performances. He was a neat, careful, tidy man, and she thought her lack of ardor might well have suited him.

Unlike Frances, for whom the hours of each day stretched endlessly ahead, Edwin was always busy. He spent the evenings either in his study sterilizing specimens or in the sitting room reading articles by eminent geologists, while she gazed into the flame of a candle or flicked halfheartedly through one of his newspapers. It was just like him, she realized, to want to preserve and categorize the things around him. Life, with its unreliable physicality and mutable emotions, was too messy for his ordered mind. His study was where the inexorable transformation of life into history took place. Putting himself at the point of this axis empowered him.

Twenty-Two

Edwin picked his way across the veldt towards the house. When he saw her he gave a half wave then dropped down onto his knees in the scrub. He must have found an insect or a lizard. Frances stifled a yawn, padded into the house, and poured herself a glass of water. She glanced in the shard of mirror which hung over the counter in the kitchen and wiped a smudge of dirt off her forehead. She had only been here a couple of months, and already she looked so different: younger and less sophisticated. Her nose and cheeks were brown with freckles. She had given up wearing powder — her face grew too damp in the heat, and besides, there were no visitors to impress — and she had taken to wearing her hair in a single plait, rolled and pinned at the nape of her neck, as she had done as a child.

When she came outside again he was still on all fours, searching in the grass. His canvas knapsack lay open, and a selection of jars stood ready. She sipped at the warm water and felt the sweat from the summer's heat drying against her skin. After a few moments he pulled something from the ground and dropped it into a glass jar. She wandered over to see what he had caught. A beetle lay spinning on its back.

Edwin shook the jar until the beetle righted itself. She realized the hot climate suited him. His face had taken on color, his hair had grown out and turned blond, and his gray eyes, when he glanced up at her, were clear. Living on the veldt liberated something in him. He didn't seem as guarded as he had in London.

"Why do you do it?" she asked.

He squatted back on his heels and looked at her, pushing the hair off his forehead. "Where I grew up, there wasn't any nature. Perhaps I'm compensating."

"Wouldn't it be more rewarding to go hunting?"

"For sport?"

She thought about William. There was a certain nobility in hunting at least. "Why not?"

"I wouldn't enjoy it."

"Because it's dangerous?"

"Because I hate to see such waste."

"Isn't that wasteful?" she asked, gesturing at the beetle, which was paddling at the sides of the glass.

"There are millions of these beetles. One will make no difference to the species."

"But killing a kudu will?"

He buttoned his knapsack and stood up, holding the jar loosely in one hand. They began to walk towards the house. "I think so, yes. There are so few kudu left in South Africa it seems a crime to kill any for the sake of a trophy on a wall."

She laughed. "But that's ridiculous. There must be thousands of them."

"That's what they said about the quagga, before they declared it extinct. Look at America. Just fifty years ago the plains were heaving with buffalo. Now you'd be hard pushed to find one in a zoo."

One evening, Edwin encouraged her to join him on a walk; there was something he wanted to show her, he said. She was restless, tired of being cooped up in the house every day by herself, so she agreed. They set out just after sunrise on Sunday to climb the *kopje* which swelled up out of the plains at the back of the house. She wore the leather walking boots he had told her to bring and a white cotton dress which Sarah had hemmed shorter the previous evening so it wouldn't trail on the ground.

The *kopje* was a difficult cluster of rocks and shifting earth. After half an hour she could feel her feet beginning to blister in the new boots, and she had to pause to catch her breath. "It's the altitude," he said, stopping beside her. "We're at four thousand feet here." It was hard to remember, under the searing heat of the sun, that when darkness fell they would be lighting a fire for warmth. The nights were so cool that when Frances came to bed in the evenings, with the casement window thrown open, she fell almost instantly into a deep and dreamless sleep.

When they arrived at the top of the *kopje* she saw a small, hollow cave about as high as her waist. "This is what I wanted to show you," Edwin said, stooping to peer inside. "It belonged to Bushmen."

"It can't have done," she said, genuinely amazed. "It's too small."

"Their women were only four feet tall, often smaller." His voice echoed off the wall of the cave as he crawled inside. He lit a candle, and she scrambled in after him, over the old remains of a fire. He showed her the walls on which the Bushmen had painted subtle, faded pictures of men holding spears, dancing around fires, disguised as ostrich, lions, impala, and elephant. She thought how empty the veldt looked now, and how sad it was that the Bushmen's world had changed so utterly. Edwin read her thoughts. "Not so long ago the plains were full of these animals — eland, gemsbok, blesbok, ostrich, wildebeest, even elephants."

"What happened to them all?"

"The Boers and game hunters shot most of them into extinction."

"For trophies?"

"In some cases. But, for the Boers, it was really about resources. They needed the grazing for themselves."

"I can't believe anyone would want this land. It's little more than a desert."

"That's what they thought at first, but they couldn't have been more wrong. These Karoo bushes are more nutritious than they look." He picked the leaves of a few shrubs that grew at the entrance to the cave and handed them to her. They were short, tough, and sapless.

"When Reitz's grandfather first grazed flocks here, there was no dam. His sheep survived for months without ever drinking. They drew their moisture entirely from the succulents and grasses. Virgin grazing. Now, of course, the soil is too dry. They couldn't survive a week without water from the dam."

The cave was eerie. It was full of ghosts, and a desperate sadness. The Bushmen must have seen the arrival of the Boers and the slaughtering of animals and known that they were being hunted to extinction just as surely as the quagga.

They emerged blinking into the light. The plain stretched out below them to the far horizon, its undulating smoothness broken only by the occasional swelling of *kopjes*. All the moisture had been burnt up out of the earth. The grasses, scorched, had turned the color of parchment. The light was so clear that you could see for what seemed like thousands of miles.

"Millions of years ago, the whole plateau — three hundred miles from end to end — was a vast lake."

"Were there ever lions here?"

"Reitz's father shot the last one thirty years ago. There are still leopard in the mountains, and the odd hyena is lurking about."

"Hyena?" Frances wasn't sure. "Is that what I've heard at night?" She was thinking of the spine-tingling wails which sounded like lunatics calling to each other across the plains.

"I saw one the other morning, near the river." He bent down to pick up a fist-sized rock and turned it over in his hand. His shirtsleeves were rolled up, and the tendons tightened on his forearm as he moved the weight of it around his palm. "It ran off when it saw me."

"Aren't they dangerous?" She was amazed that he hadn't told her.

He gave her a slow smile. "You think it would have eaten me?"

"I don't know." She laughed. "Haven't they been known to attack people?"

"Perhaps. But I shouldn't think they would unless they were provoked."

He handed her the rock, and she saw the white, fossilized skeleton of a reptile frozen into its surface. It occurred to her that permanence was an illusion; everything on earth was in a state of change. Flesh to soil, skeleton to stone; transformation was a fact of life. Even her cousins, who seemed so secure in London, wouldn't escape the force of it, and she suddenly felt less desperate being out here, so far from home. She handed the rock back to Edwin, and he said, "Frances, you're very welcome to visit the quarantine station." She didn't answer immediately, trying to make out what he meant, and he said, "I thought you might be interested to see what I do."

"Of course," she said, thinking that she should have been the one to ask, but it hadn't occurred to her. He nodded, pleased.

That evening, Edwin showed her the two tiny arrowheads which he had found in the Bushmen's cave. They didn't need to be large, he said, because the Bushmen were expert toxicologists. They tipped their arrows with poison taken from the venom of a cobra and ground it down with poisonous bulbs.

TWENTY-THREE

The Reitzes had a driver called Jantjie, who took Frances in a mule cart through Jacobsdal to the junction between the Modder and Riet Rivers, where the main transport roads from the Cape converged. He was an ancient man with a face whose skin had crumpled into the deepest shade of brown. A fuzz of white hair was cropped close to his head, and his eyes were milky with cataracts, but his body was tough, wiry, and immensely strong. Once, when they were reinforcing the dam at the farm, she saw him carrying a steel as long as his body across his back to the water's edge.

The veldt around the quarantine station had been worn to dust under the tramp of so many feet, and there was now just a flat area of sand and gravel, with no vegetation, over which men and women of all classes were milling. A stench of rotten eggs permeated the whole place. Two large canvas tents had been set up beside an old wattle-and-daub barn, and men in uniform carrying rifles strolled between them. A queue of people snaked out of one of the tents, shielding their faces with hats and shawls against the sun. They had the same resigned look as Mijnheer Reitz's sheep, waiting their turn to be watered at the dam. Along the side of the road was a motley collection of wagons and carts and a carriage, the sun glinting off fresh paint. A team of oxen had been outspanned, and a few horses, unharnessed, cropped at the parched shrubs. Their coats had hardened into dry, chalky reefs of sweat, and they shook their heads periodically to keep off flies.

It was a huge operation stopping everyone from the Cape, and Frances thought Edwin must have enjoyed the responsibility of being the man in charge. She asked an officer in khaki where she might find him, and was pointed in the direction of one of the large tents. As she approached, she saw Edwin emerging, walking quickly. He was followed by an older, stout-looking gentleman who was shouting at him. A lady ran behind them, clutching at her bonnet and tripping over her dress. She looked like a rare butterfly blown across the veldt in her fine yellow silks.

"God damn you, Sir, you'll look at me when I talk to you." The man was hot and angry, and squeezed both his fists as if he was itching to use them. The people in the queue turned to watch.

Edwin stopped and faced him. They were only a couple of yards from Frances.

"You will forgive me, my Lord." His voice was perfectly contained. "I understand your delicacy in this matter, but I cannot sympathize with it. You and your wife must be vaccinated."

The man's voice broke into a scream, and a fine spray of spittle shot over Edwin. "And I tell you we will not." He shouted to his coachman. "Harness the horses. We're leaving."

"Sir, what is it you are afraid of?" Edwin asked. "Perhaps I can reassure you."

"I'll not be called a coward!"

Edwin looked fixedly at him, and the man seemed compelled to justify himself. He lowered his voice. "I have it from a good source that vaccines carry certain diseases."

"You mean syphilis?" Edwin gave a bark of laughter. The lady put a hand to her mouth, and the man's face turned purple. Frances had heard this rumor. "If you break out in the pox, Sir, I can assure you it won't be from my vaccine."

"But it is unnatural!" the man cried out. "It is utterly contrary to nature. It's an abhorrence on the human body."

"So is wearing clothes, and yet none of us choose to go around naked."

The man took his wife's hand. "Come, Elizabeth!" He marched her past Edwin, towards his carriage.

"Sir," Edwin called after him, "the choice is yours. Either you and your wife must be vaccinated, or you will remain with us for six weeks' quarantine."

The man turned and, walking quickly back to Edwin, swung at him with his fist. Edwin sidestepped and the man's knuckles glanced across his cheek. When he swung again Edwin caught his wrist and held it, and Frances was surprised at the ease with which he held the other man back.

"Cullen! Tom!" he shouted. Two men came running forward. "Please see that Lord Rothermere is shown to the vaccination tent."

"On whose authority, you trumped-up jackass?" the man called over his shoulder at Edwin, trying to throw off the arms of the men who were leading him away. "How dare you put your hands on me. I'll see to it you appear in court!"

Edwin looked after him, seemingly unmoved, only the toe of his boot digging into the sand. Then he turned and glanced at Frances with a tight, tired smile. He had known she was there all along. This was a dirty job, she realized, and she pitied him. He might be in charge of a dozen or so men armed with guns, but he was a social pariah, disliked by the people who rode through on their way to Kimberley. It was lonely, isolated work, and she suspected that most doctors would have turned it down. She wondered again why he had agreed to come here.

"But he's a powerful man, Lord Rother-mere," she said to him later, when he·was showing her around the site. A bruise was already purpling on his cheek. "He could bring a suit against you."

"It wouldn't get him anywhere. I've had fifteen actions against my operation for various charges, including battery and assault, but they all miraculously disappear."

"I don't understand."

"The word of Mr. Baier is as good as the word of God. And behind him is the Kimberley council."

"But all this" — she swept a hand across the tents, the men, the officers — "it must cost a fortune. Not even Cape Town is quarantined with such efficiency. Does

Baier really have that much money?" Edwin didn't answer, so she asked, "Why does he care so much?"

"Seven years ago, smallpox broke out in the copper mines in Angola. The natives had such a fear of the disease that, down to the last man, they abandoned the mines. Joseph Baier is concerned that the same thing might happen in Kimberley. To use his words, he thinks that if the natives get wind of smallpox there'll be a general stampede. And quite possibly he's right. It might very well bankrupt the mines. So I prevent the entry into Griqualand West of every person coming from the Cape Province without proof of efficient vaccination."

It seemed like an impossible project. "But there must be other crossing points. Don't people try to bypass you?"

"Police patrols have occupied all the drifts passable for wheeled traffic on the line of frontier between the border of the Orange Free State and the Kalahari Desert. They have instructions to divert all traffic to cross to this drift. I have a team of thirty officers helping me. Together, we stop, examine, vaccinate, and quarantine at least twenty men, women, and children a day. We have enough beds in the camp to sleep well over five hundred."

"Has anyone died here?"

He shook his head. "So far we have only seen three true cases of the disease."

They passed a small shed, and the smell of rotten eggs grew stronger. It was a noxious, choking stink. "Fumigation," Edwin said apologetically. "Bedding, clothing, anything and anyone quarantined here has to pass through it — three minutes in a closed shed with burning sulfur. It's a horrible process, but it does seem to reduce the rate of infection."

"And is the vaccine certain?" she asked.

"Yes and no. It can corrupt in the heat, but we do our best to maintain its efficiency. Vaccination is our only hope of eradicating the disease, and I find it astounding that there are still so many men like Lord Rothermere who don't believe in it. Smallpox is nothing short of horrific, but people have become complacent."

There was a squealing noise, and they turned to see a zebra tearing its head away from the control of two men. It was trying to rear, but the men had ropes around its neck and they pulled it down. The zebra bared its lips, showing thick, yellow teeth. Another man ran up behind it and threw water at its back legs, but it wouldn't budge. Frances noticed something behind it, a furze of brown and white, an ugly little thing with a long neck and gangly legs.

They were trying to separate the mother from her foal, and she was making a sawing, hewing noise. One of the men came up and threw a blanket around her head. She stood very still, confused, her body trembling. When the men began to lead her away, she followed. The foal skittered behind, its legs slipping and sliding in different directions so it looked like a baby giraffe, but a man caught hold of it by the tail and held it back. Then a shot rang out. The mare fell back on her hindquarters, the blanket slipped off her head, and the man let go. She supported herself for a moment on her front legs, sitting like a dog, her mouth open with the huge effort of staying upright. Then she collapsed into the dust.

"Why did they kill her?" Frances asked, breaking out into a sweat. The foal was nuzzling its mother.

"Her leg was rotten. They walked her to death, to get to Kimberley."

"What about the foal?"

"It might have been worth something if they'd taken better care of the mother. They're quite a novelty for the English in Kimberley."

"But what will they do with it?"

"They can't keep it."

"You'll leave it to die?"

The foal pawed at its mother's body, then stopped and lifted its nose into the air and nickered. It was a desperate noise.

"You can't kill it."

"Even if we found a brood mare, it would more than likely die. It's severely malnourished."

But Frances was already walking away from him, towards the foal. It was too busy nudging its mother with its nose to notice her. Her body was sprawled in the dirt, blood snaking out from underneath her, congealing in the sand. Her stomach had already begun to swell in the heat. When Frances stroked the foal it pushed a bloody muzzle into her hand, butting it for milk. It couldn't have been more than a month old.

"We'd have to sell it when it grows up," Edwin said, appearing beside her and pulling the foal's long ears.

"That's fine," she said. "But for the moment we can keep it?"

He nodded, and she gave him a quick smile.

The Reitzes lent them a brood mare for the zebra, and Frances liked to sit on the *stoep* and watch him suckle. Sarah had shaken her head disapprovingly when she saw him. *"Mangwa."* Zebra. "It won't be tamed," she said in Dutch to Edwin. And the name Mangwa had stuck. Days and weeks passed, and the zebra filled out, growing into his long legs until his withers stood as high as Frances's waist. The foal was skittish and difficult to control, but over time he got used to the head collar, and after a few weeks he proved Sarah wrong and was docile enough to be walked or tied up against a fence.

Frances lost track of dates and had no notion of time. Once every two or three weeks Jantjie would deliver the post. She received another letter from her cousin Lucille. It was a flippant, breezy thing, and it set her on edge. Father had bought them new horses; they were going to the Alps in the spring; did she remember meeting William Westbrook on the boat? She had become acquainted with a good friend of his, worth £40,000 a year. She had accepted his proposal. He had investments in South Africa; perhaps they would visit.

The thought of Lucille becoming friends with William and his new wife was too awful to contemplate. Frances dropped the letter in her lap and stared listlessly across the veldt. It was Edwin's habit sometimes to

295

come back late, walking home in the gloom of early evening with the light flattening itself against the sky and the heat retreating as he came towards the house, as if he were dragging the cold air with him. She saw his shadow approaching now and felt a wave of resentment. What kind of life was he giving her here? How could she even reply to her cousin's letter? What was there to say? That she was living on the veldt like a native? That she washed once a week and had stopped brushing her hair because it was so matted with dust? That some nights the red men swarmed so thickly under the candle-light you had to abandon your supper? That she hated the boredom, the flies, the snakes, and the heat? That always, at the back of her mind, was a longing for another man?

Edwin arrived just as the frogs had begun bellowing in the dam. Dark shapes — bats or swallows — darted and swooped in front of her. It was almost dark, but she could see him moving against the light, and there was the sound of his footsteps grinding over the earth. He went straight to the back of the house to wash and returned a moment later, water dripping from his face. There was a strength — a kind of physical ease — in the way he brushed back his hair and walked up the steps towards her.

"Haven't you noticed?" she demanded, irritated that he seemed content when she couldn't be.

He looked at her, and she realized this was another of her frustrations: his constant, querying silences, which made her spell everything out.

"The lamps aren't lit. We've run out of oil."

"And the candles?"

"The candles are beside the point. It is Sarah's responsibility to make sure we don't run out of oil."

He didn't say anything, so she kept on. "I don't see why she can't be more mindful."

"I'll pick some up tomorrow afternoon."

"Yes, but it's frustrating." Sarah appeared at the door, holding a candle, and Edwin took it from her and thanked her.

"Why won't you ever admonish her?"

Edwin's face glowed ocher red in the light of the candle. "What should I be admonishing her for?"

"She's too forgetful."

"There is a lot for her to remember." He put the candle down on the small table beside her.

"But that's what we employ her for." Frances, exasperated, was losing sight of her point. "Her English is nonexistent. She

297

refuses to starch my dresses, the rooms are permanently dusty, and yesterday she burnt Mevrouw Reitz's pie to charcoal."

"A mistake, surely?"

She had the sense that she was entering dangerous territory, but she couldn't stop herself. "You are too forgiving. You feel sorry for her because you know what it's like to be her."

"Meaning what, exactly?"

Frances shrugged, wanting to rile him into an argument but not knowing how far she could push him. "At least see her for what she is."

Edwin was looking at her curiously. There was no anger in his face. She wondered if he was capable of anger. "Which is what?"

"Idle, occasionally, and careless." Frances wasn't sure this was quite true. She didn't really have a clear idea of what Sarah did around the house, but she had formed the vague impression that she wasn't working as hard as she might. Frances had caught her sleeping in the afternoons, and once she had seen her helping herself from their sugar bowl with her fist.

"Idle?" His mouth twisted, and for the first time she felt his disdain. It hit her with a small shock. In an instant she saw what he was going to say, and wanted him to stop.

"Frances, how is it that you feel you can call other people idle?" He leant his shoulders back against the post. His body was blacker than the night outside, and though she couldn't see his expression, she knew he was looking straight at her.

"Do you have any knowledge of Sarah's schedule? I do, because I trained her. She is up before dawn to light the stove in the kitchen, rolls up her bedding, and makes my tea. She dresses while the kettle boils. Sweeps the house, sets out breakfast, makes porridge and coffee, and begins on your eggs." He was speaking slowly, every word weighted for emphasis, and each one an accusation. "She cleans the shoes we put out, sets out your breakfast, washes up, cleans the knives, empties the slops into the pail while you eat, and carries them outside to the tub. Then she makes the bed, tidies the rooms, scrubs the floors, cleans out the fireplace, and walks over to the farm to pick up bread, milk, and supplies, which she carries back under the hot sun. Once home, she begins on lunch, cleans and trims the lamps, then there is supper, washing up, tea, clothes to mend, and the washing once a week, the mangling and the boiling, and God knows what else. And you want me to admonish her for what, exactly?"

The question hung between them. After a moment, she said, "You knew what I was when you asked me to come here."

"I did." There was such meaning in his words and such bitterness that she wondered what he meant.

"It's all right for you," she said. "You have the quarantine station, your fossils, and your insects, but what about me? What should I do all day?"

They stood together on the porch, with no words between them. The night loomed black and heavy, and the silence was broken only by the *chink chink* of a frog, which sounded like a tiny hammer being struck against a stone. The post creaked, and his body shifted away from her to look out towards the veldt, where the air still held a glimmer of light. After a few minutes, he seemed to collect himself. He turned back to her and said simply, "Frances, your dresses haven't been starched because we can't afford it. The starch is imported. It is expensive. Then there is the time needed to boil it up, the water used, and the expense of the fuel. I'm afraid it just isn't practical. The truth is, we have very little, and we must conserve what we have. That means, primarily, oil, fuel, and sugar." He shook his head. "I'm sorry that you aren't happier."

And he walked into the house.

On a rare overcast afternoon Frances sat on the *stoep* copying a delicate illustration of a white geranium from Sowerby's *English Botany.* She groaned in frustration. The painting was all wrong. It looked lifeless, flat on the page. Painting from the pages of a book was utterly different to painting from life. It was like trying to tickle yourself — you prodded all the right places, but you could never make yourself laugh. And she didn't have the concentration today. Her attention kept drifting back to her argument with Edwin. They had barely spoken a word over the past week. Edwin came home in the evenings polite but withdrawn and went straight to his study, and Frances, half ashamed at having sounded so spoilt, wasn't sure how to put things right — if, indeed, she even wanted to put things right. She closed the pages on Sowerby, gathered up her brushes, and went inside.

In the hall she heard a rustling on the roof. The beams overhead creaked. The noise was louder in the sitting room, and then she remembered — Edwin had said something about Sarah cleaning the chimney. There was silence for a moment, then a great squawk of surprise and a crashing sound erupted from within the chimney-breast. A thick cloud of black soot rained down into the grate. Frances froze. Had Sarah fallen down the chimney? She was too big, surely. There was another screech, and a frantic scrabbling. Rubble clattered onto the floor. Something was trapped inside. The noise grew louder, moving down the chimney, releasing a mountain of rocks and muck onto the floor below and pushing out great clouds of coal dust which rolled upwards into the room.

"Sarah?" Frances called out, apprehensive on behalf of the maid.

And as if in response, an explosion of soot ripped loose from the chimney. A black ball barreled out from the middle of the cloud, whirling through the air and colliding with Frances's chest. It was huge and soft, and it moved of its own volition. She screamed, dropping her brushes and pushing it away, but it was alive and kept coming back at her, wrapping itself around her head and enveloping her in a plume of coal dust so thick it sealed up her eyes and she couldn't see her hands. Wings beat against her face. It was a bird, she realized, caught on her dress. They struggled against each other, the bird screeching in terror until finally it tore its claws loose and flapped away. She wiped at her eyes and looked around the room. A chicken sat in one of the chairs clucking to itself reproachfully, filleting its feathers to remove the soot.

Frances looked down at her dress. She was utterly filthy — stained black, every part of her, hands, nails, shoes, and skirts as black as if she had been dropped in a coal pit. She turned, dust drifting from her clothes as she moved. Edwin stood in the doorway behind her. She shifted uncomfortably under his gaze. "A chicken," she croaked, half in accusation. She wiped the grit off her lips with her sleeve, realizing too late that it was as dirty as her mouth. "What was a chicken doing in the chimney?" she asked querulously.

He tried to reply, pointing at the roof, but he creased up as he looked at her, and his shoulders began to convulse with laughter. He put his hands over his face for a moment as if to take control of himself then, drawing in a great, gulping breath of air, he tried to speak, but as soon as he took his hands away and saw her standing there his voice broke into a deep, resounding laugh. He must have seen the whole thing. Her chest tightened. She wanted to cry, to stamp her foot and tell him to stop, but any movement — any attempt at anger — would only make her look more absurd.

"Don't," she said, shaking her head, but her throat had silted up with dust and it came out as another croak, and the croak sounded ridiculous, and before she could stop it she was laughing with him. She laughed until her lungs hurt and she couldn't breathe, finally sinking to the floor in resignation, coal dust billowing from the folds of her dress.

"They use chickens to clean the chimneys," he said eventually, wiping his eyes. "You weren't meant to be in here."

There was a shout from the roof, a question in Dutch thrown down the chimney by Sarah. They looked at each other; the laughter caught between them like some living creature. After a moment Edwin turned away. "*Ja,*" he shouted up to Sarah. Then gathering up the chicken in his arms, he carried it squawking outside.

One evening Edwin brought home a mule pack. He suggested she try it on Mangwa, and Frances liked the idea. The zebra didn't, throwing his orange muzzle into the air, laying his ears back, and lashing out with his hind feet. Edwin threw a rope around his hind legs and hobbled him, and after three days of wearing the pack,

Mangwa grew resigned to the weight on his back. They took him out walking with them on Sundays, stowing her watercolors in the pack, along with lunch — bread wrapped in paper, a round of goat's cheese, a couple of peaches, and a flask of water.

Edwin carried his shotgun over one shoulder and his knapsack on the other, crammed full of equipment. There were pocket boxes lined with cork, iron clamps, strips of gauze, and collapsible nets in different sizes. He always took with him his pocket lens, a tray of wide-mouthed vials, and a bottle of spirits. Periodically he would stop as they walked and look into the crevices of a rock or push a stone over with his foot to see what lurked beneath.

It was good to throw off her lethargy. They would walk to the river or the *kopje,* and while Edwin searched for insects or fossils, Frances would paint fragments of the landscape: the spines of a prickly pear, an ironstone boulder with dense, glistening surfaces, or the leaves of a shrub whose curious shape appealed to her. And as she painted she found the edges of a contentment she hadn't felt since she was a young girl, before the arrival of Miss Cranbourne, when she had been left to interpret the world without interference from others.

She enjoyed using her muscles. Her legs firmed up, she thought about William less, and she found she had more energy. Soon it wasn't enough to go out only on Sundays, and she began to get up with Edwin at dawn, pushing herself out of bed in the dark. They ate a quick, hushed breakfast by candlelight. When he left for the quarantine station, she would step out into the veldt. This was her favorite time of day. She reveled in the cool of early morning, the sky still cold and desaturated but the earth glowing orange as if bathed in fire.

She discovered that if you looked closely at the veldt it transformed itself into a living, breathing thing. The black, lichen-covered rock gleamed green and flickered out a tongue. Two small bushes, indistinguishable from the surrounding scrub, quivered then blew across the plain — ostrich chicks. A clump of brown and yellow soil stirred, thrust out a leathered neck, and ambled, undeniably tortoise-like, towards the dam. And the silence resolved itself into the checkered sound of insects, the beating of wings, and the wind feeling its way through the grasses. Once, a scorpion scuttled out from between the crack in a rock. She watched, fascinated, as ten miniature, translucent copies of the mother climbed off her back in military formation. If Edwin had been there, he would have scooped them into a tin and forced them into a bottle of alcohol, where, dangling lifelessly, they could be examined without risk.

They walked back one Sunday the two miles from the river past a termite mound which had been freshly raided. Soil had been turned over and flung about in rich, orange clumps. Edwin picked up something that looked like a rock and held it up for her to see. It was a perfectly preserved bulbous frog, mummified in a block of earth.

At home, Edwin filled a glass jug full of water and dropped the frog into it. Frances watched, interested but doubtful. The earth crumbled away to the bottom and the frog sank. Then, after a moment, a ripple. The water trembled, a leg paddled, and an eye blinked open. It was a miracle, and she laughed, delighted.

"It might have been there for years," Edwin said. "Hibernating. Waiting for rain."

"You mustn't kill it," she said, putting a hand on his arm. The thought of Edwin pickling this creature, after its long wait in the sand, seemed impossibly sad.

Edwin looked at her curiously.

"Let me paint it," she said, "then we can

let it go."

The next day, Frances painted their bull-frog. It sat squat at the bottom of a glass bowl blinking at her through heavy-lidded eyes. Mangwa was dozing in the shade. The silence was punctuated by the whisking of his tail as it swept over his back.

It took time to capture him. She had never drawn an animal before, only plants, and he kept moving about, so she had to get a sense of the muscularity of his body imprinted in her mind before she could begin putting her impressions on paper. His body from nose to tip existed on one plane, except for the marbled eyes. His skin was gnarled and granular, like a barnacled rock. She fed him the flies which Sarah caught for her in a little jar. When they fell on the surface of the water he extended his legs in a fluid kick and slid them off the surface with a lick of his tongue. Finally, satisfied with her draw-ing, she poured him out into the dam and watched him paddle his way into the gloom.

Frances was unsure whether Edwin would like what she had done. She thought it would hardly please the eye of a naturalist.

"It's very successful," he said, holding it up to the light and smiling at her. She was pleased. Edwin wasn't someone to give praise lightly. "But see the feet," he said, pointing. "You need to be a little clearer. I can't see here how many toes he had. And did you catch sight of the tongue?" She nodded. "Good. Well you should draw that on the side, as a separate detail."

Edwin began to give her specimens to draw: beetles, lizards, and flying insects, and in return he let her set them free.

The ewes were sheared at the beginning of April, before the lambing started, and on the Sunday Edwin was drafted in to help. Frances walked up to the farm in the late afternoon. She could hear the sheep from a long way off; a cacophony of bleating rising up into the still, hot air. The grasses on the veldt were so dry they turned to dust when she stepped on them, and the ground had begun to crack with thirst. Summer was all but over, and the rains still hadn't come.

The men were working under the full glare of the sun. Two of them managed the sheep in the *kraals,* filtering them into the hands of the others, who waited with shears, the blades huge in their hands and dull like zinc. She leant on the fence of the nearest *kraal,* watching. The men were so crusted with dirt, their hair caked to their heads with dust and sweat, that it took her a moment to make out which one was Edwin.

He stood with a ewe thrust between his knees, one hand holding both her legs and the other sloughing the wool off her swollen belly. He was talking to her in a low voice, and she lay in a stupor, her eyes half shut, her breath coming in short pants. When he flipped her upright she darted forward, a white bundle of shorn, naked angles, to join the flock. The men at the gates fed another one through to him, and the process started again. He had a quiet confidence, she realized, not just in the way he handled the ewes but in every aspect of his life. He never seemed to doubt himself. It was as if he didn't require anything, or anyone, to be complete. Frances blinked the dust out of her eyes and shifted her weight off the fence. He was whole and content as he was, and this was attractive but also faintly threatening.

On the far side of the *kraal* was a mountain of freshly shorn wool, black with flies and stinking of grease. A group of women with scarves wrapped around their heads were bagging the wool into large canvas sacks. Mevrouw Reitz was amongst them. Frances made her way over. "Can I help?"

"There's not much in it for you but bread and cheese," the woman said, but when Frances didn't move away she motioned with her head to the pile of canvas sacks. Frances worked for two hours, her hands deep in the wool, her fingernails thick with grime. The fleece was coarse and matted, and it left red welts across the palms of her hands.

When the women were done, the sun was slipping below the horizon and the *kraal* floors were a pattern of long shadows. The men had finished shearing. They washed in the trough then stood stretching their backs, pushing the wet hair off their foreheads. Edwin caught Frances's eye across the *kraal* and smiled, and she thought, We are almost friends. Then it was the women's turn to wash, and one by one they dunked their faces in the trough, scrubbing at their hands, necks, and cheeks. The water was like balm against the heat of her face, and it ran needles of cold down her neck into her dress. Mevrouw Reitz passed around a basket of bread and cheese, and the saltiness was rich and thick on Frances's tongue.

They walked back, just the two of them, past the empty *kraals,* the barns, and the farmhouse, under a gray sky emptied of light. A thread of cold air pushed over the earth. Edwin's shirt was ripped and smeared with dirt and his trousers were caked in grease. There was a looseness about him.

She could sense his tiredness, like hers, in the luxuriating slowness with which he walked and in the stretching out of his shoulders.

It was almost dark now. The night air held just a faint residue of light. "I didn't know you could shear," she said quietly.

"Why would you have known?" There was a squeak as he pulled the cork out of a small bottle and passed it to her.

"Where did you get it?" They had barely had any alcohol in the months Frances had been there.

"Mijnheer Reitz gave it to me."

She took a sip. It was peach brandy, sweet and strong after the cheese, and it pulled on the corners of her mouth. He stopped and looked up. They stood under the canopy of the fever tree. It was darker here than the sky outside, and the birds flitted like bats between the branches. The bottle was sticky, and as she passed it back to him she saw that he had left a brown smear on the glass. She took hold of his hand and turned it over. His palm had been sliced open by a blade. The edges of the wound were clogged dry with dirt, but the center still glistened.

"Does it hurt?" Her voice sounded loud in the gathering gloom.

"It's not deep," he said slowly, and although she looked at his palm she could sense the weight of his hand in hers, his gaze on her, and the taut closeness of his body. "The shears get blunt as you work."

He took his hand from her and tipped the brandy bottle to his lips, and she imagined the dark, sweet liquid gliding over his tongue.

Later, when she sat in the bedroom in her nightdress rubbing oil into her face, she felt a lump just below her earlobe. It moved backwards and forwards under her finger. She pulled a shawl from the bed and went through to Edwin's study. He sat with a glass in a bandaged hand, the brandy bottle almost empty on his desk. His eyes were heavy with tiredness and drink.

"I can feel something. On my neck," she said, standing in the doorway.

He pulled a chair over for her to sit. She let her shawl slip down her back, swept her hair to one side, and tilted her head so he could see it.

"It's a tick," he said, drawing back and looking at her with a half smile. "From the sheep."

"Will you be able to get it out?" she asked.

"Can you keep still?"

She nodded, and he lit a match, letting it

burn for a few seconds before blowing it out. Then he pulled his chair close to her and pushed one hand into her hair to hold her still. With the other he used the hot end of the match to burn the tick. She flinched when she felt the heat of the match against her skin, but the grasp of his other hand held her steady. She could smell the warmth rising from his body, the dried sweat, and the brandy on his breath. His shirtsleeve, rolled up, brushed against her mouth. For a second she wanted him to kiss her, wanted to feel him lean forward and cover her mouth with his, but he was already withdrawing his hand from her hair. He put the match down and took up a pair of tweezers, and she felt a tugging against her skin. After a moment he tapped the tick into a bottle; a swollen brown sac with orange legs.

His gray eyes settled on hers. He had consumed almost the whole bottle of brandy, but there was nothing drunk about him. He was as contained and watchful as ever. The only change was a kind of tiredness, a letting go, which manifested itself in a languorous ease. The lamp guttered, hissed, and revived. She registered as a prickling on her scalp the place where his hand had held her and her want for him to reach out and touch it again, in the same place as he had before.

"It was good of you to help Mevrouw Reitz," he said, after a moment.

"I'm not sure she noticed. Sometimes I feel she can barely bring herself to look at me."

Edwin gave a low laugh. "She told me she thought you were coming along well."

"Did she?" Frances smiled, easily able to imagine the Boer woman casting judgment. There was a small silence. She thought she ought to stand up and leave, but there was something in Edwin's stillness which made her feel obliged to offer something more. As if he were waiting for her.

"Do you ever think about England?" she asked.

"Not as much as I should." He rubbed a hand over his face. "I think about my family. I worry that they don't have enough to live on, and that I send them too little. But I don't miss living there."

"Your brothers have work, don't they?"

"In factories, yes." He leant back in his chair. "Not much of a life."

"It's been a cold winter."

"Yes."

The frozen rivers, the pinched, frostbitten faces, the gray cities teeming with people — it seemed worlds away from the hot, quiet closeness of the room in which they sat and the miles of empty veldt outside.

She spoke into the silence, needing to unburden herself. "I dreamt last night that I was in London, in my uncle's house." The dream had disturbed her, though she wasn't sure why. "I had a plant with me, a cutting from a tree which I had taken from Rietfontein. I wanted to show it to my cousins, but when I took it out of my pocket I realized it was dead. It had shriveled up into a spiny knot of thorns."

"Were you upset?"

"I was devastated. I cried like a child."

His eyes were clear as he looked at her. "Because you wanted them to see it, or because it had died?"

"That's just it." He had identified the thing which was bothering her. "It wasn't just because I wanted them to see it. I was upset because it was no longer alive and somehow it was my fault."

He didn't say anything, and she felt a wave of sadness come over her. She bit her lip to hold back the tears, and after a moment stood up and moved out of the room.

TWENTY-FOUR

Frances sat on the *stoep* watching the two men walk out of the veldt towards her. They were still far off, their figures no more than dark silhouettes against the sinking sun. Mangwa was crunching the balustrade between his teeth, occasionally curling his upper lip in distaste. She ought to have stopped him an hour ago — already there was a pile of wood chippings and paint on the floor — but it seemed pointless. The little house was crumbling into the veldt, with or without his help.

The heat made Frances lethargic, but she stood up as the men drew closer and pushed the zebra's muzzle away. She couldn't help admiring him. His brown fur was beginning to give way to the rippling, glossy coat of an adult zebra, and his body had the compact strength of a wild animal. He butted her with his nose, nibbling at her clothes with his lips, which tickled her skin and made her laugh. It was her husband, she realized, taking in the knapsack slung over his shoulders, walking with a man she didn't recognize. Frances had been sure that she would know Joseph Baier in an instant — that the influence he had exerted over her life would single him out for her — but in fact she looked at him blankly until Edwin introduced them.

He was a small man who carried too much weight, and he arrived on their doorstep panting in the heat. His eyes, sunken into folds of pink flesh, darted about with surprising speed, disconcertingly at odds with the heavy softness of his body. He must have been in his fifties, but his bulk gave him a false youthfulness. An infant's chubbiness smoothed out the lines on his face.

"So, Mrs. Matthews," he said, eyeing up the cracked plaster and warped floorboards. His voice was a nasal whine. "This is quite a change, isn't it?" He paused on the word "change," giving it an unquestionable emphasis of disdain, while at the same time smiling quickly as if he were turning a knife in a pig, hoping it would squeal.

"From London? Yes. I can't get used to the heat."

"No more gilt taps and lace curtains." He moved as he talked, thrusting his hands in and out of his pockets, adjusting his necktie and looking around the room like a prospecting landlord. He had a restless, unsettled manner. "Aren't you Sir John Hamilton's niece?" he asked.

Frances knew a little about Joseph Baier from listening to William. He was a Jew from the East End who had been one of the first to the diamond fields and made a vast fortune. She imagined he enjoyed parading William around the fields: the educated, cultured boy whom he held in check with his vast reserves of money.

"He dropped in at the quarantine station," Edwin said quietly, when Baier was washing in the trough outside. "We'll have to put him up for the night."

"What do you do, Edwin, with such a delicate wife?" Baier asked over supper. "Keep her caged up here like a bird while you go around saving lives?" Frances supposed the power Baier wielded at the Cape allowed him to say anything he liked. It occurred to her that he might allude to her relationship with William. He looked like the kind of man who might do it just for his own amusement.

"She keeps herself very well without my help."

"I've always thought women aren't so different from your beloved kaffirs. Loath to work and with a strong sense of their own entitlement." Baier laughed, nudging the mealies around on his plate. "And, of course, they can't always be trusted."

Frances watched him, transfixed, her heart thudding.

"The funny thing is, Mrs. Matthews, you could show your husband any number of diamonds in Kimberley, and it would never turn his head. Turns out I was using the wrong currency."

There was a pause where no one said anything. Edwin's face was rigid. Something was going on between the two men which she didn't understand.

"It's not a question of currency. I wouldn't do something that made me ashamed."

"Oh, I don't know about that! I think you would do a fair amount to keep your wife in comfort." There was another brittle silence. "And I thought you were a man of pride!" Baier pushed his plate away carelessly, knocking it into the candlestick. Wax spilled over the table. He produced a toothpick from his pocket and began poking it between his teeth as he talked. She could see the end was wet and bloody. "The elusive man of principle turns out to be human after all. Who would have guessed you had a weakness for the finer things in life?" He smiled at Frances. "You know, Mrs. Matthews, we thought he was terribly serious. You could never get him to laugh. He was always on some campaign or other." He paused, thoughtful, his fingers still stabbing at his gums.

"Are you still intent on saving niggers?" he asked Edwin.

"As many as I can."

"He got quite upset in Kimberley," Baier said, looking at Frances. "Took a shine to a kaffir girl. A nice piece of nigger flesh, but she wasn't quite honest. We had to take her away. Got himself into quite a state about it. And there's some in Kimberley who won't stand for that sort of thing."

Frances couldn't work out why Edwin didn't say anything. He ought to be defending himself. The man was clearly a brute, but Edwin was a coward for not standing up to him.

"And there was me thinking you had settled down, after that little debacle with the articles —"

"What articles?" Frances interrupted.

"Ah — you haven't shown your wife? And I thought you were so proud of your journalism."

"I wrote a series of articles defending the

rights of native workers on the Kimberley fields," Edwin said coldly, his eyes fixed on the table.

What was he talking about? Frances had never heard about any of this.

"I think I did you a favor, Matthews, bringing you here. Don't you think?" Edwin didn't reply, his jaw set in an effort at self-control. "It's a bit of a backwater, but you can't stir up trouble."

Frances hadn't thought Edwin was either capable or inclined to stir up trouble. Sarah brought in some rice pudding, and Baier ran his spoon through it with dismay. Then he turned to Frances. "I gather you met my cousin Westbrook on the boat from Southampton?"

"Yes," Frances said, keeping her voice level, and wondering how much he knew. She could feel the heat rising to her cheeks.

"William is quite popular amongst the young girls in the colony." Baier was talking to Edwin, but his gaze was on Frances, and he winked very deliberately, licking at his bottom lip as he did so. Edwin hadn't noticed, but she felt her blood run cold.

Blustering, she changed the subject. "He talked about importing a new generation of steam engines into the mines. Apparently it will improve your business?"

■ ■ ■ ■

After dinner they sat in chairs around the fire, and Baier lit a cigar. He stretched out his legs. "What's this?" he asked, nudging his foot against the fossil which was sitting on the hearthstone.

"Part of the jaw of a reptile."

Frances had looked at it many times, impressed by the size of the glossy teeth whose polished surfaces curved out of the rock. She had even tried to paint it.

"And?" Baier asked. "Why do you keep it?"

"Because I admire its age," Edwin said.

"Come, surely that's not all. You naturalists have a story behind everything."

"The teeth indicate that it has mammalian features."

"Which means?" Baier asked lazily, with a hint of impatience.

"That mammals have descended from reptiles. I believe this species is the missing connection," Edwin said.

"And that's it?" Baier laughed, incredulous. "You do get excited about the driest things. I hope all this talk of fossils interests *you,* Mrs. Matthews. Otherwise you're in for a dreary marriage." He laughed into their silence and drew on his cigar, and after a few moments chuckled. "Next you'll be telling us we ought not to kill crocodiles."

Edwin was up and out early in the morning. Baier had stayed the night on a makeshift bed in front of the fire, and she hadn't had a chance to talk to Edwin yet about what had happened over dinner. The shutters were still closed when she came through to the sitting room, which was unusual. Edwin usually opened them before he went out. The room was dark and smelt of stale cigar smoke and last night's dinner.

"Good morning, Mrs. Matthews."

She jumped. Baier was sitting in one of the armchairs by the fireplace. She could see the balding crown of his head over the back of the chair. "I didn't realize you were still here."

"Did you enjoy spending time with my cousin on the *Cambrian*?" he asked, without turning in his chair to look at her. She didn't reply, and he said, "I was hoping you might be able to help me with something."

"Help you?" She didn't want to be in the same room as him, let alone obliged to help.

"I've got a long journey ahead of me and my feet have already begun to ache. Could I ask you to rub them a little? Just to get the circulation going?"

She froze. He knew about William, and he was going to use his knowledge against her. The room was completely quiet, except for Sarah sweeping the *stoep* outside. She could hear the rhythmic bristle of the broom against the wooden boards. The silence was worse than talking. It seemed to connect the two of them in something illicit.

"Are you still there?" he asked.

Like an automaton, she walked over to the chair and knelt down in front of him. He had shoes on, and she had to fiddle with the laces before she could slide them off his feet. She avoided looking up at him, but she could hear his breathing. She cradled one of his feet in her hands. The sock was warm and slightly damp against her fingers.

"You'll want to take that off," he said, chuckling. She froze, for a moment undecided. She wanted to stand up and walk away, but Edwin might not forgive her if he found out about William, least of all because he was Baier's cousin. Then where would she be? She peeled off the sock. His foot was a fat spread of flesh in her palm. His breathing came heavier as she pressed her fingers into the soft, pink tissue. He wriggled his toes a little as she worked, flinching at one point when her sleeve brushed against

325

the sole of his foot. It wasn't until her fingers had begun to ache that he finally dismissed her. She stood up and walked out to the kitchen, shut herself inside, and vomited into the sink.

"Are we here because of Baier?" she asked later, when Edwin had come home.

He sat down to unlace his boots, his left hand still awkward from where he had cut it. "He offered me a position, and I accepted."

"He made it sound as if he forced you."

"He applied some pressure."

"Why?"

"He wanted me out of Kimberley."

"Because of the native girl?"

"I tried to help her."

"How? What was Baier insinuating?"

"Good God, Frances. There was no relationship between us. This was six months ago. We'd just got engaged. I was back in Kimberley hoping to take over my old practice. I'd promised myself not to get involved in politics, but . . ." He trailed off, looking at the floor for a moment. "She was brought to me for help and I couldn't turn her away. I offered her my house as a refuge."

"I don't like him any more than you do,

but I should like to know what was behind the story."

Edwin walked into the sitting room and poured himself a glass of water, then sat down heavily in one of the chairs on either side of the fireplace. She sat down opposite him and waited.

"It's not an unusual story, really — only the details set it apart. There was a girl, a domestic. You see it all the time in Kimberley. She was Sotho, and when her tribe was destroyed in the war with the Boers she left her children and walked hundreds of miles with her brother to find work in Kimberley. It was winter, and the water froze in the pots they carried. They had a blanket which they shared at night, rolled into a ball beside the fire."

Edwin passed his hand over his face as if the story exhausted him. "Arthur Gibbons hired her. He was a digger from London — a friend of Baier's — with a reputation for bad luck. He lost his eye when a dynamite explosion threw a piece of shrapnel at him." Edwin laughed wryly. "And only last year he bought a claim at New Rush. When he went to inspect it, he saw the walls had caved in and the claim was full of debris. He rejected it on the grounds that it was unworkable and bought another alongside.

A week later the original claim was bought by a man who set eight natives to work on it with picks and shovels. It took the men a day to clear off the debris and start digging fresh soil, and within an hour they were shouting and waving. Gibbons looked over and saw a native holding up a diamond as big as a bottle stopper.

"Anyway, the girl — Gibbons called her Ruth — cleaned his hut, washed his clothes, and learnt to cook roast chicken, all for less money than a maid in England would get herself out of bed for. And she gave him a lot more besides.

"Last winter, Gibbons caught red-water fever. He lay in bed for months. He had never been popular. Others had died, and he might have done the same, but Ruth went out and bought him medicine, forced him to swallow fresh water, changed his sheets, and emptied his bedpan. When his boys started coming round to the house wanting to know why he wasn't buying, saying they would take their diamonds elsewhere, she kept his business alive by buying diamonds on credit. She knew a thing or two about stones. She bought them cheap and drove a good bargain. It was a business investment — she hoped Gibbons would reward her.

"The fever broke in October and she turned the diamonds over to him. The next morning he was gone. He had taken them all. The woman was left with debts running up to thousands of pounds. Now she is in Breakwater Prison."

"When will she be released?" Frances asked.

"She won't. It's a life term."

"But you tried to bring attention to the case?"

"I wrote a letter to the governor. Didn't do much good. I might have taken it further but . . ." He shrugged, not finishing.

"But what?" she demanded, sensing what he was going to say.

"You were arriving any minute. I needed to get us settled. When Baier asked me to leave Kimberley, I wasn't in a position to refuse."

Silence settled over them. Eventually, Frances asked, "And the articles?"

"They're nothing."

"Can I read them?"

"I only have a copy of one of them. It may not interest you."

"Were they published?"

"The first two were but not the rest." He gave a dry laugh. "*The Times* in London accepted them, but it turned out Mr. Baier was more powerful than I thought."

The Diamond Field
10th February 1880
The Native Labourer on the
Diamond Fields
By Dr. E. Matthews

Our highly esteemed and admired writer Anthony Trollope visited us recently, and wrote on looking down into the Kimberley mine: "When I have seen three or four thousand [natives] at work, I have felt that I was looking at three or four thousand growing Christians." This is, I suspect, an opinion held by our dear cousins at home when they eye like magpies the sparkling fruits of Kimberley's labour. The Africans work, and in return we feed them, clothe them and offer them education. I hope to cast a more revealing light on the life of the native, but I will start by begging Mr. Trollope's forgiveness. When I stand at the crumbling edge of the mine, gazing down to the dizzying depths below, with the Africans crawling like flies over its mountainous walls, I am reminded of nothing so much as the pits of hell.

I am a medical man, not a politician or a money-maker, which gives me the advantage of impartiality. All men suffer sickness equally, regardless of race, though in Kimberley you could lay your bets on an African dying first. A native has about a one in ten chance of survival.

No surprises there, you say. After all, working the mines is self-evidently a dangerous job. Imagine a hole in the sand dug by a child. At a certain depth the walls begin to avalanche and water pools in at the bottom. So it is with the mines. If you stand on the precipitous edge of the Big Hole and gaze downwards, three hundred feet below, and you have the patience to wait there under the burning sun for a good part of the day, then you are sure to be rewarded with the sight of half a dozen Africans being swept away by a roaring landslide. I happened to be standing next to an English girl when a supporting wall gave way in a crush of rubble, taking with it four Africans and a cart pulled by donkeys.

"Oh, but the donkeys! Who will dig them out?" the girl asked, clutching at her throat in anxiety, expressing like most of her kind exactly no apprehension on behalf of the natives.

When the pumps stop working, as they do from time to time, the labourers get sucked into the pools of mud and water at the bottom, and drown. The walls of the mines are poorly made, and natives slip and fall through the rotten rungs of ladders. I have spent time at the hospital (a rather grandiose word for a canvas tent with a few beds), and it is full of men — white and black — who have had their feet blown off by dynamite. Now the miners have started to dig underground, and the heat and noise in the caves below, the terror of explosives and the smoke from the machines is unimaginable. A fire broke out a month ago, and a hundred men were killed.

Clearly Trollope is mistaken. It is not the mines themselves which turn our natives into Christians. But perhaps, you ask, the civilizing bit happens when they are not at work?

In fact, what does an African do when he is not at work?

Immediately after he leaves his shift he is ordered to strip naked. A bar is held out, and he is asked to jump over it. Then his hair, nose, mouth, ears and rectum are inspected with exacting care. His European masters are looking for stones secreted in cuts, wounds, swellings and orifices. Occasionally, if suspected, he is chained naked in a room and given purgatives. A civilizing experience indeed.

It used to be that Africans owned claims in the mines, alongside their European partners. Legislation has ensured that this is no longer possible. To be black is now synonymous with being a labourer, and being a labourer is — hardly surprisingly — synonymous with being a diamond thief.

The trend, started by Joseph Baier, is now to house natives separately, in compounds, and to keep them there for the duration of their stay in Kimberley. If an African cannot produce a certificate of registration to say that he is contracted for work, then he is classed as a vagrant. A vagrant can be sentenced to six months' hard labour, which is wonderfully convenient for a claim holder.

It works to the European's advantage if the African learns to like alcohol. After all, a native with a taste for brandy will spend his hard-earned wages procuring it. He'll stick around longer. There is not a man in Kimberley who has not returned late from dinner or a game of cards and come across two or three Africans stretched out on the grass reeking of liquor, frozen to death as they slept.

But the compounds come with advantages, Joseph Baier has been heard to argue. I ask Mr. Baier: what advantages to the African? I have been to compounds and seen men lying in filthy blankets, dying from diseases as common as scurvy, or shivering with pneumonia because there is no firewood. It is more expensive to give medical care to a sick African than to rip up his contract and offer it to someone new. If you need proof, then look on the outskirts of town, where the bodies of dead Africans litter the roadsides, dumped by men too thrifty to pay burial dues. Is this the Christian end to Mr. Trollope's parable?

For those that do survive — and I don't deny there are many — they have the honour of bringing back guns to their tribe.

South Africa is historically an agrarian economy. A rocky, barren land which — until the discovery of diamonds — was desperately poor. Is it not a startling coincidence that men like Joseph Baier have come to civilize the African just when there is a profit to be made out of it? And now we hear him arguing to reintroduce nigger-flogging at a time when the rest of the civilized world is beginning to think more carefully about the welfare of their labouring classes.

There is a cancer at the heart of the Europeans' relationship with Africa, and its nature is self-interest. The monopolies of power holding sway over the mines are controlled by Europeans — non-residents who have no vested interest in either the future of South Africa or the civilizing of its people. Why would they care about the economic development of the country, when they are single-mindedly engaged in the extraction of its wealth? What use is an educated, civilized African to Joseph Baier, when he is in need of a permanent, subdued labour force?

Mr. Baier has spent the last ten years working on the creation of a labouring class which is entirely dependent on his munificence. He has often been praised for his sponsorship of a railway which will link the Cape Coast to Kimberley, but does anyone know his real motive for such a venture? Mr. Baier wants the railway so he can undercut the native tribes who supply the population of Kimberley with firewood and grain. Goods will be imported direct from Europe, and the natives will be bankrupt in a matter of months. Then there is the sponsorship of kaffir wars, the encouragement of hut taxes, and the legal battles which force natives to sell their land in order to afford a defence in court.

Few things worse have been flown under the banner of Christianity than the exploitation of African workers in Kimberley. Only a few days ago, Joseph Baier wrote in the pages of this paper: "One of the first lessons to be instilled into them [the natives] will be to respect the laws of *meum* and *tuum.** The diamond fields have, in my opinion, done much to accomplish this." It seems that for the first time we are in perfect agreement. The laws of *meum* and *tuum* have been perfectly illustrated to the Africans who work on the mines in Kimberley.

The ferocity of the article shocked her. Here was an anger and passion she hadn't seen before in her husband. She had misunderstood him. There was fire running beneath his long silences and slow calculations of the truth. She put the dates together in her head. The article had been published over a year ago, just before he had come to London. Baier must have put pressure on him to leave Kimberley, and when he had tried to go back to revive his practice, there had been the incident with the native girl, Ruth.

* Latin: "what is mine" and "what is yours."

When he came back that evening, she was sitting on the *stoep,* waiting for him.

"Edwin — tell me. If you feel this strongly, why did you let him intimidate you into leaving? Why didn't you stay?" He didn't say anything. "Couldn't you have found someone else to publish the articles?"

He walked past her into the house.

She followed him. "He'll think you're a coward for coming here."

"Just like you do?" He turned to face her, his eyes fixed on hers. And she couldn't deny it. There was something spineless about letting another man beat you into submission.

He saw it, and said, "Frances, do you have any idea what he could do to me? To us?" Edwin made a gesture of exasperation. "I could stand having eggs thrown at me in the street, not being received into any respectable house at the Cape, but what about you?"

"Couldn't we go to Cape Town?"

"You don't get it. There isn't a thing that happens at the Cape without his say-so. The business of Kimberley drives South Africa. There is barely any other economy, and there is almost no one in the colony who wants anything except what Baier wants. He makes them all rich. Do you really want to be an outcast? Do you want to have to go back to England? Have you thought about what kind of a life we would have there?"

He turned on his heel and walked into the study. The door closed behind him. She stared after him in frustration. He had implied that she was the one holding him back. That if she hadn't been on her way to South Africa he would have stayed in Kimberley and fought harder for the girl. But it was hardly her fault. He was the one who had insisted on marrying her.

She walked out onto the *stoep*. On the distant horizon a herd of sheep were nudging their way across the veldt, the air above them churned to a dusty haze. He was right. She didn't want to go back to England. They had no capital to get them started, no house to live in. More than likely he would have to set up a practice in Manchester, where there would be little prospect of ever doing well. It would be a mean, dreary life. At least there might be opportunities in South Africa. Society was less rigid, and there were fewer doctors. He would have a better chance of being successful.

She lay in bed that night, listening to Edwin's steady breathing beside her. She couldn't sleep. They were prisoners. Edwin had made that perfectly clear. She was amazed that she hadn't guessed it before. It made sense of everything — Edwin's decision to leave Kimberley, his apparent lack of ambition, his reaction to Baier at dinner. He wasn't living at Rietfontein out of choice, and bringing her to live on the veldt wasn't an experiment in survival. The fact that he had kept all this hidden from her was a shock. She thought she had understood him completely, but it turned out he wasn't at all who she had thought he was.

What pleasure it must have given Baier to sit at their meager table, gloating over their impoverishment. Not just their impoverishment. He had dissected their marriage like a surgeon probing for cancer, knowing the great shame that was eating away at them. She felt a surge of guilt. Edwin had given up his ideals to marry her, and she had betrayed him before they were even wed. Their marriage was a sham — even Baier knew it — and Edwin had looked like a cuckolded fool. Christ knew she had more respect for her husband than Baier, and she felt a seething hatred for this man who had made a mockery of him in front of her. And what was worse, he had suggested, with his wink across the table, that they were sharing in the joke together. She shivered in self-disgust. If she hadn't compromised herself, then Baier would have no power over her. Instead, he had them both caught in a trap. She was desperate to keep Edwin from finding out about William, and Edwin would keep trying to protect her, swallowing scraps out of Baier's hand like a dog accepting gristle from the table.

Good God, was Baier right? She made a sudden movement, throwing off the sheets to keep off the thoughts which threatened to pin her down. She couldn't, wouldn't, be able to stop thinking about William, and every time she did she was betraying Edwin further. Still, she thought later, when her mind was exhausted and light was whitening the chinks in the shutters, if they could just get out from under Baier's clutches, then perhaps everything would be different.

TWENTY-FIVE

On a cool autumn evening they went to the farmhouse for dinner. Mijnheer Reitz sat at the head of the table carving a leg of Karoo lamb, and a maid ran back and forth ferrying new dishes to the table: buttered carrots, beans and salads of lettuces and radishes, and boards piled high with cheese. At the table were Mijnheer and Mevrouw Reitz, their Dutch overseer, and a neighboring farmer and his wife. A fire burned in the grate, throwing shadows over the whitewashed walls. The room was full of the smell of melting lamb fat, and Frances ate hungrily. It was a long time since she had seen such a spread.

The conversation at the table was in Dutch. She would have been content simply to eat and let the voices roll over her, but Mevrouw Reitz sat opposite and insisted on explaining. Frances listened, warily respectful of this woman who wasn't afraid of plain speaking.

"They are talking about the sheep," Mevrouw Reitz said. "The natives have lost hundreds to the drought. They can't improve their stock, the quality or quantity of meat they produce, because their sheep are always struggling just to survive. The pressures of the veldt are too extreme. You can only get . . ." She paused, unsure of the language. "How do you say it, Dr. Matthews?"

Edwin looked up at Frances with impassive eyes. He had kept his distance from her since their argument. "Variation can only take place under domestication, or in other words, if the sheep are given access to a controlled environment — constant grazing, water, et cetera. Then a lamb might be born which, say, has more meat but is less suited to surviving a drought. In a domesticated environment, removed from evolutionary pressures, this variation will survive, and it can be bred back into the herd to improve the stock."

He had told her something similar once about her father's roses — that the brilliant colors and fantastic blooms would never have existed in the wild. They were the result of the same domestication. "Presumably these sheep wouldn't be much good to the native when a drought came along?"

"Exactly," Edwin said. "There is little point in helping natives to improve their stock if they continue to be at the mercy of their environment."

Mevrouw Reitz turned to Frances, and asked her in English, "Did you enjoy the peach tree this summer?"

"Yes, thank you. They were delicious."

"Albert's grandfather planted that tree fifty years ago, when he first came here. He built the house you're living in. We used to walk the children down there every summer to pick the fruit."

"But you should have brought them down this summer! There were far too many for us to eat. Hundreds, in fact. I'm afraid we couldn't eat them all, and we had to leave some of them to the wasps."

Mevrouw Reitz frowned. "But surely you didn't let them go to waste. You were making jam, bottling them?"

Frances looked at her, embarrassed.

"Why ever not?" Mevrouw Reitz asked.

"I suppose it didn't occur to me. I've never made jam before."

There was a reproachful silence. Mevrouw Reitz began talking to the neighboring farmer in a low voice. Frances looked at Edwin, but he was eating, perhaps with

studied indifference to the conversation —
she wasn't sure, and she wondered if he was
ashamed of her. She hadn't turned out to
be at all what he had hoped she would be.

The overseer said something then to
Edwin, and he glanced quickly at her before
replying. She thought he looked caught out.
When he spoke, the table broke out into
murmurs of excitement. Mevrouw Reitz
said to her, "But you must be delighted."

"Delighted?"

"That the Cape has been declared free of
smallpox."

Frances gaped at Edwin. Why hadn't he
told her? This could mean leaving Rietfontein. "What will happen to the quarantine
station?" Mevrouw Reitz asked.

"Joseph Baier is closing it down."

"Well, that's wonderful news!" Mevrouw
Reitz said, and Frances could see that
despite their differences, the woman understood her and saw that she couldn't be
happy living here. "Where will you go?"

"We haven't decided. But more than likely
to Cape Town." Cape Town. Relief coursed
through her. There was an end to Baier's
influence after all. Once they were in Cape
Town, Edwin could start a practice, and
they would have nothing more to do with
politics or smallpox.

■ ■ ■ ■

Jantjie drove them home in the cart. The night was perfectly quiet, except for the grinding of the wheels over the earth and his gentle mutterings to the mules. The plains were vast and still, with the great amphitheater of the heavens arched over them, glittering as though God had thrown down a cinder from a fire and it had splintered into a thousand glowing shards. A fat quarter-moon hung like a pendant above them. She could see the dark outline of Edwin's figure and the white gleam of his face.

After a moment, she asked, "Why didn't you tell me?"

"Baier's letter only came today."

"And just like that we can move to Cape Town? He hasn't asked you to do anything else for him?"

"Nothing."

"Which is good news, isn't it?"

"Yes, though you shouldn't expect it to be easy in Cape Town, not at first." He paused. "I have no income now, and it will take me a few months to get up and running."

"But you have some money put aside? From your work at the quarantine station?"

"I was cheap labor for Baier. He saw my work here as a kind of reparation."

It didn't matter. He would soon have a practice established, and in the meantime they would have to make do.

The cart left them at the cottage and rolled off into the night. Edwin stood at the *stoep*, waiting for her to pass up in front of him, but she stopped for a second, close enough so she could hear the low intake of his breath. On an impulse, without thinking, she reached out her hand and touched the sleeve of his coat. Her fingers grazed across the rough wool.

"Edwin, can we start again?"

He stood so motionless that she wondered if he had heard her. Then he said, "Perhaps. If we are honest with each other." It was a statement, but, like a question, it carried the weight of implication. Did he want a confession from her? For a brief moment she felt herself teetering on the brink of telling him about William, but her heart gave a sickening lurch. They were going to Cape Town anyway. The past was behind them now. There was no need to drag it up again. There was too much damage in honesty. Edwin might never forgive her, and he was able to read her too well. He would know in an instant that she was still in love with William. They stood staring at each other for a long moment. Then she shivered and said something about the cold, and they went inside.

Two weeks later, Frances was lying on her back by the riverbank, knees making a tent of her skirts, with her head resting on one bent arm. It was cooler now as winter drew on, and today was no hotter than a cloudless spring afternoon at home. A slight breeze stirred the dappled shade of the mimosa bushes, and through the branches she could see the dark shape of a bird of prey circling.

The last of the bees droned through the sweet herbage. Although the summer rains had failed and the riverbed was dry, it was still greener here than the rest of the veldt. Soon she would be away from Rietfontein, out of the dust and the sand, but she would miss the freedom of this place. A line of ants ran through the dry scrub. She rolled onto her side to look at them. Edwin had told her once that he had counted twenty different species here in one day. He would have enjoyed that. She smiled. They would be leaving in just under a month. Edwin had already found Sarah a position on a neighboring farm, and only this morning she had written to her uncle asking if he had any contacts in Cape Town who might be able to help him get started. It would be a new beginning for them. There would be shops in Cape Town, markets, and Englishwomen who might be friends. You could buy real chocolate imported straight from England. They might have a house with running water.

After a moment, she sat up, unlaced her boots, and walked down into the riverbed. The heavy sand was hot and dry, and it prickled between her toes. She nudged her feet beneath its surface, enjoying the warm weight on her skin. Tucked into the riverbank on the far side was a tightly woven bird's nest, and inside it two halves of an eggshell. She cradled the feathery weight of it in the palm of her hand, pleased. Edwin would know what it was. She would give it to him. This was the gesture which might allow her to erase some of the bad feeling between them.

She was deeply content when she walked up to the house, her legs dusty, her arms supple and firm, her hair crackling in the heat. A horse was tethered outside, and when she went in she saw a man sitting at the table with her husband. He stood up when she came in, raised his hat to her, and said, "I'd best be off."

He was English and she asked him to stay for supper, but Edwin intervened: "He has to get back."

"Edwin," she said when the man had gone, "I wanted to say to you —" She stopped. "Cape Town. I'm so pleased." She smiled at him. "Thank you. For everything you have done."

He looked at her with a tight, closed expression. "Frances, please. Sit down." He motioned to one of the chairs around the table.

"What is it?" she asked, sitting.

"We're not going to Cape Town. At least, not yet."

He paused, and she waited for him to explain.

"There is a rumor of smallpox, in Kimberley."

"But how? The Cape has been declared free of it."

"Isaac is a sanitary inspector. He has seen smallpox before. He says some natives brought it down the East Coast from Mozambique."

"What has all this got to do with us? You left Kimberley months ago. There are other doctors."

"Perhaps not with my experience."

"Oh, Edwin, don't flatter yourself. There must be a handful of doctors in Kimberley who could diagnose someone with the pox."

"That's the problem. They are denying the disease."

"Which means it probably isn't smallpox after all."

"Perhaps. I should like to go see for myself. Besides, I thought you would be pleased. Haven't you always wanted to see Kimberley?"

She pushed her thumbnail into the soft wood of the tabletop, making a crescent-shaped groove. William was in Kimberley. If they went, she was bound to see him again. The familiar, dull pain twisted into fire. He would be married by now. Would he even be pleased to see her?

"I was hoping we could get settled in Cape Town. I have already written to my uncle. You need to get your practice started. Why delay?"

"We will do all those things, but first I have to go to Kimberley."

She saw there was no point in arguing with him. "When do you want to leave?"

"As soon as possible. Sunday, if we can manage it." It was Thursday. That gave them three days. She felt excitement, tinged with dread, stir inside her, like the uncoiling of a snake. She wanted to see William, but she knew it would only make her more unhappy.

It wasn't until she was undressing later that she found the eggshell she had brought back for Edwin tucked into her skirt pocket. There was no use for it now, and she crushed it in the palm of her hand and let the shards fall between her fingers out of the window onto the earth below.

TWENTY-SIX

"New Rush." The driver's shout woke her, and she was back with the sway of the wagon and the shouts of the boy as he flicked the oxen with his *sjambok.* She had fallen asleep with her head cradled into Edwin's shoulder, and she pulled herself upright. The canvas at the back of the wagon was unbuttoned. Edwin lifted it up, letting in a shaft of bright sunlight, and dropped off the back. After a few minutes, Frances joined him. They had been traveling since dawn, and her legs were cramped and swollen. It felt good to walk. The oxen were tossing their heads to keep off the flies, and Mangwa, who was tethered to the back of the wagon, had turned the color of rust in the cloud of dust thrown up by the wheels. She tapped the boy on the shoulder, and he pointed to a dirty smudge in the distance.

When one of the oxen stopped in its

tracks, the wagon lurched and ground to a halt. The boy lashed at it with his *sjambok*, the tuft of antelope skin flickering through the air like a hornet.

"*Rooinek,*" he shouted, over and over, whipping its flanks in a frenzy. The ox began to move, and Edwin laughed.

"What?" Frances asked.

"*Rooinek.* It means 'Englishman.' He's calling it lazy."

They walked with scarves wrapped round their faces like a desert tribe, to keep off the dust and the sun. Carcasses of animals and old broken-up vehicles littered the sides of the road. It was hours before they saw anything of note, and even then it was only a tumbled heap of Boers, searching in the dust for diamonds. They were living out on the plain in the thatched mud huts built by natives. They didn't look up when the wagon trundled past, even though it drove so close that the driver's *sjambok* could have touched their backs. Frances trailed her foot through the soil like a plow. Strange to think that you only had to turn over a stone here, and you could make a fortune. They called the sand *diamondiferous.* Further on, they passed a mound of rubbish. Native children clambered through it, knee-deep, and came out clutching glass bottles and rolls of paper.

When evening came on, they climbed back into the wagon. Edwin held out his flask of water, and she took it gratefully. She had always thought that he enjoyed the isolation of the farm, but every few minutes he lifted the side of the canvas to see where they were, and she realized he was impatient to get there. It occurred to her that she wouldn't have him to herself anymore, which was an odd thing to think, because she had never put much value on his company.

The boy ran down the wagon lighting the lanterns, and she could hear, far off, a clamoring, like the distant hum of a hornets' nest. Edwin rolled up the canvas so they could look out. The noise grew louder by the second, then lights shone in front of them, and a few minutes later they were in the midst of a throng of men. The town had swallowed them. Diggers swarmed over the road, carrying picks and spades, and leading mules — more people than she had seen in the last six months put together. Naked black men and butch, muscled Europeans swung into view as they held up their lanterns to look in at them. They were moving against the tide. Diggers, finished with work for the day, were walking out of town to the huts and wide canvas tents which clustered the sides of the road. Men pressed against them on all sides, calling loudly to one another. The oxen, uneasy, bellowed and groaned, and the boy held their heads and led them on. Then the road widened, and they were in the midst of a carnival of light. Stores and canteens, lit up with paraffin lamps, plied a bustling trade. Wood fires blazed in furnaces outside, flickering their light over the crowd of customers who bellowed to one another across the street. The air was thick with the smell of smoke and roasting meat. The wagon turned and turned again, and they entered a clearing.

"Market Square," Edwin said, jumping off the back of the wagon and lifting their luggage down onto the side of the street. He looked excited to be here, invigorated by all these people, but Frances felt a little overwhelmed. It had been months since she had set foot in a town. He handed her Mangwa's lead rope and left her standing on the steps of a hotel, one of only two brick buildings in the square. "I'll be out in a minute. Watch the luggage."

The hotel was a surprise. It looked bright and friendly, and she could see between the curtains that the front room was well lit and glowing in a shabby, welcoming way. She stood next to a window which looked into the dining room. Two tables were laid, with clean white napkins and brass candlesticks. Edwin had no income now, and she had imagined a dingy, run-down establishment on the outskirts of town. Perhaps it wouldn't be so bad after all.

She stroked Mangwa's nose while she waited. The Reitzes had offered to try to sell him, but Edwin had suggested he come along. "We'll get a better price for him in Kimberley," he had said, and she had agreed, hoping that she might be able to change his mind.

There must have been over forty oxen in the square, with natives unloading huge bundles of goods, crates, and bales of straw from the backs of wagons. Surely it was only a matter of time before she saw William. It occurred to her that he might have stood where she was standing now. Perhaps he had passed through the square today, or was about to. He might have stayed in this hotel, in the very room that she would be sleeping in tonight. Two boys darted between the wagons, running swiftly from person to person, offering pieces of paper to anyone who would take one. She held out her hand, and a pink slip was pressed into it. The lamp outside the hotel cast enough light for her to read what it said: "The disease at Falstead's Farm is not smallpox. It is a bulbous disease of the skin allied to pemphigus. Signed —." The names of various doctors were signed underneath. She felt relief mixed with disappointment. This slip was official and signed by enough men to prove without doubt that it wasn't smallpox after all. They would only be staying a few days. Which was good. The sooner they got away from Baier, the better. And yet, even though nothing could come of it, her heart was set on seeing William. A few days might not be enough time.

Two natives stood across the street, watching her. They approached when they saw her looking. One was dressed in an old woolen jumper, with bare legs and feet. He said something to her in Dutch. She shook her head to show she didn't understand, and he put out a hand to touch Mangwa, curiously, letting it rest on his shoulder. His friend, a tall boy with just a knotted cloth passed between his legs and his buttocks bare, stared at her as if she were a specimen behind glass. She took a step backwards, but the naked boy reached forwards, put out his hand, and touched her hair, letting it bristle between his fingers. She jumped away from him and he laughed, a bellowing sound showing a mouth full of long, white teeth like the keys on a piano. The boy in the jumper said something to her again. It sounded like a question. She didn't answer, and he squatted down beside their luggage and began hauling her trunk onto his shoulders. She told him to stop, but her voice was shrill. When she made a grab for the handle, he swung it effortlessly out of her way, then looked at her, grinning.

"Put it down!" she shouted, and they roared with laughter as if she were playing a part in a pantomime. She felt absurdly like she might cry.

Edwin reappeared. "You all right?" he asked, then spoke to one of the natives in Dutch.

"They'll take our luggage," he said to her, nodding to the boy carrying her trunk, and he handed the zebra to the other to lead.

"Doesn't the hotel have a room?" she asked, disappointed, as they walked away from the square.

"The hotel? Probably, but we're not staying there."

"Why not?"

He gave her a wry look. "Do you really need to ask? Mrs. Edwinson, who runs it, has a side business letting out tents on the other side of town."

They turned down a street off Market

Square, walking past corrugated-iron buildings of every shape and size, painted white,
green, red, and yellow. The tradesmen
advertised their wares on large billboards
which she could just make out by the light
of Edwin's lamp. They were mostly diamond
merchants and one-room mining offices.
Further on was a chemist, then an auction
house and a pawnbroker. They passed a
barber and a shop with a window crammed
full of bottles of carbonated water. On their
left was a row of brick buildings covered in
scaffolding. Edwin said they were being
built by the new bank.

They turned off the main street at the
corner of an architect's office and stepped
into a maelstrom of canvas and makeshift
iron houses. There was no clear road here,
and everything looked as if it had been laid
down haphazardly, with no attempt at
order, like a pack of tumbling card houses.
It was too crowded, and the tents were
pitched right up against one another. Fires
were dotted in between, and the lamps
which burnt inside the tents threw grotesque
shapes across the canvas walls, like a lantern
show.

"Why aren't there any houses?" Frances
asked, half jogging to keep up.

"They're building on the other side of

town, but it's expensive. Bricks are harder to come by in Kimberley than diamonds, and all the timber has to be imported."

They walked past a large pavilion tent which had been turned into a boarding house. Next to it was a liquor bar with a sign outside: THE DIGGER'S REST. A handful of tables were scattered in the dust at the entrance, and inside a throng of men were playing cards and drinking. A tune was being hammered out on a piano. Pools of light spilled onto the road, and two men dressed in shirtsleeves and overalls with knives in their belts swigged from the same bottle. She could smell the sweet stink of stale alcohol.

A little further on, the crush of canvas thinned, and it was here the natives stopped. A tent stood in a small yard, bolstered up with thornbush. Her heart sank. It was a squalid, dirty-looking place. There was a line for washing strung across the middle from the stark branches of a dead tree to the top of the tent, and a few barrels for water. Their luggage was brought inside, the boys were paid, and more lamps were lit. There was a small, rickety fold-out table at the front of the tent with three chairs, and a curtain which ran across the middle separating off the bed. Boards had been put down on the floor, so at least they wouldn't be living in the dust. She could stand, just about, if she was in the central seam of the tent, but not where the canvas began to slope towards the floor.

It was cold now, with winter coming on, and she pulled a shawl from her bag. She wished she had brought some woolen underclothes from London. Edwin was holding a match to a knot of kindling. She handed him the slip of pink paper. He looked at her curiously, then put it up to the light to read it. After a moment, he asked, "Where did you get this?"

"Boys were handing them out in the street. It's good news, isn't it? For the town? For us?"

Edwin shook his head stubbornly. "I can't say. Not until I've had a look for myself."

"Because of course only you would know?" she cried in exasperation.

She pushed through the curtain. The mattress was made of straw, and it had an old blanket laid on top which didn't quite stretch to the edges. She found their sheets and made the bed.

Edwin toasted some mealies which Sarah had made, and they ate them with tinned sardines. It was so cold now that you could see your breath when you talked. Through the chill night air came the sounds of other people's lives. The clatter of pots, voices raised in argument, and, further off, the tinkling of the piano at the Digger's Rest.

They had finished eating when she noticed a man appear silently in their yard. He stood looking in at them, swaying slightly like a stick of bamboo in a gentle breeze. Edwin held up a hand in recognition. The man came closer, and Frances saw from his tall frame and disheveled, old school flannels that he was English. His jacket, all faded stripes and fraying buttons, hung awkwardly from his narrow shoulders. He had a long, tanned face with a grizzled beard, and his hair, grown over to cover a bald patch, had been blown off his forehead into wisps of white cotton.

The man looked round in a nervous, hesitating way, clutching his hat in one hand. Frances, concerned that gravity was going to get the better of him, motioned to the spare chair, and he buckled into it.

"Got a drink, Matthews?" he called to Edwin, who was already pouring out a glass.

"He can be a tight bastard," he said to Frances heavily. Then, after a moment, he shouted to Edwin, "Is this your wife?" He turned to her, asking in a low voice of mock disbelief, "Did you marry him?"

Edwin handed him the glass, and the man took a long draft and seemed to revive. "I had lunch with Baier today."

"And I thought you were just here for the scotch."

"Yes, the scotch too," the man said benignly.

"Did you see the men at Falstead's Farm?" Edwin asked.

"So Baier was right. He'd heard you were coming to town. Said you'd got yourself in a twist about an outbreak of smallpox. I disagreed with him." He took another long draft and waved his hand airily. "I assured him that a few months on the veldt would have sweated your youthful ambitions out of you."

"I was told there were four Mozambicans, traveling down the east coast. Is that right? They were suspected of smallpox, were quarantined at Falstead's Farm, and shortly after, died."

"Not smallpox. Pemphigus."

"Pemphigus? I've never even heard of it."

"Well, I encourage you to look it up."

He took another sip of whiskey and sucked his teeth. "You know, we doctors should stick together, Matthews. It doesn't do to have stray sheep."

"You're a doctor?" Frances asked.

"Of sorts," Edwin replied for him.

"I'd forgotten how you love to make yourself unpopular." The man tilted his whiskey into the light. "He's right, of course. I was banned from practicing in England. Still, it's not so bad. Kimberley is less queasy when it comes to picking its professionals."

"Did you examine the men?" Edwin asked. The man didn't deny it. "And you're sure it wasn't smallpox?"

"Having never seen a case of smallpox, I don't feel absolutely qualified to say."

"But you signed the slip regardless."

"We've all signed it," he said, draining his glass. "There isn't a doctor in Kimberley who refused."

"But you don't believe it?" Edwin persisted.

The man gave a rattling cough and stood up to phlegm outside. When he came back he said, "Have you been to Ebden Street? To the new stock market?" He picked up the bottle from the chest and poured out another fistful. "You should go down and take a look. Kimberley has changed since you've been away. More than thirty joint stock companies floated in the last two months, and a handful more every day. There isn't a man in Kimberley who isn't invested. They can't get in fast enough." He waved his glass of whiskey. "Lawyers, servants, dentists, barbers, magistrates, farriers, gun runners — they're all at it. Every man a diamond digger!" he said with a flourish, then pulled something out of his pocket and thrust it at Edwin. "Look here. One hundred shares at one pound apiece bought a week ago. If I sold them tomorrow they'd go for thirty percent more than I bought them for. I'm telling you," he said, gesturing with his glass at them both, "more money has changed hands in Kimberley in the last few months than over the last ten years put together."

"And your point is?"

"You should invest."

"Thank you, but it's not my game."

"You don't need money, you fool. The Standard Bank is lending! But that's not the point." He ran a hand over his face, as if trying to clear it from a fug of alcohol. "There's an awful lot riding on the stock market. Too much perhaps."

The floorboards creaked as the man walked across the tent to set down his glass. "Think about it, Matthews. We're all sucking from the same teat here."

Then he tipped his hat at Frances, and picked his way across the yard in the dark, singing a rolling tune to himself under his breath.

"Who was he?" Frances asked, when he had gone.

"Dr. Robinson — he's a friend of Baier's."

They sat in silence, until eventually Frances said, "It can't be smallpox, Edwin. One of the doctors would have spotted it."

"Not if Baier was putting pressure on them."

"Those signatures on the slip — they'd all be prepared to lie just because he tells them to?"

"You saw how determined he was to keep smallpox out of Kimberley. He can't afford an epidemic. Anyway," he said, standing up, "there's no point worrying about it now. I'll know tomorrow one way or another."

When Frances woke she thought it was still the middle of the night. Despite the blankets Edwin had insisted on bringing, she had been chilled to the bone, and she was shivering. Edwin had lit a lamp and was already half dressed, pulling on his shirt. A baby was wailing close by, and there was the sound of a man racking up phlegm. The tent was full of smoke, and it stung her eyes. She propped herself carefully up on one elbow, trying to stop the cold air getting

366

into the sheets.

"What time is it?"

"Five o'clock." Edwin smoothed his hair down, and pulled on a jacket. "There's food in the box and drinking water in the jug. And money" — he nodded his head in the direction of the ledge above the bed — "should you need it. Everything in Kimberley is double the price it should be. Particularly fuel. So spend carefully."

A few minutes later he was gone, taking the lamp with him. Her water had turned to icy slush in the glass. She lay looking up at the holes in the canvas, turning pale and cold in the dawn light.

She slept and woke again to a drone of flies which batted against the walls of the tent and crawled across her skin. There was a foul, cloying smell which she couldn't locate in any one place, but seemed to seep out of the pores of the canvas. She rubbed the sleep from her eyes, pulled her hair into a rough knot, and sorted through her trunk. Folded at the top was her black woolen bodice; too warm to wear during the day. She pulled out her gloves and turned them over. They had holes where the fingers ought to be, and she put them to one side. She would go without gloves for the time being. At the bottom of the trunk were her two cotton dresses. They had just about survived the last six months intact, and Sarah had dyed them both brown to hide the dust stains on the fabric. She chose the cleaner of the two, but when she put it on she saw with dismay that the cotton had begun to wear through at the sleeves. She would have to talk to Edwin about having some new dresses made.

All she needed to feel half human was a cup of tea. At the front of the tent was the wooden box full of their provisions, lined with lead. The sun caught the edge of it, and the metal corners were already warm to touch. Inside was a box of tea leaves, a jar of coffee, sugar, a few cans of meat, a bag stuffed with biltong, and some powdered milk.

Tea, she thought again. There was a blackened kettle, but the fire had gone out. After a few minutes spent trying to light it, she had used up all the matches. She gave a cry of frustration. Her body craved something hot to drink. Her eyes were tired and dry, and her head throbbed. It was already too warm, and a thin, hot breeze blew sand in under the side of the canvas. She looked at the tins of meat, but had no notion how to open them. There was a chunk of yesterday's bread in the box, which splintered like wood when she broke it open, but she moistened it with some water and dried milk, and ate.

The water carts obviously didn't come out this far to dampen the earth, and when she stepped into the yard, a fine red dust sifted through the hot air and furred her tongue, dried her throat, and caught in her eyelashes. Mangwa, tethered outside, had been watered and was munching at a pile of hay under the shade of a piece of tarpaulin. A pile of rubbish was heaped up outside, spilling over the fence into their yard. There were rags, rusted tins and sardine boxes, broken wine crates, paper shirt collars, and one old boot. Flies sucked in and out of brandy bottles, their labels faded and peeling in the sun. A dog of nondescript breeding with a coat tufted with mange lay on its side on a spread of paper. It was a bitch, with swollen bags of red skin and a narrow rib cage which heaved up and down with alarming speed. Somewhere in the distance a building was being constructed, and there was the sound of a hammer, and the knocking of iron poles.

Two tents were visible, not twenty feet away. In the yard of the first she could see a thin, naked black child scratching in the soil, and a native woman holding a baby.

369

The canvas roof bulged in under the heavy weight of dust. A donkey, with hobbled front legs and withers as sharp as a mountain range, ran his muzzle hopefully through the dirt. They had a smoking fire which the woman prodded now and then with an iron. When she did, the smoke would billow into Frances's tent, making her eyes water.

In the yard of the other tent, a man dressed in overalls was rinsing a cup and pouring out coffee with bachelor efficiency. She could smell the warm, bitter deliciousness of it, and she had to force herself to look away. She stepped up to Mangwa and ran her hands over his ears, one by one. He nodded his head irritably, not wanting to be bothered while he ate. The boy in the yard opposite stood up, moaned, and squatted over a bowl.

She rested one hand on the zebra's withers and swatted away a fly. Another came to rest on her arm, and another crawled across her nose. The boy squatted over the bowl again, whimpering. When his mother shouted at him, he picked it up in both hands and walked out of the yard towards a small iron shed not far from where Frances was standing. He yanked open the door. There was a whining noise, and a thick black cloud of flies blew out into the sun.

The smell hit her like a punch, and she doubled over, coughing. That was where the stench came from then.

She found a metal beaker in the tent and dipped it into the barrel of water outside. It was warm and tasted dank and slimy, but she dipped again and drank more, washing away the smell of the place and the filth. All the debris of twenty thousand people seemed to be festering here, out in the sun. She had thought Kimberley might have a kind of romantic charm. She had read the diary of a girl who had lived on the gold fields in California, but their camps had been clean and orderly, and the diggers shared a common purpose. In Kimberley, people seemed to be barely surviving.

Later, she forced herself to visit the outhouse, pulling open the metal door and stepping into a storm of flies. There were black flies, green flies, blue flies. They settled on her face and buzzed in her ears. A pit had been dug in the soil, but newspaper and feces had clogged it up, spilling over onto the floor. Flies crawled inside the paper, gorging themselves. She stumbled outside, retching from the smell. It was too foul to stay in there for more than a second, so she went back into the tent and squatted over the chamber pot, then emptied it in the outhouse, just like the native boy had done. But it would have to be washed out. She found soap, but it wouldn't dissolve in the cold water. She used a rag to clean the bowl then couldn't get the smell off her hands. She wondered how she would ever wash in this place, or whether she would ever feel clean.

The man from the tent opposite came by later, carrying his bedding rolled up under one arm. He stood at the entrance to her yard and nodded his hat at her. He was dressed in corduroy, with hands and face dark brown and worn like the leather on a saddle, and he had a heavy, untrimmed beard. He looked worn-out but tough, his face full of small nicks and scars.

"You've just arrived?"

She nodded.

"I've got something here for you," he said, in a burring Cornish accent.

"What is it?" she called out, glad to talk to someone who was English.

"You'll have to come and get it."

She walked over, and he handed her a tin of condensed milk.

"Why?" she asked, unsure whether to take it.

"Because you look like you could do with it." His face broke open into a warm smile.

"What's a Cornishman doing here?"

"The magnates spent a fortune bringing over fancy machinery, but once they got it here they realized they hadn't a clue how to work it. So they shipped a bunch of us over to help."

"You're an engineer?"

"Not exactly, but I'm used to working underground." He winked at her and walked off, whistling softly.

Later, she found a rock and beat away at the tin until she had burst a small hole in its lid, then raised it to her lips and sucked out the sweetness. The dense sugar tasted very faintly of the metal from the tin. Occasionally she stopped to lick at the edges, cleaning the stickiness from its surface with her tongue. It wasn't until she put it down that she noticed William Westbrook watching her. He stood on the other side of the fence, stroking Mangwa's head, dressed in buckskin breeches and leather riding boots. She thought she could hear them creak as he walked into the yard. Her heart pounded and her blood beat thickly in her head. She tugged at her dress and pushed her hair behind her ears. How long had he been standing there?

His white shirt was unbuttoned a little way, and she could see a triangle of his chest covered in tight, black hair. He walked towards her, and her spine tightened. She had imagined him so many times, but it was nothing like seeing him standing in front of her, real and unpredictable. She stood up, wiping her hands against the sides of her skirts and clasping them behind her back, acutely conscious of her fingernails caked with grime and her brown, fraying dress, which looked so much worse next to the starched brightness of his shirt.

"You don't look very pleased to see me," he said, smiling.

Her mouth was dry, and she licked her lips. Why hadn't she at least plaited her hair this morning? The knot had worked itself loose, and she scraped the cloud of red curls off her shoulders. "I'm surprised, that's all. We've only just arrived." She looked around the desolate yard with its stench of raw sewage and had an image of herself as a crow perched on top of a heap of rubbish. She willed him to turn around and go, but there was no stopping him. He was already walking into the yard with the louche grace she remembered only too well, his boots stirring up small eddies of dust. He looked in rude health. His skin had turned the color of walnut in the sun, and when he smiled at her his teeth flashed white through his beard. He looked older, darker, and more solid than she remembered, not quite the same as she had thought he would be. This strangeness, coupled with the memory of his hands on her body, molding it into the shape of his desire, unnerved her, and she couldn't speak.

"Aren't you going to ask me in?"

She colored, and as if reading her mind, he said, "You should see the way some of the diggers live. It makes this yard look like a palace."

She gave him a grateful smile. "How did you know where to find me?"

"Edwin Matthews is building something of a reputation for himself. You're not difficult to find." When she didn't say anything, he said, "Frances, if you're not sure what to say to me, you could always offer me a coffee."

Her blush deepened, and she felt suddenly as if he was exposing her, coming here. She turned away from him, kneeling down and opening the box to look for coffee, but instead pressing the heels of her hands into her eyes. The floorboards creaked behind her, and after a moment she felt the weight of his hand on her neck — thumb on spine, palm on shoulder — and she made a gulping sound, somewhere between a laugh and a sob. "It's so silly," she said, "but I haven't a clue how to make coffee." She stood up, turning round to face him, clutching the jar of coffee. "I'm hopeless. I can't even light a fire."

"Hasn't he shown you?" William asked, his eyebrows raised in disapproval.

She shrugged. "We only arrived yesterday. It probably never occurred to him that I didn't know how."

He looked as though he was going to say something disparaging about Edwin, but thought better of it. He picked up a contraption that stood by the ashes of their fire, made of two tins sealed one on top of the other. She hadn't noticed it before.

"You don't need to light the fire for coffee. That's what this boiler's for."

He filled it with water from the drum. Then he squatted down in the dust, took a knife from his pocket, and cut shavings from a piece of kindling.

"Come here, look." He waited for her to crouch down beside him, stuffing the shavings into the boiler with a handful of coir. He gave her some matches, and she lit one and held it to the coir and watched it catch, the flame almost invisible in the bright afternoon light. He blew a little into the flame, and it strengthened. The kindling

376

began to crackle. She felt his fingers sweep the hair away from her cheek and tuck it behind her ear. It was an affectionate gesture, as though he wanted a better look at her face, but she flinched as if her skin had been burnt. He touched the gold chain at her neck.

"You've been wearing it all this time?"

"Yes," she said, moving away from him, embarrassed. Wearing the necklace was as good as saying she still loved him. She sat in the chair and watched while he made coffee. He poured out a cup of the hot, bitter liquid and handed it to her. "It should be better than the last one I made you."

She remembered the storm, the two of them braced against the force of it and how close she had felt to him. "Frances, believe it or not, I didn't come here to tempt you away from your husband." She had forgotten his confidence. His ability to voice her thoughts, and to say the very thing she would never dare say herself. He was all intimacy, tearing down formalities, talking to her as he had done when she had lain half naked next to him on his bunk. He knew her physically, and she felt the same vulnerability she had done then, made worse by the distance he was establishing between them. There was rejection built into the word "husband." It was too final.

"Then why did you come?"

"Because I thought you might need a friend." *A friend.* Of course. What else had she expected? And yet it pricked her pride. He was here not because he wanted to see her, but because he pitied her.

"I'm not sure your wife will appreciate the difference." She tried to keep her voice light.

"You mean you don't know?" He gave a short laugh. "Frances, I'm not married. Eloise's father called it off. He found out what a scoundrel I was and told me he didn't want anything to do with me. Baier was furious of course, but what could he do?"

She was astounded. If he hadn't married Eloise, then everything could have been different. "Why didn't you write to me?"

"What was there to say? You were already married. Then I heard Matthews was bringing you here, and I wanted to see you. I needed to make sure you were all right."

"I am all right," she said stiffly.

"You might not be when your husband starts telling everyone we're in the midst of a smallpox epidemic."

"Are we?"

William gave a scoffing laugh.

"Then why would he say it?"

His face was suddenly serious. "Frances, how well do you know your husband? He has an insatiable appetite for scandal." He stood up and looked behind the curtain into their bedroom, then glanced over the few books Edwin had piled on a small shelf beside the box. She saw it all through his eyes: the squalid yard, the thin black smoke, the stench from the outhouse. After a moment he gave a frustrated yelp. "What was he thinking, bringing you here? He must be mad, asking you to live like this. Why doesn't he take you to Cape Town?" His words stung. She realized he had no interest in her staying in Kimberley. Why would he? She had never in her life felt less attractive.

"William, I am not your responsibility."

"No, but I care about you." There was a brief silence. Then he said, "You should persuade him to leave, if you can."

"So you can be rid of me?"

"No, Frances, because I'm worried about you. Kimberley is a horrible, grubbing place full of people on the make. The sooner you are out of here the better." He came to stand over her and said with a touch of remorse, "Look, I didn't want to upset you. I'll leave now, but you must promise me — if you need help, anything at all, please

379

come and find me."

He touched her cheek lightly and walked away, but she called after him. He turned, the afternoon sun catching the tips of his black hair. "Thank you," she said, and he smiled, walking backwards a few steps while he looked at her, then turned and walked out of the yard.

TWENTY-SEVEN

She was devastated. She had expected, even wanted, to see William, but she had imagined it would be in some public place and the impact of it would be diluted by company; that she would do little more than lay eyes on him and go through the motions of a formal conversation. Instead, he had found her alone and in a moment's glance had unraveled all the resistance she had built up over the long six months of not seeing him.

She lay down on the bed and shut her eyes, but her mind was full of him. He had spoken to her with such familiarity yet offered nothing more than friendly concern. And he wasn't married to Eloise Woodhouse after all. That was the hardest thing to register. It was easier to imagine him beholden, like her, to someone he didn't love, than free to make a life on his own without her.

It was as if she had signed a contract with him on the *Cambrian.* By letting him undress her, and letting his body mark out hers, she had given away her rights to herself as an independent being. Her loyalty was all to him. It was hardly rational. In their yard, he had looked as if he scarcely cared about her. There had been no mention of love, and yet his simple presence, the way he had touched her cheek and hinted at their closeness, seemed to be reminding her of the contract between them.

Edwin came back that evening convinced that the disease was smallpox. He said he had seen two cases; and as the days went by, the number grew.

"I don't understand," Frances said one evening. "Surely these doctors have their reputations to think about."

They were sitting at the entrance of the tent on either side of the foldout table, which threatened to overturn itself every time Edwin cut off another hunk of bread. There was a brawl going on at the Digger's Rest, and they could hear shouts and the smashing of glass. The baby across the yard was crying. Through the darkness, she could see Mangwa's stripes rippling as he shifted uneasily from foot to foot. It was eight o'clock and already cold enough for the tips of her fingers to be turning numb.

"The disease is smallpox," Edwin said, opening a jar of pickle. "It can't be anything else."

"But you said yourself you hadn't seen cases of pemphigus before."

"I've looked it up. Pemphigus is extremely rare and not contagious. It would be nothing short of impossible to find so many cases in Kimberley." He cut a piece of cheese onto each plate, and passed one to her.

"But the symptoms are the same?" she asked, taking the plate from him and helping herself to pickle.

"Ostensibly, yes. There is ulceration in both cases, particularly in the mouth. But if you've seen smallpox, you don't miss it a second time. Besides, pemphigus can take years to develop, and it's rarely fatal."

"Then how do they explain the men who are dying?" she asked, beginning to eat. The pickle did a good job of disguising the cheese, which was hard and tasteless.

"They don't. The postmortems state death from other causes."

"All the same, if you're not familiar with the disease . . ."

Edwin didn't respond, and after a moment

Frances said, "Why would Baier even bother covering it up? Wouldn't it be better to just get on and deal with it?"

"And risk the consequences of closing down the mine?"

"Why not? He must be wealthy enough. I thought he owned most of it?"

"That's part of the problem. A year ago, the yellow ground, or sand, which they had been mining ran out. They hit blue ground, which was almost impossible to break up. Geologists declared it the end of mining in Kimberley. The market dropped; diggers panicked and sold their claims to anyone foolish enough to buy them. Baier took a huge risk. He started buying up other men's claims. He showed that if you leave the blue ground to weather in the sun and you water it from time to time as you would a garden, it will start to disintegrate. He brought in gangs of natives who broke up the watered ground with wooden mallets. It crumbled into soft powder. Turns out the blue ground is even richer than the sand."

"Which is why he's the wealthiest man in Kimberley."

"Yes, except it's all bought on credit. He needs results fast, but the blue ground takes years to disintegrate, unless you use machinery to break it up. He's invested a fortune in importing steam engines to work the mines — mechanical washing plants, drills, trams. He's even started sinking shafts so they can begin to mine underground. If smallpox is declared, he's terrified the natives will leave the mines and his foreign investors will pull out. Not to mention the mining companies he has floated on the stock market. He'll be ruined."

Frances considered the implications of what he was saying. After a moment, she said, "You can't take on Baier. He's too powerful."

Edwin mopped at his plate with the last of his bread, and didn't look up. "Didn't you suggest the opposite the last time we had this conversation?"

"Edwin, don't do this for my sake. You don't have to prove anything to me."

He pushed his plate away and looked at her. "Frances, it may amaze you, but not every decision I make revolves around you."

There was a long pause. Finally, she spoke in a low, steady voice. "Edwin, please, let's get out of here. It's not too late to leave. We could go tonight. Kimberley is not your responsibility. Think what Baier could do to us. You'll never be able to have a practice of your own, and there'll be no chance of making a decent living. You said it yourself. He will ruin you utterly."

"I can't pretend he doesn't exist."

He walked out to the barrel in the yard and began washing the dishes. When he came back, she stood up and hissed at him, not wanting to be overheard. "Why won't you at least give yourself a chance?" She threw up her hands. "What kind of life is this? My clothes are infested with lice and there are rats living under our floorboards." She took his hand and placed it on her head. "Go on. Feel it. It's so dry and frizzy I feel like a native, and if I don't have a new dress soon I'll be mistaken for a beggar." He drew his hand away. "I'm hungry, Edwin. I'd like a good, hot meal for once. I've forgotten the taste of butter." She sat down and put her head in her hands. "I don't want to spend the rest of my life like this."

"Frances, I can't change who I am for your sake. Oddly, it was you who proved that to me."

She had to stop herself from begging. They would have nothing — no money, no resources, no friends. It would be almost impossible for Edwin to earn money at the Cape with Baier against him. She went to bed, leaving him sitting up by the small fire at the entrance of the tent. She put down her candle, opened her trunk, and lifted out a box as long as her forearm, lined with tissue paper and smelling of tuberose. There was a rustle as she opened the leaves of paper, plunging her hand into deep, velvety cashmere. It was a rug, soft like rabbit fur, woven in a tight herringbone green. Wrapped inside it was a box of English soaps scented with tuberose. William had remembered the perfume she had worn on the *Cambrian*. The last of it had run out a month ago, and the deep, heady smell brought back memories of London, of her father, and of William.

The gifts had arrived that morning. She had been planning to send them back, but now, after her argument with Edwin, she decided to keep them. Edwin would never notice. She pulled the cashmere throw into bed with her, wrapping it between her legs to keep her warm. It occurred to her that William's hands must have touched the fabric. He would have imagined it next to her skin, and this made her feel as if he were watching her and they were sharing something forbidden.

Some time later Frances was woken. There were voices in the yard, talking urgently. Mangwa nickered in concern, and the curtain glowed as a lamp was lit on the

other side. A second later, Edwin was calling her, and she pulled a heavy shawl over
her shoulders and walked through to the
front of the tent. The body of a native was
laid out on the floor. Edwin was kneeling
over him, trying to get a response. Another
native was stoking the fire and boiling a
kettleful of water. He talked rapidly to
Edwin in a thick accent.

"Bring my bag and some cloth," Edwin
said when he saw her, "and we need a basin
for the water."

"Cloth?" she asked, unsure what he
meant.

"Shirts, pillowcases, anything we can tear
up."

She brought his medical bag and a bundle
of linen. The man was stretched out on the
boards, moaning softly. There must have
been an accident in one of the mines. His
skin was black but oily red under the light
of the lamp. His hair was slick with blood,
and his features had been smudged by some
force so huge that his lips had been peeled
off his face and his nose was the white snub
of a skeleton. It was horrible to imagine the
moment of impact. She swallowed heavily,
her eyes riveted on the body.

"Is the water ready?" Edwin asked.

The man wore no trousers. One leg

twisted at a right angle away from his knee, and a bone sliced through the dark shin. Edwin straightened it with a scraping crunch.

"Frances?"

She tore her eyes away and realized the other native had gone. Steam was blowing off the boiler. She filled the basin with water, burning her hands on the tin bowl. Edwin thrust a pair of scissors at her and told her to cut off the man's jumper. She sliced up the center and peeled it away from his body. The wool was wet and heavy, sticky with blood like the pelt of an animal. Beneath the jumper his muscled arms and broad chest glistened with the luster of fresh paint. His stomach moved up and down like a toy pumped full of air. Blood foamed at his lips. She couldn't fathom the pain he must be in. Edwin grasped her hand and placed it firmly over a wound on the man's upper arm, which pulsed a slow, viscous fountain of blood. It oozed out thickly from between her fingers as if she were squeezing an orange. It was red. Bright red. Just as if it were her own. Edwin ripped up a sheet into strips and tied a tourniquet tightly around his arm, above the shoulder. Then he took hold of her other hand and pressed it into the man's palm, telling her to hold it raised up. She gripped his hand, but it was wet and slippery and kept sliding through her fingers until she locked her knuckles into his. There was a leather strap on his wrist which had bitten into the flesh, sinking right through to the bone.

After a time the man began to gurgle as if he were drowning. His chest heaved and pink foam bubbled out from his nostrils.

"He's fighting for air," Edwin said, leaning back to squat on his heels. "His lungs are filling up with blood."

"What can you do?" she asked, but he just shook his head. The man's chest tightened suddenly, and he pulled his shoulders off the floor, struggling against something. His torso was a tight line of vibration. Frances tried to support him, to take the weight of him in her lap, but his back shuddered against her knees. She wanted it to stop, and she shouted at Edwin to do something, but he looked away. The shaking went on and on, horrifying and grim, until suddenly the tension left him and his head rolled back, heavy and still, into her lap.

"He's dead," Edwin said, feeling for the man's pulse. Frances stared down at him, her heart racing and her ears full of the sudden silence. Then she stood up abruptly, letting his head thud onto the floor, horrified by the motionless weight of it pressing against her thighs. Edwin pulled up a pallet used for carrying firewood, and with Frances's help, he levered the body onto it. The man was too tall, and they had to lay him on his side, curled into a ball as if he were sleeping. Frances picked up the wool jumper. A badge of white cloth had been sewn on the front, with a black number inked on it. She draped it over the man's waist. Perhaps it would help identify him.

She wanted to put the body outside, but Edwin said the jackals would get it. They began cleaning the blood off the floor with pails of water. It was sticky and had seeped into the wood. A sickly, thin dawn light showed boards, canvas, and pale skin smeared red as if she were looking at the world through a crimson gauze. Their breath rose like steam in the cold air. Blood had poured down the sleeves of her night-dress, seeping through the thin cotton, and now it pressed itself wetly against her arms. She shook with cold. Edwin was squatting on his heels in the yard, washing his hands in a bucket of water. He glanced up at her, catching her eye, and she felt like Lady Macbeth caught out in her nightdress, on the verge of madness.

"Are you all right?" he asked.

"Why wasn't he taken to the hospital?"

Edwin gave a short, tired laugh. "Because someone would have had to pay."

"Shouldn't they be forced to pay? He must have been working for them when this happened."

"There is a hospital tax" — he dried his hands on his trousers and came into the tent — "a levy raised for all black laborers, but the claim holders find ways of not paying when it doesn't suit them." He held out the bucket so she could wash her hands. The water was a dirty pink. "Anyway, it hardly matters. Not even a hospital could have saved him."

When she had washed and changed, she looked herself over. There was still blood caught in the edges of her fingernails, in the creases of her arms, and later, lying in bed, she could feel the texture of it, rubbing off her hands into flakes. They slept with the dead body on the floor not five feet from their bed. He had come to them for help, and they hadn't been able to save him. He had been in desperate, torturing pain, and they had watched him die without a word. Guilt settled over her. Death was an intimate thing. She had held his hand, taken his body in her lap, and now she felt his presence close in on her like a curse. She shrugged it away, telling herself that the mines were dangerous, that he was just another native hoping to make money from the white man. She didn't want to feel his agony, or have to make sense of his death. But his blood had marked her out, and she wasn't sure she was the same person she had been just a few hours before.

When she woke, the body was gone, and Edwin too. She dressed, slipping on her shoes which were worn thin, the soles peeling like dry paper away from the leather seams. The floor still held the dark, wet stain, and her shoes trod with a slight tackiness across its surface. Violence and sickness were everywhere in Kimberley: the native lying dead on their floor; the boy in the yard opposite, wasting away; Edwin, with his talk of smallpox in the compounds. She lit the boiler and made tea, trying to shake off the thought that there was something sinister and depraved about the town.

A boy came into the yard and delivered a note. It was from Anne. She had heard Dr. Matthews was in town and asked Frances to visit her at the hospital. It was such a long time since Frances had had a letter, let alone one from a friend, and she smiled as she read it, feeling her mood lift. She would visit Anne, but first she wanted to wash her clothes. She boiled more water and dissolved some soap powder in a tub, then washed her second dress, her drawers, and her petticoats, rinsed them thoroughly, wrung them out, and hung them up outside on the line to dry. She began on her nightdress, scrubbing at the bloodstains until they faded to a brown smudge, which was the best she could do. Seeing Edwin's shirt and trousers crusted with blood, she washed them as well. When she had finished, she felt better able to face the world.

It was a hot, dusty walk to the hospital. Frances weaved around piles of refuse, past tents where carcasses had been left outside to rot, stinking in the sun. Eventually she came out onto the main road. Two men, a European and a native, turned the same way. The sun burnt down overhead, and the red earth exhaled a shimmering heat. Men drove mule carts and ox wagons over the pitted tracks. When the vehicles rolled past they threw up eddies of dust which blanketed her in soft drifts of ocher snow, and she sneezed in dismay. There were no trees, and the shrubs were patchy and dry-leaved. Frances hadn't thought to bring a parasol, and the sun, brutally hot, was beginning to burn a scarlet strip down the backs of her hands. She wiped her face with her last pure white handkerchief and grimaced at the dirt which came off with it. You needed an endless supply of clean linen in Kimberley.

Up ahead was a small iron building with the word "Police" painted on the outside. She stepped in to ask directions. As she did, a scream tore loose from somewhere inside — a mixture of rage and pain that made her palms sweat. It took a moment for her eyes to adjust to the dark. Two officers were holding on to something. A shape that convulsed with elastic energy. Feet scraped off walls and a bucket clattered across the floor. There was a flash of white cotton, and someone's spittle flecked across her cheek. It was a woman. Not a native, but a European.

They had her pinned to the floorboards, a creamy mass of skirts.

"She's a live one."

"Watch her!"

"She's like a cat. She'll scratch your eyes out if you give her half a chance."

A short, squat officer straddled the woman and began sliding his hands down around her ribs. She squirmed underneath him, and he gave a gurgled laugh.

"Oh, you like that, do you?"

She flipped her face around and saw

Frances standing in the doorway. "Help me," she mouthed.

And then, in a flash, she was out of their grip. The men grabbed at her dress, but her suppleness outwitted both of them. She dashed forwards, colliding off Frances's shoulder and through the door. The officers tumbled out after her. One swiped at her on the *stoep,* snatching a handful of hair so she spun around in mid-air, and the other punched her heavily in the stomach. She doubled over, wheezing. Together, the two men wrestled her to the floor. They jammed their hands under her armpits, twisting the skin into tight rolls. Then they dragged her back inside. Frances stepped out of their way, onto the *stoep,* blinking in the bright sunshine. Two officials were standing on the road, smoking cigarettes. She asked them who the woman was.

"An English girl. She was caught ferrying five hundred pounds' worth of diamonds in the handle of her parasol."

"That's not the half of it," the other man said, dropping his cigarette and grinding it beneath the toe of his boot. "She's been sleeping with a nigger to get them."

"What will happen to her?"

"They'll try and hang her, though I doubt they'll manage it. More than likely she'll

396

end up on Breakwater."

Frances had expected more from Kimberley's hospital, but, like everything here, it was a single-story building made of corrugated iron. The main section of the hospital was finished, but the adjacent buildings were still under construction, and shirtless natives could be seen perched high up on timber frames like black rooks.

Anne came out of the hospital, looking efficient in her white uniform. She seemed to have grown up and filled out. Her narrow frame and pale cheeks had disappeared, and in their place was a softer, more assured figure, with the same neat, dark hair and serious eyes.

"Is this really the only hospital in Kimberley?" Frances asked when they were sitting on a bench on the hospital lawn under the flickering shade of a mesquite tree.

"This is it, the only one." Anne smiled. "It's not made of brick, but it's better than the one that was here before. They used to make do with just an old army tent. Jackals would crawl in under the canvas at night and maul the patients. Once, it even blew down in a dust storm, and the men were left lying in their beds in a howling wind."

Frances might not have believed this of

any other place, but it seemed possible in Kimberley.

"You must be so proud of your husband," Anne said after a minute.

"Proud?" Frances asked, confused.

"He's done such a lot for Kimberley. There isn't a nurse here who doesn't thank him for the pressure he put on the magnates to introduce the hospital tax."

Frances didn't say anything. What could she say? Edwin had mentioned the hospital tax, but he hadn't said that he had had anything to do with it. Not that it seemed to have done much good, from what she had seen last night.

Anne laughed at her silence. "You were just the same on the *Cambrian*. You never once told us what kind of man you were marrying. In fact, you were so taciturn that we all presumed you were being married off to some awful old doctor who couldn't tie his own shoelaces." Anne squeezed her hand. "I had no idea he was such a good man."

Neither had I, thought Frances wryly. Anne's empathy was misguided, but it was empathy nonetheless, and it had been a long time since she had had a conversation with someone who cared. "Anne," she began, "it's not always easy to be married to

Edwin." She paused, trying to work out how to phrase what she wanted to say.

"Of course it's not," Anne said, interrupting her. "I dare say you worry that you're not good enough for him. Well, you mustn't. I'm sure you're more of a support to him than you think."

"Perhaps." Anne had misunderstood her completely. She was idealistic, and Frances suddenly felt the hopelessness of trying to tell her about Edwin's obsession with smallpox and her concern that it was putting them in danger. "Well — what about you?" she asked. "What have you been up to in Kimberley?"

Anne smiled. "We work long hours. I start at seven and I'm often still in the ward past eight in the evening."

"Do you never have an evening off?"

"Not often, but we don't mind so much, I suppose, because we all feel so lucky to be working under Sister Clara."

"Is she the head nurse?"

"Yes. Don't you remember me telling you about her on the *Cambrian*?"

Frances did remember. Anne had said she was almost a saint.

"Hasn't Dr. Matthews mentioned her?" Anne asked.

"Should he have?"

Her friend blushed, and her eyes slid away from Frances. "No, not at all. It's only that we all admire her so much. She is one of the most influential women in South Africa. It's because of her that we have such a fine hospital now. Your husband encouraged her to establish herself here when she was visiting Kimberley. They worked together on various projects."

"What kind of projects?"

"The pail system, for one," Anne said, but Frances looked at her blankly. "It's a system for sewage disposal. Two years ago all the sewage and waste produced by the town was being dumped wherever men felt like it. Your husband wrote a report, with Sister Clara's help, which was very influential. Now we have the beginnings of a proper sanitation system, with most of the night soil being taken away from the town regularly and buried a considerable distance away. It's not perfect yet, but we're getting there. Deaths from camp fever have fallen dramatically." Anne looked embarrassed. "I suppose people don't tell you these things, because he's your husband. Sister Clara says there have been an awful lot of doctors in Kimberley since they discovered diamonds ten years ago, but they've all been in the hands of the miners. She says your husband is different. That Kimberley needs someone like him. Anyway" — Anne stopped herself, blushing slightly — "I am rattling on."

Edwin had never told her, and she had never thought to ask, what he had done when he was here. She presumed he had started a practice, but it seemed he had been more involved in politics than doctoring. Anne looked as though she were half in love with him, and Frances laughed to herself at the thought of Edwin as a romantic hero fighting for the moral health of Kimberley.

When it was time for Anne to go, Frances asked if she could introduce her to Sister Clara. She had an idea that the woman might be able to help her. Anne was pleased. "She has such an effect on everyone she meets, and she will want to see you."

Anne led her into the hospital, down a long corridor with white walls and a sloping roof. She knocked on a door and opened it. They entered a small room with a window, a desk, and one shelved wall crammed with books. A woman with a slender neck and neatly plaited, honey-colored hair was bent over the desk, writing. She looked up when they came in and put down her pen. Frances was surprised. She had been expecting someone older, but this was a woman of no more than thirty, profoundly beautiful, with high cheekbones and very pale blue eyes which looked Frances over with intelligent appraisal.

Anne introduced them and left the room. Sister Clara offered Frances a seat in the chair which sat opposite the desk, and she sat, feeling rather awkward, like a child called in for misbehaving. The age difference wasn't enough to merit it, but the woman had an air of natural authority. When she spoke, it was in a low, warm voice. "Your husband has been a great source of inspiration to me, Mrs. Matthews. It is a comfort to have him back in Kimberley."

"It may be a comfort to you, but I can assure you it isn't for me." Frances decided to be honest. "If there is smallpox in Kimberley, my husband is determined to prove it. He says natives are dying. I should like to know — have you seen any cases?"

"Not personally, no."

"But you believe the disease affecting the natives may be smallpox?"

"Your husband certainly does."

Frances nodded. "Did you know that he thinks Baier is denying it to protect himself?" The woman's face was impassive. "I'm concerned that staying in Kimberley will be suicide for him. If he antagonizes Baier, his career will be in ruins."

"Mrs. Matthews, I'm sure you don't need me to tell you that your husband is a political animal."

"Yes," Frances said, though she hadn't perhaps known this until now, "but can't he be political without endangering himself?"

"Endangering himself or endangering you?"

Frances, who had been looking down at her hands, glanced up and met Sister Clara's eye. "I simply wanted to ask if you might reason with him. The whole thing is madness. He is so determined, and I can't see why he should be."

"But I'm sure you do know why."

Frances felt suddenly as if she might cry. No one seemed to understand her situation. They were always trying to tell her something different from what she knew.

"It is not always easy to live in the shadow of other people's courage," Sister Clara said.

"I don't think I lack courage." Frances stood up, piqued by the ease with which this woman seemed to judge her. She looked around the clean, ordered room. What she lacked was the means to live. Did Sister Clara know that Edwin was working for nothing trying to help the natives in the

403

compounds? That they had no money to fall back on if it all went wrong? That her beloved pail system had failed to make it to the outskirts of town, where they were camped in squalor?

"Thank you, Sister Clara," Frances said, giving the woman a curt smile and leaving the room.

When Frances left the hospital, the sun was directly overhead. Edwin had asked her to buy some things for supper, and she headed towards Market Square. Her stomach felt tight and hollow, and as she walked a cold sweat prickled up her spine. Though the glare hurt her eyes, she couldn't feel its heat and her mouth was dry and sticky. She wiped her hand over her forehead and paused for a second by the side of the road, waiting for the feeling to pass. It was then that she saw the same two men standing a little way off. They must have gone to the hospital and come back at the same time as her. The European's eyes slid over her then looked away.

The whole of Kimberley might have been gathered in the market. It was a roar of noise; a patchwork of color and people, talking, shoving, bartering, and embracing. An auction for secondhand mining equipment was being held on the steps of the hotel. The rap of the hammer beat like a tin drum above the commotion. On the outskirts of the square, wagons full of timber, coal, and green cabbages were being unloaded. Crates of iron cooking utensils glinted in the sun. She nudged her way into the tight press of stalls, where a flow of people seethed and jostled, past Europeans, natives, Malays, and Indians. The place smelt of moldering vegetables, spices, and dried fish. Women with black, gnarled faces and strange piercings unrolled yards of fabric, their patterns fading in the sun. Malay men were squatted on the ground, dwarfed by sacks of spices full of cinnamon and cloves, smoking pipes which gave off a thick, sweet smoke.

Edwin had asked her to buy flour, meat, and sugar, but she had never set foot in a market before. In London, the cook had sent an errand boy out to buy the goods which weren't delivered to the house. It mattered to her that Edwin thought she was at least capable of buying their supper, and she wasn't going to go home empty-handed. Two near-naked natives pushed past, smelling of animal hides and sweat. There was a tugging at her skirt. A dark-skinned boy with no legs was dragging himself behind her on his hands. She turned to get away from him, but he was under her feet, and there was a soft crunch as she trod on his fingers. The boy screamed. Frances apologized, then pushed deeper into the market, leaving him behind.

She stopped by a butcher's stall. Carcasses hung from metal hooks under a canvas awning. More were piled up on a trestle table: lurid red slabs slicked over with white muscle. The meat had tightened in the heat, its surfaces congealing to a dark, ruby leather flecked with the smooth curve of a bone or tendon. Flies swarmed, rising in a cloud when the man struck at them with a stick, and the meat swung in spiraling circles on the rusting hooks. Blood dripped down into matted pools of dust. There was a metallic, cloying smell. She thought about the native lying on their floor with his shin jutting straight out of his leg. Her mouth tasted acid. She swallowed bile and spoke to the man behind the stall.

He was a Boer with a heavy beard and lank, greasy hair. He didn't appear to understand English, but when she asked for beef he pointed to a cut of meat and she nodded. There was another tug at her skirts. The beggar boy was back. He swung himself into a sitting position and held out his hand to her. His fingers were scuffed and bleeding where she had trodden on them. The butcher was talking to her. He held up five fingers. "Five," he said, in English. She wasn't sure of the currency, and pulled out a wad of notes from her purse. She took too long reading them, and he reached over and plucked them from her, sorted through them, and peeled away three or four. The boy pulled at her hand, jabbering in Kaffir. She felt guilty and handed him a note, but he took it from her, waving it in disgust as if it weren't enough, then reached up on the stumps of his legs to grab at her wrists, shuffling around her feet so she couldn't move.

She felt dizzy now. The meat was wrapped in paper, and not having a bag, she clutched it in one hand. Out of the corner of her eye she thought she saw the two men who had been at the hospital, but when she turned they had gone. All of a sudden her stomach contracted and nausea washed up inside her. A surge of vomit filled her mouth and she doubled over in front of the stall. The Boer shouted, waving his hands at her to move on. A group of Malay men, sitting in a row, watched her silently without helping. She wiped her mouth on her sleeve and started walking back through the stalls, wanting to get home, willing to forget the flour and the sugar, but the stalls were tacked together haphazardly and so many rows deep that when she tried to find her way out, she realized she was lost.

Eventually she came out onto a quiet street. She had no idea where she was, and she followed it, hoping to emerge on a road that she recognized. There were footsteps behind her, but it wasn't until she turned the corner that she realized they were following. The hairs rose up on the back of her neck. She glanced back. The European was wearing dirty overalls with a cap pushed down on his head. When he saw her watching, he smiled, and she felt a trickle of fear. She walked faster, but they kept pace. She was lost now, with no idea which way to go. Another wave of cramps ripped through her.

Two white women turned the corner on the opposite side. Frances felt a surge of relief. They would be able to help her. One of them pushed a large perambulator, and the other, tall and graceful, laughed as she told a story. They both wore white dresses, straw hats, and white gloves. They looked immaculate and refined, like polished stones glinting in a pile of rubble. A colored servant in uniform strolled behind them, shielding them from the sun with a parasol.

She called out to them, and they turned and glanced warily in her direction. Frances froze. The tall woman was Eloise Wood-house. She recognized her broad face and strong features. She was more beautiful, in the daylight, than Frances had expected her to be. Her skin was perfectly smooth, and her mouth was soft and wide as she looked at her. After a moment, Eloise took her friend's arm in a protective gesture and they kept walking. Frances hesitated before following, reluctant to be seen in such a state by the woman William had meant to marry, but fear drove her on.

"Please, stop," she cried, running across the street. She didn't want to be left alone. The men would catch up with her any minute. She touched Eloise on the shoulder. The woman turned and looked in horror at her dress, then at Frances's ungloved hand. Her fingers, bloodied from the meat, had left a pink stain on the white fabric.

"I'm so sorry," she said, taking a step backwards, mortified, but not forgetting the men who stood behind her. "If you could just help me . . ."

Eloise interrupted, saying something to the servant, who stepped between them, blocking her way. Frances stared at her, too shocked for a moment to speak. Eloise had mistaken her for a beggar.

The women began walking away. "I'm

English," she called after them, thinking that she just needed to explain. "My name is Frances Matthews. I am Sir John Hamilton's niece." But they didn't turn around, and soon they had turned the corner out of sight.

She let them go, gripped by a sudden nausea. Her stomach plunged and her mouth filled with saliva. An icy-cold sweat dripped down her spine and the backs of her legs. She doubled over on the street, vomiting.

"Madam, are you all right?" One of the men had caught up with her, and he laid a hand on her shoulder, stroking it as she retched. She shrugged it off, but he kept it there, letting it slide down to the small of her back. She was breathing heavily. "Or perhaps you would rather the comforts of my friend?"

She looked up and saw the native watching her. Otherwise, the street was empty. Dread settled like mist against her skin.

"Please. Leave me," she said, shaking her head and backing up.

"We couldn't do that," the man said, smiling at her. There was something treacherous and mean in his face.

"What do you want?" She took out her purse with clumsy fingers and held it out to

410

him, but he grasped her hand instead and it fell into the street. He unclenched her fingers, forcing open her palm. His confidence had her transfixed, like a fly caught in a web. If she moved, he would bind her closer. So she stayed very still, the hairs pricking up on the backs of her arms. He took hold of her fingers, one by one.

"This little piggy went to market,

"This little piggy should have stayed at home,

"This little piggy bought roast beef,

"This little piggy will have none,

"And this little piggy went . . . wee wee wee wee . . . all the way home" — he waggled her little finger and smiled at her — "and persuaded Mr. Piggy that he should keep his snout out of other people's business."

"What do you mean?" she asked in a whisper.

He laughed at her, dropping her hand and backing away. "Kimberley is no place for kaffir lovers, Mrs. Matthews. Your husband should have learnt that a long time ago."

He bent down and plucked the notes out of her purse. Then they turned and left her standing in the street. When they had gone she was gripped by a cramping so strong that she couldn't stop it, and she had to lift her skirts and squat in the gutter. She was too ill to care if someone saw her. Her bowels emptied, and she groaned, caught between shame and need, no better than the beggar Eloise Woodhouse had mistaken her for. When it was over she moved on down the street, filthy and scared, desperate to find her way back to Edwin. It was almost dark by the time she got home. Edwin watched her walk into the yard. His face was tense.

"The water," he said, pointing to the barrel. "What have you done with all our water?"

"I washed our linen," she said weakly, remembering tipping out great vatfuls of soapy water into their yard.

"You washed our linen?" he exclaimed. "And used all our water for a week. Do you have any idea what that water costs us?" It was so rare to see him angry. In all their time at Rietfontein he had never once raised his voice.

Frances felt light on her feet. She swayed at the entrance to the tent. "I bought some beef," she said ineffectually, holding out her bloodied parcel, which she had managed to keep with her. When she moved, her limbs felt buoyant, as if they didn't belong to her. She laughed strangely. He didn't take the meat from her, so she placed it on the table. It had been weighing her down. There had been an idea in the back of her mind, all through the horrible journey home, that Edwin would be kind to her when she got back. His anger wasn't at all what she had been expecting.

"What else did you buy?" he asked.

"There was no more money," she said, walking unsteadily towards the back of the tent. The cramps had started again.

"Frances, come back here."

She pushed aside the curtain, but somehow couldn't find her way through it. A deep sickness surged up from her stomach. The fabric felt too heavy in her hands, and her skin prickled as if her dress were full of pins. She tried to cry out, but the side of the tent was falling away from her. The world tilted and the curtain ran through her fingers as she fell.

Edwin lifted her up and placed her on the bed. He worked quickly, stripping off her clothes and wiping her down with a wet cloth. "I'm sorry," she said, over and over. "I'm sorry."

The world disappeared, and in its place was a cavernous pit which was alternately fire and ice. Her body was gripped by fever. She lost all sense of time. It seemed to her that a swarm of bugs had crawled under the canvas, the floor trembled with them, and now they seethed up the legs of the bed and over the mattress and began eating at her body. She dreamt that the earth was a living, breathing thing — she could feel the undulations of each heaving breath — swilling with filth and seeping blood and poison from its skin. The smell of the blood clung to her fingers — the native's blood — and she was sure the bed sheets, wet with her sweat, were drenched in it. Edwin's careful administrations tortured her, making her too cold or too hot. He forced her to sip water, which made her body seize, and she vomited into the bowl which he held out for her. Periodically, he stripped off the blankets, dampening her burning body with wet flannels, and she writhed with cold. Then he was gone for a seemingly infinite amount of time, and she called, then sobbed, for him to come back. She thought she saw Mariella, stroking her face and smiling too wide.

"Boudica," she said, leaning in to speak to Frances.

"What?" Frances cried. "What did you say? I don't understand."

"Boudica is gone," she said, enunciating very clearly, and Frances saw herself standing in front of William's mirror on the *Cambrian*, red hair tumbling over her shoulders, and her eyes glittering back at her, wild and unsure.

When Edwin came back, Frances watched him, convinced that in the exact tilting of his head and the movements of his hands was hidden some mathematical equation which she must — but couldn't — solve.

At some point, she heard a cacophony of voices and found herself outside. The cicadas were so loud that she put her hands over her ears. The landscape was white and leached of color, and the sun burnt her eyes. In the hot glare she saw the zebra standing in the yard with his nose dropped to the floor and his body shuddering. A red gash sliced his neck from ear to ear. Blood oozed down his chest and dripped onto the sand.

She opened her eyes one morning and felt sane and calm. There was a bitter taste in her mouth. Edwin was cleaning out a rifle. She hadn't seen him with it before. He was quiet, concentrating, his lean fingers pushing a rod smoothly backwards and forwards through the barrel. She watched, her body and mind empty of emotion.

"What happened to Mangwa?" she asked, unsure now what she had really seen.

He slid the rod from the rifle, removed a small cotton cloth attached to its end, and stood both rod and gun up against the side of the canvas.

"How do you feel?" he asked, taking her hand and feeling for her pulse.

"Better." Then, after a moment, "How long have I been sick?"

"Four days. You drank the water from the barrel, didn't you?"

She nodded, remembering now that he had told her to drink from the jug he had set aside. "And Mangwa?" she asked.

He put her hand back down onto the bed. "We'll talk about it later. You need to rest."

She fell into a deep, dreamless sleep and woke up with the evening light filtering through the sides of the curtain. Edwin was sitting by the fire, frying onions. She sank into a chair next to him, her mouth watering with sudden hunger. The sun had set behind them, and the air was full of dust particles caught in a hazy, pink twilight.

Mangwa stood in the yard, eating hay. There was a line of dried blood, like black ink, around the scoop of his neck. "What happened to him?"

"He was cut with a knife. It isn't deep."

"Why would someone do that?" Her mind

felt slow, and she struggled to make sense of it.

Edwin added a spoonful of lard to the onions, then tipped in a piece of meat, which sizzled and caught in the hot fat. "A few days ago I wrote a letter to the *Diamond News* explaining my findings of smallpox in four native compounds."

"What does that have to do with Mangwa?"

"Someone disliked it enough to give me a warning."

She paused for a second, watching the weaver birds building their untidy, sprawling nest in the dead branches of the small tree in their yard.

"Baier?"

"Perhaps."

She told him about the men in the street.

"I'm sorry, Frances," he said softly, looking at her. "From now on, you shouldn't go out alone."

"Isn't there someone you could write to? With more influence than you?"

He shook his head. "I've tried, but most people don't want to listen. It's not in their interest for Kimberley to fail. And those that do would be reluctant to come up against Baier."

"So what will you do?"

"Vaccinate as many people as possible."

"And Baier?"

Edwin turned the meat in the pot. It hissed and spluttered as it browned, and he wiped his cheek on his shoulder. His skin was dark with grime and sun. "The Cape government has formed a sanitary board. It is full of the pink-slip men. They have barred me from the compounds, and from the hospital. I'm making a speech in the town hall next week."

She wanted to ask if it was dangerous, but she was too tired. She closed her eyes. Edwin was pouring wine over the meat in the pot, and it bubbled and spat, letting off a rich, salty aroma. After a moment she got up and walked over to Mangwa.

He had finished the hay and was dozing, but when she approached he nudged her pockets and nickered softly. Frances ran her hand around the line of congealed blood, and the zebra shivered. There had been too much violence in the last few days. She wondered whether there was somewhere else for her to go, but she knew it was hopeless. The only person who could protect her was Edwin.

TWENTY-EIGHT

"What you need, Frances, is something to take your mind off things. What about a trip?"

Mariella stood in their yard, dressed in a smart, white cotton jacket with a pretty sailor's hat, looking a picture of health and cleanliness. She had arrived in Kimberley two weeks ago, and finding out from Anne that Frances was in town, she had visited, but Frances had been in the depths of her fever. Now she had returned to see how she was recovering.

"What kind of trip?"

"You know, a *voyage*," she said, throwing open her arms and lengthening the vowels into a mockery of French. "We have to get you out of this dreadful place." Mariella, curls bouncing and belly swelling with her baby, looked disdainfully at the patch of dust they called the yard. "Why ever did you agree to let him come to Kimberley?"

419

she asked. "It was a terrible idea."

"Yes, and not mine," Frances said. She had been cleaning her boots, and now she was running a file under her blackened fingernails.

"No," said Mariella admonishingly, "but you're a pretty girl, Frances. You must have influence over him. Why didn't you use it?"

Frances didn't reply, and after a moment Mariella leapt up. "There's a new bathing house in town. They've been advertising in the *Diamond News*. Towels as white as the driven snow, or so they claim. Let's go together."

Frances wiped her hands on a cloth and looked in the shard of mirror that had been hung up above the basin. Her skin was red and dry from the hot days and cold nights. Her lips were peeling and her nails felt brittle. She hadn't washed properly since she had come to Kimberley almost a month ago, and everything smelt of her sickness; of vomit and sweat. Grease and dirt had gathered in dark wrinkles in her elbows and in the creases of her groin, and her hair was matted into a ball of frizz.

"Perhaps another day," she said uncomfortably.

"Don't be silly. I'm paying," Mariella said, handing Frances her hat. "Now can we

420

please get out of here?"

The baths were en route to the better side of town. They passed a few red brick houses amidst the iron huts. Mariella said they weren't far from the Kimberley Club, where the wealthiest residents spent their time smoking, playing billiards, and gambling away their fortunes. Three women, spotlessly dressed, walked past them, and Mariella whispered, "The croquet and badminton set. More money than they know what to do with. They come all the way out here to see the mine, and realize too late that there's nothing else to do. The real highlight is being waited on by a man who is just as poor as the ones at home but has black skin instead of white."

The baths were in a corrugated-iron building, with linen not quite as white as snow but clean nonetheless. Mariella paid the attendant for two towels, and they were led into pine cubicles, each containing a cast-iron bath full of water. Frances stripped off her clothes and stepped in. The water was deliciously warm, hot enough to get slick and soapy and wash the dirt from her skin. She had lost weight, her stomach was concave, and her hips jutted out in sharp points. She leant back and shut her eyes, her head throbbing as the aching tiredness seeped out of her joints. The cloth came away from her face black with grime, and she scrubbed and scrubbed to get clean, then washed her hair and combed through oil.

"You married a good man, Mariella," Frances said, when they had changed back into their clothes. They were the only women in the room. She was curling her wet hair into a bun and pinning it up.

"And look what a state he got me into." Mariella laughed, pointing at her rounding stomach. She looked happy. George Fairley had spent six months managing a farm in the fertile valleys of Stellenbosch, and they had raised enough capital to come to Kimberley. He was hoping to find work with one of the mining companies, and Mariella had told Frances that he had already made some significant investments in diamonds.

Frances caught her eye in the mirror. "Mariella, I don't want to always be poor."

"You won't be. Edwin will abandon his zeal, you'll move to Cape Town, and he'll start a practice. Life will be so boring you'll wish this moment back again."

"Will I? Sometimes he seems so determined."

"Is he right about there being smallpox?"

Frances shrugged. "I'm not sure what to

believe."

"Be patient, Frances. Perhaps you ought to trust him. He might know what he's doing better than you think."

"Maybe you're right," she said, thinking that Mariella didn't know Edwin. She wasn't sure she was capable of trusting him. His motives were obscure, and they didn't seem to include protecting her.

After the baths, they walked down to the Big Hole. It was the largest diamond mine in the world, and Mariella was shocked that Frances hadn't visited it. "After all, you've been here almost a month, and it's the only thing in Kimberley worth seeing."

She took them along a road between clusters of low, small dwellings. Frances glanced behind her occasionally to make sure they weren't being followed. She hadn't told Mariella about the men who had accosted her. She didn't want her to worry. They heard the rumble of steam engines and walked past mountains of debris which dwarfed the tents that were pitched in their shadow.

"Should you really be walking around like this?" Frances asked, looking at Mariella's pale face reddening with exertion. She was panting slightly as they walked, and Frances felt a rush of affection for her. She made life simpler, like an experienced knitter unraveling a knotted ball of yarn. When you were with her, your problems seemed to lose their intensity. She had been lonely, she realized, and it was good to have company.

"I'm fine. It just takes the breath out of you. And I can't bear lounging around in the chair at home all day. Those rooms get horribly hot." Frances suspected Mariella was just being kind. She knew George had taken rooms at the hotel on Market Square where she had wanted to stay their first night in Kimberley. It would have been more than comfortable.

The dwellings grew closer together, pressing in on one another, and there was a swell of noise. The earth shook with the vibration of huge engines. All of a sudden, the huts stopped. As if stepping through a dense forest into a clearing, they found themselves in a wide-open space, on the brink of an immense canyon. It was infinitely larger than Frances had imagined — a giant hole, at least half a mile across, bored down into the center of the earth. Its vastness stopped her in her tracks. She had never envisaged a place on this scale. Mariella, gratified by her reaction, took her by the hand, and they walked closer to the precipice.

"Have they really dug this entirely themselves?" Frances asked. It was a dizzying experience, standing at the edge, the mine as deep below as it seemed to the clouds above; a whole world carved out of the bowels of the earth, falling hundreds of feet below them. It was so huge that the natives swarming over the surface looked like ants erupting out of a ruined nest. She remembered Edwin's description of the pits of hell.

"Yes, they dug it in a little under ten years. The problem is there are over five hundred claims and they've all been mined at different speeds. Which is why some are so much deeper than others." It was true. The ground at the bottom had no level. There were hundreds of strips of earth, each a separate claim, all at different heights. Turrets and platforms had emerged between them, with ropes and ladders linking one section to another. It had the look of a ruined underground city in the midst of being excavated.

A network of wires spun over the top of the mine like a dense spiderweb. There were thousands of threads, and you looked down at the cavernous hole through the gauzy shimmer of quivering metal. It was an aerial tramway, Frances realized, with each wire attached to a pulley system: horse-driven whims or hand-turned winches secured to scaffolding, perched precariously on the edge of the mine. An infinite number of iron pails, crates, and sacks full of soil were being hauled to the surface. The noise was deafening: the screech of wires, the shouts of the men, the bellowing of mules, the thousand tiny blows of pickaxes striking the earth in the depths of the mine.

A tram chugged its load up the wall on the far side. There was a muffled explosion from somewhere below, throwing up a thick, billowing cloud of dust. The air smelt of burning metal. When the dust cleared, a pattern began to emerge out of the chaos. In the labyrinth of ditches at the bottom of the mine, half-naked, black-skinned laborers carried wooden stretchers of soil to the pulleys that would haul them to the surface. The claims were too far beneath them to make out the faces of the men who were working there. All she could see was the flickering of their bodies as they moved. Once at the top, the earth was carried away by Scotch carts drawn by mules, their wheels plowing heavily through the deep sand. Men with wheelbarrows heaped with debris steered a path between them.

Just in front of the girls stood a tall wooden structure with a huge iron pulley system embedded into it. The scaffold was weighted down by a small mountain of sandbags. Natives climbed over it, some signaling to the men below and others, dripping with exertion, helping to turn the great handle of a windlass which was bringing a wooden crate, heavy with debris, shuddering along one of the wires. They were dressed in a ragged selection of torn shirts and rolled-up trousers, and their faces were lean and hollow.

She saw William standing below the windlass talking to a group of natives, and her heart quickened. Thank goodness she looked cleaner and more presentable than the last time they had seen each other. His back was turned towards her. Sweat had soaked through his waistcoat, turning the fawn linen black. A shotgun was slung over his shoulder, and a boy stood nearby holding his horse, a chestnut who had been worked into a lather and was shivering despite the sun. A clutch of partridge hung from the back of his saddle.

William's hands were folded behind his back, tapping a horsewhip against the leather of his polished boots. He was talking, and the men were listening to him with sullen faces. They each had a small piece of white cloth sewn to their clothes with a number painted on it. She couldn't hear what he was saying above the noise of the engines. He made a gesture of frustration and turned a little towards her. His face was tight and angry, and in a sudden movement he brought the whip from behind his back and struck the back of one of the men's naked calves with it in two hard slaps. The group immediately disbanded. William kicked at the dust in frustration, then glanced up and saw her watching him. He broke into a smile and threaded his way through the crowd to where they stood.

"Mrs. George Fairley," Frances said, introducing Mariella.

"Of course. Don't I remember you from the *Cambrian*?" William asked, taking Mariella's gloved hand and kissing it. "Are you impressed by what we're achieving?"

"What exactly are you achieving?" Mariella gave a flirtatious flick of her curls, but he didn't answer, instead bringing the back of Frances's bare hand to his lips. As his beard grazed against her skin, his fingers put a slight pressure on her own. Despite her uneasiness at what she had just seen, she was grateful for this small acknowledgment of their closeness. The bitterness she had felt before was all gone. She was determined to accept his kindness and not look for anything more from him.

He turned to Mariella. "Only the most

successful diamond-mining operation in the world."

Mariella laughed. "So, tell me," she said to him in a confidential voice. "We've bought stock in The London and South African. Am I right in saying it's one of Joseph Baier's companies? Is it a good bet?"

"There's no such thing as a bad bet in this market. When did you buy?"

"A week ago."

William laughed. "Go to Ebden Street and see for yourself. If they're not worth twice as much as you paid for them, I'll buy them from you myself. What about Mrs. Matthews?" he asked, turning to Frances. "Have you been dabbling in our stock market?"

"I'm afraid it isn't my husband's style."

"You mean you don't insist? Isn't it every wife's prerogative to tell her husband how to make money?" He spoke lightly. This was conversation without substance, but a moment later he looked away and pushed his foot through the dust. It was a childish movement. "Christ, what's the point of sitting it out in this godforsaken place if you're not going to profit a little from it?"

"Why do they wear those white badges?" Frances asked, looking at the natives turning the windlass.

"It's impossible to tell them apart. The

badges make it easier for us to identify them."

"And must you hit the men?" she asked, disliking what she had seen.

He held up his horsewhip and gave an amused smile. "What, with this thing? I'd call it more of a tickle than a blow. I use it no more than a jockey does to coax the best out of his steed, not because he wishes to damage it but because he knows it can do better."

She looked at him, appalled.

"I'm sorry. I was being conceited," he said. "But the truth is, Kimberley has a strange effect on all of us. If you spend any length of time here you begin to understand that it is absurd to apply the niceties of English law to kaffirs. Don't get me wrong. I am certainly no advocate of violence, but these are physical men. If you maintain a show of superior strength, they respect you for it. They are used to being ruled by a chief who uses brutality to keep them in check. Take the natives I was speaking to earlier. They all had contracts promising good wages in return for their work, but then some German upstart who doesn't have a clue how things operate in Kimberley offers them twice the going salary and they throw down their tools and leave.

They're always wanting more — more than they have, more than we can afford to pay them. Given half a chance they would bring us all, themselves included, to the edge of bankruptcy."

This was the way he had spoken to the reverend on the boat. There was something flippant and self-serving in his attitude towards the Africans, and it made her uncomfortable.

"What about the new native compounds?" she asked. "My husband says that they are little better than prisons. That the natives are forced to live there, that they have no access to education and no way of bettering themselves."

"And what do you think, Mrs. Matthews?"

She brushed away a fly which had landed on her cheek. "I can see his point. It seems rather unfair. It is their country after all." She swept a hand out towards the mine. "And all this — the grim spectacle of it all, with the natives in rags, being worked like animals. It's hardly the civilizing process we hear about in England."

William looked at her, his face caught between surprise and irritation. "They aren't forced to work for us. Not unless they're criminals."

She put a hand to the edge of her hat,

431

squinting into the sun to look up at him. "Yes, but what choice do they have if the law doesn't let them own claims in the mines?"

"They can own claims, Mrs. Matthews," he said in a deliberate voice, patronizingly slow. "They just need the approval of their fellow claim holders."

"Oh." This was news to her. It wasn't quite as Edwin had told it in his article. "So there are African miners?"

"Truthfully? Not many. The kaffirs who have hung on to their claims use them to traffic illicit diamonds stolen from Europeans. They pay our laborers to steal the diamonds they find, and salt their own claims with the stones so they can be recorded as legitimate. Your husband hasn't been a digger, so he can't be expected to understand. We estimate that over fifty percent of the diamonds leaving Kimberley are illicit. Anyway, I'm afraid that at the end of the day it makes little difference what your husband or I believe. The future is inevitable. Mining is not what it used to be. It takes greater resources than ever before to extract diamonds, and the days of the small claim holder, black or white, are over. They simply can't afford the new methods we're using. And the industry needs regulation — the strength of a few men to keep the market in check."

"Of course you would say that."

"Yes," he said, smiling suddenly at her, his jaw set to one side, his eyes locking onto hers. "It suits me, just as it suits your husband to have his point of view." Frances swallowed heavily, letting his gaze draw her in. For a moment she was right back in his cabin on the *Cambrian,* just the two of them, with the night unfolding ahead of them.

"And what about my shares?" Mariella asked, interrupting them and nudging Frances. "You're forgetting my fortune in the making. If it wasn't for men like Baier, there wouldn't be a stock market."

"Exactly. Not all of us, Mrs. Matthews, can afford to be as morally upstanding as your husband. Anyway," he said, shaking his head, "I don't want to talk to you about the politics of mining. It's horribly dull. I know something which will make you both happy."

He led them over to a scrawny white boy who was churning ice cream, and he paid for two double scoops of chocolate in cones. It was cold and deliciously creamy. "You know, it's worth remembering that Baier didn't have it easy either. This is how he started out, selling ice cream to the diggers. There wasn't a chance in a million that he'd make it as far as he has done." They licked their cones, and he led them back into town, to a wooden-framed building with a large sign overhead which read BAIER DIAMOND SORTING. There was a guard at the door, who nodded to William in recognition and let them pass through.

Inside were two long trestle tables. At one were seven natives, well dressed in collared shirts. Each man had a kind of trowel to help him sort through the piles of gravel. At the other were seated in a row five white men in matching shirts and waistcoats, picking through a heap of small stones. There was a shout from one. He rolled a diamond out of the pile. William bent down and plucked it from the table with some tweezers.

"Of course it hasn't been cleaned yet," he said, holding it up so it caught the light from the windows. It was a deep, clear green, the color of a lake. "Once the diamonds are assorted they're sent under armed escort to the valuators. There they are boiled in nitric and sulfuric acids to clean them of impurities. Then they are classified by size, color, and purity."

"Which is the most valuable color?"

Mariella asked, her eyes riveted to the stone.

"The pure white and the deep orange. But they come in all colors — brown, green, pink, yellow, hazel."

"And what was the largest diamond ever found here?" Mariella asked.

"There was a rough stone which weighed four hundred and twenty-eight carats."

"How large was it?" Frances asked.

"Two inches at the longest point."

"And did they manage to sell it?"

"Of course! The Maharaja of Patiala saw it in Paris and couldn't resist it.

"Look," he said, pointing to the men at the sorting table. "The natives here are wearing good clothes. They speak English and they earn respectable wages. We run a meritocracy of sorts. Those who are good at their work help us in the sorting office. Here they are free from tribal codes, some of which are unspeakably brutal. They earn salaries, and in terms of their tribesmen still living out on the plains or in the mountains, they are rich. We are bringing money to the native people of South Africa. We still have a long way to go, but it would be difficult to deny that these men are better off than they were before."

"And yet," Frances said, "they have no stake in the success of this country. The wealth remains yours."

"But you have to remember the risk is all ours as well. Baier has invested his life in these mines, and if it isn't a success he will be no better off than these natives."

She wanted to believe him. If Edwin was right, then there was too much injustice in Kimberley and it made criminals of everyone: William, the Fairleys — anyone who supported the industry.

Mariella wandered down between the tables to take a closer look, and William turned to Frances and touched her lightly on her forearm.

"You look pale." His fingers rested on the inside crease of her elbow.

"I haven't been well." She spoke with a gulping slowness, her whole being concentrated in the touch of his skin against hers. Everything else was forgotten. "But I'm better now."

"Did he look after you?" His eyes were kind, but they seemed to know too much. She had no protection when she was with him.

"Yes."

"And if he doesn't you'll come and find me?"

"Yes. And William" — she said his name delicately, enjoying the feel of it on her tongue — "thank you. For the rug, and the soaps."

"You like them?"

"Very much."

He smiled and withdrew his hand, and Frances saw Mariella making her way back to them.

"Why are you so determined not to invest?" she asked Edwin later that evening. He was writing in his diary at the table.

"We don't have any money," he said, as if it might have escaped her notice.

"We could borrow. Everyone else does." Hundreds of people in Kimberley were making their fortunes on the stock market every day, and she and Edwin had scarcely two pennies to put together.

He turned back to his diary.

"It doesn't have to be a long-term investment."

"I don't believe in buying on credit," he said, not looking up.

"Why do you always have to be better than everyone else?" she asked, exasperated. "Maybe other people are right. Maybe, for once, there's nothing wrong with making some money."

He put down his pen and looked at her. "Do you have any idea where you would like to invest?"

"Mariella gave me a copy of the *Diamond News*. Look at this." She passed it to him. It was an article on the launch of a new mining company, with shares available from Ebden Street on the following day. The journalist had interviewed a man from the telegraph office who said that the Rothschilds in London had sent a telegram requesting the purchase of two hundred shares. It was one of Baier's companies, and William had confirmed it was sound.

"So you want to borrow money and put it into the Du Toit's Diamond Company?"

"Why not?"

"Do you know who has the largest controlling interest in the *Diamond News*?"

She looked at him in frustration. It was typical of Edwin to try to teach her something. "Does it make any difference?"

"It does when the owner is Joseph Baier."

"Don't be ridiculous," she scoffed, shaking her head. "Everyone would know about it."

"Not necessarily. He is a silent investor. He wants the paper to maintain the semblance of independence. It would ruin things if everybody knew."

"Even if he is, what difference does it make?" He looked at her wryly. "Edwin!

Not everything in this world is a conspiracy. What about the telegram from the Rothschilds? Are you going to tell me that was made up?"

"Possibly."

"Once again, Edwin Matthews against the rest of the world," she said, slipping into sarcasm.

"Frances, this isn't just an issue of principle. I don't believe the stock market is resilient enough to cope with an epidemic." His gray eyes settled on hers. "Have you thought about your father's investments in Northern Pacific? He made an impulsive decision, and it ended up costing him everything he had."

"How dare you bring up my father." She stood up, her voice seething. "You barely knew him."

Edwin sighed, as if he was exhausted by her. "Does everything always have to be a battle? I made a simple point. I didn't say it to upset you. I said it because it is the truth."

TWENTY-NINE

The Theatre Royale was packed. She could hear the rabble from halfway down the street. Edwin had told her to stay at home, leaving a native *askari* to guard the tent, but she needed to hear what he had to say. She had to know how bad things were, and whether he had any support from others. It was dark by the time she arrived, and the windows of the building were glowing with light. She could hear the jeers and shouts of the crowd inside, and her husband's voice projecting over them. She pushed her way into the back of the hall. The air was warm and fetid with the breath of so many men, and they shifted against each other restlessly. She caught sight of Edwin on the stage and felt suddenly nervous for him. It took courage to stand up there in front of all these people.

"Men are dying in droves. I have seen a hundred corpses myself."

A man shouted, "White men or natives?"
"Natives."

There was a burst of laughter.

"But Europeans are starting to be infected by the disease. If we are to contain the epidemic we need to start isolating, quarantining, and vaccinating."

He was interrupted by a heckling voice. "Tell us, Doctor Matthews." The man elongated the word "doctor" for sarcastic emphasis. "Why, when every respectable doctor in Kimberley tells us this disease is pemphigus, do you insist on calling it smallpox?"

A few men shouted their approval.

"I have experience with smallpox," Edwin said, trying to talk over them. "There have been clear cases —"

"Have you ever seen a clear case of pemphigus, Dr. Matthews?"

Edwin paused. "No. But the medical journals are clear that —" He was drowned out by a laughing roar from the crowd.

"Gentlemen!" A man shouted to them, jumping up onto the stage. "Are you aware that this man has been disinterring bodies from our graveyard, and dissecting them for his practices?" The hall fell silent in superstitious horror.

"Dr. Matthews, is it true?" a voice called

from the crowd.

"Only once, where I felt a case needed to be proven."

The man on stage cried out, "And did you find smallpox on the body in question? It was a young English girl, I believe."

"Not in that instance, no."

"I know what kind of man you are," he said, spitting his words at Edwin. "You despise our community, and will do everything you can to destroy it." Frances saw that he was brandishing an old newspaper, rolled up into a baton. He addressed the crowd from the stage. "Shopkeepers, innkeepers, hoteliers, traders, hawksmen, diamond dealers, miners — you are all here today to try to better understand whether this community is under threat. Well, let me tell you, it *is* under threat. But not from smallpox. It is threatened by this man." He pointed at Edwin. "He wants you to believe that we are in the midst of an epidemic, because he knows it will destroy the industry upon which we rely. Foreign investors will pull out of the mining companies, diggers will go bankrupt, your shares will be valueless, and your livelihoods destroyed. Why would he do this? Let me quote to you from an article Dr. Matthews wrote for a London paper when he lived among us two years ago."

The man unfurled the newspaper and began reading:

"Kimberley is a filthy, debauched place where extortion is a way of life. The diamond mines disgust me. Every other type of mine in the world produces goods of some intrinsic value to mankind, whether it is coal, tin, copper, or lead. But to extract from the earth at the cost of millions of pounds, and for the wealth of a few men, these tiny crystals — just for the gratification of female vanity — shows a lust for ornamentation which is not far off barbarism."

Uproar broke out in the hall. Edwin reached out his hand to still the crowd; tried to raise his voice above their roar. Something flew out from the audience and struck the breast of his coat. He wiped the mess away, but another struck him on the face. Eggs. Yolk ran down his cheek into his mouth. A cheer went up. Then a book was thrown. It missed him, but another caught him a glancing blow on his forehead. He staggered and stepped backwards. The air was a blur of missiles. Men scrambled forward onto the stage. She tried to keep sight of Edwin, but there were too many people in the way.

She thought with a leap of horror — they want to kill him. She tried to push her way out of the hall but lost her balance in the crush forward, falling into a man wearing a felt cap. He looked at her and cried, "That's his wife!" It was the Cornish miner who lived opposite them. She didn't know the man next to him, who stopped and spat at her. Wet saliva slid down her cheek. She pushed away from them, ducking under the arms of other people until she was at the door and out into the street.

She ran until she was sure there was no one behind her, then stood wiping the spit off her face with her sleeve. Her hand was shaking. Should she try to wait for Edwin? No, it was better to head home before the men started to leave the theater. Then it occurred to her that if he did get away, they might follow him back to their tent, or go there now and wait for him. Where else could she go? There was William. He understood the situation Edwin was in. He had influence and he had offered his help. She needed it now.

She didn't know where he lived, but the note which had come with the presents he sent had been written on headed paper from the Kimberley Club. There was a good chance he would be there. It was on the better side of town, further on from the baths where she had gone with Mariella.

She hurried past private, gated red brick houses, pausing once to ask directions from a well-dressed man, who looked at her askance when she tried to stop him. She had to ask him twice before he pointed her on. Ornate turrets could be seen between the tips of blue gum trees. The streets were unlit, but each house had a gas lamp above its door and they cast a thin light on gardens bursting with eucalyptus, pine trees, and orchards. There was the sound of running water and the deep croaking of frogs, and behind it the grating of cicadas. This was a world away from the sprawl of canvas on the other side of town. Eventually she came to the Kimberley Club. It was a stately two-story red brick building with large gates. Outside were two hansom cabs, with uniformed servants polishing their brass fenders. Frances stepped up the path, which was flanked on either side by an immaculately trimmed, iridescent green lawn. It must have needed more water in a day than she and Edwin lived on in a week. Everything here told of a different world, one she no longer had access to but which could provide safety and a refuge if only she was allowed inside. She stepped up onto the wide veranda. Three ladies were standing in a group, watching her with curiosity. They were spotless in white dresses, trimmed with lace and ribbons.

"Can I help?" the manager asked at the door.

Frances straightened her black wool bodice. "I am looking for Mr. Westbrook."

"He isn't here, Madam," the man replied.

"Are you sure?"

"Absolutely." He was polite but firm, waiting for her to leave.

"It's a matter of urgency," Frances persisted. "Do you know where I might find him?"

"I have no idea, Madam."

"Excuse me."

Frances turned. One of the ladies had stepped forward to speak to her. She held a spaniel by a lead. "Did you say you were looking for Mr. Westbrook?" Frances nodded. "Have you tried Mrs. Whitley's?"

Another of the ladies laughed, a small, tinkling sound. These were the croquet-badminton-playing women Mariella had talked about. There was something surreal about their staid calm. They were too perfect-looking, like mechanical dolls imported straight from England not yet out of their wrapping. She might have known them in London, but here she was a kind of novelty, and they could barely bring themselves to talk to her.

"Where might I find her?" Frances asked, and the lady with the spaniel walked into the street with her, and pointed out the way. As she raised her arm, Frances caught a waft of bergamot. Her gloves gleamed white in the dark.

"You can't miss it," the woman said. "It's made of limed timber, imported from Scandinavia. You'll know it by the music. She's rather partial to a bit of piano.

"Good luck," she called after Frances. And she heard their laughter again, like a taunt, following her out into the street.

As she walked, she tried not to panic. William would tell her what to do. He was good in a disaster. He had helped her during the storm on the *Cambrian,* and he would have an idea now about how she could bring this situation under control. She was walking quickly towards the outskirts of town. There were fewer houses, and barely any light spilled onto the road. Occasionally, she glanced behind her, but there was no one following. Any other night and she would have turned back, but she was desperate. She had to see him.

There was music up ahead: the ribald playing of a jaunty tune on the piano, accompanied by strong male voices. A wooden house stood all on its own on a patch of earth. Outside a horse was dozing, harnessed to a cart.

A woman stood at the door wearing a scarlet gypsy dress with white petticoats and a plunging neckline. She smoked her cigarette and looked at Frances with the disdain of a real-life Carmen.

"Is this Mrs. Whitley's?" Frances asked her, stepping up onto the veranda.

The woman was much older than she had seemed at a distance. The paleness of her face had been pasted over a crumple of wrinkled skin, and her mouth, which from afar had the perfect, curving roundness of a plum, was a painted red gash.

She ignored Frances and, putting her head round the door, shouted inside, "Girl here wants to know if this is Mrs. Whitley's."

"Tell her it depends if she's willing," a man shouted.

The woman curled her head back round the door and looked at Frances. "Are you?" She raised her painted eyebrows.

"Am I what?"

"Willing?"

Frances didn't say anything. "She's not sure," the woman called back into the room.

"Are you Mrs. Whitley?" Frances asked, disliking being baited.

"The very same," the woman said in her deadpan voice. The piano inside stopped, and a gentleman shouted, "Bring her in! Let's have a look at her."

The woman nudged the door open with the toe of a heeled boot, and Frances stepped inside. It looked like a bar, not a sitting room, and Frances knew immediately that she shouldn't have come. Shabby velvet curtains hung across the window, and a group of men were gathered at a round table in the middle of the room, drinking and playing cards. The man nearest her was small and lean, and he had a girl on his lap. Her skirts had been pulled up to reveal a slab of white thigh, and his hand, which curled around her waist, was kneading the soft expanse of skin. No wonder the ladies at the club had laughed.

"Goodness me," the man said, looking up, his face breaking into a smile. She saw with a twinge of horror that it was Daniel Leger, William's friend from the *Cambrian*. "If it isn't Miss Irvine. It's been a long time since Mrs. Whitley had a piece of business as good as yours." He didn't shift the girl from his lap, and she nuzzled her face into his neck, her cropped, dark hair brushing the front of his jacket. He was the last person in the world Frances wanted to see. He knew about her affair with William and would draw conclusions. She looked back at the door, wondering if she ought to leave. Everyone's attention was riveted on her.

Finally, she nodded at him. "Mr. Leger." Then she said in a stiff voice, "I was trying to find Mr. Westbrook."

One of the men thumped the table with his fist. "Well, I'll be damned. If she isn't a proper lady!"

"Please. It's urgent."

"So is his business here," one of the men quipped in a low voice.

"How can I help?" Mrs. Whitley asked, coming inside. The door swung shut behind her, and as if on cue, the piano started up again. The men went back to their cards. Frances turned to leave.

"You're looking for Mr. Westbrook?" the woman asked.

"No. I mean, yes, I was, but not anymore." She could feel herself blushing.

The woman looked at her appraisingly. "Can I ask what business you have with Mr. Westbrook?"

"It's of a private nature."

"It always is with Westbrook," Mr. Leger said. He had returned to the card game but kept glancing at Frances. One of his hands pulled at the fabric of the girl's dress, working his fingers down into her bosom.

"Please," Frances said, looking away. "Don't trouble him."

"Hold on," Mrs. Whitley said, putting a hand on her elbow. Frances hesitated. A tall colored girl had appeared in the doorway to the right of her. She had skin the color of chocolate cream, with sloping, brown eyes. She was dressed in a gown, with bare feet, and her hair fell down below her shoulders. She looked tousled, sleepy, and very young.

Mrs. Whitley said a few words to the girl, and she slipped back through the door. A moment later, William stepped out. He held a cigar in one hand and the hand of the girl in the other. Frances looked at him, her face coloring.

"Frances," he said, surprised. He handed his cigar to the girl, who disappeared inside with it, and took a step towards her, but she had already turned away from him, walking quickly out of the door and back down the street. A few seconds later she heard the swell of music behind her as the door opened then slammed shut.

"What is it?" William asked when he had caught up with her, buttoning up his shirt with one hand. She kept walking, too mortified to speak. The cart followed behind them. It must have been waiting for him to leave.

"Is everything all right?" He put his hand on her arm, and pulled her to a stop. "Frances, please, what's wrong?"

She stood facing him. Everything was wrong. She realized that she had wanted to find him as much to comfort her as to ask for his help. And now she felt foolish. He was oblivious to how desperate the situation was with Edwin. He existed in a different world, and she was an idiot for thinking he would understand.

She turned away from him, but he caught hold of her wrist.

"Let go of me," she hissed.

"Not until you tell me why you came here."

She looked at him. "I thought you might be able to help me, but I made a mistake."

He ignored the bitterness in her voice. "Help you with what?"

"It doesn't matter."

"Yes it does," he said gently, and she felt the fight draining out of her. She needed him to say that he still cared. Nothing else mattered, not even the thought that she might have landed herself on him and now he had to pretend concern; nor the fact that she had found him in a whorehouse. She felt safe when she was with him. Edwin always asked too much of her, but William wanted to protect her. He took her hand, and she let him bundle her onto the cart. "We'll go to my house. It's quiet there, and you can tell me everything."

His house was just off Market Square. It was small and simple but clean and warm inside, made of timber, not the usual corrugated iron, with walls and ceilings clad in boards. "I didn't want one of those fancy new red brick houses out of town," he said, shutting the door behind them. "I wanted to be in the thick of things."

The sitting room had large windows on either side of the fireplace, the curtains were drawn, and there were two deep armchairs pulled up in front of the fire. He sat her down, drew a blanket onto her lap, and called to his boy, who brought bread, cheese, and hot lamb pie. She was famished suddenly, and felt her anxiety easing away as she sank into the warm fug of the room. He sat, sipping a glass of scotch, watching her eat.

"So," he said finally, when the boy had

taken away her plate, "do you want to tell me why you were wandering all over Kimberley on your own after dark?"

"I'm concerned about my husband."

"Did he hold that meeting at the Theatre Royale?"

She nodded. "It was awful."

"He didn't bring you along, did he?"

"No. I went alone. I wanted to see it for myself."

"Well, you're a fool. Christ knows what could have happened to you."

"I thought they were going to kill him."

"I don't think they'll kill him, but he might ruin any prospect of a decent life for the two of you. You've tried to stop him?"

She nodded. "He doesn't listen to me."

"He hasn't any sense. It is pure selfishness to ruin you both. If you were mine, I wouldn't risk you for a second." There was a silence. A log cracked, throwing out sparks, and William kicked a hot coal back into the grate.

"I was wondering if perhaps you could talk to Baier? Tell him to at least listen to Edwin. You're his cousin. Perhaps you could influence him."

William drew his hand over his face and sighed. "Are you aware that there isn't a single doctor in Kimberley, other than your husband, who has seen a case of the pox? And, believe me, they've been looking. Do you know what's at stake if we are seen to be taking him seriously? The whole industry could collapse. That doesn't just mean the end of Baier, it means people, real people, will suffer — miners, shopkeepers, natives — anyone who makes a living out of these mines. If the stock market collapses, it will be nothing short of a disaster."

"But I know Edwin — he isn't capable of deceit."

"You might not know him as well as you think. Did you know that they are accusing him of making money out of the whole affair? He writes his articles and gives his speeches and, inevitably, there are men and women who listen. They are terrified by his stories, and they come to him afterwards to be vaccinated. They say he is charging extortionate amounts for the vaccine." He paused. "You know yourself that he hates these mines. God knows why he insists on staying here."

She shook her head. "He isn't driven by making money. Besides, you've seen the way we're living. He doesn't have a penny."

William looked at her. Was she being naive? "He's in a tight spot, Frances. There isn't anyone who doesn't need something to live on."

She let her head rest against the soft back of the armchair and shut her eyes for a second, relishing the quiet warmth of the room. She didn't think Edwin was like most people. He was determined enough to take them both over the precipice into penury, if he hadn't already.

"Of course, it's not entirely about the money." William was rubbing a hand over his beard. "Your husband has a lot of pride. He didn't like being sent away from Kimberley by Baier. It's possible he isn't thinking clearly."

"You're saying this could be some kind of revenge against Baier?"

"Perhaps. And there could be other reasons."

She glanced at him and saw that there was a slight smile on his lips.

"What do you mean?"

"Well, he must know about us."

"No," she said, shaking her head slowly.

"Frances, everyone knows everything about everyone at the Cape."

Was it possible Edwin had known about William all this time and not said anything? The thought made Frances sick. What must he think of her?

William kept talking. "If he could suggest

Baier was covering up an epidemic, it would be a scandal. Everyone in England would know about it. Baier's political prospects would be ruined, not to mention the state of his finances. And naturally that wouldn't leave me in a very good position."

"But when they find out it isn't smallpox?"

"I imagine your husband will be hoping a rumor is enough. Once foreign investors hear the word 'smallpox,' they'll pull their finance, as will the thousands who have invested in the stock market. Baier would be bankrupt. Then there's the labor market. The natives have a mortal fear of smallpox. So much as mention the disease and they'll be out of here. Think what that will do to confidence in the market."

Frances felt the power of William's argument. It wasn't impossible that Edwin was fanatical enough to try to bring down Baier. Certainly if he knew about her affair with William, then that would explain his almost suicidal decision to stay in Kimberley. "What if you're right?" she asked, staring into the fire. "What kind of man does that make him?"

"Not necessarily a bad one," William replied. "Just misguided."

It made sense. Edwin hated Baier, and he hated the mines. This was an effective way of sabotaging both. She stood up to go. There was nothing William could do to help her, and it was best if she went home. He didn't stand up when she did. She pulled her shawl off the back of the chair. "Thank you, William, for all you have done."

He reached forward suddenly, taking hold of her hand. "I don't want you to go back there." His skin had a rough warmth. He rubbed his thumb over the inside of her palm, and she wanted nothing more than to curl up against him.

"What choice do I have?" She thought about the cold, stark tent with its stench of filth, of Edwin's anger and determination, and, worst of all, saying good-bye to William. Once she left this house she would never come back.

He let her hand slide through his until he was holding just the tips of her fingers. "What if you stayed here with me?"

She gave a bitter, nervous laugh.

"I can't bear the thought of you going back to him. Matthews is too wrapped up in his own ambition. He won't be there to look after you. And besides, this is all partly my fault."

"It's not your fault. I knew perfectly well what I was doing."

"Did you, though?" He looked at her with

a slight smile, and she felt the blood rush to her cheeks.

"I want to make amends if you'll let me."

"There is nothing you can do now which will help me."

"Perhaps there is," he said, pulling her down onto his lap so that they were very close suddenly, her legs between his. She didn't fight it. His arms circled over hers and took hold of her wrists. She let her head fall into his shoulder, giving in for a moment to the pleasure of being held by him. "Frances, there is something I haven't told you," he continued in a low, warm voice. "I'm leaving soon, to go to Johannesburg."

She sat up, looking at him. "What's in Johannesburg?"

"Gold. They've discovered the largest reefs in Africa. There's more gold there than they ever found in California, and there's barely anyone mining it."

"Well, that's wonderful for you," she said, trying to stand up, but he closed his arms around hers, pulling her back down. "You don't understand. I want you to come with me."

She stared at him, her heart quickening. "To Johannesburg?"

"No one will know you there. We can make a fresh start."

"What about Baier?"

He shrugged. "We've quarreled. He treats me like his messenger boy, always giving me his dirty work. He has me on an allowance and monitors my spending. He thinks I can't keep a handle on my outgoings. What does it matter, when my work in the mines more than pays for what I spend?" His voice was flecked with anger. "Anyway, it was his idea for me to go north. He wants someone he can trust to buy up claims. But it won't all be for him. I have money of my own that he doesn't know about."

"But, of course, he won't approve of me."

"You don't understand, Frances. I've grown up. I don't care anymore what he thinks. Besides, Baier is desperate to get rid of me. He thinks I need a dose of hard work to cool my enthusiasm for life. He's bored with my restlessness and he wants to see me settled."

She knew she should put an end to the conversation — it was nothing but fantasy — but she couldn't help herself. "And Edwin?"

"Matthews has too much pride to cause any trouble. I'm sure he'll let you go. What does he want with a wife when he has so many campaigns to fight?"

"What do you want with a wife?"

"I adore you, Frances. I can't live without you." He lifted up one of her hands and covered the inside of her wrist with kisses. She laughed at his exuberance, pulling it away. "This is a dream, William. A ridiculous dream. It could never happen."

"Why not?" he asked, drawing her deeper into his lap and kissing her on her forehead, on her nose, and once, very quickly, on her mouth. "I'm good at making things happen. Everything is in place. All I need is for you to say yes."

She didn't want to think about what he was asking. All she wanted was for him to kiss her again, but she was scared that he might, and that if he did she might never bring herself to stand up and leave. She pulled away from him, trying to think clearly about what he was asking. She wanted to let herself believe in him, but now that the moment had come she wasn't sure she could trust him. How well did she know him, after all?

"And the girl you were with earlier?"

He laughed. "I'm not a married man yet, Frances, and I'm far from perfect. You'll have to forgive past indiscretions."

"You'll soon get bored of me."

"Well, you'll just have to work very hard at making sure I don't." She looked at him sternly, and he laughed and said, "How could I ever be bored of you?"

"How do I know I can trust you?"

He held one of her hands and looked at her intently. His face was serious. "You don't, Frances. There is no way of telling. That's the whole point of trust — it requires faith. But I promise to look after you." He squeezed her hand. "You will benefit from my every success. I will make sure you have your own servants, horses, a good house. You will never want for anything."

"Do you remember that afternoon on the *Cambrian* when we played blindman's buff?" she asked suddenly. It was the last time she had been truly happy. "Why couldn't life always be like that?"

"It can be, my love. You just have to have the courage to give it a chance." He tried to kiss her, but she moved her head away. Her mind was filled suddenly with a picture of Edwin being mobbed by the crowd in the Theatre Royale. What if he had been seriously hurt? And if he wasn't, surely he would be worried about her. She needed to know that he was all right, and she wanted to find out if the things William had said were true.

"But you do love me, don't you?" William was demanding. His voice was petulant.

She looked at him. His black hair fell down over his forehead, and his green eyes shone with a roguish self-belief. He was too persuasive. He held such power over her. She wanted to trust him, but she needed time to think.

"Please, William. Let me go," she said, twisting out of his grip and standing up. He stood up with her and putting his hand on her jaw pulled her chin round so she was looking at him. Tears streamed down her cheeks. "Yes, I love you," she said, as if it had been forced out of her.

He kissed her on the forehead and called to his boy to take her home in the cart.

There were no men lurking outside the tent with rifles and pitchforks, as she had worried there might be. She walked into the quiet yard and saw, with relief, Edwin sitting just inside the tent, writing a letter. He had changed his shirt. He looked up when she came in. The skin had been scraped off his cheek, and one eye was closing up. A dark bruise, like dirty fingerprints, smudged the skin. The *askari* was squatting in the yard, cradling his gun. Edwin didn't ask her where she had been. She sat in a chair, staring at her hands while he wrote. Her heart was thudding. There were too many alternative truths pounding through her mind, and she needed to find out which ones were certain.

"You're hurt," she stated eventually.

"It's not serious," he said, glancing up briefly from his letter. Silence dragged out between them.

After a few minutes, she said, "Edwin, do you truly believe there is smallpox in Kimberley?"

He put down his pen, folded the letter, and slipped it into an envelope. She had his full attention now. His hands were folded in his lap and his eyes seemed very cold. "I'm surprised you should have to ask."

"There are rumors that you are making a profit out of selling the vaccine."

"Do you believe them?"

"It's hard for me to know what to think," she said uneasily. "You are always so closed."

He looked at her, waiting for her to say more. She was wary of him, but finally she said, "Either way, I think it's wrong to keep on trying to prove it."

"Why?"

"Because Baier will have you killed if you don't stop. Because smallpox will be a disaster for Kimberley. Because I don't think I can stand much more of this."

"Smallpox is a disaster for Kimberley,

whether I have anything to do with it or not."

"Why this stubbornness? Why won't you listen to me?"

"Why do you think?" he asked, looking at her intently.

"Because you blame me," she said, staggering through the words, "and bringing down Baier is the easiest way for you to get revenge."

The words had been said, and now they lay between them, ready to be grappled with. The words which would change everything.

"I blamed you, Frances, yes. I blamed you for being seduced by a man who any girl with an ounce of sense would have seen is a fraud. I blamed you for not being honest enough to tell me about it before we were married. I blamed you for continuing to love him when he had proved himself beyond any doubt. I blamed you for being naive enough to think the whole of the Cape wouldn't know of your indiscretion. But don't be conceited enough to think for a second that you are the reason I am here." He drew a hand over his eyes. "Christ, Frances. We are in the middle of an epidemic. I have seen ten men dead this morning, and you have the temerity to suggest that somehow my involvement is because of you? This obsession with yourself confounds even my familiarity with your condition."

She was speechless and sat staring at him, letting his words roll over her. There was something terrifying about Edwin when he felt liberated to tell the truth. He seemed to have more of it at his disposal than most people. He stood up, looking out into the yard, with his back to her. "I told myself to be patient. I said that in time you would grow up and take charge of your life. That you would stop looking to me to be somehow responsible for your happiness. That you would forget Westbrook and begin to see the merits of the life we were leading. It was frugal, but I thought it had its charms. But you were stubborn and slow to change. Still I thought I saw glimmers of hope. You began to paint, to walk, and to laugh more often. I hoped when we got to Cape Town you would put your old life aside and start again."

She wanted to say, Yes, you were right, I was ready to do that, but then you took me to Kimberley, but she couldn't speak.

"When I heard about smallpox in Kimberley, Mrs. Reitz offered to have you in the house at Rietfontein. But I wanted you to come with me. Is she capable, I thought, of rekindling a passion for Baier's cousin? I wanted to find out. I needed to know for sure if I could trust you." There was a pause, and he said with great bitterness. "And now I know."

"What do you know?"

"Don't think me a fool, Frances. I know where you were this evening."

"I went to him because I thought he could help."

"Help? How could William Westbrook possibly help?"

"I thought he might be able to persuade Baier to listen to you."

"Good God, you're naive!" Edwin gave a short, despairing laugh. "Well? Was he willing to talk to Baier?" She was silent, and he said, "And you asked for his help and left?"

She blushed, guiltily remembering the conversation between her and William, him holding her in his lap, his kisses, and her declaration of love. Then she rallied. After all, it wasn't entirely her fault. "You knew when you asked my uncle for my hand in marriage that I wasn't willing. You knew that I would be forced to say yes. Yet you asked for it anyway. You lured me into it, and you shouldn't blame me now if it hasn't been all you hoped it would be. I wasn't given a choice."

"Neither was I."

She looked at him sharply. "What do you mean?"

"Frances." He said her name almost tenderly, affectionately. "You are an intelligent girl, but the world is a more complex place than you have ever believed it to be. I can't protect you from it, as your father did." He looked at her for a moment, as if expecting her to grasp what he was about to say. "Has it never crossed your mind that your uncle may have written to me first?"

"Why would he have written to you?" Some truth was nagging at her, but she couldn't quite grasp it. "He called on my debt to your father's charity." Still it wasn't clear, though she felt the edges of its awfulness. "He asked me to take you off his hands."

She looked at him in confusion. The whole prism through which she viewed herself and him was changing, as if she were seeing him through the shifting patterns of a kaleidoscope.

"But you wanted to marry me. You loved me," she said, as if it were an incontrovertible fact. She thought back to their conversations in London. "You may not love me now, but I know you did then. You asked to marry me before my father died."

"I did," he said, as if it changed nothing, and she remembered finding her father with him that night in the drawing room, when he had been unwell. What had her father said to him? Had he known then about the crisis with Northern Pacific?

"Your father asked me to make sure you were looked after. I think he thought it would be better if you married me than went to live with one of your aunts." He passed his hands over his face. "Of course, it was impractical for me to bring you here, and I knew you would find it hard. I tried my best not to ask too much of you."

Her world was breaking into fragments. The sense had been drained out of things. Edwin wasn't at all the person she had thought he was. She had made him up, and he had gone along with her fiction. Why? Because he had wanted her to come to an understanding of her own accord. Because he had thought she would see things as they were, if she was given enough time.

"Frances." Edwin was talking to her. Every part of his face seemed crystal clear to her now, as if she were seeing it for the first time. The sharp cheekbones, the blond hair pushed back from the bruising that ran down one side of his face, and his clear, gray eyes, which looked at her as if he knew her better than she knew herself. She was watching him but couldn't focus on his words. She kept thinking, I haven't known you at all. You are a stranger to me.

"I have found someone to fund a hospital to manage the epidemic. I will be sleeping there from now on. They need me around the clock — at least until I can get government support for the project." He picked up the envelope and handed it to her. "Here is a letter for you to bring to Rietfontein. Mevrouw Reitz will take you in for a fee." Things were moving too fast. It was as if there was some invisible line beyond which their marriage ceased to exist, and she had unknowingly crossed it. She needed a chance to catch up with the truth, but he was already standing up. "You may be relieved to know that I have no wish to see you for some time. I shall be in Kimberley for at least six months. When it is over here, I will come to Rietfontein and we will discuss the future." He had it all planned out. He was banishing her. He put his diary into his canvas knapsack, and she realized he had already packed his things. She hadn't noticed before that his pile of books was gone from the shelf and his two bags were lined up at the entrance of the tent.

"I won't be going to Rietfontein," she said,

standing in front of him, trying to grasp control of the situation. "William has asked me to go to Johannesburg with him."

Edwin didn't even flinch. She thought she might see a flicker of pain cross his face, but there was nothing except perhaps disappointment. He sighed. "It is no longer my duty to protect you either from others or from yourself. Presumably you know what kind of man he is?" She had wanted to push him into anger, but he was talking to her as if he were a disinterested party, with just a touch of pity.

"I love him," she said with force, as if to admit no doubt.

"Then you're a fool," he said, more in dismay than anger.

"You have always treated me like a child!" she cried.

"Frances, you have always treated yourself like a child."

"You're jealous," she said, angry now. "He may not be as moral as you, but he is more human."

"The man who died here," Edwin said. "He was under their employment."

"And? It was an accident!" she said, her voice seething.

Edwin shook himself as if to throw off the conversation, swung his knapsack over one

471

shoulder, and picked up his bags.

"Where are you going?" she demanded.

"To the hospital. I am late already, and was only waiting for you to come home. I have asked Tom to watch over the tent this evening." He nodded to the *askari* in the yard. "I trust him. Tomorrow you should pack up your things and leave." He put a few banknotes down on the table. "If you decide to go to Rietfontein, I will forward what money I can." He walked out of the yard without a backward glance.

When he was gone, she sat down, her head buzzing. Her future was mapping itself out without her having made a decision one way or another. She was too wound up to try to sleep. She brought Mangwa closer to the entrance of the tent, tethering him on a long lead rope. The shape of him in the dark was reassuring. He was company of sorts. He stood, resting one hind leg, until at some point in the night he turned a circle and lay down at her feet with his neck outstretched in the dust. Occasionally, the *askari* shifted his weight and spat into the dirt. She sat huddled under two blankets until dawn broke, cold and icy. Mangwa rose instinctively in the pale light and shook himself. She fed him a few handfuls of oats and left.

She went to find Mariella to get her advice. She needed her sanction before she went to William. Two men were standing outside the Fairleys' room in quiet conversation. They looked up when she approached. One of the men she recognized as George Fairley. His face was drawn into tight lines of worry. The other, dressed in a grubby flannel suit, tilted his hat at her and gave her a crooked smile. It was Dr. Robinson. She could smell the whiskey on him from ten feet away.

"I am worried, Sir," George said, after greeting Frances. "She doesn't look well."

"I assure you, Mr. Fairley, that there is nothing to be concerned about. Pemphigus often looks worse than it is. She should make a full recovery. Of course, there is the child to be concerned about, but I have every hope that she will carry it."

"Is there any risk of contagion?" Frances asked him.

"No. There is no reason why you shouldn't see her." The doctor smiled generously at them both. "Now, Mr. Fairley, we said last time that you needn't pay me right away. Perhaps we could settle now?"

George took the doctor a little to one side. Frances heard him say, "If you could just wait until Friday, I'll have cash then."

"It's all in stocks, is it?" the doctor asked.

"Yes," George admitted. "I can show you the receipts." There was a rustling of paper.

"I'm afraid receipts are one thing and ready money is another."

"I can't get at it now," George said, with withering self-reproach. "The market's taken a bit of a dip."

"We'll leave it for today, but I'm afraid I shan't be able to see her again unless I can expect to be paid. I'm sure you understand."

"Can I see her?" Frances asked, when the doctor was gone.

George ushered her into the bedroom.

Mariella lay on her side, the sheet pulled in around the swelling of the baby. Her face and the backs of her hands were covered in a rash of flat, red spots. Some of those on her cheeks had swollen into white sacs, like the bodies of ticks. She opened her eyes when she heard them come in, and smiled, and Frances saw that her lips were covered in ulcers.

"I feel better than I did." She moved her mouth delicately around the words. "The fever, at least, has gone."

"How long have you been ill?" Frances asked, smoothing Mariella's hair out of her eyes. It had sealed itself in dark, wet lines against her face. She had only ever seen it teased into glossy ringlets, and it was a shock to see it lying flat and lank on the pillow. It gave her the appearance of an overgrown baby.

"A few days. The doctor says I will be all right."

"Of course you will," Frances said, but she was concerned. The rash itself didn't look as bad as the pictures she had seen of smallpox, but she didn't trust Dr. Robinson.

"Have you considered the possibility that it might be smallpox?" she asked George when they were outside.

He shook his head. "How can it be?" She remembered the vaccination office in Cape Town. Could you catch smallpox if you had been vaccinated? She remembered Edwin saying something about it corrupting in the heat.

"Initially, I thought it might be," he was saying, "but Dr. Robinson ruled out the possibility. He was very reassuring. He said the symptoms seemed similar but the disease would soon pass of its own accord. And, so far, he seems to be right. The fever has gone, and she is already feeling a little better."

"I think you should get a second opinion. Send for my husband. He will set your mind at rest." She grasped his hand. "Promise me you'll do it?"

He nodded, taking his hand back and smiling to reassure her. "Of course."

She went to William then. It was late morning by the time she knocked at his door, and his boy let her in. She sat in the armchair and waited, trying not to rehearse what she would say because every time she got to the part where she asked him if she could stay, her heart started thudding uncontrollably. Would he really be happy to see her when he realized she had nowhere else to go? His proposal had been made on the spur of the moment. He might have changed his mind. Periodically, she heard voices outside, but they always passed by. She waited all day, watching the sun shift across the floor until it had slipped behind the house and the windows grew dark. The boy seemed to have forgotten her. He didn't draw the curtains or light the fire. It was very quiet, and evening drew on. When it got to nine o'clock, she was hungry and anxious and had almost given up hope of him coming home. Perhaps he had already left for Johannesburg.

Then she heard voices outside. She recognized William's deep laugh. The door was thrown open, and it crashed against the wall. In walked Leger, followed by William. It took a moment for them to see her in the darkness. Leger spotted her first and said quietly, "Hey, hey, look what the cat dragged in."

She stood up awkwardly, and saw William turn and lock eyes with her. She wanted Leger to be gone and for it just to be the two of them and for him to say he was glad she had come.

Leger swung himself down in the chair opposite hers, grinning at her and stuffing his pipe.

William took her hand without speaking and led her through a door on the far side of the room. He lit a candle. There was a simple double bed, and he sat her down on it.

"Are you here to stay?" he asked, looking down at her.

"If you'll let me," she said softly.

He grinned at her wolfishly. "I'll let you." Then he said, "Leger and I have some business to settle. You'd best wait here."

She waited a few moments, sitting stiffly on the bed, listening to the murmur of their voices. When it was clear he wasn't coming through any time soon, she unlaced her boots and lay back on the deep feather pillows at the head of the bed. She blew out the candle. Moonlight filtered through the small window. If only Leger hadn't been here. She disliked the way he looked at her, as if he knew what she was. It made her feel cheap and worthless. There was a plaid woolen blanket at the end of the bed, and she pulled it over her knees. She woke some time later, groggy with sleep and still alone in the room. There were footsteps on the boards in the sitting room, and the low voice of a native. When he had gone, she heard Leger laughing, then shortly afterwards he left as well.

The bedroom door opened and William came in, without a lamp. She saw the dark bulk of him in the dark. He sat down on the bed. She pushed herself up into a sitting position and rubbed the sleep out of her eyes.

He watched her, nudging the hair off her forehead with the tips of his fingers. Her blood beat high and fast in her throat. When he didn't say anything, she asked, "Are you glad?"

"Glad?" He looked at her for a moment then leant forward and kissed her. The smell of wood smoke was caught in the folds of his shirt. His tongue flickered across her upper lip. Then he pulled back. "Shouldn't you have changed for bed?"

"I wasn't sure if I would be staying. All my things are still in the tent."

"Still" — he said, looking at her. She could just make out his eyes in the dark — "it's no excuse for not undressing." He tipped her chin up with one finger and began undoing the high collar of her black bodice, easing open the buttons from her throat down to the last one at her waist. She tried to kiss him when he had finished, but he shook his head then undid the buttons at each sleeve and drew her arms through, letting the bodice drop back onto the bed. His fingers trailed along the line of her collarbone until they found the eyes at the top of her corset. He unhooked them one by one then slipped her out of it. With each layer he took off came the residues of her old life. He stood her up, and she raised her arms like a child and let him slide her chemise over her head, shivering as the cotton brushed over her breasts. She was glad that there was little light. He wouldn't see the graying fabric, nor — when he got to them — her torn flannel petticoats. He untied her skirts and stepped her out of them. Finally, he pulled down her drawers until she stood completely naked in front of him. Then he kissed her delicately, searchingly, and drew her down onto the bed.

They lay together in a tangled knot of sheets. William lit a candle and produced a small stone from his hand. He held it up to the light. It was about the size of a large pearl, with uneven edges. He unfurled one of her hands and pressed the stone into her palm. "For you," he said, smiling at her. "Not quite a ring, but the sentiment is the same."

She felt uncomfortable taking it, lying there naked next to him. It was as if he was paying her for what they had just done. And then she realized that of course this was the way it was going to be: her always feeling indebted to him, doubting him, and worrying that she had to rely on him for everything. She handed it back to him, and he laughed, propping himself up on one elbow.

She shook her head. "I don't want it."

"What do you want then, Frances?"

She thought for a moment. "Anything?" she asked.

"Anything."

She smiled. "Something to eat?"

He gave a roar of laughter. "You've not had supper?"

"Nor lunch."

"How long were you waiting for me?"

"Most of the day."

He stalked naked to the bedroom door, opened it, and bellowed to his boy.

"What happened with Matthews?" he asked, coming back into the room.

She shrugged. She didn't want to have to explain about the hospital. "He let me go."

The boy knocked on the door, and William got up and took the tray from him. There was a tureen of soup and a loaf of bread. He sat on the floor, pulling her down next to him, along with a heap of sheets, so she was propped up against the bed with her hair falling about her knees. She ate hungrily. The soup was mulligatawny, thick and hot with a deep spiciness, and the butter dripped off the bread down her fingers. She was starving and ate with intent, aware of him watching her closely. He took the tray away before she was finished.

"You can have the rest later," he said, burying his head in her neck, under her hair. He groaned. "I can't bear to look at you without touching you." She smelt the sweet sweat of him, and the salty heat of the chillies was in her mouth. The sheets felt cool and strange, and his hands were warm against her skin. His fingers began exploring her again, touching the soft, hidden places of her body, pulling at the sheet until it fell down around her waist, and she laughed, turning to get away from him, but he pinned her down, kissing her soft belly. His lips moved down between her thighs, his beard brushing against the smoothness of her skin until his tongue, like the flick of a knife, unlocked a sudden, sweet pleasure inside her.

The next morning she woke before he did and wriggled her arm out from under his chest. She wanted to get dressed before he woke up, but he snatched at her hand as she was slipping out of bed and pulled her back down again. "Wait," he said, and the next minute the door had opened. She pulled the sheets over her head, but her hair spilled out from under them. The boy left tea, hot toast, and muffins. When he was gone, William pulled back the sheet and grinned at her. Sunlight streamed between gaps in the curtains. She smiled shyly at him.

"What do you call him, the boy?" she asked.

"Halfwit."

She laughed, unsure. "You're not serious?"

"Perfectly." He smiled at her disapproval. "What? There's too little humor in Kimberley. And besides, it's not as if he knows what it means."

"But still . . ." she said, frowning in distaste.

"Frances, one thing you should know about me is I don't do disapproval. I don't judge others, and in return I don't expect to be judged. Now," he said, giving her a gentle push, "I'm desperate for a cup of tea." She tried to take the sheet with her, but he pulled at a corner of it, and she was left standing naked. He smiled at her, watching her pad across the room. She could feel her breasts swinging and her hair shifting across her back. She blushed when she bent down to place a cup beside his bed. He pushed open the sheets and took her in against the warmth of his body, curling her into him.

"Do you think this is entirely appropriate?" he asked, holding out her left hand. She was still wearing her wedding ring. He held her finger up to his mouth, flicked his tongue over the ring, then slid it over her knuckle. He dropped it into the teacup, and she laughed.

"Are there problems with the stock market?" she asked after a moment, thinking about George Fairley's conversation with Dr. Robinson.

"Nothing we need to worry about," he

said, murmuring into the skin on her shoulder. "I've sold all my stock."

"But the market isn't doing as well as it was?"

"It's down a little."

"Because of fears of smallpox?" she asked.

He laughed. "No, not because of smallpox. Matthews has so far failed to sell the idea of an epidemic. The market's a little nervous, that's all."

They lay in silence, his breath falling warm against her shoulder, until she asked, "When do you think we can leave?"

"Not for ten days or so. In the meantime, you should stay in the house." His fingers tiptoed down the crease of her underarm, and along the soft fold of her waist. "Can you bear ten days as my prisoner?"

"How do I know you'll look after me?" she gulped.

"I'm not sure I will." His hand brushed across the top of her buttocks, and her spine tightened with pleasure. "I intend to take complete advantage of you."

William left her £5 and kissed her goodbye. "You'll take the diamond, Frances," he said as he left, placing it on the small table in the sitting room. "I like people who look after themselves."

"William?" she called after him when he was almost out of the door. "The zebra we brought from Rietfontein. He's tethered up in the yard. If we leave him there, Edwin will sell him. Do you think we can keep him?"

He smiled at her. "Of course. I'll tell the boy to fetch him."

When he was gone, she wrote out a letter to George enclosing the £5 note. She wouldn't have any chance to spend it herself in Kimberley, and Mariella would need it more than her. Then she put her wedding ring in an envelope and began writing a letter to enclose with it. She wanted to explain to Edwin everything which she had felt since she had come to South Africa, but after a few sentences she realized that her need for his understanding was inappropriate, and she tore up what she had begun. It was too late now for reconciliation, and she sealed the envelope without a note. She gave the letters to the boy to carry. In the afternoon he came back with Mangwa and her trunk with all her things. The zebra was tethered in the yard. She stood at the back door and watched him drink, his flanks hollow from dehydration and his body trembling as he drew on the water in a long draft.

She felt better once she had her clothes,

485

her watercolors, and the photograph of her parents. It made her feel less isolated in this new house. There was a letter from Anne, delivered with the rest of her luggage. It must have arrived that morning. Wasn't she excited by the breakthrough? An Englishman agreeing to fund the smallpox hospital was surely good news. Sister Clara was moving a division of nurses to help set up and run the place, and she was going with them. Frances put the letter aside. She didn't want to think about Edwin working with Sister Clara. His world was no longer her world.

THIRTY

The days in the house alone felt long. Frances became restless and unsure of herself. She chewed her nails down to the quick, something she had never done before. When William saw them he tutted and called her a naughty girl. "We'll have to keep your hands in gloves until you can learn better," he said, producing a pair for her the following day and pulling them on over her hands. He told her not to take them off until he told her to. That evening, he came home and sat her on his lap, slipped them off, and kissed each fingertip in turn.

He bought her new dresses, a riding habit, hats, and petticoats. She felt like a doll, being dressed for his pleasure. It made her fretful and anxious waiting for him to come home and — when he did come home — completely enthralled to him physically. She was subsumed by him. He wanted this infatuation from her; she saw it pleased him, but she was terrified by it. At times, when she was on her own in the house, she realized that he left no room for her to breathe, that there was nothing left of her except what he had made her.

She told herself that this would change in Johannesburg. They would be on the same footing, husband and wife. She thought he had promised her this, but found she couldn't remember his exact words. In the mornings she would set up her easel to begin a painting, but by the end of the day she wouldn't have sketched in more than a few lines. All the calmness she had felt at Rietfontein had gone. Although she laughed about it when she was with him, she had a residual terror that he would cast her off and she would have nowhere to go. She was entirely dependent on his goodwill. This is what mistresses do, she thought, digging the coarse diamond out of her pocket. They hoard the things they are given so that, when the end comes, they can survive. He had said the diamond would take the place of a ring, but in fact it was just the opposite. A ring was a public statement. The diamond he had given her was only the guarantee of a private contract.

And there was one thing she hadn't reckoned on. Leger. He followed William round like a dark shadow, turning everything that was good and honest about their relationship into something sordid and shameful. When he looked at her his mouth curled into an expression of mocking knowingness. He did what he could to keep William away from her, lounging around the house in the evenings, drinking whiskey, until the early hours. She consoled herself that they would soon be leaving him behind. He wouldn't be coming with them to Johannesburg.

She thought about Edwin when she was on her own, more than she ought to have done. He had been asked to marry her, and he had obliged. But had he ever loved her? He had been attracted to her in London, she was sure of it, but was that the same thing? At the back of her mind lurked an image of Sister Clara, sitting at her desk with her plait of honey-colored hair falling over one shoulder — gentle, industrious, and beautiful. Anne's letter had said she was supporting Edwin with the new hospital, and the idea kept catching at the back of Frances's mind. She shouldn't care, but it disturbed her to think of them working together.

She read the letter over and over, and wondered whether Edwin had been right about smallpox, and if he would eventually give up on his campaign to try to prove it. He would know by now that she had decided not to go to Rietfontein. She was upset by the idea that he thought badly of her, then confused that she minded what he thought.

And she kept remembering her father. She had always thought that he would have been ashamed to see her married to Edwin, living such a frugal life in South Africa, but in fact he had approved of Edwin, and had wanted them to be married, and this was a difficult readjustment.

In the evenings Frances would go to bed soon after supper, leaving William and Leger to sit up drinking. Some hours later there would be a knock on the door and the voice of a native talking quietly. There was a safe inside the bedroom, and once or twice William came in to take out cash. When she asked him what it was for, he shook his head at her and said, "Curiosity, Frances, can be a dangerous thing."

William came home one evening keyed up and full of a restless energy. When he kissed her his breath smelt of beer and cigar smoke. Leger hovered at the door.

"I won't be staying for supper," William said, wolfing down a plateful of bread and cheese that the boy had brought for them.

"Where are you going?" she asked in the bedroom, as he fumbled with the safe. She had been looking forward to him coming home and didn't want to think about the long evening ahead of her, alone in the house.

He didn't answer, kissing her on the forehead instead. "I won't be back until late."

Her eyes flickered to Leger, who was looking in at them through the open door with a slight smile on his face. She wanted William to reassure her that he wasn't going to see the young colored girl at Mrs. Whitley's, but she had too much pride to ask.

She was asleep by the time he came back. He sat on the edge of the bed, unlacing his boots. "What time is it?" she asked.

"Come, sit with me," he said, kicking off the boots and taking her by the hand. She let him lead her through to the sitting room and watched him pour some whiskey into a glass. The boy was lighting the fire.

"Why are you in such a good mood?" she asked as he pulled her onto his lap and wrapped his arms around her. He kissed her neck. "Because I have the most beautiful woman in Kimberley sitting on my lap and I can summon her from bed at will." She laughed, and he put his hand into his pocket and pulled out a handful of notes. "And because I just happen to be the best card player in Kimberley. I didn't lose a game all evening."

"You've been playing cards all evening?" she asked.

"I've been playing cards."

"I thought Baier had told you not to."

"Is this disapproval I'm sensing?" He held both her arms in one hand and tickled her so suddenly that she squirmed with laughter and shouted at him to stop.

There was a knock at the door. William let go of Frances and motioned to the boy, who looked through the window. She glanced questioningly at him.

"Stay here," he said, taking a sip of scotch and passing her the glass. He stood up. "You may as well see what I do for a living."

The boy opened the door, and a native came in. He was what they call raw — half naked, with bare feet and no trousers. He spoke rapidly in Kaffir, then stepped forward into the light and spat a stone into his hand. William took it from him. He wiped it against his trousers and held it up to a light, then carried it to the scales on his desk and weighed it. They negotiated over the price,

William's boy acting as translator. William bargained hard, and the native, looking disgruntled, finally agreed. Money changed hands, and he left.

"Stolen diamonds?" she asked in a tight voice when they were alone in the room. He had let her in on something, shown her a new side of himself, and she didn't like it.

"Does it bother you?" he asked.

"Isn't it dangerous?" Illicit diamond buying was the most talked about crime on the fields. It carried as high a sentence as murder.

He shrugged. "I try to mitigate the risk."

"But you're encouraging the natives to steal."

"The natives are born opportunists. They will steal whether or not I'm in the game. I need money, and this is the fastest way to get it."

"But you have money. Baier has given you money, legitimate money. Why take this risk?"

He snorted with derision. "I don't know about legitimate. There isn't a diamond dealer in Kimberley who hasn't made his money from buying illicit diamonds, and Baier must be the worst of the lot. Anyway, you may as well know that there isn't much money. Not anymore. Baier has me on a tight leash. He expects me to have the morality of a saint when he has been the very devil himself."

"I don't blame Baier," she said, standing up and walking towards him. "You're worse than a common thief."

The slap shocked her. Her face snapped round and exploded into fire. Tears stung her eyes, and she stood with her mouth half open, gaping at him.

"Don't forget your position in my house," he said in a cold, still voice. "As my wife or my mistress, I expect your submission and respect. What did you imagine, coming here, living off my money? That I would be as squeaky clean as your husband?"

He left the house then, and when the door slammed behind him she felt empty. Remorse battled with resentment. She crawled into bed. He came home just before dawn, reeking of liquor, his breath sour, his thick hair full of sweet smoke, and she let him turn her over in the dark onto her stomach, the weight of him holding her down, pressing her into the mattress, sealing himself to her as a second skin. His body burnt itself across the backs of her legs, her buttocks, the dip in her lower spine. One hand pushed under her chest and the other grasped the back of her head, driving her face into the pillow. He thrust into her and she gave a muffled cry, struggling to get free, but she couldn't move from under the weight of him and he lunged deeper, his breath falling hoarse and damp against her cheek. She cried silently afterwards, the tears running down her face, gulping back the sobs so he wouldn't hear.

The next morning he was conciliatory. "I need to make money if I'm ever going to break away from Baier. I have a hundred thousand pounds' worth of diamonds which I'm going to take across the border. Do you know what that can do for us? When we get to Johannesburg I'll buy up the gold fields and start an empire of my own."

"When we talked on the *Cambrian* you said you wanted to go into politics. You were going to achieve great things for South Africa."

"And I will. But I need money to do them. Money is power. Without it, I am nothing." How like Baier he sounded. And yet there was an undeniable logic to his words. Edwin had no money and no power, and look what a mess he had made of everything. William put a hand to her chin. "We are none of us perfect, Frances. There is always a sacrifice to be made. And this is yours: to loosen that schoolgirl morality of yours just a little. Can

495

you do that for me?"

She nodded, wary of him now.

"I don't particularly like Baier," William was saying, "and I don't admire the way things are done in Kimberley. With the money I have made we can be independent. Start again. You do want that, don't you?" he asked, cradling her waist with his hands.

"Yes," she said, hoping it was true. But last night had frightened her. She didn't trust him. "Of course I do."

"Good." He kissed her lightly on the mouth. "That's better."

He told her that they would be leaving in three days. The diamond police were jumpy, he said. They had been making searches at Baier's offices, and they had been through his books. Men were being stopped and searched leaving town. They would have to be careful.

"How are you going to get the stones out of Kimberley?" Frances asked. "What if you're caught?" If the police stopped them and found the diamonds, then they would send William to Breakwater, and possibly her as well. He kissed her on the tip of her nose. "Don't worry about that. Leave it to me. I'll take care of everything."

There was a knock on the door while they

were eating supper. Frances glanced at William. They were leaving the following morning, and she was jumpy. He motioned to his boy, who opened it a crack. They heard a murmur of conversation, then the door swung open and a native boy stepped inside. Frances didn't recognize him. He couldn't have been more than thirteen, his lower lip was thrust out, and she thought he might cry. He shifted his weight nervously from board to board. William asked him a question, then grasped his jaw, but the boy just made a sobbing sound and failed to meet his eye. He kept holding up a stone between two fingers, as if it were burning him. She could see from the armchair five yards away that it was no ordinary diamond. It was larger than the tip of his thumb. If it was real, it would be worth a fortune.

She wanted to tell William to send the boy away, but he would be angry if she interfered. He shouldn't be taking the risk, not when they were so close to leaving. William stepped outside. She heard him walk down the *stoep* into the street. The young boy was left standing awkwardly in the center of the room, holding his diamond. When William came back he asked Halfwit to send for the inspector. He tried to refuse, but William raised his voice and eventually he went out.

497

The boy's shoulders began to tremble, and his chest heaved. William plucked the stone from his still-outstretched hand, slipped it into his pocket, and took out a cigarette. Silence settled over them. There was just the gasping noise the boy was making, and the rasping of a match as William held a flame to the tobacco.

All of a sudden the boy flung himself at the door, opened it, and bounded through. William leapt after him, as if he had been expecting it, and threw out his foot. The boy tripped heavily. Frances ran to the door and saw him sprawled, with his head in the dirt of the street. William plucked him off the ground by his collar and dragged him inside. The boy slithered down the wall into a squat and stayed there until the inspector came and took him away.

Afterwards, William's boy spoke angrily to William, but he waved him away.

"He's annoyed," William said to her, as if to excuse himself. "The boy was his cousin."

"Why couldn't you have let him go? He was almost out of the door."

"My, how your morality changes," William mocked. "I thought you didn't like thieves?" She looked away from him, angry. He drew on his cigarette, then after a moment said in a more serious voice, "I thought it might

498

have been a trap. It was the safest thing to do."

"What will happen to the boy?"

"You know what will happen to him, Frances," he said, turning away from her and walking into the bedroom. "Don't always make me responsible for the things you don't want to hear."

She lay awake for a long while, listening to the deep rhythms of William's breathing. She had thought that by coming to live with him she wouldn't have to see the brutal side of Kimberley; that she could escape the feeling of injustice which had first settled over her when the man lay dying in her lap. She hadn't wanted Edwin to be right, she realized. She had hoped there was a legitimacy to William's business, and a strength of logic, which made sense of the mines. But the feeling of injustice had followed her here, and when she thought about the boy being dragged off to Breakwater she couldn't justify William's behavior. Illicit diamond buying was a cutthroat business, with every man out for himself. It undermined the civilized pretensions of the whole industry.

Edwin, she realized, would have been able to articulate her misgivings better than she was able to, and she kept seeing William through his eyes: a tougher, lazier, more selfish man than she had imagined. She felt more trapped now than she had ever done before, and she suspected Edwin had guessed that this was how it would be.

And she knew she wasn't immune from risk either. What were the chances they would make it across the border without a search? She had heard stories of the diamond police ambushing men fleeing with diamonds, of gunfights before the border, and men racing for their lives across the veldt, dropping stones as they ran, but she had never thought that anything like that could happen to her. The terror on the boy's face and his complete helplessness as he was carted off by the inspector had made the danger of their situation very real.

William was under suspicion, but he seemed confident they wouldn't be caught. He said they would ride out dressed like a hunting party, insisting she and Mangwa come with him, to make it seem more like a leisure tour. The border was only half a day's ride away, and their luggage would follow later. He was levelheaded and he knew the risks, and he wasn't about to take an idle chance on twenty-five years as a convict at the Breakwater. And yet the fact remained that he was going to try to smuggle £100,000 worth of diamonds out of Kimberley.

"I'm going out to see to the horses," William said, shaking her awake. He slipped out of the bedroom door. She pressed the nauseous tiredness from her eyes with a damp cloth and dressed quickly in the dark. The new riding habit he had bought for her was blood-red and tight-fitting. It was too provocative, and she felt self-conscious. She would rather have worn something simpler, but William had insisted. When she came through to the sitting room, Leger was standing there, leaning against the window frame, smoking a pipe. When he saw her he gave a low whistle.

"What are you doing here?" she asked.

"Didn't he tell you? I'm coming with you."

Frances stared at him. Leger was coming with them? How could William not have told her? She had hoped never to have to see him again. Now they would be sharing their every second with him. There was no chance of her ever feeling like William's wife when Leger was there to remind her otherwise.

"That was a good bit of business Westbrook did last night," he said in his thin, reedy voice.

"Turning the boy in to the police? I wouldn't call it business."

"But the stone," he said. "The size of it!"

"It was clever of him to hand it over." She straightened her hat in the glass which hung over the desk. "It wasn't worth taking the risk."

He looked at her for a moment, then gave a low chuckle. "You mean he didn't tell you?"

"Tell me what?" She glanced at his reflection. Leger knew something she didn't, and he was enjoying it.

"He swapped the boy's stone for one a tenth of the size, of negligible quality. The inspector was none the wiser, and Westbrook is considerably richer. The stone was a Goliath. We haven't seen one like that for months."

It took her a moment to grasp what he was saying, and when she did, she understood something about William. He was utterly ruthless — far more ruthless than she had imagined. He would stop at nothing to get his own way. Of course, it was just like him to coolheadedly take advantage of the situation. And what damage did it do the boy, if he was turning him in anyway? Still, she didn't like it. He had been too comfortable sending the boy off to a lifetime in prison, and the ease with which he had lied horrified her.

She stepped out of the back door into the yard. The air was cool and the sky was lightening to a bluer shade of black. She saw shadows and heard the scuffing of horses' hooves as they shifted under the weight of their saddles. Quickly, not wishing to be seen, she pulled off her gloves and knelt down by the door. There was a brick, which she moved aside, and underneath it a piece of wood, buried in the earth. She levered it up and dug out the diamond that was hidden beneath it. She hadn't wanted to take it across the border, but Leger's story had changed her mind. She wasn't sure she could trust William. The value of the diamond had to be considerable, and she needed something more than just William's promise of protection. Back in the bedroom she shut the door, unraveled her stocking, and tucked the diamond into the groove of her big toe. She wove a ribbon around it to keep it in place, then put her stocking back on and over it her boot. Her hands, she realized, were shaking.

"Frances." William stood in the doorway. "What are you doing?"

"Nothing," she said, pulling on her boot.

"Come on. We're ready to go." He paused for a moment. "And for Christ's sake, if you do have anything you're taking with you, make sure it's well hidden."

She followed him into the street and mounted the little palomino pony he had bought for her. The breath of the horses clouded in the sharp dawn air. It was the first time she had been out of the house since she had arrived, ten days ago. So much had changed since then. She glanced back once as they rode away and felt a sudden, sharp misgiving at the thought of leaving Kimberley. She shook it off and kicked her pony on. William rode ahead and Leger behind, their horses laden with haversacks and flasks for water. Both men carried rifles, and pistols in their belts. Two boys rode with them on mules. The sharp edges of the diamond ground against her foot, and she made a silent prayer that they wouldn't be stopped.

Market Square was quiet except for the shuffling of oxen and the hollow knocking of the horses' hooves on the hard earth. They rode past two men offloading timber from a wagon, swearing softly under their breath. When they had crossed to the far side, Frances heard voices. A group of natives, wearing uniforms, leant up against a wall, smoking. They watched them ride by, sharp-eyed and alert. She wondered what they were doing up so early and whether they belonged to the diamond police.

The painted, corrugated houses gave way to a sprawl of canvas tents. A noisy brawl of men swarmed over the road, walking towards the mines. They were mostly diggers, squinting into the first rays of sun, picks swinging from their shoulders. Makeshift canteens had been set up in large tents pinned to shacks. The place smelt of burnt fat and the damp of early mornings; of sweat, and over it all the filth and noise of too many men living in one place.

When the road widened they were free of the town, riding into the shimmering expanse of the Karoo. Leger rode up beside William, and Frances allowed her pony to fall in behind. The sun had risen, and their shadows stretched out in front of them. She glanced over her shoulder. Arid scrubland extended to the far horizon on every side, broken by the russet-brown tops of aloes which thrust up from the ground like sentinels. There was no sign of the police. Mangwa, a perfect apparition of white and black, walked on a lead rein alongside William. His gait was shorter than the horse's stride, so that every few yards he broke into a trot to keep up. The flies bothered him, clustering up his eyes like bees in a comb, and he tossed his head to throw them off.

She could see William's hand resting on his saddlebag. His wide, calloused fingers ran backwards and forwards over the canvas. There was a pocket at the front which was stuffed full, and he traced his thumb in a smooth pattern along the contours of the bulge, across the leather trim, and down the wide strap to the clean brass buckle. William seemed calm. Too calm, she thought, for someone who was carrying £100,000 worth of illicit diamonds. Her stomach twisted with fear.

Up ahead, piles of rubble erupted from the ground like vast termite mounds. She saw a Boer family scrambling over one of them, sifting through the sand and gravel. They would be lucky to find anything. This was earth that had been worked through on the mines and dumped here as worthless. The side of the heap collapsed with a grating noise, and a small girl emerged, running down the shifting gravel towards Frances with an outstretched hand. Her skin was brown with dust, and the whites of her eyes shone like marbles from a dark face. Frances reached into her pocket for a few pennies and threw them down to her.

The sun was higher now, and they rode past low *kopjes* which swelled up out of the earth, softening the contours of the landscape. Still the police didn't come, and she began to hope they might not be stopped. William reined in up ahead. A group of four or five bodies lay twisted together at the foot of a *kopje.* Vultures squatted on top of them. She saw a tangle of limbs and a movement, as though one of them were trying to stand up. It was only when she drew closer that she realized it was a cloud of flies which settled then rose as the vultures moved, cloaking the carcasses in a shifting mantle. The bodies were naked. They were natives. One man lay towards them, draped over another man's legs. His head was tipped to one side in the dirt. A vulture had ripped out his throat, but his face hadn't been touched. The skin was covered in white pustules, a mass of them which had seeped together and were drying in the sun to a crust which was beginning to peel away from the flesh beneath. She covered her nose and mouth against the sweet, noxious stink, and swallowed to stop herself from retching.

"That's the pox, all right," Leger said, kicking his horse on and spitting into the dust.

"I thought you didn't believe it?" Frances demanded, riding up to William.

He glanced at her but didn't speak.

"You said you were sure it was pemphigus."

"I said the doctors were sure it was pemphigus."

A cold and horrible understanding seeped into her. "So you knew it all along?"

"None of us knows anything, Frances. All we can do is speculate." His voice was barbed with anger. She had been slapped by him before. She knew the warning signs, but she needed to be sure. "So you knew Edwin wasn't making a profit out of it?"

"What does Matthews have to do with anything?"

"You persuaded me against him."

"Good God, Frances, he was your husband! I think you could make up your own mind."

"But how could you suspect it was small-pox and do nothing?"

"Use your common sense," he said. "Do you have any idea of the expense involved in quarantining thousands of natives? With no business for six months, the mines would collapse. Every man in Kimberley is invested in mining stock, most with borrowed money. The whole of South Africa is in on the racket. This isn't just about a few men making a profit; this is the fate of a country riding in the balance. If speculators, international investors, banks get wind of smallpox, the whole damn thing will implode. Then where will I be? Where will you be? Where will Matthews's goddamned natives be?"

"You have influence over Baier," she said, barely listening to him.

"Whether or not there's smallpox in Kimberley is not my responsibility."

"But you can't just leave, knowing the epidemic will escalate."

"Why not?" he said. "You have a wonderfully infuriating habit of blaming other people for the truths you can't handle. You were married to the man, for God's sake. If anyone should have believed him, it ought to have been you. I hate to break it to you, but you're just like the rest of us — you didn't want to know." He kicked his horse on, and rode up to Leger. He was right, she realized. She hadn't wanted to know, and that made her just as guilty as him.

The sun was overhead when her pony pricked its ears and let out a shrill whistle. She turned and saw a boiling cloud of dust and, just ahead of it, two men on horseback bearing down on them. William wheeled

509

around and watched as two more officers rode in from the other side, cutting off their route to the border.

"Stay where you are, Sir!" the sergeant called out, reining in his horse, which stamped and tossed its head, throwing specks of foam into the air. Mangwa wrenched at the lead rope, almost pulling William from the saddle. He turned on his hind legs in a tight circle, eyeing the strangers with the whites of his eyes. Her heart pounded.

The sergeant had a rifle slung over his shoulder, and his men carried shotguns. Frances saw William swing his rifle off his shoulder, cradling the weight of it loosely in his right hand. He glanced at Leger, who grimaced back at him, holding his rifle in one hand and making a low clicking noise with his tongue. She made a silent prayer that William would give himself up quietly. He was outnumbered. There were four guns to his two. He would be mad to try to fight his way out, but when she looked at him his face was frozen into an expression of contempt.

"Mr. Westbrook. We need to make a search. I have reason to suspect . . ." The sergeant paused to catch his breath, wheezing as though the dust had silted up his lungs. He swept his hands over their group in a futile gesture, and his eyes flitted nervously over William. To her surprise, William slung his rifle over his shoulder, dropped his reins, and dismounted, motioning to Leger to do the same.

The sergeant didn't go straight for William's saddlebag. Instead, he started by searching the men. When he had finished he beckoned to Frances. Her legs buckled when she dropped off her pony, and the sergeant put out an arm to steady her. Then he ran his hands over her body, starting at her hair, pushing his thumbs round her ears, down her neck, and into her collar. She could see William watching. The tips of the sergeant's fingers were at her waist, pinching along the seams of her dress, and she had to stop herself from taking a step backwards. His face was no more than an inch from hers, and she could smell the biltong on his breath. She lifted her eyes and saw him staring at her. He asked her to remove her boots. Her throat made a choking sound as she bent down to unlace them.

She stepped each foot into the dust, hoping he wouldn't see the color of the ribbon through her stocking, and handed him the boots. He slid his hands into the warm, soft leather, checking for stones, then handed them back to her. When he thanked her she had to turn her head away to hide her relief. He wasn't going to check her feet, and — shaking — she pulled her boots back on. William, seeing that he had finished searching her, spat into the dirt at the sergeant's feet and walked out into the veldt with Leger, where they crouched down, hats pulled low over their heads, their backs to the officers. They talked quietly. She stood at a distance, unsure whether to join them.

The officers took the saddles off the horses, feeling round the corners of the leather. Finally, with studied calm, the sergeant removed the saddlebag and unbuckled the three straps. He dipped his hand inside and pulled out a handful of something which glinted in the sun. He pushed them round in his palm. His shoulders relaxed, and his face seemed to lose its tension. This was it. He must have found the diamonds. But a second later he let the contents fall through his fingers into the sand, and she saw that what she had thought were stones were in fact nothing more than cartridges.

The sergeant scraped the sweat from his forehead, and William turned his head and gave a gruff laugh. "You didn't think they were diamonds, did you, Sergeant?"

The sergeant turned to his officers. "Search the boys."

The two native boys offered themselves up. She knew the routine, and though she had turned her back when they were stripped, she heard the glucking of open mouths as the officers slipped in their fingers, feeling round the inside of the boys' cheeks and down the backs of their throats until they retched and coughed. They would probe the boys' ears and run hands down their bodies, checking for small slices in the flesh which could be turned into pockets. There was a clinking noise — the unbuckling of belts — and protesting grunts as they were bent forward so the officers could slide their hands round the boys' buttocks.

"Nothing, Sir. What should we do?" The sergeant's men shuffled nervously in their pockets for cigarettes and looked at him accusingly. Their brash confidence was dissolving fast. Now that they had lost the possibility of bringing down a great diamond trader, they were ashamed, disowning the enthusiasm for scandal that had gripped them just a few moments before. And there was an undercurrent of fear rippling through the group. Baier would protect his cousin, and he had a reputation for reprisal.

The sergeant paused. The veins in his neck

were swollen, and a thin trickle of sweat ran into his shirt. "Mr. Westbrook," he called to William, "you're free to go. Thank you for your patience."

"Didn't find what you were looking for, Sergeant?"

The officers swung up into their saddles, turned their horses east, and rode back to Kimberley.

They rode on under the searing midday sun. Frances's shawl was too hot, and she let it slip back onto the saddle. The soft, red hairs that ran up the backs of her arms began to singe and curl. Her lips were dry, and her tongue, thick with dust, kept flicking moisture into the corners of her mouth.

In a supple movement, William swung round in the saddle to look at her. She blinked at him through the heat. He watched her carefully, unsmiling. He hadn't forgiven her. Her blood stopped, then returned with a rapid pulse. One hand fluttered nervously at her throat.

"Water," he called to one of the boys, who dug his heels into his mule and trotted up alongside, holding out a flask. He looked straight at her while he drank, liquid spilling down his chin, mingling with the sweat that stained his shirt dark. When he pushed

the flask away from him, his face creased
and his lips stretched. It was a smile of
stealth, and though she was so thirsty her
tongue had sealed itself to the roof of her
mouth, she couldn't bring herself to ask for
water.

When they arrived at the straggle of
corrugated-iron shacks that marked the end
of British territory, William pulled up his
horse and waited for her to ride alongside.
He took her hand. "They frightened you?
Frances, surely you didn't imagine I would
hide the diamonds where they could find
them?"

A laugh spilled out of her, and he smiled
back. She was relieved that they had made
it. And William seemed conciliatory. He
swung himself off his horse, his rifle hanging loosely across his back, and helped her
dismount, holding Mangwa's lead rope in
one hand while he supported her with the
other.

Then he pulled Mangwa towards him,
grasping his head tightly in one hand. She
watched him run his hands down the zebra's
muscled flank. The stripes rippled under his
fingers. Sweat, like froth on a shore, had
smudged the perfect lines of his coat, leaving a wave of salt. Mangwa moved nervously
under his touch, ears flicking back, stamp-

ing his back legs and crossing them away from him.

He handed the zebra to a boy, who led him to the *kraal*. Mangwa nudged his pockets, sensing he was about to be fed. The boy slipped off his halter, and the zebra trotted past him to the manger, snatching at the hay in greedy mouthfuls.

William walked towards the *kraal* and in a swift movement swung the rifle off his back. She realized, suddenly, what was about to happen, and cried out to Mangwa. The zebra jerked his head up and looked over at her. She was running towards William when the shot rang out. The zebra leapt into the air, jerking awkwardly like a puppet on strings. A tremor ran through his body. He groaned, and his hind legs collapsed against the fence of the *kraal*. It buckled under him with a sharp crack. She reached him just as he fell. There wasn't any blood, but the eye that faced her was white and sightless.

She managed to lift his head and untwist it so that the weight of it was in her lap. A soft mucus oozed from his mouth, flecked with blood, and his lips were drawn back, clenched round his teeth. She heard William talking behind her, and one of the boys came into the *kraal* carrying a panga.

"Get out," she shouted at him, but the

boy just stopped and stared at her with his mouth half open. William ducked under the *kraal* fence, and her voice broke into a hoarse scream. "What do you want with him? Leave him alone!" She stood up and threw her fists at him, hitting him on his chest, on his shoulders, digging her nails into his neck. He grasped her hands and held her off. Arms were wrapping themselves around her waist, pulling her away. It was Leger, dragging her backwards. William crouched down beside the boy and put a hand on Mangwa's withers. Frances kicked out at Leger's legs, screaming with rage, and threw her head back against him, hoping to connect with his jaw. She missed, and his hand clasped her open throat. His fingers tightened their grip until she could scarcely breathe, then he slowly twisted one of her arms behind her back. Her shoulder socket locked in a sickening, overwhelming lurch of pain, and she stopped shouting.

"That's it," Leger said, his breath moist against her ear. He pushed her up against the fence, his weight crushing the air out of her lungs. Something slid down her neck, and she saw out of the corner of her eye the gold chain William had given her uncoil itself and land in the dust at her feet. She struggled again, but he held her down and gave a slow, satisfied chuckle. "I didn't think you'd have so much fight in you."

She couldn't move her body, but she could turn her head. The boy was in the *kraal.* He took out his panga and slit the zebra open from chest to sheath. It was a neat incision. The stomach sac spilled out onto the ground, swollen and white and shiny, like a deformed fetus; then the guts, in a purple trail. The boy ran the tip of the knife down the smooth white membrane of the stomach, and it split under the gentle pressure of the blade. There was a sigh of exhalation, and a green-brown chaff pushed out onto the dirt of the *kraal* floor. William leant forward, his head resting on the ribs of the zebra, and thrust his hand inside the stomach. He grunted and worked his arm in further, until his elbow disappeared and then his shoulder. Finally, he gave a cry of triumph. His hand sucked out, and with it came a small package wrapped up in a tight ball. Then a second, and then a few moments later, a third. She knew what they contained.

Thirty-One

Frances didn't speak for three days. They stayed in a grotty boarding house waiting for their luggage to catch up with them, and she watched with gritted teeth as two natives heaved Mangwa's body onto a cart and took it away for meat. It was her fault that he was dead. She had brought him here, and she had failed to protect him.

William treated her silence as he would the spoilt willfulness of a child, barely acknowledging her. He spent every waking minute with Leger, coming to bed at dawn and snoring heavily through the hours when she lay in bed, trapped between him and the peeling plaster wall, wondering how she could have got it all so wrong.

On the third morning, she woke hot-headed and thick with sleep. The muscles in her body were tight and sore, and when she bent to lace her boots the blood beat heavily in her head. William came in and began packing his things.

"We're leaving," he said, glancing at her sitting on the bed.

"I'm not going," she said quietly.

"She speaks," he exclaimed, in mock wonder. "Look, the wagon is packed. We've got to be out of here in half an hour if we're to leave today. I suggest you hurry up and start getting your things together, or you'll be running after us." He spoke in a light, practical voice, as if nothing had changed between them. He even smiled at her, passing a hand through his hair, which was very slightly damp with sweat. "And I don't advise running in this heat." He turned to leave, then paused at the door. Perhaps he was disconcerted by her continued silence. When he spoke, it was in a serious, conciliatory voice. "Frances, we've got money now. We can do anything we please. I'll buy up gold fields in the north. We'll have everything we could ever want in Johannesburg. You'll feel better once you get there."

She didn't say anything, and taking her silence as progress he came and sat on the end of the bed, next to her. She didn't like to have him sitting so close. "You'll think I should have told you, but how could I have done?" he asked tenderly, tucking a stray strand of hair behind her ear. "You would never have let me. And besides, we were lucky I did. It was pretty close with those officers. Other men might have been caught." He took her hand and she let him hold it, and he took this as a positive sign.

"Really, you should be thanking me," he said. She felt as if she didn't belong to her body, as if she were listening to him from far off. She could feel the touch of his hand on her skin but couldn't relate it in any way to herself. "Don't you see?" He kissed her knuckles. His lips were cold. "This is our ticket to freedom."

"At what cost?"

"Frances, be practical. I know you liked the zebra, but there were more important things at stake."

"You let Leger touch me."

"You were hysterical," he said in a soothing voice. "You needed calming down."

There was silence for a moment. William, looking as if he thought the conversation was over, stood up. She realized that the whole thing bored him. He had no instinct for the change that had taken place in her.

He headed towards the door, and she spoke to his back in a low voice. "A man came to my husband when we were in Kimberley. It was the middle of the night. He was a native and he was hurt, bleeding. Do you know what it was about?"

He turned to face her. The laziness had gone from his face. She had caught his attention. "How should I know about every wounded kaffir in Kimberley?"

"Because he had a number pinned to his shirt. He was one of Baier's men."

"Baier has hundreds of natives working for him. I can't tell one from another most of the time."

"Number sixty-four," she said. "He died in my lap. His injuries were horrific. Surely you would have heard about it?"

He swore under his breath. "Is this some game of yours? Always trying to pen me into a corner?"

"You knew?"

He looked steadily at her, his jaw set to one side, his face solidifying into an expression of brutality. "Yes, I knew."

She was beyond being scared. She needed the truth. "What happened?"

"He was caught with a diamond sewn into his thigh. Baier wanted him punished."

"Who did he ask to do it?"

He turned his back on her and opened the door. "We're leaving in ten minutes. If you intend to come with us, you should get a move on."

"There was a leather strap on his wrist,"

she persisted. "What was it for?"

"I don't know. They probably dragged him about a bit."

"On horses?"

"Yes, on horses. Christ, the man was a thief, Frances. He knew full well what risks he was taking."

She paused. Something had occurred to her which she hadn't seen before. "Was he one of your boys?"

"Meaning what?" he asked, in a voice that was flat with a dangerous sarcasm, shutting the door again.

"Were you paying the man to steal diamonds from Baier's claims?"

William didn't say anything.

"What would Baier have said if the man had told him?"

"The boy was a consummate liar. He was trying to play me off against Baier."

"So you had him punished?"

"Are you coming or not?" he snarled.

"Why am I here?" she asked, seeing everything clearly for the first time. "I mean, it's obvious you don't love me. So why have you brought me along?"

He gazed at her, anger battling with something that looked like sheepishness. He looked caught out. "Don't be a fool. Of course I love you."

She stared at him in amazement. "Is this just you doing Baier's bidding again? Bringing me here? Because it suits him, doesn't it? You taking Dr. Matthews's wife away from him."

"Of course this isn't about Baier," he said in a gentler voice. "It's about us. What do we care if it suits him? As long as we are together."

Realization. Like the sky clearing after a dust storm, the truth was visible to her in perfect clarity. She felt nothing for him. Everything had been a fantasy. He might care for her financially, as long as it suited him, as long as it was a victory of sorts for him to have her, as long as Baier said that it was all right. But there would be no love, no compassion, no trust. He was a brute and a coward, and she wanted to get away from him as quickly as possible.

"Frances," he was saying, "I'll make it up to you later, I promise. But now we have to go."

"Please leave. I don't want anything more to do with you."

"Do you understand what you're asking?" he said, sparking into anger again. "I won't take you in when you come crawling back to me." She stayed silent, turning her face towards the wall. He didn't move for a moment, and she could feel him watching her, waiting for her to relent. Eventually he swore, wheeled round, and walked quickly out of the room.

The door swung back on its hinges, and she got up and shut it, then sat down on the bed and put her hands over her face. She had been wrong, utterly wrong. How could she ever have thought that she loved him? A man who cared about nothing but himself and his own ambitions, who hung on the shirttails of his cousin and was afraid to breathe without his say-so? She dug her nails into her forehead. There was a time when she had thought he had courage because he lived impulsively. But in fact he was riddled with fears, a pantomime Romeo whose indolent restlessness needed a constant variety to satisfy itself. She had loved him because he had so convincingly loved himself, and now — too late — she saw him for what he was: an overgrown, willful child, dangerous in his determination to get his own way.

She waited until William and Leger had ridden out of town, then packed up her things. There wasn't much, not more than would fit into the small portmanteau which had come with her from England all those months ago. Her trunk was on the wagon with William. She sent the boarding house boy down to get her pony ready, but he came back up shaking his head. William had taken the pony. She gave a cry of frustration. She had no money, no way of getting back to Kimberley, and she was desperate to see Edwin. Nothing else mattered. She needed to hear him say that he had forgiven her. And yet, why would he? She had gone to bed with a man he despised, betrayed their marriage, misjudged him in every respect, and refused to believe in the smallpox epidemic, simply because the implications of him being right had terrified her. She wanted to tell him — if he would listen — that she had been scared in Kimberley, daunted by the strength of his resolve, but she knew it wasn't enough. She needed to convince him that she had changed.

She left the room, clutching her portmanteau, and stepped out into the searing sunlight. Her eyes ached, and her spine felt bruised and tender. It was strange, this feeling, as though her body was succumbing to sickness but her mind was still detached from it. She shivered despite the heat, and a trickle of fear ran down her spine. The carcasses on the side of the road — they had died of smallpox. Did that mean Mariella might have caught the disease? Was it

526

possible she had caught it? Frances pushed her fingers into her eyes to ease away the pain; more than likely she was suffering from a lack of sleep.

The border town was a straggle of houses, *kraals,* and iron sheds. A small acacia tree stood forlornly outside the boarding house, and a group of natives lounged in the shade beneath it. There was a corrugated-iron shack, barely larger than an outhouse, which advertised itself as a diamond buyer. The trader was American — young, cocky, and, by the looks of his shabby dress, not doing particularly well. He eyed the expensive riding habit which William had given her, and she cursed herself for wearing it. She rolled the stone out onto his desk, and he held it up to the light.

"Almost valueless, Madam," he said, handing it back to her.

"I don't believe you, Sir."

"Well, perhaps we can come to some agreement halfway between your disbelief and my needs."

"What can you give me?"

He named his price.

"You would be robbing me," she said, thinking that it was barely enough to get her back to Kimberley.

"No, Madam, I would be doing you a

favor." He looked pointedly at her. "You're in a tight spot, and I can get you out of it. I won't pay a fortune for the privilege."

He counted out a handful of banknotes, and she took them, not feeling well enough to argue.

She hired a Cape cart. It used up most of the money, but she didn't care; it was the fastest way back to Kimberley. The wheels clattered along the uneven road, and she gripped the wooden armrest to keep her balance. It was difficult to get comfortable, and her tongue was thick and dry in her mouth like cardboard.

A splinter pricked the skin on her palm. She sucked off the small ball of blood, cursing her misguided self-conviction. All this time she had been looking for other people's protection, refusing to accept the injustice of her father's death, her uncle's rejection, the brutal reality of the mines. Now she saw that it was Edwin's refusal to protect her from the truth which should have given her strength. He hadn't spelled things out for her. He had wanted her to see for herself. He had waited patiently for her to wake up from her childish infatuation. And finally he had brought her to Kimberley so she could see what corruption really was, and still she had failed to see things as they were.

In his article he had talked about the absurdity of the English girl who looked into the Big Hole and failed to see the suffering of the laborers. That was her, she realized. Her naïveté astounded her. It was as if she had woken from a fairy tale and found herself in a world that was starker and more brutal than she could ever have imagined; a world in which she would be held to account. She had never felt the weight of such responsibility before, and now it pressed heavily on her.

The cart struck a pothole, and she lurched in her seat. Her back ached and her legs felt heavy. She noticed that her skin, where the dust blew in through the window, had broken out in goose bumps. She shifted on the hot leather. The backs of her legs had begun to sweat.

She knew, suddenly, that she wasn't being honest with herself. She didn't just want Edwin's forgiveness. She wanted him to reach out and pull her towards him. She wanted to hear him whisper in her ear that he had loved her at Rietfontein, and that he loved her still. She wanted him to need her, and she knew that it was only through the touch of his hands that she would feel absolved. She remembered the night in the cottage, after the sheep shearing, when the brandy had loosened something in him. He had looked at her with his cool, gray eyes — the night outside pressing in against the window — and she had yearned for him to kiss her.

She loved him. The truth hit her with a small shock. Perhaps she had loved him for a long time but had simply not known it. She bit her lip, terrified that when she got to Kimberley he might refuse to see her, and that if he did she wouldn't be able to bear it.

The Cape cart let her out at Edwin's makeshift hospital. Pavilion tents stood stark and motionless in the hot, still air. There were a handful of sanitary police in canvas uniforms carrying rifles, crouched under the shade of a tarpaulin, and a mule cart with a native man offloading stretchers onto the sand. She recognized the smell of sulfur from the quarantine station. There were no other houses here on the outskirts of town, and the place held the quiet of the veldt in the heat of the day. The only sound was the knocking of stretchers as they were piled one on top of another. She walked across the scrub towards the hospital, jumping when a *korhaan* took off into the sky from under her feet with a clattering cry.

"Can I help you, Madam?" A nurse appeared in the shaded porch of the nearest tent.

"I'm looking for Dr. Matthews," Frances said, peering past her into the gloomy interior.

"I'm afraid he isn't here."

"Are you sure?"

"Quite sure."

Frances was clammy and light-headed. She tried to pull herself together, but she didn't feel quite right. Her head was pounding and her legs felt unsteady. "Where will I be able to find him?"

"I'm afraid I can't disclose the whereabouts of our doctors."

"But you must. I'm his wife."

The woman drew down the corners of her mouth in an expression of distaste, and Frances wondered if all the nurses here knew that she had left Edwin for another man.

"Frances?" Anne was standing on the porch behind her.

"Have you seen Edwin?" Frances asked. "It's urgent. I need to find him." Her hands were clasping and unclasping at her sides, and she felt hot and overwhelmed.

"He's not here," Anne said.

"When will he be back?" she asked, trying

not to sound desperate.

"Frances, you're not well." Anne took her hand and led her away into the cool shade of a smaller tent which acted as a kind of reception. She was looking at her strangely.

"What is it?" Frances asked, putting a hand to her hair. "Why are you staring at me?"

"I think you should sit down." Anne pointed to a hard-backed school chair and poured her a glass of water. Frances's hand shook slightly when she took the glass. After a few sips she felt calmer. "Have you seen Mariella?"

"Mariella?" Anne's mouth twisted in dismay. "Haven't you heard?"

"Heard?" Her voice echoed in her head as if she were underwater.

"Mariella died last week."

Frances felt the shock deep in her stomach. She took in air and asked, "Of what?"

"Smallpox."

"Was she here?"

"Not until it was too late."

"But I told Mr. Fairley to send for Edwin."

Anne asked sharply, "When were you there?"

"I don't know. About two weeks ago."

"You'll have to be quarantined, Frances."

She shook her head. "Anne, don't you

remember? We were all vaccinated. In Cape Town."

"And it didn't help Mariella. They've had problems maintaining stock of efficient vaccination. Sometimes it can be unreliable in this heat. We've all been revaccinated here at the hospital." Anne put a hand to Frances's forehead, her face concerned. "Have you been feeling all right? You're quite hot."

But Frances shook her head. She felt fine. She was fine. Just a little warm. "I feel all right, honestly; it's just traveling in this heat. It's worn me out. I don't understand why Mr. Fairley didn't bring her here sooner?"

"He paid a fortune for a doctor who was quite convincing. He promised Mr. Fairley it wasn't smallpox. By the time she got to us it was too late." Frances had an image of Dr. Robinson, shabby and mercenary, drinking whiskey in their tent. She nodded. It made sense. She should have known that George might not listen to her. Everyone mistrusted Dr. Matthews.

"Anne, I need to speak to my husband. Do you know where he is?"

"He's in Du Toit's Pan, at one of Baier's compounds. There's a bad outbreak there. He won't be back until much later. But Frances, you can't leave." Anne put a hand on her arm. "I'm afraid you really will have to be quarantined."

But Frances was already moving away from her, ducking under the canvas, out into the glare of sunlight. Anne called after her, running to keep up. The sanitary police looked up as she ran past them, waiting for Anne to tell them to stop her, but the girl let her go. Frances didn't turn her head to look back. She kept walking briskly towards town, and soon she realized she was on her own.

Mariella was dead. Her friend was gone, and she was partly to blame. When the realization came it was brutal, and she found herself standing in the road, eyes squeezed shut to hold back the shock of it. William had been right about one thing. She was always blaming others when she should have been taking responsibility for herself. If she had listened to Edwin, Mariella would probably still be alive.

It took her two hours to walk to Du Toit's Pan, and an intense thirst raged through her as she walked. By the time she found the Baier compound the sun was low in the sky and she was worried he might have already left. A high wire fence surrounded a shabby, dirty-looking yard, and two natives with rifles patrolled the wire, stirring up dust with their boots. A few horses were tethered to a post outside. She asked at the door if Edwin Matthews was there, and the man at the gate signed her in and nodded her through. The yard was a bare, flat patch of red earth, littered with cigarette butts, rusting tins, and broken bottles. There was a row of large canvas tents across one side and a few corrugated huts on the other. A white official lounged outside one of them with his legs sprawled out and his head thrown back, asleep. The late-afternoon sun shone in a deep golden strip across the yard, glinting off the iron roves, the wire fence, and the tips of the men's rifles. She had never been inside a prison, but she imagined this was what it would feel like.

There were no natives in the yard — they were still working the mines. It was utterly quiet. She stepped inside the first tent. She couldn't see anything in the dark. The air was hot and tasted of sickness. She pulled her shawl over her nose and mouth. Edwin had said you could tell smallpox just by the smell. After a moment her eyes adjusted and shapes began to emerge from the gloom. There were no beds, just rugs which stretched in lines across the wooden boards. A groan rose in the still air, and she stopped. When it came again her heart thudded darkly but she couldn't turn away. The man was lying on his back, naked, without a blanket. His body was covered in a close rash of white spots, startlingly luminous on his dark skin, as if he had been flecked with paint. She watched him put a hand near his face to brush away the flies which crawled over him.

His face was a mass of ulcers weeping fluid, and his eyes were swollen to cracks where the pustules had grown together. He moaned again. He was asking for water. There were no glasses that she could see, just a rusted barrel in the corner of the tent. She dipped a tin into the tepid water and carried it to the man, who took it from her, his dry fingers brushing hers, gulping thirstily. The next tent was the same, and the one after that. The stench in each was overwhelming. These men were clearly dying. No one could see them and deny it. Where were the doctors and nurses to look after them?

Frances stood in the yard, swaying slightly, her mouth dried up with thirst. Her hands were heavy at her sides, fat with blood, and she felt unsteady on her feet. Bright spots danced in front of her eyes. She could hear men talking on the other side of the yard. She walked towards the corrugated huts.

One had a half-door at the front and looked as if it served as a canteen. It was empty, but she could hear voices coming from behind it. She stepped past the sleeping official, down the shaded alleyway between the huts, and into a sheltered inner courtyard.

Initially, all she could take in was Edwin. She was transfixed by the sight of him. He stood half turned towards her, the evening sun turning his hair the color of copper. He was holding a woman to his chest. Frances could see her shoulders trembling. He stroked a hand over her hair and pressed his lips to her forehead. It was Sister Clara. She wasn't wearing her nurse's cap, and her white pinafore was crumpled and filthy. The thick blond plait which swung down her slender neck had worked loose of its knot and was unraveling into glossy curls down her back. It took Frances a moment to realize that Sister Clara was weeping. Only when someone cursed did Frances look past them, and then she wished she had never come at all. A knot of bodies lay piled one on top of another as if for a bonfire. Four sanitary police were untangling them. Limbs, hands, and faces were contorted into the impossible positions of acrobats. They had been thrown together haphazardly, a jumble of broken fingers and snapped spines. It looked like the remains of a massacre, except the bodies were blistered with the pox.

Edwin looked up and caught her eye. She willed him to say her name, or to acknowledge her in some way. But instead he pushed Sister Clara gently away from him. "Get her out of here," he whispered, loud enough for her to hear, and Sister Clara turned and saw her standing there.

The nurse approached.

"Edwin," Frances said, but he turned away from her. She tried to walk towards him, but he seemed suddenly to be a long way off. She said his name again and managed to walk forward a few steps, but before she got to him her legs gave way from under her.

THIRTY-TWO

The next moment, someone — a woman — was talking to her, saying her name, and shaking her lightly on the shoulder. Frances forced her eyes open. The room was full of shadows. Light filtered dimly through cracks in the iron roof above her. She was lying on the floor of a hut. Immediately in front of her were the legs of a table and a pile of dirty blankets. She couldn't recollect how she had got here. Someone must have carried her inside. She felt dizzy and thought she might be sick. Her mouth stung and her throat had tightened. She was struggling to breathe. Sister Clara was crouched beside her, half supporting her body, holding a glass of water to her lips.

"Where is my husband?" Frances asked, pushing her hand away. She needed to speak to him; needed to tell him that she had been wrong. She tried to sit up, but her head swam and she was instantly and violently sick, vomiting a thin stream of bile onto the ground. It burnt at the back of her nostrils, and her mouth turned sour. When she swallowed, it felt as though her throat were full of broken glass. She lay back down again, chest heaving, on the floor.

"He's asked for you to be taken to hospital," Sister Clara said in her low, melodic voice, and even then Frances noticed how perfect she was: the porcelain lines of her face, the soft mouth, the intelligent eyes. The anxiety she had felt at William's house, when she thought of Edwin running the smallpox hospital with this woman, came flooding back, and she recognized the feeling now as jealousy. It was possible that Edwin loved this woman. He might always have done, long before he came back to London and was coerced into proposing to Frances. After what seemed a long while, she was lifted by two men onto a stretcher and carried outside to a cart. Darkness had fallen, and the yard was full of men — native men, with picks and axes, carrying lanterns and swilling beer, calling to one another under the blackening sky.

The stretcher was placed in the back of the cart. She could smell the grease of the mules, and something else, metallic, like blood left out to dry in the sun. She shut her eyes to keep the nausea at bay, but it was no good. The cart lurched into motion and her mouth filled with saliva. She forced herself up, doubling over, her stomach gripped by a series of rapid contractions.

She was taken to the smallpox hospital. Flickering candles marked out the stretchers which lay on the floor in rows on either side of a pavilion. It was hot under the canvas, even at night. The place smelt of carbolic acid, and beneath it there was a stench of putrefying flesh. Two nurses lifted her onto an empty stretcher, and she wondered if her predecessor had come out alive.

A high fever coursed through her, and her mouth broke out in ulcers, but after a few days it subsided. She felt as if she was recovering but then remembered that Mariella had said something similar. It was agony to swallow, as if she had a nest of stinging bees caught in her throat, and when she touched her lips she saw that her hands were covered in a rash of fine red spots. An acid fear seeped into her stomach. Sister Clara came, holding a bedpan.

"Where is Anne?" Frances asked, reluctant to have this woman, who was so close to Edwin, handle her body.

"They're short of nurses in Kimberley Hospital," Sister Clara said, levering the bedpan underneath Frances. "She has had to go back." Frances swallowed thickly. It would be harder without Anne.

"And my husband?" she asked, looking at her hands and trying to keep the emotion out of her voice. Edwin still hadn't been to see her. "Will he be coming to the hospital today?"

"The disease has spread to one of the villages outside Kimberley. He has had to go there to vaccinate."

Frances released a thin stream of urine into the metal dish.

"Why do I feel better?" she asked, when Sister Clara had removed the pan.

"This is the first stage. I'm afraid you'll get worse before you get better."

"If I get better."

"You've a good chance. The previous vaccine you were given should help."

Frances pressed her. "How good a chance?"

The nurse gave her a straight look. "About two-thirds of our patients survive."

After two days, her skin began to itch and burn, and the rash of red spots, which had seemed innocuous before, swelled into bloated pustules. Blisters erupted on the palms of her hands. She waited for Edwin, but he never came. The fever returned, more strongly this time, and the world fractured like glass into a thousand shining pieces which wouldn't fit together. The blisters spread down the inside of her arms, across her stomach, and over the soles of her feet. They began to swell and grow and were hard to the touch. When she felt them, round and firm beneath the surface of her skin, she became convinced that they were egg sacs and would hatch, each one disgorging a million translucent spiders crawling over her body.

Her skin felt too small for her body, shriveling and crackling like a roasting chicken, leaving the raw flesh beneath. The pain was excruciating, as if a butcher were easing it off with the tip of a sharp knife, and she couldn't stop herself from whimpering. Her eyelids, swollen and raw with pustules, closed up, trapping her in the dark. Her mouth felt as if it had been scraped raw, and her whole body was on fire. The moaning of other patients troubled her sleep, and the sweat under her arms smelled like the juices of decaying meat.

Time passed slowly, then frighteningly fast. She woke once in the night, and it seemed as if it had been dark for a year and the sun would never rise, and when she woke again it was dusk and the light was fading. She dreamt she was drowning in a pool of thick, sluggish blood. Edwin was standing nearby and she tried to call to him, but she couldn't keep herself afloat for long enough. The blood ran down her throat into her lungs, bloating her stomach and suffocating her shouts into scarlet, foaming gulps. She woke up shouting his name. The nurses came, looking concerned, but they didn't seem to understand her when she spoke. Her sentences became long, slippery things which didn't make sense, and they hushed her into quiet.

Some time later the fever broke, and she was conscious of herself again as a fixed being with a mind and a body separate from each other. It was possible to think clearly. She was able to open her eyes a little, and she lay for a long time, exhausted, staring at the canvas walls which glowed yellow under the beating sun.

"Good, you're awake," Anne said, crouching down beside her stretcher.

Frances managed a faint smile. "I thought you were working back at Kimberley Hospital?"

"Just for a week," she said, holding out a cup of water. Frances lifted herself onto one elbow and took it from her. It was good to see a familiar face. The metal beaker clinked against her teeth, and the sores in the corners of her mouth were needles of pain as she opened her lips to drink.

"And my husband? Is he here?" she asked, lying back on the stretcher, exhausted from the effort of sitting up.

Anne began straightening the bedsheet, and Frances realized her friend was embarrassed. She must know what had happened with Edwin. "He left for Cape Town yesterday evening. The governor had asked to see him personally." Frances blinked back her disappointment and watched Anne pull an envelope out of the pocket of her pinafore. "He left you this," she said, handing it to Frances. The paper was dry and sharp against the sores on her fingers. Anne stood up, but turned before she walked away. "Your skin, Frances, it will heal. It won't be as bad as it seems now."

Frances slipped the letter out of its envelope, and a flutter of banknotes fell onto the sheet. She gazed at the writing on the thin paper.

I have written to your relations in England letting them know that you have been unwell, and that the climate in South Africa doesn't suit you. Your aunt will no doubt agree to take you in on the same terms as previously agreed. Enclosed is enough money for your passage back to England, and for a few weeks' stay at the sanatorium in Cape Town so you can recover before the journey. I shall return to Kimberley in three weeks. It would be best if you were gone before then.

She closed her eyes. The letter was completely cold, void of sympathy or concern, and she understood now that he wanted nothing more to do with her. She folded it and laid it on the floor. Then she put a hand carefully to her face. The sores on her cheeks were turning into scabs. They were pitted and hard, and when she touched them it was like turning a tooth. They seemed to have roots which went deep into the surface of her skin. How could Edwin ever love her now? As a child, she had thought that people scarred by smallpox were erupting with maggots, as if they were rotting from the inside out.

She wouldn't leave Kimberley until she had spoken to him. She needed to see him again, just the two of them alone in a room together, as husband and wife. But what if he forced her to leave South Africa and return to England? It would mean never seeing him again, and this was too awful a possibility to contemplate.

He agreed to meet her three weeks later in a small tent adjacent to the main hospital pavilions. Sister Clara stepped out as Frances was about to go in, and gave her a warm smile. "Mrs. Matthews. I hope you are feeling better?"

"Yes, thank you," Frances said, feeling her confidence drain away at the sight of this woman, with her austere, impeccable beauty.

Edwin was seated at a small wooden desk in the center of the tent. He stood up when she came in, holding her gaze steadily but not moving to take her hand. There was a look of huge compassion in his eyes; of integrity and honesty; that he would look any evil in the face and come out of it unchanged. Was it possible that this man had been her husband and she had blindly pushed him away? They both stood perfectly still. She was aware of her skin, pitted with scars, and of Sister Clara having stood here a few moments before. She wondered what they had discussed, whether he had looked at her with the same intensity, and whether he had liked what he had seen.

All the things about Edwin which had frustrated her before had only done so, she realized, because she had been threatened by them. His capacity for stillness; the careful way that he watched her, assessed her, tried to figure her out; his persistence in talking to her about the things he cared about; his patience in waiting for her to understand. He had known her better than anyone else; better than her father, who had seen her as an accomplishment. Edwin had dared to expose her, tried to make her more than she was, and she had hated him for it. Now she wanted to plead with him to forgive her and take her back, but she didn't dare.

He broke the silence, gesturing to the small canvas chair facing him. She sat, remembering suddenly their meeting in London, when she had accepted his proposal. How long ago that seemed, and how different things were between them now. She had assumed that he was coercing her into marriage, against her father's wishes, and she had resented him for it. Now she knew he had felt obliged, but the knowledge had come too late.

"Have the nurses looked after you well?" he asked, sitting down at his desk. He was too polite, and she knew he wished she had gone on to Cape Town without requesting this meeting.

"Yes, they have been very kind."

"You were lucky. The scarring is not so bad."

She knew this was true, but it was hard to be grateful. Her face might not have been as damaged as some, but it was still a shock to see herself in the mirror. Her eyes and nose were unmarked, but the skin which used to stretch so finely over her cheeks and forehead had turned livid and raw, the surface riveted with small craters. Anne had told her that over time the marks would lessen, but she knew her face would always carry the mottled thickness of heavy scarring. Any claim she might have had to beauty was gone.

"Have they told you to use coconut water?"

She nodded. It made her uncomfortable to hear him talking to her with the medical concern of a doctor. She wanted to have a conversation with him as her husband.

"Was your trip to Cape Town a success?" she asked.

"They're finally taking the matter seriously, which is progress. I hope they'll be sending an independent health inspector to visit us. We'll see." He smiled at her, a gentle, kind smile, but one that suggested no closeness between them. The last time she had seen him sitting at a desk, it had been at Rietfontein. He had leant over and pulled out the tick which had buried itself in her neck, and she had smelt the sweat drying on his body and felt the firmness of his hand as he held her head. She looked at his hand now, resting on the desk, and she felt a choking, maddening desire for him to reach forward and touch her, to lean into him and feel the hard warmth of his body.

She forced her eyes away, trying to bring herself back to the present, and saw his canvas knapsack leant up against the desk. "I suppose you don't have much time for collecting insects?" she asked, remembering their walks at Rietfontein.

"No," he said, waiting for her to come to her point.

She was silent for a moment, looking at her hands; then, unable to bear it, she glanced up at him. "Edwin, I want you to know how sorry I am. I thought I under-stood what I was doing. I thought I loved him. But I couldn't have been more wrong." How to tell him the awfulness of what she now knew about William? But he knew already. He had known all along what Baier's world was really like. "Can you forgive me?"

His gray eyes settled on hers. "You don't need to ask for my forgiveness."

He didn't say anything else, and she became desperate. "Edwin, I don't want to go back to England."

"Where would you go instead?"

"What if I stayed in South Africa?"

"How would you support yourself?"

"You are my husband," she said in a low voice.

"I think you forsook the right to call yourself my wife some time ago." His tone was cold and practical. His finality frightened her.

"Will you not give me a second chance?"

"I brought you to Kimberley."

"Did you never care about me?"

"Yes," he said, "I cared about you. I even thought I loved you."

"Because of the way I looked?" Her eyes stung, and she bit her bottom lip to hold back the tears.

"Because there seemed to be something raw and untouched in you. I thought South Africa would set you free."

"And now?"

"And now I think it is time for you to go back home. To England. You have suffered enough here."

"I don't want to go back," she said, her voice catching on a sob. She was aware that she was covering the same ground. That there was nothing left for her to say. "Edwin —" she began, but he interrupted her.

"Frances, don't do this to yourself. We wouldn't be happy, either of us. There isn't enough respect on either side. It wouldn't be good for you or for me."

"But if you loved me once . . ."

"Perhaps my love was no different than yours for Westbrook." It hurt to hear him say the name so casually. The thought of William clearly didn't affect him at all. "We were both of us caught up in a fantasy. I thought I saw something in you which I wanted, but in the end I couldn't find it."

He stood up, signaling an end to the meeting, and she realized that this would be the last time she would see him. Time was running out. She stood up herself, wringing her hands. "Can you blame me for not understanding?" She took a deep breath. "Nothing was ever explained to me. You talked to me once, a long time ago, about my father's roses. Domesticated plants — 'monstrosities,' you called them. They grew in a controlled environment, protected, mollycoddled, grafted onto the stronger roots of other plants so they could survive; deviations from their true form in nature. They might be highly decorative, you said, bred for dazzling colors, but essentially they were monstrosities." She was speaking faster now, the logic of her words gathering force as she spoke. "I asked you — do you remember — what would happen to them if they were left to grow wild? Whether they could survive?"

He stood with one hand resting on his desk, looking steadily at her. "And I said they would die."

"No. You said either they would die or they would be forced to change. They would revert back to their aboriginal stock." She stepped forward, her heart pounding, her palms sweating. "Don't you see? I am just the same." The truth of her words was overtaking her. "I am a monstrosity. I can pin my hair in five different styles; I can paint, embroider, and play the piano; but what else can I do? What merit do I have outside in the real world where people live and die? Where there is disease and corruption? What purpose do I have? You offered me a world of truth. Can you blame me if I shrank from it? I had no familiarity with the truth. It terrified me. I thought it would destroy everything that I was." Her cheeks were wet with tears, and her mouth was full of the taste of salt. "You are the only person who ever thought I could be something different. Who thought I could change. I have felt like a weightless, hopeless thing my whole life, except when I have been with you."

He stood watching her, not saying anything. She might have seen a sadness in his eyes, but nothing that suggested he would change his mind. She knew she had lost, and she brushed at her tears, composed herself for a second, and walked out into the bright sunlight.

THIRTY-THREE

She traveled in a mule cart. Blackened earth, a road of dust and bones bleached to perfect ivory. This was the drought which they had talked about in Kimberley. It was spring now, the days were warmer, and farmers were said to wake weeping in the night at the thought of another summer without rain.

It wasn't the drought that woke Frances up, weeping in the night, but the thought of England. It took on the quality of a nightmare. Her aunt had written to her saying she would take her in as a nurse, but the damp, cramped house with its tiny attic room shared with two children filled her with bleak despair. She hadn't forgotten the gray skies and the ugly, sprawling city with its vast factories pumping smoke into a charcoal sky. The poverty, the pain, and the grime, and a crippling morality that kept each person fixed in his place. Her every second would be a lesson in humiliation. There would be no one who saw her as anything other than a burden; someone who should give affection without expecting to receive it; a woman who had failed, with not a thing in the world to call her own. And she knew she would torture herself with regret, and the certain knowledge that while each day increased her longing for Edwin, it would bring him closer to forgetting her.

So she went instead to Rietfontein. It was her only chance. The cart dropped her outside the house, almost a year after she had first arrived, and she stood for a moment in the yard with the chickens pecking at her feet, breathing heavily. The farm looked desolate in the midst of the barren plain. The fever tree no longer cast its shade over the house. It had been sapped of life, its branches withered so that it looked like a spiny skeleton of its former self.

She made a silent prayer before knocking on the door. Everything depended on Mevrouw Reitz. She could have written, but she suspected the woman would have turned down her appeal. There was little reason for her to like Frances. She had been churlish and spoilt when she had lived here before, refusing her offer of help and holding herself apart. Now she had to convince her that she could be useful.

Frances waited for Mevrouw Reitz in the sitting room. When the woman walked in she stopped and stared. Frances had been expecting it, but it hurt nonetheless, and she had to stop herself from bringing a hand to her face to feel out the scars with her fingertips.

"Where is Dr. Matthews?" Mevrouw Reitz asked. Frances had anticipated the question, but still it made her flush, and she hesitated.

"You've had a disagreement?"

"He wants me to return to England."

"But instead you came here."

"Yes." Frances paused, realizing the ridiculousness of what she was asking. Why would this woman want to help her?

"I thought . . . or at least I was hoping that you might take me on as a governess."

"A governess?" Mevrouw Reitz asked, as if she didn't understand the word.

"I could teach your boys English, French, and drawing."

The woman stood up, brushing down her skirts. "I'm sorry, but I cannot help you."

"Please, if you would take a moment to consider."

"Mrs. Matthews, I cannot —"

"He needn't know that I am here," she said desperately.

Mevrouw Reitz stopped abruptly and looked at her. "Madam, you are missing the point. Have you no sense? This is a drought. The cattle are dying. There is no water for the sheep. And you come here offering to be a governess?"

"But you have the dam. You said it had never failed."

"The dam?" Mevrouw Reitz laughed faintly, and Frances remembered the landscape she had driven through, scorched as if by fire, scrub receding from the earth like the shriveling hair on an old man, and the dead bushes, uprooted, blowing over the parched ground. "It has been over two years since the last rains. My Jan has never seen them."

"You needn't pay me," Frances said, fear knocking at her ribs. She could feel her future slipping through her fingers. "Is there nothing I can do here?"

The woman gazed at her, and Frances felt the weight of her reproach. They both knew she was of little use.

"Can you cook?"

"I can learn."

"Have you had any experience with laundry work? Keeping poultry? Can you make dresses?"

Frances shook her head in dismay.

"Why here? Why don't you go home?"

What could she say? That there was no home. Not anymore. She could see the confusion on the woman's face. She didn't understand why a girl who was clearly so out of place on the veldt would want to stay. She didn't understand that she wanted to learn to love this place because Edwin had loved it.

Mevrouw Reitz stepped away from her and went to stand by the window. "You must have done something terrible for him to have left you. I never knew a man more honest."

"Yes," Frances said. "But look at me now. Is this not punishment enough?"

There was a long pause. She looked at the woman's strong, broad back, at her graying hair, pulled into a tight bun. Somewhere in the house a child began crying. After a moment the woman spoke. "Where would you sleep?" she asked, more to herself than to Frances.

"In the cottage," Frances said quietly, her heart swelling with hope.

"On your own? Don't be ridiculous." The woman gave a bark of laughter. "And we can't have you out with the native servants either. You would have to sleep in the house."

She turned at the window and looked at Frances. "And you are happy to work?"

Frances nodded. "Of course."

"Well, it seems you have luck on your side. Our Dutch maid left us a week ago. Scared we won't feed her and the baby if the drought doesn't break. And she's probably right. We can scarce feed ourselves. But as I said, we're short of a maid. There won't be much in the way of wages. You'll help with the children and you'll work in the kitchen. You'll sleep in the house, but don't expect anything else that's any different from the other servants."

"Mevrouw Reitz, thank you."

"You should call me Mevrouw, not Mevrouw Reitz," the older woman said, efficiently establishing the new terms of their relationship. "And you'll have to learn to speak Dutch."

THIRTY-FOUR

A ladder led up to the attic. Untreated wooden floors which creaked and splintered on bare feet. Dried hams hung from the ceiling, and the room smelt of animal hides and old paper. The floor was taken up with crates of peach brandy and boxes of kitchen instruments. Suitcases of shredded clothes were stacked up beside piles of old newspapers. The mattress had to be rolled out, and she shifted the crates back against the wall to create space, working carefully, wary of scorpions. Her mind kept touching on a great sadness, like a finger pricking on a pin. Edwin had cut his ties with her. No one knew she was at Rietfontein, and there was no one to tell.

She shook out a sheet over the bed and began tucking in the corners. It was made of coarse cotton, rough against her fingers. Mevrouw Reitz had given her a hessian sack for a pillow, which she stuffed now with handfuls of shredded clothes. She had imagined herself sleeping in the cottage. It would have afforded her a degree of independence. Instead she was a maid of all work, and her time would not be her own. She would have to swallow what was left of her pride, and work hard and learn quickly if she was going to survive.

A window looked out over the veldt towards the dam and the setting sun, and the leafless branches of the fever tree shivered over the pane. The thorny tangle of stems looked all but dead now, and she wondered if the tree still offered the birds its protection. When she had rolled out the mattress and made the bed, she stood and watched the sky turning from pale gold to deep yellow like the spilled yolk of an egg. The tall stump of a quiver tree, black against the fading light, stood alone on the veldt as if it were the cloaked outline of a figure watching the house. In a drought they self-amputated, Edwin had told her, constricting their branches until they became so dry they dropped off. Then they drew water down into the depths of their trunk and waited for the rains.

The light seeped from the horizon, leaving thin strips of color. She had no candle up here — that was another thing to ask for. Bats flickered through the darkening sky like pieces of charred paper turning in the wind. She felt as if she were seeing everything through his eyes. She breathed deeply. It wouldn't be easy, but she was content to be here.

Frances was worn-out by the disease, drained of energy both emotionally and physically, and the work she was given at Rietfontein exhausted her. It was hard to believe that scarcely a year ago she had had the temerity to complain to Edwin about Sarah. The woman had single-handedly put every meal on the table, washed every article of clothing, mended and darned, and still managed to keep their house immaculate. It was no wonder she had napped in the heat of the afternoons.

At five, Frances brought tea to the Reitzes in bed, dressed the younger children, served the family breakfast, cleared the table, and washed the dishes, but not the pots and pans — the boy did those. There was lunch to be prepared, and more washing of dishes afterwards, then tea and dinner in the evening. When she wasn't helping in the kitchen, or watching the children, she was with Maria, the Xhosa maid, making soap and candles, stuffing mattresses, and polishing the brass. There were the chickens to be fed, the butter to be churned, and the lamps to be filled and trimmed. At first she was clumsy and slow at everything, and her fingers blistered with all the burning and chafing, but she soon learnt.

On Mondays she helped Maria with the washing. They boiled hot water in the tall copper, plunging their hands in until they scalded and turned purple in the heat, kneading the fabrics and beating out the dirt. The drought meant that washing was kept to a minimum, but even though there was so much less than there might have been, she dreaded it. The linen had to be boiled, bleached, scrubbed, rinsed, and wrung into buckets which they carried out to the garden and tipped over the vegetables. Her shoulders would stiffen up the following day so that it hurt when she dressed, and her hands turned soft and flaky then hardened into bony scales.

There were four boys still at home. The twins were identical, large-boned and athletic with white-blond hair, broad thighs, and pure blue eyes which gazed skeptically at Frances as if she were a strange new species. They were old enough to help on the farm, and they spent most days ranging over the veldt with their father, shearing, dipping, and herding the vast flocks of sheep. They rarely returned of their own accord, and in the evenings Frances would be sent out to bring them in. More often than not, she would find them squatting in the yard torturing something. They baited spiders out of holes with long twigs and plucked the wings off hornets. Once, they dropped two scorpions into a bowl and laughed as they danced around each other, stings poised in a deadly duel. Frances watched over their shoulders, fascinated by the creatures' brilliant ferocity. Another time she found them poking sticks into a box full of fawn-colored worms — except they weren't worms, she discovered later, but miniature cobras which drew back their heads, tails flickering, and darted at the sticks with lethal precision. When Mijnheer Reitz discovered them, he threw the snakes, box and all, into the furnace. Frances, standing by, thought she could hear them screeching as they fell into the white-hot flames.

Piet had grown into a shy, slight, solitary boy with a wad of dark hair, pale skin, and large brown eyes. He was the very opposite of his brothers' brutality, and he brought home a slew of wounded animals. There was an elephant shrew mauled by an eagle, and a baby bird dropped from its nest, throat transparent and taut, which he carried home cupped between his hands with an expression of profound concern. Inevitably they died, in the night, and he would show himself the next morning, stoic in the face of tragedy. His father was often angry with him. When he caught him playing with his lead soldiers or scratching out letters in the flour dust outside the bread oven, he would cuff him round the head for idleness and say, "There's a drought on," as if the boy were somehow culpable. Frances thought he probably blamed himself for the boy losing his fingers. Then there was Jan, the youngest, who spent most of the day sitting in the cool corners of the house with a colored nurse who plaited a kind of willow for the backs of the chairs.

The drought was one of the worst in living memory. The men, armed with rifles, guarded the dam day and night to stop the game from drinking. Every day the water receded further from its banks, like a puddle drying in the sun. The ground blistered and dried in the heat, its surface cracking, so that it looked like the gnarled, leathered skin of a crocodile. She had always considered the Reitzes to be wealthy — their land stretched as far as the mountains in the distance — but she hadn't understood that the veldt was so poor that when the drought came and their herds began to die their wealth would fall away from them like coins poured down a drain.

Mevrouw Reitz kept water turtles in a glass bowl in the kitchen and said that when they rose to the surface it would rain. A dog went missing on the farm, and they found the carcass behind the native huts. The natives had no crops, and Maria said that they were so hungry they were grinding down the bones of dead animals to survive. The water they drank in the house was dank and brackish and always warm. Spring rolled into summer, and everyone waited. The veldt turned from dun to brown, and began to blacken in the sun as if it had been singed by fire. Frances walked down to the river with Piet one afternoon, and they dug their feet into the deep, heavy sand in the riverbed. It was hard to imagine water had ever flowed here. There were no insects or birds. Only the cicadas still grated out their song. Even the mimosa bushes had dried up and lost their green. A few goats were nibbling at their lower branches. She had been told that the leaves would turn their milk sour and the kids would stop suckling, but when she tried to shoo them away they butted at her legs and kept on eating.

Her great struggle was learning to speak Dutch. Mevrouw Reitz was the only person who spoke English, but she refused to speak it to Frances now that she was a servant. Frustrations were quick to show when she didn't understand. The difficulty was finding someone to teach her the vocabulary. But here she found a friend in Piet, who loved to explain the meaning of words, never losing patience, perhaps understanding with a child's intuition that her position in the house rested on her ability to grasp the language.

There were two other servants who worked in the house. The cook — a small, silent man with two missing front teeth and sad eyes — and Maria, the maid. She was the daughter of Jantjie, the Reitzes' driver, who had been born on the farm over eighty years before. Maria had high cheekbones and a brush of hair cut close to her scalp like a man. A stream of children would come to see her at the back door of the kitchen, and Frances never worked out how many of them were her own. She was straight-backed and strong, with capable hands, and she took control of Frances as if she were a child, not necessarily because she liked her, but because someone had to assume responsibility. It was Maria who showed her how to polish the brass, how to make coffee — grinding down the beans with dried figs — how to gut a fish without slicing open her palm, and how to mix bleach into the water without burning her hands.

It was Frances's duty to darn and mend. The only sewing she had ever done was embroidery, and during her first week in the house she looked with mounting panic at the linen piling up in the workbasket. Maria taught her how to darn socks, fix the seam of a dress, and put a new collar on a shirt. She would place her hands, dry and warm like leather, over Frances's own, the fabric jammed between her fingers, molding itself into the neat folds which always evaded Frances when she tried by herself. If Frances slipped a stitch or knotted the thread, Maria would admonish her in her own language, a tumbling flow of clicks and vowels.

Frances ate in the kitchen — mealies, which stuck in her teeth, smeared with gravy from dinner. Occasionally, in the evenings, Jantjie would come and stand just outside the open door of the kitchen, packing his pipe and talking to Maria, and he would nod at her politely.

For a few hours every afternoon, it was her responsibility to look after Piet. She walked with him to the dam most days. It was a ritual for all members of the household, master and servant, to see how far the water had fallen. Some days the twins would come with them. They wrestled on the muddy banks, bodies jammed against each other, rolling over and over in the earth until one had pinned the other to the ground, knees on elbows, jaw open in triumph. Piet avoided them, content to be on his own, and this reminded her of herself as a child. He would squat down on the mud, watching the natives beating the sheep away from the water's edge, or stretch out on the burning earth, tempting birds to come closer with specks of bread. His brothers treated him as a curiosity. When bored, they loved to taunt him, and occasionally their bullying turned to violence. He would scramble out from under them with a nose trickling blood or a bruised eye purpling as it swelled shut.

In the afternoons, wisps of clouds would gather, forming tumbling mountains in the sky with the sugary whiteness of meringues, and the household would look up, daring to hope for rain when they had promised themselves not to. The sun would slip momentarily into shade, and the earth would exhale in gratitude. A moment later the plains would be cast again into a blaze of heat, and they would watch despairingly as the clouds dissolved into a hazy sunset.

Frances's fate was inextricably bound up with that of the whole household. If the rains failed, they would all fail, and she would have to go back to England. But she found to her surprise that she wanted the rains to come not just because her survival depended on it but because she was beginning to respect the life at Rietfontein. Mevrouw Reitz was brittle and coarse, but she had purpose. She was never still, with Jan on one arm, pulling weeds out of the garden, or in the kitchen, bottling and preserving and pounding down herbs into medicines for her children. And out of her labor came this extraordinary family, thriving in this hostile place.

Frances wondered at the single-mindedness, at the passion and the pleasure to be had from such an existence. Life had been so different in England. She and her cousins had prided themselves on being idle, boasting about not having to lift a finger all through the long summer afternoons. But in the Karoo, merit rested on one's ability to be useful: to cook, to clean, to sew, to mend. Everyone was hard at work, and they seemed happier because of it. They treated Frances for the most part well. She fell into bed every night beyond any exhaustion she had ever known, and found to her surprise that she was, if not content, then satisfied. Her muscles ached in the mornings, and there was pleasure in being busy. More than that, she was learning: about how to create things; how to transform this barren, desolate place, through human endeavor, into a thing of beauty.

A few trees had been watered through the summer, and they yielded fruit. Frances helped Mevrouw Reitz in the kitchen making jam. She reveled in the process, carving out the peach stones and boiling up the soft chunks of wet yellow flesh in a huge copper with sugar and water until the room throbbed with an aching, bodily sweetness. She loved to watch it thicken, eventually letting a drop fall from the spoon onto the slab of cool marble, where it proved it would set. It was her job to spoon the oozing amber jam into jars, and when it was done she licked the sticky residue from her burnt fingers with satisfaction.

Her Dutch improved until she was able to understand the Reitzes and hold a conversation with the other servants. She particularly enjoyed talking to Jantjie. His quiet strength and fascination with nature reminded her of Edwin. He would tell her stories about the veldt, bringing it teeming into life. He talked about the droughts which had lasted years and left the land a desert, of the floods which followed when the water ran off the plains and burst the dam, and the swarms of locusts which arrived in the wake of the rains. He told stories of hailstorms which struck in midsummer with stones as large as fists, and the snow which fell one winter three feet deep. Lightning stories weren't unusual, but Jantjie's was the best. He had seen a team of oxen all struck dead by one bolt which hit the metal harness.

Maria called him a *slangmeester*. He had, so she said, rubbed the venom of snakes into wounds in his skin to give him immunity. There was never any proof of this, though he did once hold up a scorpion in front of the children and let it sting him again and again, and he showed no pain or ill effects. He told snake stories as school-girls told ghost stories, and the children sometimes crept to the door to listen to him. There was the time when Maria was still a child. She had pushed open the door from the *stoep,* and a snake, asleep on top, fell down in a noose about her neck. She froze in fright as the snake uncoiled itself and slithered down her back, leaving her unharmed. Jantjie spoke with such conviction that Frances could never tell when he was blurring the lines of truth. He told her about the snakes that had a thirst for milk — he had seen one with his own eyes drinking from the udders of a cow — and the Xhosa woman who had fallen asleep underneath a tree suckling her child and woken to find a puff adder clamped to her other breast.

Frances avoided looking in mirrors, but she couldn't always help catching a glimpse of herself in the reflection of a window or in the glass in the hall. She noticed over time that the scars were losing their redness. They weren't as deep and pitted as they had been before, but her skin had taken on the indelicate quality of roughly worked clay. Oddly, in her dreams, she was never scarred, and she wondered whether that would change, like those who — living in another country — begin to dream in a different language.

She longed for news from Kimberley, but few newspapers made their way to the house, and visitors were rare. Occasionally, men stopped in on their way to or from

Cape Town, and she would eagerly listen in on their conversations, but she heard nothing of any interest. Only once a trader spent the night, and she overheard him saying business was bad. Smallpox had been declared in Kimberley, and though there was no mention of Edwin, she was pleased that he had succeeded.

THIRTY-FIVE

Frances saw that Piet liked her, and was gratified by it. He brought her bugs to examine in matchboxes, chocolates from the dinner table, and one evening, when she was cutting his fingernails, he asked her cautiously whether it was true that her husband had left her.

"Yes," she said, thinking he must have heard it from his parents.

"Why?" he asked, his head tilted up to look at her.

She held one of his hands in her own, the stumps of his missing fingers round and hard in her palm, and snipped the crown off the tip of his forefinger. "When we married we didn't know each other well enough." She held her lower lip between her teeth, and blinked back tears. "By the time we did, it was too late."

When the older boys rode out onto the farm with their father in the afternoons, she and Piet would read or walk. One afternoon, she asked him if he could keep a secret. If I take you to a special place, will you not tell a soul? He nodded solemnly, pleased to be included in an adventure.

They took a parasol to keep off the sun and a flask full of water. Piet thrust his dry hand into hers, and she clasped it. A fierce, hot wind blew up dust devils which flew across the veldt like miniature tornadoes. The land shimmered and danced in the heat. Piet kept his eyes riveted to the ground. He was looking for the blue-headed lizard, which could be seen staring north in the advent of rain.

When Frances saw the cottage she was torn between joy and sadness. This was the place where she had known Edwin best. Returning here was a way of pretending that nothing had changed. It was an indulgence. As she climbed the *stoep,* memories flooded back. The door was slightly ajar, and she swung it open, wary of snakes. Piet held on to her hand, fascinated by this old, empty shell of a house weighted down with history. The rooms were shuttered and dark, and the hall smelt dry and faintly aromatic of the camphor Edwin had used in his study. She stood breathless for a moment, Piet dangling from her arm, impatient but

577

fearful. Then she stepped into the bedroom. The brass bed had gone. Fingers of light escaped through chinks in the wood, casting a delicate pattern on the bare floor. The beating of wings startled her. A bird flew in frantic circles around the room, dashing itself against the shutters in a bid to escape. Frances lifted the latch and threw them open, letting in a flood of sunlight, and the bird darted outside.

She looked at the worn boards and the peeling, plastered walls. These rooms had been a prison to her before, but now the isolation and simplicity seemed full of opportunity. Why had she refused the possibility of happiness here? It had been growing inside her, a sense of contentment, but she hadn't acknowledged it. Instead she had resented Edwin for bringing her to Rietfontein and thought about nothing but William. She stepped into the sitting room and gave a low cry of surprise. The piano still stood in the corner. It was the only piece of furniture left in the house, and she wondered why it hadn't been sold. When she pulled off the sheet a plume of dust rose into the air. She sneezed, then lifted the lid and pulled out the stool which was tucked beneath it. The piano smelt of an English drawing room — of wax and the raw underside of furniture. It was just as out of place as her, this piece of England cast up on the veldt.

It was then that she saw the music book in the stand. She hadn't noticed it the first time she had sat at the piano. Inside was an inscription: "To my wife. 1880." Regret welled up inside her. He must have bought it for her, and he would have expected her to see it, but she had been too preoccupied.

She didn't recognize the sonatas, hadn't even heard of the German composer. She began to play the first, feeling her way slowly through the music, faltering at times. It swelled and filled the room, a wonderful, lilting, nostalgic piece, strangely delicate in this tumbledown wreck of a cottage in the middle of the vast plains, miles from the civilization which had produced such refinement, and she thought of all the times she might have played for Edwin but had willfully refused. He had bought her the piano — a gesture of huge generosity — in the hope that it would be something they could share together, but she had assumed, instead, that he had wanted to gloat over the talents of the girl he had secured in marriage. Of course, she had been thinking only of herself. He must have wanted the music too, the release of it. It might have taken them to other places, opened doors between them, but she had shut down the opportunity.

There were times over the past year when she had been ashamed of the fact that she couldn't turn herself to any practical purpose. She had felt useless and lacking in some way, but as she played, she remembered something different. The music was exquisitely beautiful, a thing beyond value, and it poured from her fingers. Her pride expanded, stretching inside her, and she remembered that this too was worth something, and he had wanted her because of it.

When the piece came to an end she put her head down on the lid of the piano. She was aware of Piet standing behind her, watching her, but she couldn't turn around quite yet. She was tired — tired of polishing, of washing, of serving another family and not having her own. She was tired of blaming herself, and tired of wanting Edwin. For a moment she felt overwhelmed. Her body shuddered, gripped with longing for a past that could not be re-created. Her marriage had played itself out here, and she had made nothing of it.

A hand touched her lightly on the shoulder. Piet stood holding out a golden feather. She wiped her eyes and smiled, taking the

feather from him. In the old, warped cupboard in the kitchen, she found a tin of
Swedish anchovies. The two of them sat on
the *stoep,* and she knocked a hole in the lid
with a rock and prized open a jagged section of metal. They ate the anchovies with
their fingers, delicious and salty rich, and
washed them down with gulps of warm
water from the flask. A lizard crawled out
from behind a rock, the only living creature
in a vast empty plain of blackened ant
heaps. She had hoped that Nanny might appear, but there was no sign of her.

They took a different route home, walking
up the slight incline of the *kopje* until they
had a good view of the veldt, the cottage
behind them and the farmhouse ahead with
its *kraals* and barns. To their right was the
dam, shrunken now to a pool that barely
reflected the sun on its muddied surface.
Vultures wheeled in the air above. Frances
had heard they were slaughtering lambs
today, to save the ewes.

When they got home, the twins were waiting for them. The brothers were animated.
Hendrik held a box, which he promised to
show. It mewled and chattered and threatened to overturn itself until he planted
himself firmly on its lid. A baboon, Hermanus said, had been driven down from the

mountains by thirst. It had ripped the udders from two ewes, sucking them dry for milk. Mijnheer Reitz had shot it, and when they approached they saw she held a baby to her chest.

On cue, Hendrik hopped off the box, flipped off its lid, and pulled out a baby baboon. It was a scraggly, ugly thing, no bigger than a rat, which grappled at his arm and screeched in fear. It had pink ears and a pink face, wrinkled and hairless, the very replica of an old man's, with tufted eyebrows and a dog's nose. Its head was bald, and the hair was so thin across its body that you could see the fleas crawling over its skin. Piet tried to take hold of it, but his brother laughed and hurled it at the other, who caught it — or, rather, the baboon caught hold of him, sticking like a burr. It tried to cling on but was thrown back again. Piet took great gulps of air, trying to fathom their cruelty, until Frances intervened. "Let him have it," she said. "You have played with it all day." And they reluctantly obeyed.

The baboon, which Piet called simply "Baboon," was bottle-fed until it was able to suck from a bowl of milk. Then it would crouch, hands on either side of the bowl, only rising, snorting from the white froth, when it remembered to breathe. Piet was the only person in the house who had any interest in it, and the baboon adored the boy, reluctant to ever be prized away. When the twins came close, the baboon swiped at them until they learnt not to touch it. At night, when the family was gathered in the drawing room listening to Mijnheer Reitz reading from the Bible, the baby baboon sat by the lamp catching moths, stuffing them into its mouth with a puff of powdered wings.

Thirty-Six

The Reitzes had stocked the dam with fish many years ago, and they had multiplied. Now the water, a fraction of its former size, became a broiling mass of bodies. Every day it receded, and the fish were crammed more closely together. They flipped and turned, scales glistening through the mud, in a desperate bid to keep their bodies out of the sun. Mijnheer Reitz said that any man on the farm was welcome to take them away, and in the afternoons native boys could be seen wading into the water, grasping at them with their hands, shouting and laughing as the fish pumped and slid out of their tight fists like writhing chunks of muscle. They tossed them into canvas buckets and took them home. Hundreds were hauled out of the water with nets and left on the banks to die, mouths gulping under a hot sun, wet scales sticking with dust, and their eyes drying up in seconds to a hardened crisp.

At the house, Frances was asked to help the cook gut the barrelfuls which were brought in from the dam, still alive. She stood in the kitchen, her hands glistening with slime and her arms covered in scales, knocking the heads of the fish against a corner of the zinc tabletop. Occasionally, one wriggled from her grasp, flipping onto the kitchen floor, where it lay motionless, gills heaving with knowing desperation. She sliced open stomach after stomach, spilling the guts into a bin. The Reitzes and their servants ate fish soup, fish pie, fish curry, fish balls, fish ten different ways, and still they weren't rid of it. The cook jarred bottles of fish pickle and fish sauce, and every room in the house reeked of it afterwards.

Every day, Mijnheer Reitz came back with blood on his shirt and stories that told of life disintegrating on the farm. When the men had watered the sheep, herds of springbok pushed down amongst them to draw water from the dam. The springbok wouldn't move away, even when the men began shooting at them. Still the springbok pressed down to the water's edge. That night they carried home thirty or forty animals, and for days they skinned the carcasses, butchered the meat, and hung sheets of biltong up to dry. Mevrouw Reitz said they ought to have saved the bullets for the cattle. They would need them before long. Ostrich, great shabby balls of feathers, gathered on the plains and strutted round the house, rapping on the windows, and Frances was reminded of stories of the Irish famine — the starving tenants of the rich being refused admission to the feast — except no one was feasting here. Everything was locked in a battle for survival. If the rains failed again, the Reitzes would be finished. The land would be impossible to farm.

One afternoon, Frances discovered Maria shredding a newspaper, and she stopped her, asking if she could read it. She took it up to bed with her. It was three weeks old, from Cape Town. The front page was dominated by the fall of share prices in Kimberley: thousands bankrupt, the bottom fallen out of the market, banks refusing to lend. "Moneylenders are finding out that they have killed the goose that laid the golden egg," the journalist declared. Property prices had fallen by 1,000 percent. She felt a thrill of satisfaction. Baier must be suffering.

Inside, there was an article about a jailer

at a prison in Natal who had deliberately starved to death half his native prisoners, dousing them with freezing water and beating them with clubs, while keeping the other half in perfect luxury. Then another article about Boers abandoning their farms because of the drought. Her heart stopped when she read the name Dr. Edwin Matthews in a headline on the third page. The article declared him a hero: "He has worked tirelessly to expose one of the most shameful medical scandals in British history." An inspector had been sent to Kimberley from Cape Town and had instantly declared the disease smallpox. A handful of Kimberley doctors had lost the right to practice, and Baier had been taken in for questioning. She read the article over and over, smiling each time she came to the bit about Edwin. It was the news she had been waiting for. He had been vindicated, and Baier — even if he managed to escape justice in court — would be financially crippled.

But when her pleasure at reading the news had worn off, she was left feeling more alone than ever. Edwin's success accentuated their separation and her failure to show courage when he had needed her to. She wondered whether he was still working with Sister Clara. They had been side by side for so long, and their companionship, and the faith Edwin clearly put in her, might surely have turned into love. The idea tortured her, and she woke up in the night, palms sweating, throwing off the covers, trying to get away from the thought that he had found happiness with someone else.

In the long, hot afternoons, when there was nothing left to do and the house settled into sleep, Frances would walk with Piet to the cottage, Baboon riding on his back, clutching his shirt with neat adroitness. The boy seemed to love the peace of the place, and he would bring a handful of toy soldiers and line them up on the crumbling *stoep* outside. Frances went immediately to the piano. Touching the keys worked on her as a kind of drug. She made her way through the book of sonatas, imagining as she read the music that she was playing for Edwin. There were six in total, and they were difficult — technical and unfamiliar — and it took her time to master them. The first was delicate, but they became increasingly dynamic, full of startling life and a brutal sadness. This music had meant something to Edwin. He had wanted to share it with her, and as she brought it into being, it was as if he were there talking to her, telling her about himself. It took their relationship out of the realm of memory into new territory. It was a gift, and she was grateful for it. Her sanity began to rest on being able to come here and place her fingers on the cool, ivory keys and conjure a different reality into being. But when it was over and silence had reclaimed the house, the fantasy receded and she was all alone in the empty room.

THIRTY-SEVEN

When Frances came in one morning from
the henhouse, she found the kitchen quiet.
The cook had his back turned, sweating
onions for the soup. She put the basket of
eggs down on the table, brushed the wisps
of straw from her skirt, and went through to
the dining room to clear breakfast. The family had left the room, and the table was its
usual muddle of spilt tea, yolk-smeared
plates, and scraps of meat. It wasn't until
she turned to the sideboard that she saw it:
a carcass ripped open and spread-eagled,
front legs stretched out in front of it. She
thought at first that it was a rat, but it was
too large. It took her a moment to see the
pink ears, the fingers, and the tiny, wrinkled
toes, and then she felt sick to her stomach.

"Does he know?" she asked the cook,
walking back into the kitchen. He nodded
sorrowfully.

Mijnheer Reitz had killed the baboon at

the breakfast table with a knife when it clambered onto the sideboard and took a fistful of porridge. Piet had watched it happen. It's a drought, his father had said apologetically, and we've no room for hangers-on. The boy had run out of the room, and no one had seen him since. The general opinion was that he would reappear in time for lunch.

Frances was kept busy all morning beating dust out of the mattresses and hanging out the sheets to air, because they couldn't spare the water to wash them. The air was hotter than usual, humid and close. There was no sign of Piet at lunch, and it wasn't until Frances walked into the kitchen laden with dirty dishes and was scraping the greasy remains of roast lamb into the bin with her fingers that Maria nudged her. The girl pointed outside. Low on the horizon, so far off they were still translucent, she could see clouds. They were banking in the distance. Even as she watched they moved closer, gathering in height and substance.

By the time the dishes were washed, the clouds were purpling. The sun illuminated them from beneath so that the plains glowed, iridescent, as if lit by a lamp. There was a flurry of movement outside. Men ran past the kitchen door, and the barn doors swung open with a clatter. They were bringing in the sheep. Frances looked at Maria, and saw the woman was grinning.

"Will it rain?" she asked, even though she didn't need to.

Jantjie appeared. "They should find the boy," he said to them both, "before the storm breaks."

Mevrouw Reitz burst into the kitchen. Frances had never seen her look so frantic. "Have you seen Piet?"

Frances shook her head.

"Isn't it your responsibility to be watching him?" she demanded.

"But he's been gone since breakfast," Frances said, confused suddenly. Ordinarily, he was her responsibility, but the whole family had known he was missing, and no one had suggested they were worried or had asked her to look for him.

Maria was dispatched to look for Piet in the outhouses, barns, and *kraals*. Frances searched the house with Mevrouw Reitz, turning over every inch of space. She was aware of the sky darkening outside. By four o'clock there was still no sign of the boy. The expectation of rain had infected the whole household with a kind of fever. Everyone wanted to know if the dam would hold, and what they would do if it burst.

Outside, the men were herding the sheep off the plains into the barns and battening down the roofs. Mevrouw Reitz went out to find her husband, to ask him to help in the search. Frances was left alone in the kitchen. The air which blew in off the veldt was icy cold, filleting the humidity. It smelt of melting snow. The wire door on the kitchen suddenly swung back on its hinges and clanged shut.

It occurred to her where Piet might be. Was it possible he had gone there by himself? If she was right, then it was her fault. There wasn't time to fetch her shawl. She had to leave before the storm broke. She ran back into the hall, down the *stoep,* and out onto the plain. The temperature had plummeted. It was freezing out here, unnaturally cold. A gust of wind carried the smell of wet earth, and a streak of lightning flickered across the bruised sky. She paused for a second listening, transfixed. It felt like the prelude to something on a huge scale. There was a clang of metal and the shrill whistle of a horse as it kicked against the iron bolts on the stable door. A loose shutter banged against its hinges — then a door slammed shut. In the distance, a wind pump was turning a manic circle. She saw one of the Reitzes' collies cowering under the *stoep,* whining, and all the time the wind was in her ears, threatening to bowl her over, bringing weather so cold it felt arctic. Could she get to the cottage before it broke?

She began to run, tripping over the scrub. A low rumble of thunder, and the sky glimmered. The wind pushed at her back. A dark shape — an eagle, she thought — wheeled above her, and for a moment she saw herself from his height, being blown across the plains into the storm. If Piet was at the cottage, then he would be frightened. Hopefully too frightened to try to make his way back. A crack of thunder tore through her, and the ground tremored. Then a bolt of lightning, like the lash of a whip, struck the earth twenty yards from where she stood. She had a sudden intimation of the vastness of the sky and the power it could unleash. She ran faster now, her lungs burning, racing against the storm. The cottage loomed up ahead. A moment later she saw him, running down the *stoep* onto the veldt. He stood for a second against the sky turned black, then sprang towards her, his mouth open, arms held wide in joy at the storm, shouting, "I saw it — the blue-headed lizard. And now it's going to rain."

There was a roar of thunder, and lightning forked directly overhead, striking the ground between them. A moment of silence, as if the world were holding its breath. Then out of the silence came the hail. A thousand tearing, brutal missiles unleashed from the sky. Rocks, flung down at them, from a thousand feet. Not rocks, she realized scrambling towards Piet, but hailstones, as large as cricket balls, with jagged edges like knives, bouncing over the earth. She threw her arms over her head and staggered forward. Piet was down. A blow struck her on the cheek as hard as a brick might have done and sent her sprawling into the dust. She pulled herself up, clambering on her knees to reach the boy, then lifted him into her arms and staggered forward until she was under the roof of the *stoep.* But the stones sliced in at them, and now the corrugation was being torn down. There was a thundering sound, as the hail ripped through the iron. The noise was immense; louder than the deafening clamor of huge factory machines.

She pulled open the door and pitched inside, dragging the boy into the empty bedroom. The clatter of stones on the roof was overwhelming. She couldn't hear her shoes moving across the floor or her voice as she shouted to Piet. The force of the hail stepped up a notch. The shutters were being ripped off their hinges. Hailstones tore into the room, skidding across the floor. She carried the boy down the corridor, into the study. It was on the lee side of the storm, and the window here was protected. It was dark in the room, and it took a second for her eyes to adjust. Two crates leant against the wall. Inside them, someone had stuffed some hessian sacks. She lifted Piet onto the crates and pulled his legs into the sacks to keep him warm. He wasn't moving, and she willed him not to be dead.

There was a gash on his forehead, and blood was seeping down his face, across his mouth. She put her sleeve to the wound to try to wipe the blood away, to see how deep it was, but more blood dripped onto his face. Her hand was soaking. Not with the boy's blood, but with her own. It was hard to tell in the darkened room where it came from. Her clothes had been shredded; they were wet, and so was her hair, drenched with blood and water. She called Piet's name, squeezing his hands until he moaned slightly and half opened his eyes; a rush of relief. He was still alive.

Footsteps behind her. She swung round. A figure was standing in the doorway, a saddle slung over one arm. She couldn't get a clear picture of him, and when she did she didn't believe it. The hail was like thunder, and her ears roared with the sound of it. She stared, rooted to the spot. Swallowed. A moment of fear. She didn't trust herself. Edwin was saying something. She couldn't make out what it was — too much hail. Then she felt the brush of his shoulder against hers as he walked past her into the room, flung the saddle down, and knelt beside Piet. After a few seconds, he opened one of his saddlebags, took out some fabric, and bandaged the boy's head. There was a crashing inside the house, and the roar of hail grew louder. The roof must have given way over the sitting room. She prayed it would hold over their heads. Then a different sound beneath the hail — a juddering of notes, a clamoring of keys. The piano, she realized. It was being torn apart.

Edwin gave Piet a sip of brandy, took off his jacket, and laid it over him. Then he turned to her and pushed her down so that her back slid along the wall and she was sitting with her knees bent. He crouched beside her. His hands ran over her head, her shoulders, her face, feeling for breaks or cuts. His eyes were flashes of white in the darkening room, and she willed him to look at her. Then, quite suddenly, the hail stopped. There was — for a perfect moment

— a complete and profound silence. It seemed to stretch far out across the plains. A second of astonished stillness. She could hear Edwin breathing, the dripping of water and the brush of his shirt against her dress as he moved his hands down over her arms.

Then, a moment later, it started to rain. She heard the soft, gradual falling of raindrops like fingertips over skin.

He put a wad of cloth in her hand and motioned to her to hold it against her cheek. She felt a sharp, throbbing pain as she put pressure on the wound. The rain began to fall more heavily; a luscious, rushing sound of large, fat raindrops growing every second more forceful until it sounded as if they were standing beneath a waterfall.

Edwin stood up and left the room. A few minutes later, he came back.

"Will he be all right?" she asked in a whisper.

"He should be fine. The important thing is that he doesn't get cold or wet. We can't carry him back. The ice is nearly three feet deep. I'll go for help when the rain stops." Three feet deep. Was that possible? She had thought the worst was over, but now she felt a tremor of fear. The ice would be halfway up the door of the cottage, and if it didn't stop raining soon they would be flooded.

He came and sat beside her with his back to the wall. The room was pitch black. Night had come on. They sat with their shoulders a few inches apart. Now she felt the cold, and her body began to shake. She let the bloodied cloth fall into her lap. Her hands were numb, and when she tried to warm her fingers, rubbing them on her skirts, she couldn't feel them against the fabric. Water ran off the ice into the room, swilling around their feet.

"So," he asked, "are you going to tell me?"

"Tell you what?"

He didn't reply, and there was a moment of quiet between them. Then she said, "I couldn't go back to England."

"And so?"

"And so I came here. Mevrouw Reitz took me in."

"Under what pretext?"

"She needed a maid." A thread of panic was weaving through the seconds that she was with him. The throbbing in her cheek, the freezing water rising over her feet — none of it mattered. Her whole existence had crystallized into the simple pleasure of having him near, and she dreaded him leaving.

"But you don't speak Dutch."

"I have learnt."

"Why is it any better than living in England with your aunt?"

What could she say? That she hadn't wanted to leave him behind? Instead, she said, "You loved this place, and I wanted to know if I could love it too."

"And do you?"

"Yes," she said simply.

Again, a silence, while the rain came down outside. Icy water was soaking through her skirts, and she couldn't feel the tops of her thighs where they touched the boards. Her teeth began to chatter. A trickle of water, like a tap left running, was pouring from the ceiling.

He sensed her moving. "Half the roof is down," he said, "and the rain is running straight off the ice."

A moment passed. "What about you?" she asked eventually.

"I was on my way to Cape Town. The Reitzes are holding some money for me, from the sale of the furniture."

"But not the piano."

"No, not the piano."

Because it was our wedding present, she wanted to say; you asked them to keep it because it was ours. He rubbed his hands together — she could hear it in the dark —

and she wished that he would reach out and touch her. "When I got to the farmhouse the storm was blowing in and the boy was missing. They said you had gone after him. We went looking. I wasn't far off here when the hail came. My horse was making to bolt, but I slipped the saddle off him. The saddle saved me."

She was shivering, convulsing now with cold, and she pushed her head forward onto her knees, pressing the water out of her clothes, squeezing herself into a ball to keep warm. The room was freezing. They were, to all intents and purposes, encased in a block of ice. The water deepened across the floor, rising over the sides of her shoes. It was filling up the house like a dam. At least Piet was lying on the crates. They would keep him dry. Time seemed to slow down. She heard Edwin moving around the room. When he came back, he slid down the wall, so close that his shirt was touching her arm and she could feel the warmth of his body. When he moved his foot, it made a slight splash in the water. She let herself lean into him.

The rain kept falling. Her arms were numb. She saw the white of her sleeves against her wrists but couldn't feel them. She had the impression that they were in a sinking boat, the sea pouring in the leaky joints. She wondered if she had been asleep when she felt him tugging at her hands. He was crouched in front of her, massaging her palms with his fingers. They ached with cold, and she winced when he pushed too hard.

"How is the boy?" she asked.

"Sleeping." Her hands shot with pain as he pressed his thumbs into the joints. "Thanks to you, he is still alive. You were brave coming here."

She tried to laugh, clenching her jaw to stop her teeth from chattering. "Not brave, foolish. I'd no idea the storm was going to be so bad."

He stood up, placing a candle and a box of matches on the edge of the crate. "Light it only if you have to. I'm going now, to get help."

"But it's still raining."

"It's slowed down a little."

She didn't want him to go, but he was already moving across the room. It was dangerous outside on the ice. What if he didn't come back? What if he decided to leave her here to die? The idea that he might hate her enough to do this filled her with sudden horror. She stood up, keeping a hand to the wall for balance. "Edwin. Can you forgive me?" Her question was spoken into the dark. She couldn't make him out.

After a moment, he said, "Is it a question of forgiveness?"

"Every day I wake up wishing it could have been different. Wanting to start over again."

"You have started over," he said gently. "You should be proud of what you have achieved."

But she wasn't proud. All she felt was a profound sadness. He left, and she sat down against the wall. Her skirts stuck to her legs, soaking and cold. The water had risen above her ankles, swilling over her thighs. It was logical to think she might die here. She hadn't imagined it was possible to feel cold like this. It was as if the flesh had been stripped from her bones and ice was being held against her raw nerves. It burnt.

She opened her eyes with a jolt. Edwin was crouched over her, slapping her awake. She was stretched out on her back, staring at an opal sky. She couldn't feel her body, but she could see it, lying perfectly motionless. The shivering had stopped. The veldt was silent. It wasn't raining anymore. Edwin said her name, over and over, until she blinked at him and tried to shift her muscles into recognition, but he was already stripping the wet clothes off her, pulling them from her body. He dressed her in a woolen shirt and thick cotton trousers, sitting her upright, pushing her arms through the sleeves as if she were a child. The surface of her skin was entirely numb. She could hear the rustling of fabric, but like a porcelain doll she felt nothing, just the vibrations, the movement as he picked up each limb in turn.

He brought a bottle to her lips. She drank and felt her body firing into life. The sky turned mauve, then azure blue. She didn't think she had ever seen anything so beautiful. Ice floated on the surface of the flood. He wrapped her in blankets. They were on a cart, she realized, as it began to move. There was the sound of oxen splashing through water. The land as far as she could see was white, and the sun, beginning to rise, sent shards of light glittering across its surface as though the veldt were made of quartz.

A fire was crackling, fiercely hot. Where was she? Not in her attic room. Edwin was sitting on a chair by the bedside, watching her. When he saw she was awake he leant forward, picked up her wrist, and took her pulse. Her skin prickled, hot with fever. She couldn't bear his professional concern.

"When I was sick," she said, feeling herself ripping open from the inside, "with small-pox. You never came." She had felt so alone, and so close to death, but it was only now that she felt the full force of his rejection. "You didn't care if I lived or died." Tears coursed down her face, over her mouth, onto the pillow. She knew that he would abandon her as he had done before, and she wasn't sure that she could bear it a second time.

His fingers pressed into the soft part of her wrist, burning tunnels into her flesh. "Frances, I did come. I sat through the night with you. I didn't leave until I knew you were going to pull through."

A gulping, tearing sob ripped through her. "You didn't want me to die?"

He put her wrist down on the bed and smiled. "No. I didn't want you to die."

"I should have trusted you." Her voice was choked with tears. "But I was scared. Of what Baier would do to us. Of your determination. Of all the terrible things I had seen in Kimberley."

He put a hand to her forehead, stroking the scarred skin. "Frances," he said softly, "it's not your fault." And his words, and the touch of his hand, unburdened her.

She woke some time later. It was night. The room was dark, and the fire threw shadows flickering across the wall. Edwin was sitting on the bed, watching her. She could see the dark outline of his shoulders. The fire spat and burnt. Her body was hot, but her skin was wet. There was a dull ache from the wound on her cheek, and her mouth was dry. The weight of the sheets made her skin crawl. She couldn't see his face, couldn't read his expression. He was perfectly still, and she sensed his expectation. She swallowed, and he must have heard because he reached out a hand and touched the flannel shirt at her waist, just above the jut of her hip. Her skin froze and then rippled outwards from his touch. His fingertips tugged at her nerves, as though they were sticking on a network of ice. He nudged up the fabric, circling her rib cage with one hand. Her breath came heavily. She tried to sit up. There was a burning in her chest. His palms slid up her damp body, his skin slicing into hers. She put her hands on his belt and undid the buckle, and he waited as she slid the shirt off his shoulders. He felt entirely new to her, as if she had never touched him, and his skin against hers was like fire, obliterating everything that had gone before.

Afterwards, they lay looking at each other. She touched his face, wondering at the feel of him under her fingertips. He watched her for a moment, then said, "I should have been more honest with you, right from the beginning. I hated myself when I heard you were sick. I had been angry with you for so long, but I barely knew it."

"And are you angry now?"

"No," he said, smiling, taking hold of her hand and drawing her towards him.

She slept and woke again, each time putting out a hand to feel for him and going back to sleep only once she knew he was there. Fingers of light crept into the room. She watched him dress. He put a hand to her cheek. She let him go without speaking. There would be time for talking later. She slept again, and when she woke it was broad daylight and her fever had gone. On the table by the bed was a gold ring. She turned it over in her hand. It was her wedding ring. Edwin must have kept it with him all this time. Smiling, she slipped it onto her finger.

Mevrouw Reitz was in the kitchen, peeling potatoes. When Frances came in, she looked up and beamed, enfolding her carefully in her arms. Frances was surprised by this sudden show of affection. She had thought she might be blamed for Piet's escape to the cottage. After all, she had been the one who had taken him there.

"Is he all right?" Frances asked.

"Thanks to you. If you hadn't gone after him . . ." She opened her hands in a gesture of futility.

"We were lucky that Edwin was there."

"Yes. But you knew where to find Piet." The older woman squeezed her hand. "You must take it slowly for a few days. Make sure you recover. And I want you to know, there will always be a position for you here."

"Thank you." Frances smiled back, but she didn't want to think about that now. Edwin was here. What had happened between them in the night — the things he had said and the way he had touched her — had changed everything. "And my husband? Has he already eaten?"

Mevrouw Reitz looked at her strangely. "Yes. Did he not say good-bye?"

Frances swallowed. Her sense of things was falling away from her. Mevrouw Reitz scraped the potato peelings from the sink. Frances would be asked to take them out to the pig later.

"He was gone by five o'clock. I was lucky

to catch him. I said he was foolish to ride out with all this flooding, but he was in a hurry to get to Cape Town."

She had given him the last of herself. She felt empty. Used, and burnt up. All the strength she had stored up since she came to Rietfontein was being torn from her. There was no future that she could imagine without him. She felt the weight of the ring on her finger and wondered why he had left it, if he didn't want them to be together. She told herself that he would come back for her, but it seemed like little more than a fiction invented to console herself.

The aftermath of the storm, like the relief that follows a near tragedy, gave way to a hysteria of storytelling. The overseer had been looking for Piet when the storm came. He hid from the hail under a rocky outcrop. The hailstones came down on all sides, sealing him up behind a wall of ice. He had to hack out an air vent with a stone to stop himself from suffocating. Three hundred sheep had been lost on a neighboring farm. They had been left out in an open *kraal* when the hail came down, and the stones had butchered them all. The veldt was littered with dead animals: birds, snakes, and antelope killed by the onslaught. The roof had been ripped off the dairy, and the shutters on the house swung uselessly on their hinges. But the mood was joyous. Frances watched, and in their smiles and laughter she saw reflected only her deep sadness.

The ice melted, and the dam filled to bursting, but the walls held. When the rains had disappeared, the plains broke out into flower. It was spectacularly beautiful; a carpet of yellow blooms sweeping over the earth. Grasses thrust up green and succulent from the ground, and the veldt came heaving into life. The air throbbed with the hum of insects, and butterflies washed over the flowers in swirling white clouds.

Frances constantly thought back to their night together. It had seemed to her at the time that Edwin had unfolded a part of himself, and let her come close to him. That he had found something in her that he needed; a place in her that satisfied him. But now she began to doubt herself. She remembered his hands on her body. Had they been kind, not passionate? Was it possible that the feeling of communion had been all hers? Perhaps he had tried to love her out of a feeling of duty but had found, in the end, that it was impossible.

Summer turned into a mellow autumn, the weather cooled, and from her room in the attic she could see the swallows leaving in droves. Her heart ached with disappointment, and she wondered if she should leave with them. Go back to England.

Then, one day, two months after the storm, a letter arrived for her. She recognized the handwriting. It was from Edwin. Her hands shook as she tore open the envelope.

Frances. Forgive me for taking so long to write to you. We have had enough false starts, and I wanted to settle things in Cape Town first. My work in Kimberley has earned me the respect of some, and they have asked me to take up a position in the government here. There is a house with a view of the sea, and a fig tree in the garden. You once asked me if we could start again. If you are still willing, then don't write back. Leave Rietfontein and get the next coach to Cape Town.

She put down the letter and smiled. The drought was over, and the rains had come. Her work here was done. She would begin packing her bags immediately.

AUTHOR'S NOTE

The Fever Tree first spoke to me on a dark winter's afternoon in the British Library. The hush in the reading room was broken only by the turning of old pages and the soft tapping of keys. I was researching the history of English colonials in South Africa, and amongst the books stacked on my desk was an old canvas-bound diary. The spine creaked as I opened it, and the gilt lamp spilled a pool of light onto its thick yellowing pages. The diary had been written by a doctor at the end of the nineteenth century, and it told the extraordinary story of a smallpox epidemic that had ravaged the diamond-mining town of Kimberley. Extraordinary because — reading on — it became clear that the epidemic had been covered up by the great statesman Cecil Rhodes to protect his investment in the mines.

The disease raged for over two years, killing thousands of men, women, and children, mostly African laborers. The tragedy was that the epidemic could have been brought under control in just a few months if the doctors had quarantined and vaccinated patients instead of denying its very existence. The doctor writing the diary had fought — at great personal risk — to bring the epidemic to the attention of the authorities in Cape Town. It was later reported as "the greatest medical scandal in the long and honourable history of British medicine." Dr. Jameson, one of the doctors who was paid to deny the presence of smallpox, went on to become prime minister of the Cape colony, as did Rhodes himself.

I could scarcely believe what I was reading. Cecil Rhodes was a man with vast colonial ambition, but nonetheless a figure generally talked about with respect. He had established the Rhodes Scholarship at Oxford University, an award of immense prestige. Was it possible that he had been responsible for such horrors? If so, how could history have forgotten? The smallpox scandal in Kimberley seemed to lie at the very heart of Britain's exploitation of the resources and people of South Africa under the banner of "civilization." It was a tale of greed and corruption, exemplifying a complete disregard for human life. But it was also a tale of courage. The story gripped me. I couldn't let it go, and, before I knew it, I had begun to work it into the pages of a novel.

The landscape of southern Africa wasn't new to me. A few years before, I had been to Namibia with my boyfriend (now husband). We had rented a Land Rover, filled it with enough food and water to last a few weeks, and set out to drive the length of the country from Swakopmund to the Angola border. We free-camped, and tackled the infamous van Zyl's Pass, vertigo steep and strewn with boulders the size of oxen. We put up our tents on the crocodile-infested Kunene River and lurched into hidden valleys where the Himba still live in their beehive huts, dressed in animal hides, their skin thick with ocher, their lives unchanged for hundreds of years. We saw leopard prints by our fire in the morning, and in a dried-up river valley I touched the carcass of a giraffe hollowed out by drought and burnt to leather.

My residing memory, over and above the staggering beauty of the landscape, was the dust, which found its way into every crevice, coated every surface, and gritted in our teeth. One day towards the end of our journey, we drove past a high wire fence cordoning off a diamond mine, and I remember thinking, What would life have been like for the first Europeans who came to these desolate places to try to profit from the land?

I wanted my lead character, Frances Irvine, to mirror something of my own journey through the wilderness of Namibia and my growing sense of anger, and political enlightenment, as I came to understand the mercenary and often brutal exploitation of South Africa at the hands of the English. But what would drive her to such a place? Would she go willingly or would she be pushed? And what kind of life would await her?

Frances led me down a rabbit warren of research — a world of dust, diamonds, and disease. I read political pamphlets from the nineteenth century that discussed the million surplus women living in Britain and the emigration societies which specialized in shipping them out to the colonies to work. I dipped into guidebooks on the Cape published in 1880 and sifted through Victorian women's magazines — turning over patterns for embroidered glove boxes and lace cushion covers — just as Frances might have done. I delved into manuals on social etiquette, cooking, botany, and what to bring on a hunting expedition to the Transvaal. I found old pictures of Kimberley, which showed women sorting diamonds, camping in the dust and filth of the town alongside their husbands. It wasn't long before Frances emerged, a living, breathing character with a story of her own.

I went back to southern Africa one last time before I began writing *The Fever Tree,* driving from Johannesburg to Cape Town, over the vast arid plains of the Karoo, a landscape of extraordinary beauty. I spent a few days in Kimberley, and stood giddily on the edge of the Big Hole, the largest hand-dug diamond mine in the world. But what stayed with me — the indelible impression — were the quaint little Victorian towns, with their whitewashed Cape Dutch houses, and always on their outskirts the sprawling corrugated townships with their story of apartheid, disease, and poverty. I have traveled to many parts of Asia and Africa and seen disparity and hardship of all kinds, but nowhere has a place seemed as desolate as those I witnessed in South Africa. Here, in the twenty-first century, were the all-too-visible legacies of the English speculators who had mined Africa for a profit. *The Fever Tree* is my response to that history.

ACKNOWLEDGMENTS

Thanks to my editors, Venetia Butterfield and Amy Einhorn, and all the staff at Penguin Group, without whose help this novel would be a much less worthy book. Thanks to my brilliant agent Araminta Whitley, who made it all happen, and to Harry Man, Alice Saunders, and the rest of the staff at LAW. Likewise thanks to Stephanie Cabot at The Gernert Company, and to Nicki Kennedy, Sam Edenborough, and their team at ILA.

The Fever Tree couldn't have been written without the resources of the British Library, which made available to me countless diaries and firsthand accounts of life on the diamond fields — my gratitude goes out to the men and women who wrote them.

Several historians have written very well on the politics of Kimberley. Particularly useful for my research were Martin Meredith's *Diamonds, Gold and War,* Robert Vicat

Turrell's *Capital and Labour on the Kimberley Diamond Fields, 1871–1890,* and William H. Worger's *South Africa's City of Diamonds.* I have taken liberty with a few dates, and an earnest historian might notice that certain events took place a couple of years before or after they appear in this narrative.

The austere beauty of the Karoo inspired me to write this novel, but I couldn't have brought its stories to life without the help of three books: Lawrence Green's *Karoo,* Eve Palmer's *The Plains of Camdeboo,* and Pauline Smith's wonderful collection of short stories, *The Little Karoo.* Thanks also to Ailsa Tudhope, who was so generous with her anecdotes of nineteenth-century life in Prince Albert.

I'm indebted to all those of you who were either willing or coerced into reading the book in draft form: William Beinart, Suellen Dainty, Colin Edwards, Kylie Fitzpatrick, Deborah Gaitskell, Kirsty Gordon, Tessa Hadley, Brett Hardman, Richard Kerridge, Angela Lett, Jack Wolf, and Moogie Wood.

I couldn't have asked for a more committed writing companion than Duke, who heard the novel being read out loud countless times, and steadfastly managed to sleep through every word.

To my father, to Charlie, Whitney, and

Dorrie, and most especially to my mother — thank you for setting me on this path. And to Dave, the greatest thanks of all.

ABOUT THE AUTHOR

Jennifer McVeigh graduated from Oxford University in 2002 with a First in English literature. She went on to work in film, television, radio, and publishing, before giving up her day job to write fiction. *The Fever Tree* is her first novel.

The employees of Thorndike Press hope you have enjoyed this Large Print book. All our Thorndike, Wheeler, and Kennebec Large Print titles are designed for easy reading, and all our books are made to last. Other Thorndike Press Large Print books are available at your library, through selected bookstores, or directly from us.

For information about titles, please call:
  (800) 223-1244

or visit our Web site at:
  http://gale.cengage.com/thorndike

To share your comments, please write:
  Publisher
  Thorndike Press
  10 Water St., Suite 310
  Waterville, ME 04901